KARMIC WINDS

Dreena Whiteley

Copyright © 2022 Dreena Whiteley
All rights reserved.
ISBN: 978-1-7384286-1-8

Dedicated to my nephew, Matt
28/12/1976 – 26/2/2022

1

A vortex of emotions swirled around Marcia's mind as she imagined the thousands of kilometres that lay ahead, not knowing where the Karmic winds would ultimately take her.

After the two-hour flight from Alicante to Charles de Gaulle airport in Paris, she waited in the airport lounge for the three-hour stopover.

Marcia settled into the business class seat on the Air France flight, realising that it was an extravagance. However, both the economy and premium class sections were full.

She felt exhausted as the Boeing 777-300ER moved down the runway, and she immediately fell asleep, only to be awoken hours later by the vibration of the aircraft as it fought its way through turbulence. She looked out of the window at the majestic icy mountain peaks that loomed below. Glancing at the flight tracker on the screen in front of her, she saw the outside temperature was 40° below zero.

Marcia pondered how could something that looked so magnificent could be such a killer – a destroyer that pulled with such magnetism. She thought of Eamon O'Donally who exerted a similar attraction for her.

From the beginning, he had lured her with his good looks. He had a magnetism that Marcia couldn't resist.

She had faced the challenge of stepping into his dangerous world of violence and crime. Although at times their relationship had been a roller coaster ride, their deep love had withstood the ups and downs. Furthermore, they had been happy throughout their relationship. Marcia giving birth to their sons was the icing on the cake for them both. Although they wanted more children, it hadn't happened. Nevertheless, the couple were content, that is, until Eamon's decision regarding the boys' future.

That's when the rumbling began. Cracks appeared in their relationship and tremors shook the foundations of their love when he'd sent the boys away to boarding school. Because of the world of crime that he was immersed in, he said that their safety was paramount. But for Marcia, it was like her whole world had been taken away. She struggled with feelings of deprivation and separation until finally, she had enough, and fell headlong into the abyss. Now she was alone, facing unknown demands that she sensed lay ahead. Marcia glanced back at the splendiferous beauty of the mountain, fading into the clouds.

The vision of her small sons' faces appeared before her, and a heavy sensation, like a concrete block, hit her solar plexus. She fought against the feeling of despair, the futility of being unable to get to her boys.

They were locked away behind the imposing walls of the boarding school. Marcia inhaled, looking out of the window, sending out a silent prayer to the Universe, mentally envisioning wrapping a cloak of protection around all three of her sons, who were all lost to her.

Her thoughts turned to her eldest boy, Reuben. He had just turned 18 years old when he was taken from her on his ill-fated trip to Asia, which she had assumed was just a backpacking holiday.

Marcia mused how incarceration came in various forms. Her eldest son's internment was unlike that of his two younger half-brothers. His sentence was self-inflicted.

She was brought back to the here-and-now by the pretty, young flight attendant asking if she would like to order anything from the menu.

Marcia asked for Voss mineral water. However, she declined the menu, although she hadn't eaten since the previous day. The thought of food nauseated her.

She had never been someone to wallow in self-pity. After the loss of her parents in an accident when she was a teenager, she learned how to control her mental anguish.

She had been sent to live with an aunt who resented having a young girl under her roof and made it known to Marcia that she was an inconvenience.

At age 16, Marcia married Andrew and became pregnant. Andrew was kind and took care of her and their young son Reuben until his sudden death when Marcia was 24 and Reuben was only 7. Nevertheless, she was determined to provide for her child on her own.

Yet now, the loss of all three of her sons, and Eamon, was just too much to bear. Marcia didn't think she would be able to cope this time and felt that her life no longer had any purpose.

She turned to look out of the window. The aircraft flew over the dense tropical vegetation of Bangladesh. She recalled another flight across the continent that lay below when Eamon had accompanied her on the return journey. He had flown from Spain to be by her side when their first son Niall was born in Jomtien, Pattaya, Thailand, where Eamon had sent her to live because his criminal activities had made it unsafe for her to be with him in Spain at the time.

She had been overjoyed to see Eamon, feeling that she was safe with him there by her side.

Marcia couldn't fault him as a husband and father. He was protective and solicitous to their sons' welfare. Eamon's generosity surpassed anything that she'd ever encountered, giving her carte blanche to buy anything she desired from fashion designers that she favoured.

However, Eamon's decision to send the boys to a boarding school without her consent turned her against him and they hit a low point in their marriage. Marcia saw him seeking solace in another woman's arms, which had destroyed her.

Marcia wiped away the unbidden tears. Her mind was weary and her resolve to overcome adversity was now broken.

She thought about Jane, who she decided she would contact once settled in at the wellness retreat in the mountains. She wouldn't disclose her location as she knew it would put Jane in an awkward position if she was questioned by her man Billy, who was one of Eamon's trusted and loyal men.

Marcia's financial situation wouldn't be an issue for a while. She had accrued a substantial nest egg over the years, albeit with Eamon's benevolence, which would enable her to be financially independent while she established herself.

She knew that the problem she would face with her work in a foreign country would be the language barrier, and she realised that she would eventually need to return to England.

Marcia decided that once her mind became clearer, she would look on the Internet for rented accommodation in the UK. She was aware that her psychic gift would enable her to survive the next chapter in her life.

2

Early that morning, just before 5 am, Michael, the owner of the Irish bar, put an intoxicated Eamon O'Donally into the back of the taxi, which he had paid for in advance, telling the driver that if there was any damage to the car, to bill it to him. The cab pulled up outside the large, ornate gates of Eamon's villa. Seeing no movement in the backseat, the driver jumped out and opened the backdoor. He shook his head when he saw the man slumped in the back seat. He pulled and heaved until he eventually got Eamon sitting upright. Eamon stared blankly at him, fumbling in his pockets.

The cabbie swung Eamon's arm over his shoulder as support when Eamon's feet touched terra firma. Stumbling two paces forward, Eamon fell against the iron gates, gripping the bars for support. The driver stayed with him, directing Eamon's hand to the keypad on the concrete pillar. Duty done, the taxi driver left Eamon to it.

On the third attempt, Eamon got the combination correct and the gates slowly swung open. Falling to his knees, he half crawled, then tried to stand, finally making it to the steps. Sitting on the top step, he brushed himself down, realising the knee on his left leg trouser leg was torn. After what seemed an age, he steadied the key with both hands and inserted it in the lock, staggering, then righting himself, as the door swung open. The Belgian shepherd wagged his tail and intelligent almond-shaped eyes fixed on his master, waiting for a command. The dog side stepped when Eamon tossed his jacket aside.

The dog's ears pricked up at the sound of Eamon calling out to Marcia, the echo of his voice resounding throughout the expansive rooms. As Eamon headed towards the bedroom the dog's claws tapping on the marble tiles was the only sound to be heard.

Eamon's foggy brain was trying to make sense of the pregnant silence.

"Shush!" Eamon said, putting his finger to his mouth, directing the dog to be quiet upon opening the bedroom door. Trying to focus, he moved back to the lounge, going into each of the downstairs rooms, calling out,

"Marcia!"

Returning to the empty bedroom, Eamon's eye was drawn to the dressing table, where the diamonds and emeralds twinkled back at him.

Marcia's engagement and wedding rings lay alongside the American Express card that he had given her for personal use. His muddled mind wouldn't allow him to comprehend that she had left him.

He made his way towards the walk-in wardrobe. Top drawer, second right, he told himself upon opening the drawer. He fell to his knees, discovering that she had taken her passport.

Enveloped in mental anguish, he curled up on the bed in the foetal position and howled, setting the dog off, who joined in with a mournful cry.

A short while later, alarm bells rang. He knew that he had to find her – post haste.

He placed a phone call to Dan and Billy. They did not ask if it was urgent; the time of the morning and their boss's urgent tone brooked no query.

The men were on their way.

The icy blast from the powerful shower heads helped Eamon to clear his mind. He quickly dressed while forming a plan in his mind.

He made a pot of black coffee to help stimulate his brain so he could see his way forward.

He pressed the button to open the gates for Dan and Billy when they arrived. They both looked on the ball and were ready for action, although it was 6.35 am. The men did not pass comment on his appearance. Eamon knew that they could see that he had been drinking heavily by his bloodshot eyes.

He didn't normally speak about his private life with his men, however, this time it was crucial.

"Marcia has left. She has taken her passport and left behind her rings." He tried to keep the desperation that he was feeling from his voice.

"The situation needs yer urgent attention." He continued, "Marcia's car, as youse have noticed is outside, therefore, she has…"

Billy interjected, "Sorry to butt in, boss. Do you think she could have booked a flight on the Internet?"

Eamon replied, "To be sure. But I have looked at her laptop and there appears to be no sign of any recent purchases. Nevertheless, I know that my wife is savvy about computers, and she could have wiped the history!"

Billy stated eagerly, "I can take the computer to my pal Leo if you want me to ring him, boss. He's brilliant and there isn't much that he doesn't know about IT."

Eamon checked his watch.

Billy smiled and said, "Don't worry about the time, boss. For a few quid, Leo will look at it! If Marcia's booked a flight, Leo would find it."

"That's grand," Eamon said. "Give the man €500 as an incentive, Billy!"

Within minutes, Billy had called his pal and went on his way with the laptop to meet him. At that early hour, he knew that there would be hardly any traffic on the roads.

Dan got straight on it and began phoning local taxi companies. The sixth company came up trumps. One of the drivers had taken a woman from that address just after 3 am that morning to Alicante airport terminal N.

Eamon felt sick to his stomach, as the thought struck him that Marcia could have already left the country. He prayed that she had made the reservations on the computer and Billy's man Leo could retrieve the booking.

Fifty-three minutes later, Eamon opened the villa door to a smiling, triumphant Billy, who held out a printout with all the flight details. "It's all here, boss!" Billy said.

Eamon thanked both men, stating that he'd phone them later.

Pouring himself another cup of black coffee, he took the paperwork and sat at the lounge table. He was stunned as he read that she had booked three flights. His heart sank as he looked at the time of the first flight from Alicante to Charles de Gaulle airport in Paris.

Checking his watch, he realised that she would be in the air.

. . . .

Her connecting flight from Paris was business class to Suvarnabhumi airport, Bangkok. Then she'd booked an hour-long

14

domestic flight to Chiang Mai International in the north of Thailand.

Exhaling, he ran his fingers through his hair, shaking his head in disbelief at the great distance she had flown to flee from him.

He couldn't believe his stupidity. "Why didn't I see it coming?" he chastised himself. He realised that Marcia had been devastated when the boys went away to boarding school. Nonetheless, he knew he had no other choice. How could he risk his boys' lives, knowing that they could be brought down or harmed by his enemies? His world was a dangerous one, and at any given moment he could end up in prison. Why couldn't Marcia understand that he felt the loss as much as she did?

He perused the paperwork, studying her hotel reservations in Asia. He noticed the wellness retreat that she had booked for 21 days. He exhaled wistfully. At least time was on his side.

Underlining the name and phone number of the Chinese doctor who ran the business, he read through the information about the retreat, which promised isolation and peace of mind. The building was tucked away in a country setting with views of the mountain Doi Suthep.

He thought of her being all alone, travelling thousands of kilometres. Her desperate plight tore at his heartstrings. He knew what he must do. Furthermore, he realised he had to play it carefully because of the fragility of the situation.

He needed an ally, and he hoped that the Chinese doctor at the wellness retreat, with a certain level of understanding, and also with some financial persuasion, would assist him by preventing Marcia from leaving before Eamon could reach her.

Eamon leaned back in his chair, musing upon the happiness that Marcia had brought into his life, from the first time they had met over six years ago. She had turned his life around just when he was at an all-time low. It was after the devastating revelation he read in his dead wife's diary, that she and Jimmy Grant had been having an affair. He had thought that he would remain childless when he was married to Eve, who had told him that she had a medical problem that prevented her from becoming pregnant. He had found her contraceptive pills hidden in her chest of drawers and then the writings in her diary detailing how she planned to have Jimmy Grant's baby.

Fate then played its hand and Marcia moved into his heart. His depth of love for her was something he had not experienced before. Marcia became pregnant very quickly after they had got together, and then 10½ months later after Niall, she gave birth to another son, Quinn. Both boys were his mirror image. He had never known such happiness and contentment. His sexual passion for her was returned; they consumed one another with a deep love.

He looked over the two-acre grounds of his villa surrounded by palm trees, fronds swaying languorously in the early morning breeze – the beautiful villa that not so long ago was filled with children's laughter, and the pool that Marcia swam naked in whenever he was there to watch over her. Their home, once full of love was now void of happiness. He had had the luxurious home built especially for Marcia.

"There is no way that I'm going to throw it all away!" he vowed aloud. Checking the time difference to Thailand, he picked up his phone and dialled the wellness retreat.

Eamon felt more at ease after he had spoken to Dr Li Qiang Cheng, who had reassured him that he would abide by his wishes regarding Mrs Marcia O'Donally's welfare. The financial donation to the retreat that Eamon offered had persuaded the doctor. He had agreed to give a daily report on his wife. Furthermore, the doctor would ensure that she would be monitored

24/7 and that her passport wouldn't be released. Dr Cheng said that he had influential contacts in the Chiang Mai province who would prevent Mrs O'Donally from leaving until further instructions from Eamon.

Eamon battled with himself. Part of him wanted to rush to her side, pleading with her to return, however, common sense prevailed. He decided to leave her for a couple of days to regain her equilibrium.

3

Marcia smiled at the young woman behind the customer service desk at the airport. She explained that she was looking for the domestic connections hub for her flight to Chang Mai.

The young woman pointed towards a sign and both women pressed their palms together in a prayer-like fashion, bowing their heads in the Thai tradition of greeting or gratitude. Marcia hurried towards the directive signs; she could see the shimmering lights on the runway. The air-conditioned building had not prepared her for the oppressive heat outside, although she had previously been to Thailand and knew how hot and humid the climate was. Marcia walked up the steps of the domestic flight which would whisk her away to the north-east Isan region. There she would be able to cleanse her mind and body in tranquil mountain surroundings where the air was free of pollution, far away from the exhaust fumes and heavy traffic of Bangkok.

Forty minutes into the flight she looked out of the window at the overgrown dense vegetation of the impenetrable jungle that spread out below. The lush green carpet bordered the hotel grounds where she would stay for the next 21 days. The seatbelt sign flashed red and the aircraft began to descend.

Marcia braced herself as her inner fears took over. Her anxiety levels rose, and her heartbeat sped up. Taking deep breaths as she did with her yoga routine, she gradually felt calmer. Nevertheless, she couldn't shake off a feeling of apprehension of foreboding. She tried to put her feelings to one side, knowing that the lack of sleep and food would affect her negatively.

She came out of the Chiang Mai international departure, putting on her sunglasses to shield her eyes from the sun's powerful rays. Suddenly, exhaustion took over and she felt her head start to spin. To her left, she saw a bench and walked towards it. She had just sat down when she heard a voice calling her name. She waved her arms at a cheery-looking, young Thai man bearing a placard, who walked purposely towards her.

Marcia steadied herself, she felt dizzy as she rose from the bench, trying to smile politely.

Taking her hand luggage, the young man gesticulated and spoke in broken English. He opened the rear car door for her, and she slumped onto the seat.

The animated young driver told her his name was Tye. On their way to the wellness centre, he chatted with her about his life. He said his family lived on a farm where they had cows, pronouncing it as 'clows'. He continued to inform her that they had rice paddies as well as rubber trees. "You come see," he invited her. "My two days off soon," he said, beaming. He waited for Marcia to reply, watching her in the rear-view mirror.

Marcia smiled at him despite how she was feeling. She didn't want to hurt his feelings by declining his invitation, knowing that the Thai people were welcoming, even to strangers. Placing her palms together, bowing her head, and smiling appeased Tye.

"You rest, then later, I tell you days off," he responded.

Marcia nodded throughout while the driver spoke of his wife and two children and how clever they were at school. She couldn't help but warm to him as she did with the other Thai people that she'd encountered on previous stays.

"You love Thailand. Good for you." She was used to the questions and directives being intermingled.

"First time you come?" Tye asked.

Marcia held three fingers up.

A beautiful smile accentuated his cheekbones. "I see you love Thailand, like me."

Pointing ahead, he proudly said, "Look, beautiful" as they approached the wellness retreat.

He bowed his head when she gave him a €20 note tip.

"I haven't any Thai baht," Marcia stated.

"Mai pen rai (no problem)," Tye responded, leading her up the steps to the reception desk. Bowing, he took his leave.

Marcia gave her name to the receptionist, passing over her passport and bank card.

Checking her reservation, the receptionist handed Marcia a medical form.

"You complete, tomorrow you see doctor!" she said, proffering a seat at a nearby table.

Marcia ran her eye over each question, placing a cross in the relevant 'no' boxes as she went. There weren't any ailments that she suffered from. Once she completed the form, she handed it back to the receptionist, who, in return, gave her the fob to the door of Marcia's room.

When she reached the dark wood door of her room, Marcia slipped out of her shoes as was the Thai custom. On entering the room, she placed her handbag and small case on a chair and walked across the large room. The feeling of the wooden floor beneath her bare feet and the quiet hum of the overhead fan brought her some relief. The large, elegant bed overwhelmed the otherwise sparsely furnished room. There was a small table and two chairs, and a picture of Thailand's revered king placed prominently in the middle of the wall.

Sliding open the balcony doors, Marcia stood in awe as she took in the stunning view of the majestic mountain Doi Suthep, which spread out before her. She inhaled; the tranquil setting would enable her to find peace of mind. She turned back to go inside. She knew that she should eat something. She rang room service, ordering Tom Yum vegetable soup, jasmine rice with cashew nuts and fresh coconut. She decided to shower before her food arrived.

After her ablutions, Marcia wrapped herself in a light cotton robe and dried her hair. A sharp rap on the door indicated that her meal had arrived. Thanking the young girl who served the food, Marcia took the tray and placed it on the table. Although she wasn't hungry, she ate every morsel, drinking the liquid from the coconut, which quenched her thirst. Feeling weary, she decided to rest and reclined on the grand bed.

Marcia hadn't realised that she'd immediately fallen into a deep sleep. Six hours had gone by since she lay on the bed. She had momentarily forgotten where she was. When she realised this, a feeling of drowning suddenly engulfed her, as she remembered the all-encompassing loss of everyone she loved.

With the three-hour stopover in France, the long flight to Asia and the five-hour time difference, it had been over 24 hours since she had left Spain.

To clear her mind, she decided to go through her yoga routine. She tried to empty her mind of thoughts of desperation. Upon finishing the routine, she didn't feel mentally lighter as she normally would. She felt numb, but she knew that would assist her in coping with her situation.

She switched on her mobile phone and watched as texts came through from Suzette. The numerous missed calls were from Eamon. She suddenly felt the desire to contact Jane but thought she would go to the hotel restaurant and have breakfast first before deciding to involve her friend.

Following the signs to the dining area, Marcia crossed the reception area and went out the patio doors into the sunshine. She found herself in a beautiful floral setting with a picturesque backdrop of the mountain. On cue, elephants trumpeted in the distance.

Half a dozen middle-aged women who were a mixture of nationalities and races were sitting alone at tables, and two young men of Mediterranean appearance were laughing together. Various species of birds pecked around on the ground at titbits that guests had thrown to them. Looking around for a table at the far end of the large terrace, a waving hand caught her attention. The attractive young redhead with a long plait that hung to her waist, waved cheerily, her smile infectious as she beckoned Marcia.

"Are you on your own?" the young woman enthused when Marcia approached.

Marcia nodded. Although she wanted time on her own, she felt drawn to the young woman, who looked like she was in her early twenties.

"Please join me. I'm sorry, let me introduce myself. I am Rosalind, although my friends call me Ross, which in truth is what I favour," she said as she held out her hand, smiling.

Marcia took the woman's outstretched hand, noticing that her nails were bitten into the quick, and she sat down opposite her.

"Hi, I'm Marcia," she said, without adding anything further.

"I live in Saint Ives in Cornwall, in England. I have been staying here for two weeks. I return home in two days. I have been struggling to try to sort out my mind and body. I have an addiction to narcotics, which has been a battle," Ross said candidly. "This is my second visit here in two years," she added, "which Daddy financed."

She handed Marcia a menu. "I have ordered already. I can recommend the omelettes. They are delicious." She continued, "What is your story? Are you from England?" she queried. "How long are you booked in for?" She thanked the server who placed a plate of food before her.

Marcia felt nauseous at the aroma of the fried omelette. She ordered fruit, natural yoghurt with almonds and fresh orange juice.

Marcia said, "I live in Spain. I have booked in for three weeks for some rest."

Ross looked up as she cut a slice of the omelette.

"Do you have an addiction?" She raised an eyebrow as she began to eat.

Marcia smiled gently despite herself.

"Not an addiction. My life has been rather stressful of late."

"I do hope you don't think that I am prying!" Ross gave a soft laugh. "I have been starved of the English language and someone to talk to for two weeks."

"Not at all," Marcia replied.

Ross ate enthusiastically, however, she went on talking, "I can show you the sights before I leave. The trip up the mountain is impressive. The 14th-century wat at the top is impressive." She did not wait for a reply. "Tomorrow you will most probably see the doctor. There is nothing to it, just a general health check. The appointments are usually the day after arrival."

"I am booked in at 10.30 am," Marcia confirmed.

Marcia thanked the server as she laid her breakfast on the table. She ate while Ross continued to question her. She sensed the girl was troubled.

"Do you like yoga? We have a session at noon." Ross finished her food and leaned back into her chair.

"Yes, I practice regularly at home," Marcia replied, drinking the pure orange juice, hoping that the sugar would help energise her.

"The yoga session is at the back of the retreat on the veranda. We will not be able to speak as the instructor is extremely softly spoken and one cannot hear her instruction. Also, her English is difficult to comprehend," she grinned.

"I am going to miss the retreat. I love being here. I feel free," Ross said, looking wistful. "Although I miss my boyfriend, I do not miss him encouraging me to join him. He is an addict." Ross exhaled, smiling thinly, and said, "I am also addicted to him, much to Daddy's chagrin."

Marcia took note of the needle marks on the woman's arm. Her heart went out to her.

"Do you like markets? There is a nice one at the top of the mountain near the temple. If you are not too tired after yoga, we could visit the Wat Phra That Doi Suthep, hire a taxi, and take in the view?" Ross enthused.

Marcia felt that she couldn't refuse her invitation.

"Thank you, I will enjoy that, Ross."

"If we meet up at about 2 o'clock in reception, I will order a taxi from the front desk." She gave a small laugh, "Out here in Asia, it's commonplace to use pickup vehicles with seating in the back in place of a taxi, where one has to hold on tight, as the drivers, for the most part, tend to drive erratically."

Marcia did not let on that she had previously been to Thailand; she did not want to go into too much about her life. Ross's girlie giggle lit up her beautiful blue eyes. She pushed her chair back as she rose to leave. Marcia noticed how thin she was.

"I must go now to prepare for yoga. See you there. Bye, Marcia."

Marcia ate slowly, looking around at the garden with its vibrant variety of orchids. The serenity of the setting helped to ease her troubled mind. Her thoughts turned to the young woman. She hadn't mentioned a mother, only a father. Marcia felt her troubles paled in comparison to the young woman's narcotic addiction and having a boyfriend who was also an addict. A recipe for disaster, she concluded.

Upon returning to the solitude of her room, the low hum of the air conditioning filled her with a disquieting despondency. She sat on the bed and took out the photos of her three sons. She ran her finger across their faces. She picked up her phone and wrote a text to Jane, asking if she was free to speak, her heart pounding while she waited for the reply. After what seemed like an age, the ping of Jane's response came through.

"Yes."

Marcia rang her, withholding her number in case Billy discovered that she had called.

"Jane!" Marcia said, "I just needed to speak to you. I have left Spain. I will not tell you where I have gone to because Billy might question you." Her voice faltered as she tried to control her emotions.

"Please let me help you, Marcia. Do you need any money? I have enough to spare that I would transfer if you ever needed it?"

"I have enough to see me through but thank you, Jane."

"Marcia," Jane exclaimed, "I sensed that something like this would happen. You've been on the verge of breaking ever since the boys went to the boarding school!"

Marcia could not contain her tears as she went into detail about the build-up and the final straw of seeing Eamon with the woman in the Irish bar the night she had left.

"Marcia please try to let it go. I know that it must be extremely difficult. Nevertheless, once you have recuperated and gathered your thoughts, then you and I can get our heads together. I am here for you, no matter what." She encouraged Marcia to stay positive.

"I know that Billy must have gone to see Eamon because he received an early morning call yesterday, and he jumped out of bed, rushing to dress without showering, which is unheard of with Billy unless his boss required him urgently. But that's all I know!" She laughed softly, "But, I can imagine that the topic of conversation must be about you leaving!" Jane advised, "The important thing is that you rest. Your mental well-being is a priority. She paused. "If you text me at any time, day or night, I will find a way to speak to you. I will not ever leave you to face this situation alone, Marcia," Jane reassured her.

Marcia promised Jane that she would relax and said that she would contact her the following afternoon around 3 pm Thai time when Jane said that Billy would be at the gym.

4

The second yoga routine of the day was complete. Marcia stretched, then returned a head bow to the instructor. Catching Ross's small hand wave, she smiled giving a slight nod.

Marcia couldn't help but smile at the young girl's gaiety as they travelled up the steep incline in the back of the pickup truck, where she held on for grim death as the driver took the sharp bends, driving too close to the edge for her comfort. Looking at the drop below made her feel dizzy, so she looked ahead, trying to kerb the feeling of travel sickness.

Marcia temporarily forgot the heartache of what she'd left behind as the vehicle took them higher up the mountain. She was struck by the beauty of the wat, standing regally on the mountain top.

Marcia insisted on paying the driver who said that he would return in two hours.

"The dragon's tail below, leading up to the wat has 300 steps – if one was energetic!" Ross laughed as they looked over the edge." She took Marcia's hand in hers, leading her to the temple.

Slipping their shoes off, they moved quietly across the tiled floors. Rows of people bowed their heads in prayer as the shaven-headed monks in mustard-coloured robes chanted. The elder of the Buddhist monks, covered in tattoos, swished water in blessing across the people's heads in the front rows. Marcia prayed, asking for the spirit world to help watch over her three sons, to keep them safe from harm and to guide her to do the right thing. She asked for the strength to overcome her mental anguish. She included a prayer for Rosalind.

"Did you pray? Ross queried as they left the temple, moving to the protective walls.

"Yes," Marcia replied.

"My mother died when I was five years old," Ross said, sadly. She turned to face her and asked, "Do you believe in the afterlife, Marcia?"

Marcia exhaled. "I have a strong belief in the afterlife, Ross and that we are surrounded by spiritual loved ones. They never leave us!" she assured her.

"You speak with such conviction," Ross replied.

Marcia smiled knowingly and said, "In times of weakness or trouble, if you call to them, they will hold you up, enabling you to regain your strength."

Tears welled up in Ross's eyes, although she smiled thinly. Hugging Marcia and crying quietly on Marcia's shoulder, she said, "I don't know why, but I believe you, Marcia." She sighed, wiping her face with the back of her hand.

"When my boyfriend rings me, I am not going to answer. I will text him to inform him that I want no further contact unless he checks into rehab."

Marcia returned her hug, genuinely happy for the young girl, sensing that Ross finally would move forward, with or without her boyfriend.

"Daddy will be thrilled," Ross beamed. "You must come to visit our home if you come to England. Saint Ives is such a beautiful place."

Putting her arm through Marcia's, she gently guided her to a concrete platform where they could take in the vista. "We are 3,520 feet above sea level!" Ross informed Marcia, while they took in the sight below. Chiang Mai province was covered in a haze; however, it did not take away its beauty, Marcia thought.

"I am so pleased to have met you, Marcia. May we exchange telephone numbers?"

Marcia smiled and said, "Certainly, let's do it now." Taking their mobile phones out, they exchanged numbers. Marcia felt a warm affection for Ross, and she was glad that she was able to help her.

"Isn't it magical? So mysterious, it is sacred to the Thai people," Ross said softly, putting her arm around Marcia's shoulders.

"It is as if my prayers are out there on the wind." She splayed her free arm. "Did you pray for something special?"

"I included you in my prayers," Marcia responded, not elaborating any further.

"I feel I have known you forever. You are a beautiful soul, Marcia!"

"You are too, Ross," Marcia replied. "You should always value yourself, Ross!" Marcia advised.

"I am going to listen to your advice and live a fulfilling destiny!" Ross exclaimed, beaming.

Marcia felt an inner sense of other worldliness descend, wrapping its tendrils of protection around her. Suddenly the feeling of aloneness lifted, and the cloak of despair flew into the ether.

Doi Suthep Mountain would have a special place in Marcia's heart. It was here that the pretty young woman, Ross, regained her life.

The following morning, Marcia went for an early morning swim. The pool was not heated, and she had found the chilly water stimulating. Then she went to the outdoor breakfast area before her 10.30 am appointment with the doctor.

She was finishing her meal when a beaming Ross skipped gaily to her table, taking a seat. She gushed, "It worked, Marcia. After I dismissed Alexander's phone calls, he texts me 28 times, I ignored them. Finally, after getting the picture, he left a voice message promising me that he would book himself into rehab if I would only answer his calls. I didn't telephone him, Marcia. I replied with a text, that if he breaks his promise, we are finished for good!" She laughed and said, "I spoke to my father." Her wide smile radiated her newfound confidence. Then her tone became more serious. "I informed Daddy as to how you helped me. He asked me to tell you that he would welcome you to our home."

Marcia smiled. "Ross, it has nothing to do with me! You have stood strong all by yourself!"

"I could not have done it without you, Marcia, and also the spirit world. I cannot thank you enough, and I will never forget you."

"I will not forget you, Ross. Always remember that you owe it to yourself…," she paused, "to become the powerful warrior within you."

"My taxi will be here to take me to the airport within the hour. I do hope everything works out well for you!" Ross said as she reached across and hugged Marcia. "Don't forget to call me," she called out as she went out through the veranda doors.

Marcia gave her a small wave.

Marcia knocked at the door with Dr Li Qiang Cheng's name on the brass plate. A smiling Thai nurse in a white uniform, opened, smiling and bowing her head, bidding Marcia to enter.

The big man behind the desk rose to his full height. Although he did not smile, his eyes were friendly and ever watchful, Marcia thought when she took the proffered chair, placing her bag on the floor.

"How are you experiencing the retreat?"

Marcia smiled. "It is beautiful, extremely peaceful." She sat back as the doctor glanced at the completed questionnaire on the desk.

He gave a sharp nod, picking up the form and leaning into his chair as he studied her. Marcia did not miss his fleeting glance at her bare left hand.

"Mrs O'Donally, you have no ailments, no medication? Are you prescribed contraceptive pills?" He held her eyes when she shook her head.

"I see that you have three children. What form of contraception do you use?" he glanced back at the paperwork.

Marcia blushed. "I have not fallen pregnant since my last son was born five years ago." She adjusted her position, feeling uncomfortable under his gaze.

He cocked an eyebrow and said, "Therefore, there is a possibility that you could be pregnant?" He leaned forward placing his forearms on the desk.

Marcia shook her head, smiling thinly without replying.

"Hmm," he said, directing the nurse to take Marcia to the examination room for a blood test and a urine sample.

"Please be seated!" he stated upon her return. The nurse passed him the readout of her blood pressure. He nodded to himself. "All appears to be fine; however, we can investigate your well-being tomorrow when your results from the tests come back. I will see you at 10 am." He smiled and added, "If you require anything, please call. The number is on the telephone in your room."

He stood, head bowed as Marcia thanked him and left. "That will be all!" he stated to his nursing assistant.

Sitting down at his desk, the doctor telephoned Spain with the early morning report as had been agreed.

5

Marcia had spoken to Jane, giving her an account of her trip to the mountain and the tests she had undergone. Jane had nothing further to say, as Billy was a closed book. Marcia was going to phone her the following day.

Marcia sat by the pool on a sun lounger, under a large umbrella that shaded her from the sun. The languorous breeze brushed her skin and helped to ease the sense of dread that she could not seem to shake off ever since her appointment with the doctor. She tried to relax by reading a book that she had picked up in the reception area that previous visitors had left behind.

She ate lunch at a nearby table, taking a coconut back to her sun lounger. Sipping the juice, she suddenly felt tired. Throughout the long night, she had tossed and turned, the yearning for her children preventing her from sleeping.

Her thoughts turned to Eamon. When she switched her phone on again to speak to Jane, there had been no contact from him. She felt sad about how easily he had forgotten her. He had other interests now – his new woman. There had been a further text from Suzette, however, she could not bring herself to ring her. She couldn't bear Suzette saying that she had always been right about Eamon and that he was no good for her.

After falling asleep just after 3 am, Marcia awoke the following morning at 7.35 am. She did her morning yoga routine, which lifted her spirits. She would join the others for another session this afternoon and try to make conversation, although most of the other women, from various countries, appeared wrapped up in their thoughts. However, at least the two young men who were staying at the retreat appeared friendly. They waved and smiled at her.

She knocked once on the doctor's door. She stepped inside and the nurse greeted her. She disappeared when the doctor asked Marcia to be seated. She tried to read his look but to no avail. A feeling of apprehension filled her as she faced him.

"Sitting back in his chair with a hint of a smile forming at his mouth he asked, "May I ask you when you last menstruated?"

Momentarily surprised by his question, Marcia stumbled, trying to remember.

"My periods have always been irregular." She stayed silent for a minute, then asked, "What is the reason for your question?"

"There is no doubt from the test results that you are in the first or very early second stage of gestation."

Her eyes searched his trying to comprehend his meaning.

The doctor sat upright, smiling. "Mrs O'Donally," he said, smiling, "You are pregnant!"

She heard a rush of wind, her head spinning, her heart racing, and perspiration forming on her brow. She clutched the arm of the chair.

Dr Cheng pressed a buzzer; the nurse entered and went to Marcia's aid.

Taking her pulse, he placed Marcia's head between her legs.

"Take deep breaths!" he advised.

"Nam!" he ordered.

The Thai nurse returned with a glass of water.

Shaking, skin pale, Marcia sipped the water and was helped to stand up. The doctor checked her pupils, nodding.

"You must rest. My assistant will take you to your room and check on you at regular intervals."

In a zombie-like trance, Marcia allowed the nurse to lead her by the arm.

Marcia lay on the bed in the darkened room, with curtains drawn. Her sobbing, along with the hum of the air conditioning was the only sound to be heard.

Three hours earlier, when Dr Cheng had read the blood and urine test results, he placed the international telephone call.

It was 3:47 am in Spain when Eamon's mobile phone rang. Groggily, he reached for his phone, sitting up when he saw the international number.

"Not at all!" he said, standing up as the caller continued to speak. Running his fingers through his hair, he moved towards the bathroom, thanking the caller. He immediately punched in Billy's number.

"Set the plan in action, 'tis urgent!" Eamon directed.

Eamon could count on one hand the number of times in his life that situations had caused him to panic. This was one of them.

6

Marcia felt stupefied by the revelation that she was pregnant. Lying on the bed, she stared into the darkness. A nurse who visited every two hours had tried to coax her to eat, noticing the untouched tray of food on the table.

Sleep evaded her throughout the night. Her mind was worn out with the desperation of her plight.

Rising from the bed, she crossed the floor, drew back the curtains, and slid open the door and mosquito screen.

She took in the beauty of the scenery. The tiny lizards, known as chit-chats, flicked their tongues, devouring insects, and birds chirped in the mango trees. She gazed into the distance at Doi Suthep Mountain. Her thoughts turned to her second pregnancy, with her and Eamon's first son, who she had given birth to in Pattaya, Thailand while she was staying with Aye. She knew that it was not a coincidence with this pregnancy. She knew that Thailand was significant.

She could stay in Thailand; however, she would require a translator to help her build a future. Her best hope would be Bangkok where there would be English-speaking tutors for hire. She could hire a nanny to help mind the baby while she worked.

Closing the screen doors and retreating inside, she headed to the shower.

She shook her head when she saw herself naked in the full-length bathroom mirror. She noticed the dark areolas and the small mound of her abdomen. How had she not noticed previously? This was the baby that she and Eamon had desired to have after the two boys. They had not used any form of contraception from the first time they had made love. The boys had come in quick succession, then for five years with no further pregnancy, they assumed that was it. Ironically, now that she faced her future alone, she carried a part of Eamon O'Donally within her.

Dressing, she thought about Karma and the seven-year cycles of life. It suddenly dawned on her that it was over six years ago that she and Eamon began their relationship. This baby would be born into a new cycle. The Karmic winds of Saturn would take her to a place where she could restructure her life. She tied a silk sarong around her waist and adjusted her sleeveless white, light weight top. She exhaled, picked up her bag and left for the outside dining area.

There were a few women who sat alone at their tables and did not look up, engrossed in their own world. She sat near the edge of the tropical gardens taking in the ambience of the setting.

She sat waiting for the server, who had acknowledged her from the doorway. She placed an order for mango, kiwi, and yoghurt with a large coconut. She thought that as soon as she finished eating, she would phone Jane, although she was undecided as to whether or not to tell her that she was pregnant.

"May I join you?" The handsome man who was normally with another guy asked.

"Please do!" Marcia returned his smile.

37

"My boyfriend is resting. We had a late night at the Chiang Mai bars last night." He held his hand out.

Marcia took it and he kissed the back of her hand as he introduced himself.

"I'm Lucas." He pulled the chair out to sit.

Marcia introduced herself. She was surprised by Lucas's English accent, which didn't match his olive skin tone.

Marcia ate while he told her that they lived in Richmond in Surrey and that they visited the retreat twice yearly. Lucas went on to say that they owned two flourishing hair and beauty salons and that having amazing managers allowed them to take vacations and relax at the retreat while knowing that their business was well cared for.

"My family is Greek, and my partner is from Rome. Neither of us goes back to our native countries because of old family values!" He smiled wistfully. "Our people find it difficult to accept our relationship." He added, "The problem has been ongoing for 20 years."

Marcia did not reveal anything about her life, and Lucas did not pry.

After placing his food order, he asked how long Marcia was booked in for.

"Three weeks."

"We are leaving tomorrow afternoon. Our night flight from Bangkok is something that I'm not looking forward to!" He laughed.

Marcia looked at his strong jawline and the dark shadow of a forming beard. He reminded her of a younger Eamon, although he was tall and lean, whereby Eamon had a heavier, muscular build.

"If you would like to join us tonight, Marcia, we are going to a restaurant in the town. The journey is just over 15 kilometres, but you do get to see the wonderful views."

Marcia thanked him. "I am feeling rather tired, however…" she smiled, "if I give you my room number–"

He interjected, "If you change your mind, meet us in reception around 5 pm. Then before dark, you can enjoy the ride, and maybe spot a few elephants."

Marcia took her leave, thanking him once more and she returned to her room.

A feeling of tiredness came over her. Marcia lay on the bed. She would leave phoning Jane until later after she had rested. She drifted off to sleep with the vision of her sons' faces. Tears fell as she held out her arms to embrace them.

The knocking became louder as she slowly came out of her slumber. Sliding from the bed she answered the door. A young Thai boy stood with a huge bouquet of electric blue, pink, and white orchids in his arms. He bowed, slipping off his shoes as he entered, placing the flowers on the table. Marcia went to her bag and took out some Thai baht to give to the boy. He placed his raised palms together in thanks.

She could not understand who had sent them. There was no card from the sender. A sharp knock on the door broke her musing.

Marcia knew that the nurse would be checking on her, as she had ever since her last visit to the doctor.

Opening the door, she gasped, and her hands inadvertently went to her abdomen.

"May I come in and speak wit ye, Marcia?" Eamon asked quietly.

She slowly stepped back, as Eamon removed his shoes and entered the room.

He surveyed the room, walking towards the veranda doors. The silence of their thoughts was hanging in the air. Stepping outside, he glanced around and then slowly turned to face her.

She could not trust herself to speak. A tight band of trapped emotions restricted her vocal cords. She fought against the tears that were battling to reveal her heartache.

"Marcia, please let me put tings right between us. I would not ever hurt ye!" he continued, "I know that it has broken ye since our boys went to boarding school. Nonetheless, I am begging ye to understand that it was for their protection!" He shifted his weight. "It was the hardest decision I have ever had to make. It broke my heart too; my love equals yours for our children!" he stated, moving back into the room.

He moved closer to her. He was in her body space, and she put both palms on his chest to prevent him from moving any closer. He cupped her chin, wiping the falling tears with his fingertips. "Ye are my life, Marcia," he breathed, as he looked deep into her eyes.

"You forget that I saw you in the bar with that other woman!" Marcia cried.

"To be sure, she was after me, bothering me each night. However, I only wanted an ear to talk to about ye, Marcia. I had the drink in me, and I was heartfelt because ye turned away from me. All I wanted was for ye to love me, as you always have. I will swear to ye that not only have I never strayed from ye, since we have been together, I have never wanted anyone but you in my arms."

She softly exhaled without taking her hands from his chest, and she looked into his eyes.

"Marcia, I have never pleaded with anyone, but I beg ye to give our marriage a chance. I will investigate a school nearer to us. Anyting," he added.

He slowly played his fingers across the back of her hands. She did not withdraw. She moved her arms around his neck. He pressed into her, encircling her in his embrace as they kissed.

Lifting her to the bed, he untied her sarong, lifted her top off and released the hooks on her bra.

With his free hand, he slid her panties down. As she stepped out of them, he undressed, watching her. He placed his white linen shirt and black trousers over the chair. Marcia observed him as he removed his underwear. His powerful physical presence never failed to excite her. She gazed at his peppered grey body hair and his resting penis as he approached the bed. She lay back on the soft pillows and he knelt over her.

"Eamon," she faltered, "I am having another baby!"

He did not answer. His penis hardened as he covered her. Her legs involuntarily opened. He guided his rock-hard erection into its harbour, filling her, moving with deliberate motion as he spoke to her.

"This is the baby we have been trying for many years!" Marcia said. She raised her hips to aid deeper penetration, holding his face in her hands as each stroke inside of her gave her comfort.

"We'll make a fresh start with this child," Eamon breathed, cupping her rear, and drawing her closer.

She gripped his arms, which he had placed on either side of her face. He took his body weight as she quietly gasped. Her nails dug into his flesh, and he watched her in the first throws of orgasm.

"l love ye, Marcia." He kissed along the nape of her neck, clamping his thighs, holding her. Their juices flowed, orgasms deepening with the soul kiss.

A while later, Marcia straddled him.

Lying back, arms locked behind his head, Eamon observed her, as she rode him with her head thrown back. He could see the familiar signs of pregnancy; the darkness around her nipples and the baby bump, although it was small due to her weight loss. The doctor had reported the test results to him early the previous morning. He had been taken aback when he was informed that Marcia was pregnant and could be in the initial stages of the second trimester. It had been bittersweet news that the longed-for baby was planted. She had left him without knowing that his seed was growing inside of her. Dr Cheng had also telephoned him after breaking the news to a very distraught Marcia. She had been under strict observation while Eamon's private jet was being booked and prepped to take him to Chiang Mai.

"Would ye like me to pleasure ye?" he smiled, "perhaps twice."

Lifting her off him, he gently opened her legs as she lay back. His hot breath and flicking tongue brought the first orgasm. Before she reached the plateau, he moved inside her. "The second time I'll come wit ye.

. . . .

As they went to check out of the hotel the following morning, Dr Li Qiang Cheng came into the reception area as Eamon settled the bill.

"You appear to be more rested," the doctor said, smiling at Marcia and glancing at the diamonds and emerald rings on the fourth finger of her left hand.

He gave a sharp nod in Eamon's direction, who returned it.

"Marcia!" a male voice called out. She turned and waved at Lucas, who blew her a kiss.

Eamon cocked an eyebrow at Marcia. Sucking air through his teeth, he turned his attention towards the handsome, dark-haired guy.

"Please wait, Lucas!" his partner appeared, playfully slapping his rear, and slipping his arm around Lucas's shoulder.

Eamon nodded, smiling knowingly at Marcia, guiding her to the waiting taxi.

A languid breeze blew across the tarmac as they approached Eamon's charter jet, wrapping its tendrils around Marcia's white linen dress, revealing her early pregnant form.

Eamon held his arm protectively around Marcia's waist as they walked towards the waiting concierge at the top of the private jet's airstairs.

"Mr hunky Emerald Isle has an attractive pregnant woman with him who's wearing the crown jewels on her left hand," he said out of the side of his mouth to the two pilots, who laughed.

"Stop being envious, you old queen!" the co-pilot countered.

"Not so much of the old!"

The concierge broke into a perfected Pan-Am smile when his male passenger's hardened look caught his eye.

"I don't want to be disturbed," Eamon directed, "until I need ye!"

The concierge acquiesced by bowing his head.

Joining the pilots in the cockpit he fanned himself.

"That accent is orgasmic. The lucky cow!"

Ollie the captain smiled, shaking his head.

7

Eamon had an intense work schedule with the partnership in the Hawk Wind adult club, which he had invested in with Greg Davidson. Greg and Eamon went back a long time. He knew that the man could be trusted. Nevertheless, it was his woman, Suzette Greenaway, that Eamon knew was only out for herself. However, this new venture would aid him to become financially legitimate, notwithstanding the problems he faced with the Eastern Europeans who were trying to stake a claim on the narcotic scene by bribing his HGV drivers to transport drugs out of the country.

The constant threat of being arrested because he was on the Law's radar weighed heavy on his shoulders. Furthermore, there was another canary 'singing', whose name Eamon desperately required.

He had insisted that Marcia have further health checks with Dr Saggio on their return to Spain. They had been back from Thailand for three weeks and Marcia's fatigue had increased along with the size of her baby bump. To his mind, she was further along in her pregnancy than she first thought. He was taking her to the ultrasound scan appointment. They had both agreed that they would like to know the sex of the baby. Although he would not mind if it were another son, Eamon hoped that for Marcia's sake she would get her wish for a girl.

He thought that she looked radiant. She had blossomed – pregnancy certainly suited her. Her contentment was infectious. Furthermore, they made love more often. Marcia's libido had increased, and her sexual appetite had become insatiable.

She had agreed with him that the boys should not be uprooted yet from the boarding school. The principal had informed them that Niall and Quinn had settled into school life very well and were excelling in various subjects.

Eamon moved behind Marcia as she sat at her dressing table combing her hair. Leaning down, he kissed the nape of her neck, taking in the scent of her perfume. She smiled into the mirror at his reflection, turning to face him and placing her hands on his chest. He looked into her dark eyes while she began slowly unbuttoning his shirt.

"No wonder ye get tired, Marcia," he smiled, "I don't tink it's only the size of yer belly that has increased but also yer need for sex. My wife has become a nymphomaniac!" He added, "Not that I am complaining." He raised her chin, kissing her softly, as she released his fly, caressing and stroking his resting penis.

"This is for your pleasure," she purred, the tip of her tongue teasing across the eye, sensually drawing and withdrawing him into the warm wetness of her mouth. Moving her hands to his hips, Marcia took him deeper.

Watching her in the mirror, he held either side of her face as she took him to the plateau, adjusting his stance when her motion increased. Her fingertips played over his scrotum. Lost to her, he involuntarily shuddered.

She turned, then passed him a tissue from the box on the dressing table. He pulled her up, cupping her rear and wiping her mouth.

"Ye wonder why I chased ye to the other side of the world," he said, tongue in cheek, grinning.

"Is it sex that you want me for?" She cocked her head, straightening her dress.

"Maybe 'tis I that should be asking ye that question?" he playfully slapped her rear. "We spend more time in the bed than out of it with ye wanting me to pleasure ye. To be sure, this baby will have an easy birth with the amount of its father's sperm to aid its passage," he laughed.

....

Doctor Saggio gave Eamon and Marcia a welcoming smile as they entered his office, asking them to take a seat.

"Mrs O'Donally, if you would like to go behind the screen, the nurse will assist you with a surgical gown."

A few moments later, Marcia lay on the couch and the nurse raised Marcia's gown.

"Do you both wish to know the sex of the baby?" she asked.

They both nodded.

"Also, we will have a clearer idea as to how many weeks into the pregnancy you are."

Eamon observed the nurse spread the ultrasound gel over Marcia's abdomen and move the transducer over the baby bump.

Doctor Saggio looked closer at the screen's images. Using his stethoscope, the doctor listened carefully to the baby's heartbeat.

Eamon caught the fleeting look between the nurse and doctor, and he shifted uneasily in his seat.

"Thank you," Dr Saggio said to the nurse, who helped Marcia to a sitting position. The doctor sat at his desk scribbling notes.

Eamon twiddled his thumbs while Marcia slipped back into her midi dress.

Marcia sat alongside Eamon, and he took her hand in his.

"Congratulations are in order!" the doctor smiled from one to the other. "You will have two baby girls in a matter of 16 weeks or so."

Marcia gasped, putting her free hand to her mouth. Eamon squeezed the other, smiling at her.

"Thank you, doctor!" Marcia's voice broke with emotion.

"I imagine that it should be your husband, and not I, that should be thanked," the doctor said, rising to his feet and smiling when Eamon pushed the chair back to take his leave.

Marcia couldn't contain the overwhelming joy that she was pregnant with twin girls. They sat facing one another in Eamon's car after they left the clinic.

"Eamon, I am so happy!" she exclaimed, placing her fingertips on either side of his mouth. Leaning across, she kissed him.

"Ye know that I'm not a man that does tings by halves. Ye wanted a baby girl," he grinned, waggling his head, "therefore, I give ye double." He returned the kiss. "However, my little mystic," his tone became more serious, "I want ye to rest. Yer only a small woman and by the looks of our baby girls they are going to take after me." He rested his hand on her stomach. "Ye have a way to go!"

"The boys will be thrilled, especially Quinn. Aye returns the day after tomorrow from Thailand. She will be over the moon to have two more babies to help care for."

Eamon nodded. He knew that Quinn would be happy with the news, but he didn't think that Niall would show any enthusiasm, however, he kept his thoughts to himself.

Marcia was in the pool, and Eamon was drinking a glass of wine at the garden table when his phone rang. Going back into the villa, he took the call in his office.

"I have the security in place for the club, boss." Dan said. "There are some mean-looking fuckers among them!" he laughed. "If anyone tries to start any trouble, these boys will put a stop to it before anything kicks off."

"That's grand, I'll be wit ye tonight." Eamon clicked the call off, and as he was about to leave his office, Billy's number came up. He sat on the corner of the desk as he answered.

"I have just received the call that you have been waiting for, boss!" Billy continued, "Thomas Harper-Watts has just received a phone call from his father Lord Arthur, whose contact, Chief Inspector Ross Lowe, imparted all the inside information about their informant."

Billy paused for a few seconds, then said, "The grass is out here in Spain. Vic Greyland – he has all the rundown on Jimmy Grant and many others' previous dealings. Although your name was mentioned, the old Bill hasn't got any evidence yet that you played a part in any crime. However, the Chief Inspector is ever hopeful that you can be brought down. Obviously, boss, you know of Vic Greyland."

Eamon sucked air through his teeth. "That pox-balling cunt! I never liked the slimy bastard. Nonetheless, Jimmy Grant would not listen to me. But he went off the radar years back!" Eamon shook his head, exhaling, running his fingers through his hair.

"I'm up for sorting him out. Dan will assist me," Billy offered.

"Don't ye worry. I have the right man in mind to take care of Vic Greyland," Eamon stated. "I will need ye to be at the club because there is a lot to be sorted there before the opening night. I will get the ball rolling myself with Greyland. Tell Thomas Harper-Watts that he is in for a large drink. It goes without saying, Billy, that I will show ye my appreciation for yer help. Come to my office tonight."

....

Eamon went to his safe, removed the sim card from his phone, and exchanged it for another before punching in the number. He heard the familiar cockney voice answer. Eamon gave him his request, stating that it was urgent. Once the fee was agreed upon, Eamon promised a bonus upon completion.

Eamon returned to the terrace. He felt optimistic now that he had one of his men on the trail of the grass. He had not been surprised to discover that Vic Greyland had been hanging all and sundry out to dry to save his skin. Once he was out of the way, Eamon would be able to rest easier until the next 'canary' warbled.

Putting the situation to one side, his thoughts turned to Marcia. He had agreed that she could help at the club. He didn't want her working with Suzette Greenaway at her beauty salon where Marcia conducted tarot readings. Having her at the club instead was the lesser of two evils. But then the thought of his wife being caught up in any fray if it kicked off at the Hawk Wind club weighed on his mind.

He poured himself another glass of sauvignon blanc and took a seat, putting his long legs up on a chair and observing Marcia as she contentedly swam. Although he was as pleased as Marcia that they would have two baby girls to complete their family, the thought of how he would protect them troubled him. Luck had been on his side up until recently. He had been in the narcotic import business for too long, having been Jimmy Grant's right-hand man for many years. He had been the one to sort out the deals from both sides of the pond, but that was before Marcia and his children came into his life. Now with his fold increasing, he had too much to lose. He felt like a cat on a hot tin roof while he was waiting to hear that the grass had been dealt with. Eamon knew that his man wouldn't waste any time unearthing Vic Greyland. Nevertheless, he couldn't afford to get too comfortable.

Marcia brought him back to the moment.

"Eamon come join me in the pool!" She stood up, wearing the black bikini that barely covered her full breasts. He could see the rotundness of her pregnancy beneath the water. The familiar ache in his groin sent the blood rushing and he adjusted himself.

"Are ye going to behave yerself?" He stood up as he spoke, undressing, leaving his underpants on, smiling as he walked towards the steps.

"Ye are not playing the game fairly," he laughed while she released the bikini top.

"I'm definitely not." Her arms went around his neck, her lips brushing his.

"Tink of the babies," Eamon breathed, softly nipping the nape of her neck, his hands roaming her naked body.

He held her hand fast as she went to remove his pants. "They are staying on, my little temptress."

Her hand fondled.

"You are hard," she said, smiling. "Are you going to waste it?"

"To be sure, I will give ye what ye want," he smiled, "However, ye are pregnant wit two precious baby girls in yer belly. Therefore, there will be no sex in the pool."

Marcia smiled pressing into him, kissing along his jawline. Eamon lifted her, carrying her up the steps. He picked up a towel and wrapped it loosely around Marcia's shoulders.

He went into the villa. "Stay!" he commanded the dog at his heels as he kicked open the bedroom door. He laid his wife on the bed.

Kneeling over her, he slowly caressed her abdomen. His finger trailed between her parted legs, teasing back and forth. She moaned, bucking towards his tongue while he pleasured her.

"Let me straddle you. You can video us," Marcia said.

Eamon switched the iPhone on to record while Marcia guided him into her. She had waxed, but he knew that it would not be too long before she would not be able to see below her growing baby bump.

Eamon observed Marcia with her head thrown back – her full breasts and belly big with his babies. He had not seen anything as beautiful as his pregnant wife rose and fell, with him deep inside of her. He controlled himself, the measured movement throbbing, fighting to thrust. He did not want to hurt her or the babies. In one swift movement, he lay her on her side, moving in behind her, filling her, encasing her in his embrace, his finger aiding.

Her hands reached for his face, searching for his mouth. As he took her, her breathing became rapid as they climaxed together. He stayed inside of her until their breathing slowed.

"I think that it is sensual to see us making love," Marcia snuggled into him as he replayed the recording.

"Hmm," he smiled down at her upturned face, kissing the tip of her nose. "To see me pleasuring ye, is something private, between us." He paused, then said, "If something like this ever fell into the wrong hands…" His voice trailed off as he watched the video and heard Marcia's voice calling his name over and over, as the spasms of orgasm overtook her – the intimacy of their union playing out before them.

He exhaled. "I will transfer it to another sim card. It will be locked in my safe." Eamon realised that the recording could be easily smuggled into prison if he were ever detained. He had plans in place with Dan and Billy if the worst-case scenario should happen. Although his brother Patrick was his most trusted friend, who Eamon knew that he could rely upon if needed, he did not want to involve him in the world of crime. Patrick and his family were safely tucked away in County Armagh in Northern Ireland. He had seen to making provisions for him via his bank manager, Felipe Hortez, who was on his payroll as his adviser. Eamon kept his legal banking separate from his other dealings.

Eamon knew that the man he had hired to track down the 'canary', Big Dave Broadbent, could be relied upon to obliterate the scummy cunt. Nonetheless, Eamon was aware that Big Dave would need to act quickly before any whispers reached Vic Greyland. Eamon knew from experience that the warning drums could reach him at any time.

Marcia was in the dark about Vic Grayland's betrayal. Eamon wanted her to enjoy her pregnancy. The revelation that she was having two baby girls had given her such joy. He hoped that he would be a free man to be able to welcome his daughters into the world. It was not the financial aspect that was of concern, he had seen to it that Marcia would always be provided for.

A pang of guilt momentarily overcame him as they lay in each other's arms. He had wanted Marcia from the moment he was over Eve, his previous wife, who had died. The revelation in Eve's diary of her betrayal with Eamon's boss, Jimmy Grant, had put paid to their marriage.

Eamon had not wanted to become involved with anyone else after that as he could not bear to be betrayed again. He had become very mistrusting of women, but there was something about Marcia that drew him to her. Marcia had been in a league of her own.

He was aware that Marcia had been pulled involuntarily into his life of uncertainty. He knew that at any given moment he could be arrested and put in prison, and Marcia would be left to care for their four children on her own.

"I am needed at the club!" Eamon stated without resistance, feeling her warm breath and her tongue circling over the tip of his flaccid penis.

Laying back, he put the phone on record again. He wanted to cherish the time that they had together.

After Marcia had pleasured him, Eamon moved behind her. She was on all fours and began to succumb to his tongue, his finger and the heel of his hand, which deepened her orgasm.

"This is going to be locked away!" Eamon said as he slapped her rear playfully, phone in his hand, sidling from the bed.

8

The following day at Suzette's beauty salon, Marcia waited for her next client. There was a rap on the door, but it opened before she had a chance to even say 'come in'. The formidable presence of a short-haired, blonde woman filled the room. Marcia judged her to be in her 60s. Her figure was slim and curvaceous. Marcia thought that she could be an attractive woman if it wasn't for her projected hostility. The woman closed the door and approached the desk. She pulled out the chair, placing her expensive-looking designer bag on the floor beside her.

"I want answers, which I am told that you can tell me. My mate has recommended you!" she directed, her piercing blue eyes, boring into Marcia's.

Marcia smiled, picking up the pack of tarot cards. "I will answer your queries once I have completed the reading!" Marcia took note of the woman's irritation. Her neck flushed scarlet at her directive. She sensed that the client was used to giving orders, not receiving them. She handed her the cards. "Shuffle them until you feel the need to stop!"

The woman shuffled the pack as if she were playing at a casino, sliding them back across the desk.

Marcia began, "If you would like to record the…?"

The woman interjected, "In my world, love, you do not record anything." She added," Prying eyes!"

Marcia had the woman's full attention. She proceeded to lay out the cards. Marcia could see that she had to tread carefully when the first card revealed deception.

"You are about to make a life-changing decision which will see you falling flat on your face. However, if you bide your time and keep your tongue in your head, then you will end up the victor!" Marcia fleetingly looked at the woman. "I sense that this relates to a relationship which has hit a rocky patch." She continued, "You are no stranger to heart-ache. The turmoil that you face will be resolved within the next two months. Do not try to push a situation – let it unfold because there will be a parting of the ways that will be favour-able for you."

Marcia placed her finger on the card of The Star. "This card represents the planet Uranus," she tapped it, "an unexpected disruption in your life will bring a windfall, not only financially, but something that you desire which will see a new pathway opening for you."

The woman put her hand up. "Let me stop you, love!" she said, her tone now softer. She leaned forward putting her forearms on the desk, looking at the layout of the cards. "I can take it. What you are telling me is what is going on in my life. Furthermore, to enlighten you, my old man has knocked up his young bird. She is 25 years younger than him. I cannot take anymore." She said with an element of wistfulness, sitting back looking resigned.

"How can I compete with all that? He has always been a player – I put up with that!" she exhaled. "But not this. She has hooked him, with the kid she is carrying!" She contin-ued, "My old man, Les Booker, knows your fella, the Irishman.

Mind you, it was before you when he was married to the blonde tart that was shagging his boss, Jimmy Grant!"

Marcia froze but did not respond.

"They all get up to it!" she smiled. "However, from what I hear, you have straightened the good-looking Dubliner up, and given him babies!" She glanced at Marcia's stomach, waggling her head. "Let's get back to me and my old man, and my decision to leave him."

Marcia hesitated before saying, "I am only advising you that if you keep a still tongue, the winds of change will blow in your favour within two months. The turmoil in your life will be removed."

"FINITO!" the woman exclaimed gesturing with her forefinger, swiping her throat.

"Yes!" Marcia nodded, smiling.

The woman guffawed, "This will be a first, me keeping my mouth shut! She waggled her head. "However, my mate followed your advice, much to her happiness now." She threw in, pursing her lips. "Why not!" She picked her bag up as she rose to leave. "When's your baby due?"

"I am having twins – girls," Marcia smiled.

"I am no psychic, however, for you to be able to turn that man of yours around from the previous life he lived, before Jimmy Grant's demise," she smiled, "I'd say that you two are in for the long haul. You may look sweet and innocent, a touch demure, but you're no fool, pretty lady!" the woman grinned.

"You will have the contentment that has evaded your life sooner than you think…" Marcia paused for a second. "Watch and wait."

"You have made me a happy woman," she smiled wistfully. "I'm listening!" She opened the door imparting a nod in Marcia's direction.

Marcia sat at her desk mulling over the woman's words regarding Eamon's previous wife, who she said had been having an affair with Jimmy Grant. She realised that it had been common knowledge, and Eamon was the last to know. Marcia knew that Eamon's previous jealousy stemmed from his insecurity because Eve had betrayed him. Her thoughts went to the woman's husband, who knew Eamon. She realised that if Eamon discovered that she had given a tarot reading to Les Booker's wife, he would put a stop to her continuing to work.

Suzette popped her head round the door, grinning. "Your last client obviously had a satisfactory reading. She came in like Attila the Hun," she laughed, taking the seat opposite Marcia, "however, she looked like she had just won the lottery when she left. Whatever did you tell her, Marcia? She left this tip for you." Marcia smiled when Suzette handed her the €50. "She said that she was going to recommend you!"

Marcia returned it. "Put it in the staff tip box. The boys and Cindy work flat out."

Suzette crossed her legs, leaning back in the chair, smiling softly. "Who would have thought that seven years ago when we came to Spain…," she paused for a second, looking momentarily uneasy, both women knowing that Marcia had not had much choice in the matter. "Still!" she laughed, dismissing the awkward moment. "I know that man of yours is not the one I would have put you with." She shook her head, her immaculate hair, cut in a bob, falling back into place. "Nevertheless, he makes you happy. Your handsome sons will compliment those two baby girls that you are carrying."

She rested her gaze on Marcia's stomach, exhaling. "There are times that I envy you, with your children! However, I am not including your stud!" Suzette laughed. "Eamon O'Donally is too controlling, like most of the men in our world.

Although I know that he adores you. As Gregg does me, but Greg is a big old pussy cat, unlike your roaring lion!" She stood to leave, straightening the skirt of her black Chanel suit. "There is one thing in your man's favour that I must hand to him, at least he appreciates haute couture and keeps you in the style that you have become accustomed to!"

Marcia smiled fondly at her friend. Fate had sent Suzette to Marcia for a tarot reading seven years ago. Their relationship had started off on an unsure footing, but Suzette had proven to be a loyal and generous ally, much to Eamon's chagrin. Marcia could understand why Eamon disliked her; in the beginning, Suzette had used Marcia for her own ends. Nevertheless, without Suzette's plotting and scheming, Marcia would not have found herself in Spain or met Eamon.

She placed her hands on her stomach – the babies moved. She did not have any regrets. Marcia heard her mobile vibrating – she had switched it to silent mode when she began the first tarot reading three hours ago.

"Are ye available for yer man to take ye out to lunch, my little mystic?"

Marcia relaxed back in her chair.

"Or maybe if ye want me to make us a salad, we can relax by the pool at home, and I will give ye a back massage." he offered. "The wee babies must be weighing ye down."

Marcia still found Eamon's Dublin brogue sexy. She found everything about him desirable. She sometimes wondered, though, especially since he had gone into partnership with Greg at the adult club, whether being near all those scantily clad pole dancers on a regular basis would tempt him to stray from their marital bed. The thoughts had recently played on her mind as her baby bump grew.

Marcia replied, "I would like us to eat at home. Also, the massage sounds very inviting." She added, "I have purchased luxury Neom oils with a CD for restoring health. I will massage your back – you need it, Eamon!"

Eamon laughed, "It seems that our lunch break may be turning into a steamy afternoon, my little hot-sexy wife."

Marcia giggled, as she put her phone in her bag and got ready to go home.

The languid breeze from the open terrace doors in their bedroom gave little respite to the heat. Their bodies entwined, his legs clamped hers, and his hand caressed her mound. "Relax," he breathed, "Let me take ye again!" He continued with deliberate gentle thrusting, Marcia slotting in with him, allowing him to take over. After the first time, he had not withdrawn. "I want us to flow together." His fingertips moved to her erect nipples, giving them soft tweaks. With his warm breath on her neck, he smiled, "I can feel ye beginning." Releasing with her, they tumbled into bliss.

Withdrawing, he turned her to face him, cupping her chin. "Ye give me so much pleasure." He held her dark eyes. "More than I've ever known." He ran his fingertip along her top lip.

Marcia kissed him, knowing that Eamon was not usually a man to disclose his feelings. However, his reassuring words gave her comfort.

9

Vic Greyland received a telephone call from his long-time pal Kev Green. Although they kept in contact over the years, he hadn't heard from him for a while. They had a brotherly bond. Kev had been in with Vic's people in the past. He had been the man who had shifted the stolen goods. Vic knew that he was someone to be trusted. Kev had gone on the straight road, working a nine-to-five job, while Vic had continued his path until the gang he ran with got caught in a jewellery heist. Fortunately for Vic, his wife had gone into premature labour that night and he hadn't been with the gang. Way before the trial, Vic and his family scarpered to the Costa Blanca.

"Long time no hear!" Vic said cheerily when he answered the call. "What you been up to mate? How is the 'smoke'?" he asked, referring to the East End of London where Kev lived.

"This is not a social call, Vic." Kev's tone was distant, unfriendly.

"What's the problem mate? You sound like something's eating ya."

Kev replied, "It's not my problem that's bothering me." He continued, "I have been mulling it over as to whether or not to ring ya, however, due to us having a past, I felt like I owed it to ya."

"Don't sound so serious, Kev. Nothing's that bad. They abolished hanging years ago!" Vic laughed.

Kev Green replied tersely,

"I am doing you a favour, mate, by marking your card. I had a little bird chirp in my ear that there is a price on your head. Some people want you out of the way."

"WHAT THE FUCK!" Vic raised his voice.

"Listen up! Don't start on me. I'm doing you a good turn," Kev said.

"And who the hell is your source of this information?" Vic asked.

"Well, it turns out my girl, Louise, is getting married, you see. She recently disclosed to her mother that her intended Nathan's cousin is a certain Detective Inspector Ian Blackmore. More to the point, he joins the lads on the stag do, they have a few bevvies, and the detective discloses to Nathan that he's got a feather in his cap due to a 'grass' giving him inside informa-tion. Your name came up. Nathan informs my girl, who, as you know, realises that my old buddy Vic Greyland is one and the same."

"What a load of bollocks – fucking Chinese whispers!" Vic yelled. "The Bill might have brought my name into some-thing that connected me to the past, but I'm telling ya—"

"DON'T GIVE ME YA BOLLOCKS!" Kev shouted. "This is fucking kosher. Ya can't worm ya way out of this one mate. Please don't insult my intelligence by trying to deny it! You're fortunate that my Louise is savvy. She doesn't let on too much to her fella, only her mum, who isn't a happy bunny because her half-brother Leroy has recently been pulled in on an investigation on a past blag that you knew about..." Kev paused. "I'm sorry that it had to end like this. Nevertheless, mate, I can't associate with ya anymore."

The burring of the dial tone informed Kev that his message had been loud and clear.

Vic Greyland didn't waste any time. He instructed his wife Janis to throw a few things into two suitcases, no questions asked. She kicked off, stating that she wasn't leaving her beautiful villa, but she changed her mind when Vic shouted that he would end up as shark bait as there were people after him. Vic got on the phone to book a flight to a bolt hole that he had in place for a time such as this.

Vic Greyland went on the run with his wife, not realising that Big Dave Broadbent was already hot on his tail.

Eamon shook his head when Big Dave informed him that Vic Greyland's villa was vacant.

"There's no sign of him. However, the Greylands were spotted by the old fella who lives opposite getting into a taxi with two suitcases. He was out watering his front garden and had waved to them, but they had ignored him.

"Obviously, someone has marked the cunt's card," Eamon spat.

"Luck's on our side!" Big Dave said. "The old boy was angry at being ignored and fortunately the taxi company's name was on the side panel. To cut it short, I phoned with the address and the receptionist said they dropped off those passengers at terminal N at Alicante airport. She also remembered that they had to rush as the flight to Pathos, Cyprus was leaving within two and a half hours."

Both men laughed.

Eamon needed Vic Greyland's address in Cyprus. He had only one way of finding it, and that was through Thomas Harper-Watts's father, Lord Arthur. Eamon realised that time was of the essence. Big Dave needed to reach Vic before the Bill in London discovered that their 'canary had flown the coop'. He knew that once they set an international arrest warrant in place with the Cypriot police, all would be lost.

Eamon phoned Billy, who sprang into action, contacting Thomas, who in turn called his father Lord Arthur. The peer placed the phone call, inviting his 'friend' Chief Inspector Ross Lowe to his London gentleman's club for a lunchtime tipple the following day.

The invite was immediately accepted.

Eamon sat at his desk at home contemplating what could happen if the Law in London had gotten wind of Greyland's bolt hole before he did. But with the resources Eamon had to hand, it would not take long to discover the address.

Lord Arthur plied the Chief Inspector Ross Lowe with the Asbach 21-year aged brandy that he liked, which assisted in getting Lowe to impart the inside information.

Eamon knew that it was a waiting game. He hoped his luck continued and the address in Cyprus would come back to him. Then it would only be a matter of 24 hours before Big Dave would be able to solve his problem. Then he could rest easy, until the next time.

10

Eamon and Marcia's sons were returning home from the boarding school for the summer holidays. It was the first time that they had left the school since their enrolment. Eamon read Niall's report – the situation had deteriorated. Niall's disruptive behaviour had increased. Eamon had spoken to the principal, who informed him that Niall required a firm hand. There had been two incidents when Niall behaved in an intimidating way towards his fellow students. The principal warned that the school would not tolerate any further incidents. Eamon assured him that he would deal with his son.

On the other hand, Quinn had a glowing report. Both of his sons excelled in many areas, but Niall's disruptive behaviour was getting him into trouble.

Eamon exhaled, putting the reports on the desk that had been faxed to him earlier. "How in hell can my two boys who are identical in looks and who are treated equally to so much love and attention be so different," he mused, running his fingers through his hair.

There was one thing that he was not going to tolerate – that was his boy's bullying behaviour. He was determined to nip it in the bud before Niall hit his teenage years. He realised that he would need to try different tactics with Niall. He thought back to how his brother Patrick used to be. Eamon had helped to give him and his family a new start by purchasing him the small holding in County Armagh, Northern Ireland. His brother had moved away from the previous life of crime in Dublin to the fresh country air and seemed to have a happy life, although he knew that Patrick's shotgun wedding to the quiet Catholic girl who was besotted with him would not have been by choice. However, Patrick had made her pregnant. One night when Patrick had returned home from his regular haunt, the Bar-Code club in Clontarf with the drink in him, Rosie McConnally was on the corner waiting. "It was only one shag up against the wall!" Patrick had confided woefully to Eamon. Nonetheless, Rosie's irate father convinced him that he had to do the right thing and marry her.

Unfortunately, after a few months into the marriage, Rosie miscarried, but later down the line, they produced a beautiful dark-haired daughter who was the image of Patrick. They were told that the baby was autistic. Then a couple of years later, Rosie gave birth to a son, Conner. Patrick doted on them both.

Eamon ensured that his sibling and his family did not want for anything. He could not make out why his eldest son was not of the same mind. It certainly was not due to Eamon trying to instil it in him. Eamon concluded that Niall was jealous of his brother Quinn.

. . . .

Eamon and Marcia entered the principal's office. The tension in the room was palpable. Eamon glanced at his sons. Niall stood, head down, alongside his smiling younger brother.

Eamon returned the principal's brusque nod.

The principal said, "We have come to an agreement that Niall will report any potential situations of conflict," he smiled smugly in Niall's direction, turning his attention to Eamon, "before he decides to take it into his own hands."

His charming smile was lost on Eamon; however, Eamon's Arctic glare wasn't lost on the principal, who shifted his stance.

Marcia put her arms around the boys' shoulders as they walked from the building.

"We are going to have a wonderful holiday," she pulled them into her. Quinn skipped alongside, beaming, while Niall looked ahead. Eamon sensed that something was amiss with his son.

"Your tummy is big, Mummy!" Quinn said.

Marcia smiled. She was going to wait until the boys were settled in back home before telling them the news, but she blurted out,

"I have two baby sisters for you both in my tummy."

Quinn stopped walking, looking at Marcia's stomach. "How did you get two baby sisters in your tummy?" his innocent dark brown eyes searched hers.

Marcia fleetingly looked at Eamon, a smile forming at the corner of his mouth.

"Papa will explain," she smiled at both boys, "when you are grown up."

"You are still pretty with a big tummy, Mummy!" Quinn held her hand, smiling at both parents.

Niall kept on looking straight ahead without acknowledging his mother's proffered hand.

Eamon nodded to himself as he observed his son, sensing that something was amiss with Niall. Whatever it was, he was determined to get to the bottom of it.

Throughout the journey home, Quinn fired many questions about the forthcoming baby girls. He said that he was eager to teach them to swim.

When they arrived in the Spanish town of Benissa, on seeing a restaurant, Quinn chirped, "Papa, may we have pizza?"

"To be sure!" Eamon smiled, pulling up outside the restaurant.

"Do ye want to look at the menu here, Niall?"

"May I have a steak?" the boy asked.

"That's ye and me sorted!" Eamon said, placing his hand on his son's shoulder, and guiding him through the restaurant doors.

Back at the villa, the boys wanted to swim so Eamon told them to change into their swimming trunks. Marcia went to help them, but Eamon placed his hand on her arm, smiling. "Let them be, Marcia, they are taught to be independent at school."

He pulled her to him while the boys went to their rooms. "Ye will have the baby girls to see to shortly," he grinned, brushing her mouth, kissing her softly. "If that's not enough to keep ye busy, we will have enough time to make another one."

Screams reverberated around the villa. Eamon raced up the stairs two steps at a time.

Bursting open the bedroom door, he was momentarily taken aback by the vision of Niall astride Quinn's chest, holding a fistful of hair, banging his brother's head on the floor. In two strides, Eamon picked both boys up. Setting them down, he glared at Niall. The small boy's dark eyes held his father's. Quinn sobbed, his nose running.

"What in hell is going on?"

"Niall said that he is going to hurt the baby girls!"

Eamon knelt to their level, and he exhaled. Marcia came into the bedroom, startled by the mess. Quinn made a move towards her. Eamon placed a firm but gentle hold on him. "Marcia, let me deal wit this!" He gave a sharp nod for her to leave. Quinn held his arms up towards her. "Mummy, please!" Quinn cried.

Marcia stepped forward.

Eamon raised his brow at her while putting a protective arm around Quinn.

Marcia closed the door.

"Niall, go to ye room. I will be in to ye shortly!" Eamon said firmly.

Niall, head down, left the room.

Eamon sat Quinn on the bed. He sat down next to him. Quinn sniffed, eyes brimming with tears.

"I want ye to tell me what's going on, Quinn. Don't be frightened, because Papa will put a stop to it!"

"Niall tells the students that we are not true brothers. He says that I am adopted. But Papa, I am not, am I?"

Eamon exhaled. The question was ridiculous to him, as his boys were so alike in appearance that they could be twins, however, he realised his small son wanted confirmation.

"Ye are mine and Mummy's son, as Niall is. When Mummy gave birth to ye, Niall was not a year old," he ruffled Quinn's hair. "Niall is tormenting ye."

Eamon stood up. "However, I will not tolerate Niall hurting ye! Does Niall hit ye at the school?" Quinn looked at the floor. Eamon nodded, sucking air through his teeth. "Get changed, Mummy is waiting on ye!" he smiled.

Entering Niall's bedroom, Eamon closed the door. Niall sat on the bed, still wearing his school uniform. Eamon sat at the end of the bed facing him.

"What is it wit ye Niall? Ye are saying bad tings. Striking ye brother!" He held his son's dark eyes. "I am telling ye, Niall, that I will not tolerate my children being at war wit one another!"

He paused for a minute, watching Niall. "We are a family. Ye are my eldest, my first!"

Niall looked away. Eamon gently cupped his chin, easing his head to face him. "When ye are older, ye are going to be responsible for ye siblings. Do ye understand?"

Eamon stroked his goatee beard. "However, until that day comes, I want ye to tell me if ye or Quinn have any problems." Eamon smiled, standing to his full height. He ruffled Niall's hair. "Get changed for the pool. Maureen and Dom will arrive tomorrow. We are going out on the boat for the day."

Eamon took note of the interest at the mention of Maureen coming to visit. He knew that Maureen loved both boys, however, it was Niall she favoured.

Eamon realised that he was going to change tactics with Niall. *Let's see if this way works*, he thought to himself as he opened a bottle of wine. Taking the wine, he took it out to the terrace. Marcia was standing near the pool watching the boys jumping onto the inflatables, laughing gaily while Aye gave them instructions regarding their evening meal. Quinn waved to Eamon as he came up behind Marcia.

His free hand removed her sunglasses, placing them on her head.

"The boys will be grand!" he soothed at seeing Marcia's watery eyes. He could see she was upset. She smiled wistfully.

"Eamon, I sense that there is something wrong. I know that Niall requires more attention. However, I feel that there is also–"

"I have it in hand!" he broke in, putting his arm around her shoulder, and pecking the nape of her neck. Gulping a large mouthful of the wine, he placed the glass on the table, caressing her stomach. "We are going to have a perfectly balanced family!" he smiled softly. "Two boys and two girls." He pressed his groin into her baby bump and felt the babies move. He smiled, "They can hear their papa!"

"Perhaps it is your intrusion they can feel!" She put her arms around his neck, head cocked to one side.

"I will soothe my babies to sleep while I massage ye – once the boys are in bed!" He reached for the wine glass, finishing it in one gulp.

"Khao jai mai, kin khaw kan!"(Do you understand, let's eat) Aye called out when she came back through the terrace doors with the boys' towelling robes, hand on hip, shaking her head. They both hurried out of the pool.

"Khao jai," Quinn replied, telling Aye that he understood.

Eamon and Marcia smiled at each other as Aye ordered the boys to the table for their dinner.

She mumbled under her breath in Thai as she ushered the boys inside. Niall and Quinn both nodded. Aye smiled.

"I tink that Aye has more control of the boys than me!" Eamon smiled. They both sat down at the garden table. Eamon studied Marcia. "Do ye tink that yer up to it – helping at the club? Yer baby bump has doubled in size. Yer also working at the salon giving tarot readings…" he paused. "To my mind, ye shouldn't be working right now." He raised his hand, palm facing her, to stop her from protesting. "Hear me out, Marcia," he said softly, smiling, "Ye have a bank card that gives ye carte blanche to buy whatever ye need. The amount of money that ye earn advising clients about their lives, to my mind it does not warrant the fallout that ye could come up against. The type of people in our circle are not yer everyday regular sort of 9–5 people. The majority of yer clients, I should imagine are criminals' women!" He cocked an eyebrow.

Marcia reached across the table for his hand. "I know that you are generous to me." She held his eyes. "Nonetheless,

Eamon, I need my independence." Her fingertips played over the back of his hand. "I only work at Suzette's for two days. I can help Suzette at the adult club with employing the dancers until the latter stage of my pregnancy."

He sucked air through his teeth. Taking her hand in his, he replied nodding, "Okay! But listen to me. Ye can be in the club only when I am working there. I won't take the risk of ye getting hurt if any of the men wit drink in them kick off."

Marcia moved around the table, leaning into him, and wrapping her arms went around him. He pulled her onto his lap. "Don't tink that I am giving into ye, because when those baby girls arrive ye will have four children that will require yer attention." He smiled. "I also need ye."

He returned her kiss. "I will go to see the boys. Then ye will have my full attention for a few hours before I meet Greg and the men at the club. I must run through a few tings wit them."

11

The following morning, after Dom and Maureen's arrival, Eamon noticed that Niall's previous heavy mood had lightened when the cockney woman started fussing over the boys. They were heading for the marina where the yacht that Eamon had purchased for a 'song' from Lenny Decker's widow after Lenny had died, was docked. Eamon had also purchased their villa, which he had quickly sold. The profit had covered the cost of the vessel. It was a perfect way to make some 'clean money.'

Eamon had given the day off to the two Spanish brothers who maintained the vessel for him. Dom O'Reilly was an expert seafarer and knew the waters well, so he would be taking command of the boat. They were being joined by Thomas Harper-Watts and his family, as well as Billy and Jane and Dan and Cindy. Eamon had been grateful that Suzette and Greg hadn't been able to make it. Her presence at the Hawk Wind club was as much as he could tolerate, and he only did so because her husband Greg was Eamon's business partner.

Maureen helped the children with their life vests and ushered Niall and Quinn and Thomas's boys into the lounge/diner. The rest of the women sat talking on the deck. Billy, Dan, and Thomas headed to the stern, where the bar was situated. Eamon followed Dom up the steps to the bridge.

"What a lovely piece of kit!" Dom stated as they moved out from the marina.

Eamon's mind was elsewhere, he was deep in thought about Vic Greyland's bolthole. He had hoped to hear some news from London by now. Previously, Lord Arthur had always come up with the information that Eamon required. He did not doubt that if the Bill at London's HQ knew of Greyland's whereabouts Lord Arthur would coerce his 'friend', Chief Inspector Ross Lowe to spill the beans. He realised that he had to be patient.

"The weather forecast is fine until late this afternoon. It might get a bit choppy on the way back. But as we head for Denia, I know of a lovely cove in Las Rotas where I can lay anchor. There are dolphins and occasionally whales in that area." Dom held his arm out indicating the boat and the scenery. "What more could a man want!" The sun sparkled across the Costa Blanca waters. He pointed to the Serra Gelada Natural Park in the distance on the starboard side. "That heavy cloud won't reach us for a few hours, if at all. The forecast is not always spot on. However, with the women and kids on board, I won't take any chances." Dom smiled. "She rides these troughs with ease." Dom grinned turning his head towards the women below. "I must congratulate you, lad. My Maureen informs me that your wife is having twins – baby girls? You must have plenty of lead in ya pencil to keep knocking them out," he laughed.

Eamon nodded, smiling. "My wife wanted a girl, but we were surprised to find out that there are two!"

Dom interjected. "You were never a lad to do things by halves. The wife wants a girl, you give her double. Nice!" He chuckled. "I miss that…" he paused, "a good romp in the haystack. Mind you, there's still a good tune on this old fiddle!

Dom's tone took on a serious bent. "I wanted to speak to ya about something that's being whispered about a grass!"

Dom had Eamon's attention. He knew that Dom had a lot of powerful connections in the UK, and also Spain.

"I have heard a couple of names mentioned. A lot of my old pals are feeling uneasy due to someone 'singing'. You know how it is lad. We are all in the same boat, if we aren't fully involved, we have dabbled in the past. You were up to ya neck in it with Jimmy Grant – the prick!" He added, "The likes of us can never rest easy, although, like me, you went straight after you met your woman and had ya family!"

Eamon pursed his lips, nodding.

"We can all play the guessing game, however! Danny Harvey, as you know, is doing a long stretch in Belmarsh Prison after having been on the run for a good few years. He is married to one of Vic Greyland's wife's sisters. The Harveys were a hard lot, women included. Nevertheless, Danny Harvey had lived a clandestine life in Andalusia, tucked away in the hills, when suddenly he gets the proverbial tap on the shoulder from the Law, who takes him back to the UK." Dom pointed ahead. "Denia and Javea's coastline." Dom rubbed his paunch, grinning. "My Maureen was up late last night cooking our favourite Irish grub." He rubbed his brow. "Where was I?" Shaking his head, smiling, he said, "The name that takes my money is Vic Greyland. Never trusted the man. Greyland was linked with Danny Harvey's older brother who had his collar felt at the same time as Danny. Vic Greyland had too much inside info, yet Greyland remains free!" Waggling his head, Dom exclaimed, "None of it adds up to me." He steered the yacht into Denia's cove.

Eamon listened without responding.

He turned, catching sight of Niall and Atticus, Thomas's son, wrestling over a game console. Eamon saw Atticus leaning across the table glaring at Niall and gripping the item that both boys desired, before Maureen intervened, giving Atticus a replacement. Eamon smiled to himself. Young Atticus was a good match for his son.

Walking onto the deck, he caught Marcia's eye. He winked. She smiled.

Eamon could hear the laughter as he approached his guests. Billy was no doubt entertaining the men with his ribald jokes and tongue-in-cheek banter.

Thomas saw Eamon come over and extricated himself from the group. "Can I have a word, boss?" Both men moved out of earshot.

"My father called today and gave me some information regarding your runaway. The Chief Inspector told him Vic Greyland's bolt-hole address, and even detailed his early morning regime." He smiled.

Eamon nodded, placing a hand on Thomas's shoulder, smiling. "That's grand. Please thank yer father."

Eamon felt as if a huge weight had been lifted from his shoulders. Billy passed him a glass of red wine. "It's not your usual, boss."

"No problem." Eamon was feeling elated; he did not care if the wine was not the usual. As soon as the information on Vic Greyland was received he would telephone Big Dave, and the cat-and-mouse game would begin.

Eamon strolled across the deck, stopping near the lounge. He glanced inside to see the boys listening to Maureen singing an Irish lullaby. Niall was sitting on the leather seating, comfortable in the arms of Maureen. He inhaled. *My son has a weak spot for the older Irish woman,* he thought. Marcia came alongside him. "Would you like to eat? You must be hungry, as you skipped breakfast."

He put his arm around her shoulder, looking down at her.

"Ye fulfilled me last night when ye were beneath me!" His eyes twinkled. Marcia blushed. "Ye may act coy, however, ye appeared to enjoy it. Yer soft moans of delight are all on record. Therefore, my wee mystic, ye innocent looks don't wash wit me!" Eamon kissed the top of her head.

Marcia laughed, putting her arm around his waist. She turned to look at the scene of Maureen with the children. "Niall loves Maureen!" she said wistfully.

Eamon nodded.

"I need the bathroom!" Eamon patted her rear turning his attention to Dom moving towards him, wine glass in hand.

"When ya get tired of this new toy," he gulped the wine, "give me a bell. Not only does she handle smoothly over the troughs, but the twin Volvo engines also give a good thrust. Like a good woman!" he chuckled. "Speaking of women," he sank half of the wine, "when does this adult club of yours open, ya lucky bleeder? All that young, bare flesh – I would not get any sleep just thinking that I could make hay while the sun shines. Quick leg over in the office. Mind you, I should imagine that your woman looks after ya." He smiled. "Mine is a different ball game. He exhaled. "That's the reason I have had to find my entertainment outside."

"The club opening is tomorrow night. The sale of the yearly membership has been through the roof. If it is anything to go by, it appears that the club will be successful." Eamon said.

Dom shook his head. "I don't have any doubt that the club will take off. However," he glanced in Marcia's direction who was chatting with the other women. "I'd be worried if I were Marcia, and my old man was surrounded by pole dancers. That's a lot of temptation for any man, let alone a good-looking bloke like you. The women will be after ya like bees to a honeypot. Put yourself in her shoes. Or, if she…", he nodded towards Marcia, "was surrounded by near-naked young males. How would…"

Eamon interjected, placing his hand on Dom's arm, "That's never going to happen!" He gave a sharp nod, directing Dom to the galley. "Let us eat your wife's lovely Irish food!"

12

The following morning, Eamon phoned Big Dave Broadbent with the details of Vic Greyland's address in Cyprus and the details of his regular early morning walk that he took before 9 am along the cliffs near his home.

He smiled to himself as he stepped through the terrace doors. Marcia walked down the steps of the pool. The black bikini she wore looked sexy. Her pregnant belly was protruding, and her full breasts filled the top. He would have joined her in the pool; however, he had an appointment with his bank manager Felipe Hortez. He checked his watch. The bank manager was flexible with Eamon; they had come to an understanding ever since Eamon began paying him a stipend. Eamon had unearthed the man's secret double life. His mistress had given him three children. Furthermore, Felipe Hortez's father-in-law was the CEO of the bank. Felipe Hortez had agreed to aid Eamon in investing the undisclosed one-hundred-and-fifty million euros that he received after the disappearance of Jimmy Grant from the deal in Miami nearly seven years ago. The Cayman Islands and Gibraltar became Eamon's clandestine financial haven. Eamon wanted to set up a trust fund for his wife and children.

He walked to the edge of the pool. Marcia looked up.

"Have you got time to join me?" she said as she continued to swim.

"Unfortunately, I can only spare ye 30 minutes. My appointment cannot be put off!"

Marcia stood up. "The boys won't be back from Thomas's villa until after lunch. I can swim later. It would only take me a few seconds to remove my bikini," she said enticingly as she climbed out of the pool and made her way back inside.

"I am always up for that!" Eamon said, following her to the bedroom.

He lay her on the bed and climbed atop her. She took him in deeper and her fingertips caressed his scrotum. There was an involuntary jerk as he released. He knew that he needed to control himself as he didn't want to hurt her. However, the spasm of pleasure accelerated as she aided him, with her free hand upon his shaft.

Easing from her, he said, smiling, "I do hope that no one ever sees these videos of us – my heavily pregnant wife on her back pleasuring me." He kissed her.

"I like to please you," she said.

"I am sorry it was short but sweet!" he said, winking at her as he dressed. "I will transfer this and lock it in my safe."

Later that evening, Eamon's Byredo cologne, which Marcia had introduced him to, with its lemon, floral, musk, and sandalwood scent, filled her senses. She moved in behind him as he buttoned his suit jacket.

"You look handsome and suave," she said, speaking to his reflection in the full-length mirror. Eamon turned, placing his hands on either side of her baby bump.

"I want ye to rest tonight while I am at the club. There is no telling what time I will be back because ye cannot tell what the night will bring wit men wit drink in them!"

She placed her palms on his chest, their dark eyes fixed on each other. Eamon pressed into her, kissing her softly. He smiled when he felt the babies move.

"Ring me if ye need anyting…" he paused cupping her chin. "Upon my return, I will try not to disturb ye!"

"I want you to disturb me!" Her fingertips stroked his goatee beard. "Whatever the hour!"

Eamon smiled, nodding, and brushing her mouth with a brief kiss.

"Ensure that ye get some sleep. Then I won't feel guilty for wanting ye in the small hours!"

Marcia closed the door after watching the entry gates close behind Eamon's Maserati. The dog followed her across the room towards the terrace doors. Aye was in her room watching her favourite television programmes, although Marcia knew that she would be alert to the boys' monitor.

She sat at the garden table. The dog rested his head on his forelegs – his intelligent almond-shaped eyes forever observing.

The panoramic scenery of the twinkling waters of the bay stretched out before her. The picturesque Sierra de Bernia Mountains, which protected Altea created an especially mild climate. She scanned the luxury villas that housed many ex-pats, associates from Eamon's past when he worked for Jimmy Grant. The beautiful vista never ceased to fill her senses with its majesty. Eamon had given her all this. His generosity knew no bounds. He had revealed to her some snippets from his childhood, and she guessed he sought to ensure that his family did not experience the poverty that he had experienced as a child.

Nevertheless, she still felt as if her life was shrouded in uncertainty. Although Eamon did not reveal it to her, she could sense his constant concern regarding his criminal past catching up with him. His dark brown eyes, which reflected hers, spoke to her. She exhaled – the dog raised a curious eyebrow. She ruffled his coat. "I would give all this up, Roman, to live a life with him and my children in obscurity!" The dog listened, ears cocked.

Marcia pondered upon their frantic lovemaking. Their coupling was filled with a knowing that their time together could be snatched from them at any given moment. "I ask you to keep all of my family safe!" she included her eldest son Rueben as she spoke to the Universe. "Eamon was a lost soul before I met him. Lord of Karma, if you make him pay for his past sins then all will be lost!" Marcia quietly pleaded her case to the unseen deity.

Marcia locked the doors. Directing the dog to stay in the lounge, she left her bedroom door ajar.

She lay on the bed, her thoughts turning to the dancers that she and Suzette had interviewed. She suddenly felt a pang of vulnerability. She ran her hands over her belly, feeling the baby girls that she had so desperately wanted. Eamon said that he loved her pregnancy, although her growing belly was making some positions difficult. Even with all her yoga training, she was unable to bend and twist as she used to during their lovemaking, so they adapted their methods.

Marcia realised from the beginning that she couldn't take Eamon's love for granted, even though his desire for her had never waned. Nevertheless, Eamon was a passionate man – powerful and handsome. She knew that the women at the club would have no scruples and would try to seduce Eamon. They were attractive, young, sexy women ranging from a sultry Somalian, two red-headed Irish sisters, a blonde, a brunette, and Mediterranean. Marcia could sense their predatory nature. Suzette was overseeing the pole dancers on the opening night. She knew that her friend would be on the phone in the morning to fill her in on the details of the evening. She picked her book up; a distraction from her thoughts was what she needed. She was the second page in when the book slipped from her hand, and she drifted off to sleep.

13

Eamon looked at the testosterone-filled crowd filing into the Hawk Wind club. *I must hand it to Suzette,* he thought, begrudgingly giving her the praise that was due. Her business acumen with advertising had paid off. The place was buzzing. Eamon had made it a rule that the security men and the dancers should not mix. Relationships between them, he reasoned with Greg, would mean trouble. From Eamon's point of view, the tough men would not be able to tolerate seeing their woman, nearly naked, enticing other men with their provocative dancing.

He checked his watch as he walked to the office. He sent a text and waited to see if it had been read. He knew that the unread message meant that Marcia was asleep.

His two-way radio crackled into life. He locked the door and strode to the other side of the club. The two bars were five deep. His men were alerted to a mouthy young guy near the stage. Eamon caught Greg's look of concern. Eamon gave a sharp nod in Suzette's direction as she came out of the dressing room. Greg marched towards her. Suzette immediately turned on her heel and went back in.

A moment later, Jenny, the dancer, tried to move back as a hand tried to grab at her thong. She stumbled backwards. Billy,

Dan, and Thomas jumped into action, and the security guards surrounded the crowd. The pals of the perpetrator who were egging the guy on were seized by Thomas and Dan. Billy yanked the lad back, lifting him off his feet. Billy smirked, frog-marching the troublemakers out of the club.

Eamon nodded at Jenny who professionally resumed her dance routine. He followed the men to the exit. Another ruckus had kicked off outside of the club. While Billy's attention was momentarily diverted one of the lads being thrown out struck the side of Billy's head with his fist. Billy didn't flinch but the retaliation punch was instantaneous. The lad reeled then staggered backwards. His buddies rushed to help him. Shaking them off, he walked away, shouting threats, "You has-beens are going to have to watch your backs. That big Irish tinker that owns the place, won't reign long. The club will be petrol bombed!" The security team laughed at the retreating lads, however, Eamon remained serious.

"Do any of youse know who that mouthy pox-balling prick is?" he asked, keeping is eyes on the retreating back of the lad who continued to shout at them.

Dan piped up, "He is Dougie Dugan's boy, Tommy. When I was running through the yearly membership subscription I clocked the name. I have already made a few enquiries. The flash sod is trouble. He drives a yellow Lotus, all down to his father's generosity." He smiled, "However, due to his old man being who he is, I thought it best to not rock the boat by refusing his membership application."

Eamon sucked air through his teeth. "I don't doubt that we will get a visit from Dougie and his brother when the kid runs home screaming."

"Odds on!" Dan declared.

Raising his brow, Eamon said, "I will cross that bridge when I come to it. The night is still young! Let us get back inside to see what else is in store."

The group of guys at a stag party, who had been some-what rowdy but without getting out of hand, thanked Eamon and Greg for a great time.

"We've made a killing!" Greg beamed, turning to face Eamon. "You are legal now. No more looking over your shoulder!" He cocked his head. "At least with the taxman anyway. I can't help you with the 'canary'. Thank God I got out of that game, way back." He smiled fondly. "However, we both know that it will always be part and parcel of our lives. Once the grass is unearthed it will be only a matter of time before the next bird will start singing." He placed his hand on Eamon's shoulder. "You have one thing in your favour. With Jimmy Grant gone, at least he wouldn't be able to put you in the frame. He was the main man!"

Eamon smiled thinly. "I will wrap it up here. You and Suzette should go home. The crowd has thinned out. There is plenty of backup if needed!"

Eamon leaned back in the office chair. Deep in thought about Vic Greyland. The rap on the door brought him back to the moment.

"Come in!"

Jenny stepped inside and closed the door, smiling at Eamon.

He proffered her a chair.

She is certainly sultry, he thought, glancing at her red panties. As she crossed her legs the short dress rode up. Her full breasts strained against the tight dress. She exuded confidence as she flicked her thick hair from her bare shoulder, her false black lashes enhancing her blue eyes.

"How can I help ye?" Eamon smiled.

"I came in to thank you. The men saved me from that lad. It was quite unnerving. However, it was over before it even began!" As she adjusted her position her panties caught his eye again. "I noticed that your wife wasn't at the opening night. She's quite heavily pregnant now, isn't she?" She continued, "I should imagine that with the heat and the burden her small frame carries that she must find it difficult. If I could help you in any way!" Her wide smile invited.

"My wife, for her safety, and under my instruction, is at home waiting for me." He glanced at his watch, resting his forearms on the desk. He smiled. "Thank ye, Jenny, for the offer, however, I have sufficient help with my requirements at work. My wife, although not too far from her due date, gives me all that I require at home!" Eamon said, sitting back in his chair.

Jenny rose, straightening her dress. "Anytime you feel that you might need a little distraction I am available!"

Eamon did not reply. He shook his head after she had left.

He checked his phone. The text hadn't been read.

. . . .

The stillness of the villa was palpable. The dog wagged his tail and Eamon patted him. He placed his keys on the side table and removed his jacket before going to the bedroom. He stood in the bedroom doorway for a moment, watching Marcia in deep slumber. The shaft of light from the moon highlighted her silhouette. Eamon checked the boys' monitor, smiling with satisfaction at his two handsome sons, Quinn, asleep with his thumb in his mouth.

He stripped and then entered the ensuite bathroom.

He tried not to disturb Marcia as he slid into bed alongside her. As he raised the cover, he noticed her silk nightie had ridden up above her waist. She murmured as he gently raised her leg. His now erect penis sought her. He slotted in along her bare buttocks and breathed softly into the back of her neck.

"That is so nice!" she said sleepily, opening her legs for Eamon to gain entry.

She reached up for his face as he filled her. Holding his hand beneath her big belly, he did not move inside of her. "How long did ye sleep for?" he kissed down the nape of her neck.

"I fell asleep not long after you left," she murmured.

He began moving with deliberation, cupping her breasts, fingers teasing her nipples.

"Not yet!" he whispered feeling her heart beating faster. "Fall into me, I'll give ye depth."

The back of her head rested on his shoulder. His fingertip brushed her clitoris like butterfly wings, working in unison with each motion. Marcia gripped and released his arms as each spasm took her. He gently bit her neck when she cried out.

"I'm about to join ye!" Eamon turned her face, seeking her mouth, pumping without force.

"From yer cries of pleasure, I don't need to ask ye, if it was deep. He smiled at the welts from Marcia's nails on his forearms.

"I have slept for hours!" she turned on her side to snuggle into him. "Are you hungry?" her hand moved, her fingers encasing, her fingertip playing across the opening of his flaccid shaft.

He relaxed, lying back, hands locked behind is head. He watched her mouth engulf him.

"Ye have yer answer!" He adjusted his position to make it easier for Marcia to take him.

14

Dave Broadbent arrived at London Gatwick airport on an early morning flight with time to kill before his connecting journey to Pathos international airport in Cyprus. Knowing that he would not have another chance to eat until after he had completed the mission, he made his way to an eatery.

He found a table at the back of the restaurant and ordered a vegetarian omelette. Placing his hand luggage on the seat next to him, he studied the people around him. He was grateful that he looked like a regular Joe. He was known as Big Dave due to his previous weight being 114 kilos. However, a previous health check-up came with a warning that his blood sugar levels indicated borderline type two diabetes. With his wife's encouragement, he joined the gym she went to and followed her healthy eating regime. Eight months later, Dave weighed in at 70 kilos. Standing in stocking feet at 185 cm he was the fittest he had been in 20 years.

He couldn't say that he normally enjoyed his work. It allowed him to travel, sometimes taking him to various countries. However, he was looking forward to this job. The man was someone who had previously caused a problem on Dave's uncle's turf in Harrogate. He had gotten away with a slap, due to his uncle's friendship. Nonetheless, Big Dave didn't forget or forgive. It wasn't in his nature.

Dave's wife Lorraine thought that he was a business trouble shooter. He did not like to lie to his wife, but he reasoned that he only stretched the truth. If everything went according to plan, he would be back in Spain within 24 hours.

After the four-and-a-half-hour flight with only a carry-on bag, Big Dave headed towards the car hire kiosk. He had pre-booked and the young guy at the desk handed him the car keys as he slid the signed contract across the desk to him.

He had researched his destination on Google Earth beforehand and didn't need to use the satnav in the Mercedes C class convertible he had hired. The cost of the car, which he knew would be reliable, came out of his expenses. He wanted to enjoy the scenic route.

He turned the radio on for company as he drove out of Pathos international airport, taking the route to Skouille, which was 41.5 kilometres away via the E606 – about an hour's drive. With plenty of time to spare, he settled back in the seat and prepared to enjoy the scenery on his fleeting visit.

Big Dave parked up and changed into a short sleeve shirt, light weight combat trousers and walking boots. He carried no arms. He never required them on missions such as this. He took his sunglasses off – light reflection could be a giveaway. He began the trek up the incline.

Half an hour later, he had reached the peak. There was a sign warning that the cliff edge was only two meters away. From his obscure vantage point, he observed a solitary figure slowly walking up the hill towards him. The target appeared to be an unfit man, panting with the exertion. He stopped, caught his breath, and then carried on.

There was no time to feel any shock, no time to scream out. The smash to the skull from the piece of rock rendered him immediately senseless. He was a lightweight and it required no effort to lift him past the sign and drop him over the cliff edge. Dave watched the body strike boulder after boulder and land lifelessly at the foot of the cliff. Big Dave waited a few minutes. Satisfied with a job well done, he smirked at the warning sign. "You should have paid heed to the path that you took before you took up singing," he said aloud.

He knew that the contractor would be pleased. Also, many other associates that he knew would rest easy once the news was out.

15

The boys had gone to spend a week of their summer holiday at Dom and Maureen's home in Marbella. Eamon had warned Niall regarding his previous disruptive behaviour at school. At first, he was reluctant to allow Niall to join Quinn at the O'Reilly's. However, he gave in to Marcia's pleading to let Niall go. I thought she could do with a rest anyway. Her due date was only a few weeks away.

However, against Eamon's wishes, Marcia had gone out to work at Suzette's beauty salon. She had three tarot reading appointments booked. *The woman is an enigma*, Eamon smiled to himself on the way to his early morning appointment. She would earn six hundred euros, plus tips, which is not something to be sneezed at under normal circumstances, but hardly anything when you considered the price of some of her recent purchases. The multi-coloured midi dress, wedge sandals, and other items that had recently arrived from London must have cost thousands of euros. He had insisted that she needed to purchase some new clothes, as her girth had doubled as the babies got nearer to their delivery date, and that he would pay. It irked him that she felt the need to work when he gave her free rein with his bank card anyway.

Eamon's Maserati entered the N332 del Mascaret tunnel. His return journey would bring a new chapter, a breathing space. The destination was one that he had previously used for a drop when he had worked for Jimmy Grant. He made sure to keep to the speed limit to not draw any unwanted attention – he could not afford to be stopped and searched, due to what he had on him. After driving through Benissa onto Teulada, he exhaled.

Reaching Javea, he took the road that led up through the hills, with the villas on either side, until he saw the sign for Playa de Ambola. He took a right turn down the cliff road towards the isolated beach below. The turquoise waters of the bay twinkled in the early morning sun. A cooling north-easterly breeze blew through the open window offering some relief from the heat. He was minutes away from gaining freedom. A black Audi A1 was parked by the crash barrier, beneath a large sign warning of rock fall. Eamon smiled thinly to himself. He did not know what was more hazardous, the risk of falling boulders or the man who was sitting in the parked car. The man did not turn as Eamon pulled up alongside the Audi. Eamon dropped the package through the open passenger window. Reversing, Eamon glanced at the scenic view, which he hoped he would be seeing for the last time.

Parking up outside Suzette's beauty salon, Eamon sent a text message to Marcia to let her know that he was waiting for her. He was taking her out to a restaurant. He did not want to enter the building, to avoid Suzette. It was enough that he had to endure Suzette's company at the Hawk Wind club. His mobile rang and he put on his newly acquired black-framed spectacles to see who the caller was. Dan spoke to inform him that he and Billy had taken the Belgian shepherd for an unexpected visit to the haulage company. Although a few of the HGV drivers seemed a bit edgy when they arrived, there was no evidence of contraband.

Eamon thanked him. From out of the corner of his eye he spotted Marcia coming towards the car. Jumping out to open the passenger door for her, he glanced at her ankles, which were visibly swollen. Adjusting her seatbelt for her as she settled in, he brushed her lips with a warm kiss. "After lunch, I want ye to rest. I tink that it's about time that ye called it a day." He fired up the engine, looking at her. "Ye need to use common sense. The swelling indicates that it is time for ye to hang yer hat up."

Marcia nodded. He smiled and said, "Ye and our baby girls are more important than yer independence!"

"You look far less stressed than you did earlier. Did your business meeting go well?" Marcia asked, smiling.

"Extremely!" he replied as he drove towards the marina. Eamon had given some thought to selling the yacht to Dom. Although their previous family day out on the boat was enjoyable, he started to rethink the danger and risk of all his family being out at sea. He knew that Dom would understand that he couldn't do an under-the-table deal. A legit sale would enable him to show the taxman that he was above board.

The maître d' walked briskly across the restaurant as they entered. Marcos welcomed them, showing the pair to their table. Even though Marcos had been the manager of the restaurant for years, Eamon still hadn't let on that he was the silent owner. Eamon had Jimmy Grant to thank for that. He had signed up to the deal with Jimmy Grant putting the money up front for the purchase. With the money he got from the Miami deal that he had overseen for Grant, Eamon was going to pay Jimmy for his 50 per cent share of the ownership. However, Jimmy Grant's demise cleared that debt. Eamon rewarded his accountant and solicitor, who Jimmy had also previously used so that they would 'cook' the books in Eamon's favour.

Once they had ordered, Eamon leaned across the table to hold Marcia's hands. "Yer rings are tight!" He studied her hands. "When we leave here, I will phone the doctor!"

Marcia began to protest, but he put his hand up to prevent her from disagreeing.

"Marcia bear wit me!" he smiled. "I don't want ye to exert yerself in any way. Even like ye did in bed last night. Yer too near yer time…" He paused for effect. "I mean it!" he chastised playfully. "Ye being on top might be pleasurable for us both, however, it could hurt the babies," he said softly.

Taking her hand in his he said, "Marcia, the boys return to school next week. Before we know it, the babies will be here. Ye must heed the fact that ye are eight months pregnant. All I am trying to say is that once the girls are safely delivered, and as soon as ye feel up to it, we can resume, but not until then!"

She interjected, "There are other ways, Eamon!" she adjusted her position stretching her back. She cocked her head and said, "You look suave and sexy in those black-framed spectacles!"

"Stop yer flirting wit me!" he grinned, removing the glasses and sitting back in the chair as the waiter approached with their meals.

Eamon quietly inhaled, watching Marcia. He had overcome another hurdle by having Vic Greyland removed from the picture. Eamon had previously fought numerous battles, nevertheless, he realised that he would need to practise restraint when it came to his desire for Marcia. Sleeping apart from her at this late stage wasn't an option. However, whenever he sidled into bed behind her at night, he realised that it was not his head that he needed to try to reason with. The fight that he had on his hands this time was with the automatic erection that sought its port, Marcia seeking him, slotting into him, the jigsaw complete.

"After I have seen the doctor, I promise you that I will adhere to his advice," Marcia said before she began to eat her salad.

Eamon's mobile phone rang. He put on his spectacles. Not recognising the number, he switched the phone to silent mode. When he put it in his pocket, it began to vibrate. He checked it again and this time it was Dan. "I had an irate Dougie Dugan and his brother Roy stop by the club when Billy and I were changing the barrels in the bar. He demanded your number. To prevent trouble, I gave it to him. Furthermore, he said that they would be returning tonight to speak to you!"

"Ye did right!" Eamon replied, putting the phone away and smiling at Marcia. He did not want her to notice that he was concerned that there could be trouble looming.

Later that afternoon, they had returned from Dr Saggio's office. Marcia's blood pressure was fine and the babies' heartbeat was regular. However, Marcia was instructed to keep her legs elevated as much as possible.

Although Marcia could not swim due to the weight of her pregnancy, she continued to exercise in the water. Eamon sat under the awning, hands locked behind his head, legs stretched out, observing her. Marcia finished her routine and walked slowly up the pool steps. At the top, she glanced out towards the vista. Eamon caught a wistful look as she dried herself. The vision evoked memories. Marcia had recently come to Spain with Suzette. The men were sitting at the garden table, and Eamon had been half listening to Jimmy Grant, observing from his vantage point, Marcia as she stood in the same position after she had swum in Jimmy's pool. That same look seven years ago had intrigued him. He nodded to himself. He remembered how she had looked up and caught his eye, blushing.

Marcia turned to face him. A smile replaced her pensive countenance as she moved towards him.

"Ye have had only an hour's rest before ye resumed yer exercise," he chastised. "Aye has left two cushions with instructions that ye put them under yer legs." He picked up the thin, white cotton dress, placing it over her head. His hands encircled her, releasing the bikini top, moving down, and helping her out of the bottoms. Their eyes locked. He smiled, smoothing the dress over her baby bump. He picked the bikini up. "That barely covers anything anymore!"

Marcia smiled up at him. "Please join me. It is not often that we can relax together. Aye is meeting Cindy at the beauty salon where she is being treated to a restyle."

Eamon pulled up a sun lounger next to her, turning on his side, head propped up on his arm, facing her.

"Before you go to work later could you give me a massage with the oil that helps prevent stretch marks?"

"If ye behave yerself!" he countered.

Marcia placed her hand on his chest beneath the unbuttoned white shirt, smoothing his skin. "Eamon, I know that we need to be careful!" her fingers played across his nipple, however, we did not refrain when I was pregnant with Quinn!"

His nipple hardened. Eamon did not move.

"The abstinence that I endured while I was in exile in Thailand for the months when I was pregnant with Niall was unbearable," she pleaded her case, "I need you!"

"Marcia," Eamon spoke softly, adjusting his position. His hand reached for her, trailing his fingers down her arm. "Ye know that ye cannot contain yerself as ye reach the peak. Yer heart races!" He tilted her face towards his. "Ye have to consider yer blood pressure!" he said, concerned.

"If I lay back on the bed with you astride me, I can pleasure you without any exertion!" Her hand moved, releasing the button on his fly. The zip slid down with ease, she dipped her hand in and her fingertips stroked. He exhaled.

"If ye assure me that when I return the favour, ye accept it without exhilaration!" He helped her up.

Roman followed them back inside through the terrace doors, stopping outside the boundary of the bedroom door.

"There cannot be any foreplay. It will increase yer pulse rate!" He knelt above her as she lay on the bed. Her mouth enclosed the rock-hard tip of his penis, her tongue darted as her fingers moved through the pubic mass. He allowed her to take him, practising restraint when she caressed his scrotum.

"Follow my lead!" he instructed from between her legs, placing each one upon his shoulders. His fingers opened her, tongue teasing. Marcia bucked.

"Relax!" he said firmly, continuing. The heel of his hand aided his finger. They watched one another while he guided her. "Let it take you. Fall into it!"

Marcia's stomach moved as the spasm began. Eamon placed a caring hand on her abdomen throughout the climb to the peak of her building climax. He smiled into her eyes, observing the pleasure that he was giving her. She lay back, arms splayed, letting the ecstasy consume her.

"Don't move!" he kissed between her thighs.

Marcia sighed contentedly when he lay alongside her.

"Have ye informed Suzette that ye won't be back to work today?"

"I will ring her!" Marcia replied.

"Ensure that ye do because it will be better coming from ye!" He kissed her. "I received a phone call from the husband of one of yer clients."

Marcia's eyes darted towards him.

"Ye gave his wife some advice."

Marcia slowly sat up, her mind racing.

"Les Booker informed me that ye must have something special to cause his wife to alter her aggressive attitude!" Eamon paused. "Les Booker's words, not mine. His wife informed him that ye gave her some sound advice, which she adhered to. She forgave him for his past indiscretions. They are going to renew their wedding vows in the Maldives in a few weeks. We have been given an invite." He smiled. "Nevertheless, I declined, explaining to Les that the twins are about to be born." He cocked his head. "Ye obviously have a way wit words, my wee mystic."

When Marcia did not reply, Eamon added on a more serious note, "That is one dangerous man to mess with!"

"I was extremely careful with my advice," she said, sheepishly.

Eamon nodded, pursing his lips.

"For Les Booker's wife to listen to ye, ye must have something special!" His eyes twinkled. "She is a match for any man. Nevertheless, my little pregnant mystic, yer wings are clipped for the time being. These women can sort out their problems."

16

The sharp rap on the Hawk Wind club office door informed Eamon that this was not a social visitor.

"Come in!" he had left it unlocked knowing that at some point that night Dougie Dugan and his brother Roy would come calling.

The two men entered; the tension was palpable. Eamon rose to his full height, offering them a seat. There was no introduction or pleasantries as they sat opposite the desk one leg crossed over the knee, reclining back, eyes fixed. Roy's fingers began drumming on the armrest.

"You know why I am here!" Dougie stated. "My old woman has been giving it to me in the ear about the black eye that Tommy came home with from his boys' night out at your club!" He exhaled, chewing the corner of his lip. "Nonetheless, I want to hear it from you. If you was that slimy cunt Jimmy Grant who you previously worked for, I would have taken immediate action!" he threatened, then smiled. "But you, lad, are a different ball game. Let's hear you out!"

Eamon went through what had happened. "The young dancer was scared. Your lad was strong. He gripped her thong, trying to get to her on the stage. Thankfully, my men intervened," he continued, "These dancers are only trying to earn a living, Dougie. Ye have got girls yerself, as I will have shortly. They have got to be protected!"

Roy glared. Dougie's piercing eyes were not directed at Eamon. He slowly nodded as Eamon resumed. "Yer boy did not go quietly, unlike his pals. Once outside the club, there was another ruckus, which my men had to see to. Your boy takes the opportunity to give one of my men a dig, my man retaliated. Your boy shouted the odds with threats to sort the Irish tinker out and burn my club to the floor."

Dougie sucked air through his teeth. Shifting his position, he tugged at his bottom lip. "I guessed as much. It had to be something along those lines. The boy has got out of hand, most probably on the 'Jack and Jills'. Not that I can tell his mother that I know he is out of his head on the white stuff half the time. She is blind to it." He rose to his feet, and Roy followed suit.

"The little cunt will make an apology to the girl, and you!" He added, "Like we have not got better things to do!" he proffered his hand to Eamon, but Roy didn't. "I'll be in touch," Dougie said, hand on the door handle.

Eamon leaned into the chair, momentarily closing his eyes, stretching. He thought about the dancers, and how vulnerable they seemed up on the stage. The security men protected them throughout their routine, however, most of them were actually man-eaters. Jenny had winked at him earlier – he ignored it. Sunni also left no doubt that she was available. Her suggestive look and movement on the stage around the pole in his direction was not misconstrued.

He put his glasses on, unlocking the desk draw. He removed the club's accounting books. He perused the bookings. "At this rate," he mused, smiling to himself at the number of pre-booked stag nights, "It should not take too long before my debt for the 50 per cent share of the Hawk Wind is repaid to Greg."

He pondered on the suggestion that Suzette had put forward to Greg, that the club allow hen parties. Greg said that there had already been numerous enquiries. He waggled his head, tossing around the idea. "One night a week," he concluded. Two light knocks on the door brought him back to the moment. Closing the book, he put it away and said, "Come in!"

"Problem?" he asked, without returning Jenny's smile.

"I know that you have a lot on your plate." She took a seat. Eamon leaned back in the chair, trying not to glance at her underwear that was directly in his line of sight.

"I have a slight problem with one of the punters."

Eamon cocked an eyebrow. "Because I have been friendly, there's this guy who seems to think that I am interested in him outside of work." She added, "He bought me a drink and gave me a big tip. I said that my next routine would be for his eyes only!" She gave a soft laugh. "You know how it is in this game!"

Eamon removed his spectacles, putting them on the desk. "If ye don't mind me asking, how much did he give ye?"

"Five hundred euros, which may seem a lot, however, I have received far more from others on other occasions, without any expectations." She leaned forward revealing her enhanced, full breasts. "I saw him outside my apartment. I live on my own with my child. It is scary!" She held Eamon's eyes. He looked away.

"I cannot get involved with anything that happens outside of the club, however, if ye give me the guy's name, I will get him checked out. A warning should be sufficient." He put his glasses on when she gave him the man's name and description. "Now, if that is all…" He sat back. "I need to sort out a few tings!"

Jenny picked up her shoulder bag. Eamon dismissed the further show of cleavage. Jenny smiled at him as she got up.

"Thank you, boss!" She turned to leave, then stopped. "If you don't mind me saying, you look extremely sexy wearing the glasses!"

Eamon did not respond and showed no reaction. He shook his head after she had left. He knew that Jenny was one of the most popular dancers. Her good looks, coupled with having enhanced curves in the right places warranted the men's attraction to her. She had brushed herself off from the encounter with Dougie Dugan's lad. Nevertheless, he could not allow the punters to step over the line. He made a mental note for Billy to sort the stalker out.

There was another knock before the door opened. Greg entered the office, smiling, and locked the door behind him. "Sorry that I am a bit late!" He pulled a chair out. "Did I just see the Dugan brothers leaving in a Jaguar?"

Eamon smiled weakly, nodding. He went into detail. "I don't tink that we have heard the last of Dougie's boy, although his father is going to give him a rollicking. Furthermore, the lad is going to be made to apologise to the dancer." He leaned forward, forearms on the desk. "And also to me!"

Greg raised his brow, pursing his lips.

"That's going to hurt the lad's street cred!" he smirked.

"Indeed!" Eamon grinned, cocking an eyebrow.

"It's a good thing that we are straight men who do not stray from the marital bed," Greg grinned, "It is on offer out there!"

Eamon scratched his earlobe, "I have noticed!"

"How are things going with Marcia's pregnancy? Suzette said that she is still working."

Eamon bristled. His face reddened. "I have told Marcia to inform Suzette that she is terminating her work at the salon. I am not going to let her risk her health or the babies' health at this stage." He stood up. "Ye tell me, Greg, what the fuck does Marcia tink that she is doing? She is going to rest up!" he stated firmly.

"Take it easy, mate! I understand your concern. I will speak to Suzette tonight. She will only think of Marcia's well-being. They are good friends!" He patted Eamon's shoulder. "Look, at the first sign that Marcia needs you with her, bell me. Whatever time, day or night!"

"Niall and Quinn are away at Dom's place. They return to school next week. I know that the doctor said that twins can come early, therefore, I don't want Marcia tired out. The babies are a fair size for her small frame, and although she is fit, she is a mature mother. I don't want any problems.

"Class it as sorted!" Greg assured him. "Your daughters will soon be here. Then your troubles will begin," he joked. "If they have the good looks of their brothers, you have done well with your brood," Greg complimented. "Now, get back to your wife and enjoy the rest of the night."

Eamon entered the hubbub of the club. He spotted the two Irish sisters who danced at the club, chatting together at the bar. Billy was at the far end speaking to Thomas. He passed the girls, nodding in their direction. Martha smiled, and Bridie, the younger sister, winked.

Eamon had given Thomas a bonus for the information that his father Lord Arthur had passed on, which had allowed Eamon some breathing space. Giving Billy the run down on Jenny's problem, he passed him the details.

Getting into the car, he put his glasses on, sending Marcia a text to say that he was on his way home.

"I have given my notice in!" Marcia told Eamon when he stepped out through the terrace doors with the dog, who had come to greet him. Relief washed over him. He smiled warmly without mentioning that he had had words with Greg regarding her stopping work.

Eamon thought that she was a vision as she stood by the pool; the breeze captured the long, sky blue dress she wore, wrapping around her pregnant form. He felt himself stir, heat filling his loins.

"I telephoned Suzette this evening, and then I checked on the boys. Although they were already in bed, Maureen said that they had both had a fun-packed day. She said that because they had been good, she took them shopping. Maureen is a wonderful woman!" She added, "How was your night?"

He kissed her, replying, "Grand! Greg has taken over! Take a seat while I get some wine." He went back inside.

Marcia had felt a few twinges earlier. She wondered if they were Braxton-Hicks contractions. However, she decided not to inform Eamon unless they continued. He returned with a glass and the bottle of wine, having removed his jacket and tie.

"Have ye put yer feet up tonight?" he queried while opening the bottle and pouring himself a full glass. He sat down opposite her at the garden table. "Aye insisted that I rest, so I read my book for a while. Then Aye made me a spinach and fruit smoothie, and she stood over me to make sure that I ate the mackerel salad," Marcia laughed. "Aye has cooked various Thai curry dishes for you, also chicken satay."

"Did you transfer the money for her family?" He took a mouthful of wine.

"As soon as you left for work, I did that. Aye said to thank you. She told me that her family asked if I could visit her village in the future to give them tarot card readings. I explained that you did not like me to read the tarot cards!" she smiled when he frowned.

"How did she respond?"

"In her usual brusque manner. She said that men were babies!" She knew that Eamon would accept Aye's declaration with humour.

He laughed, shaking his head.

Eamon showered while Marcia prepared for bed. He turned the tap on cold, killing the erection that had been straining for release. He was determined that there would be no love-making tonight.

The Frédéric Malle Portrait of a Lady perfume, which was one of Marcia's favourites, filled his senses. He took in the low lighting and leaf-green silk negligee she had put on and realised that he was not going to win this war with his wife. He dropped his towel, moving towards the bed.

She smiled, her eyes roaming, resting on his penis, which was standing to attention.

"Ye don't play fair!" Eamon breathed. The silk against her bare perfumed flesh was too much for him to resist. Slowly approaching her from behind, he bit gently into the back of her neck, surrendering to her. "Do as I tell ye, and allow me," he instructed.

His powerful legs held her, "Fall into me!" he coaxed kissing her shoulder softly, "Enjoy the pleasure wit me as I join ye!"

Eamon held her without withdrawing. "Let yer heart rate come back down!" He turned her face towards him kissing her. "The babies were moving when we came together!" he smiled.

Eamon held her in his arms. "I have had some battles in my time, wit at least a fifty-fifty chance of winning!" he said, "but, wit the weapons that ye use against me, I have no choice but to surrender to ye, my foxy wee mystic! Now get some sleep!" He kissed her good night.

17

The boys returned home, laden with gifts of clothing and games consoles. They were now happily playing in the pool, while Marcia sat on the top step, dipping her feet in the cool water. "Come in, Mummy!" Quinn called, "I will help you!"

Niall, who had not been very talkative, looked up. "Mummy needs to rest, Quinn!" he said sternly to his brother.

Eamon, who was sitting with Dan at the garden table, caught Marcia's eye. She turned to the boys and said, "After your sisters arrive and you are next home for half-term, Mummy will join you both in the pool!" Marcia thought that she noticed a fleeting dark look in Niall's eyes. It perturbed her, even though he carried on swimming and diving to the bottom of the pool. She adjusted her sunglasses and wide-brim sun hat, leaning back, letting her arms take her weight. She observed Niall. Both of Eamon's sons were like him, and yet in some ways, Niall reminded her of her eldest son Rueben. She prayed that Niall's future would not be like his half brother's. The boys were not aware that they had an older half-brother. She thought of Rueben as she looked out at the bay and her heart travelled far beyond the Sierra de Bernia Mountains to wherever he was. She dismissed her thoughts, feeling her eyes fill with tears. She discreetly brushed away the trickle.

"Let me help ye!" Eamon's shadow blocked the sun as he came up behind her, taking her weight. He removed her glasses and looked puzzled as he noticed her teary eyes. He took her by the hand and led her to the garden table.

She did not realise that Dan had gone.

"Tomorrow night, I have booked us a table at the restaurant. While Thomas and I drive the boys to school, ye can take it easy." He studied her. "It won't be long now until those baby girls are ready to come out!" He kissed her hand.

. . . .

After a tearful farewell to the boys, Marcia had dried her tears and composed herself by the time Eamon had returned from dropping the boys off at the boarding school.

"Ye look stunning! Very sexy!" He came towards her as she adjusted the emerald and diamond studs in her ears. The matching bracelet complemented the midi black sleeveless Yves Salomon dress.

"I do not feel sexy, especially in comparison to the near-naked dancers that you see most nights at the club," Marcia lamented.

Sitting her down on the dressing table stool, he helped her slip on the low-heeled mules. "Ye are my woman, carrying my babies. Believe me, there is nothing more beautiful than you are when you are naked. There is no contest!" he countered.

Eamon helped her into the passenger seat, leaning across and adjusting her seatbelt. "If I get much bigger the seatbelt won't be able to attach!" Marcia exclaimed.

He brushed her lips, kissing her softly "Enjoy yer pregnancy. As I do." He winked.

Marcos bowed when they entered the busy restaurant, welcoming them both. He guided them to Eamon's regular table at the back of the restaurant.

The young couple at the neighbouring table, who appeared to be celebrating their engagement stopped their conversation abruptly when the guy turned his gaze towards Marcia as she was seated. Tommy Dugan smiled, running his eyes over her cleavage, down to her stomach, until he heard the familiar Irish accent of the man speaking to the maître d'. His look of admiration turned to one of hatred, as he moved his gaze towards Eamon.

"Tommy are you with me?!" Amy, Tommy's fiancée queried, snapping her fingers in front of his face and turning to see what he was looking at. She gasped, "That is the woman who predicted my future and our baby boy. She is amazing!" Jumping up from the table, she straightened her short dress. "Won't be a minute!" Before Tommy could stop her, she teetered on her five-inch stilettos towards the seated couple.

Eamon's back was to Amy, however, Marcia caught the beaming smile of the approaching young woman. Amy stood alongside Eamon, facing Marcia. "Sorry to interrupt. I don't know if you remember me. I came to you for a tarot reading a while back. I just wanted to tell you how good you are!". Amy gushed, patting her stomach proudly. "My fella has a bit of a problem, and I was having trouble getting pregnant!" She said.

Eamon turned his head to face her, raising his brow.

"You predicted that I would be pregnant within three months and that my baby would be a boy. The scan last week revealed our boy," Amy said, beaming. "My fiancé is thrilled, hence the ring!" she thrust the diamond nearer to Marcia's face. "Although it's a bit loose now. It will have to be made smaller." She stopped talking when Marcia leaned back in her seat.

"Wow!" she exclaimed. "I did not realise that you were pregnant when I came to see you. When is your baby due – at any moment by the size of your bump?" she laughed.

"My babies are near to term," Marcia replied.

Amy raised her hands excitedly. "Babies, plural!" she exclaimed. "You are having twins! How wonderful." She continued, "Do you know the babies' sex?"

Marcia caught Eamon's bemused look as she replied, "Girls!"

Amy placed her hands on her stomach. "You predicted two for me. One of each sex."

"Sorry, love!" she turned her attention to Eamon. "Your wife is gifted." She smiled at Marcia. "I will need to get back to my table, otherwise my man won't be a happy bunny."

Eamon leaned forward, forearms on the table, taking Marcia's hand in his. "Ye appear to make a lot of people happy," he raised her hand to his lips. "Including me!"

Marcia placed her free hand on top of his. "Have you ever had any regrets, ever since that first time that you stepped into the shower with me?"

"That vision of ye naked in the shower will stay wit me always. My nightly fantasies of ye, which prevented me from sleeping, fulfilled my expectations. The only regret that I have," he said, squeezing her hand, "Is that I should have made my move earlier!"

"That is beautiful!" Marcia said, looking into his eyes.

"The vision of you standing by the shower door, having stripped off, and your powerful arms around me, fulfilled my previous fantasy of being with you for the first time," Marcia confessed.

Eamon nodded. "We have got a lot of living to do. If all goes well, this time next year, we could add another baby to our fold!" He kissed her fingers.

"WHAT IN HELL!" Tommy raised his voice, annoyed with Amy when she sat back down at their table. He clicked his fingers to the waiting staff. "BILL!" he demanded, lowering his tone slightly, his temper simmering beneath the forced smile he projected towards Amy. He wanted to keep her sweet. She was wanting to have the diamond ring made smaller; however, he had received it as payment for a cocaine deal and he knew that it came from a burglary. Although the stolen goods were not local, he did not want to take the diamond ring to a jeweller in case it was recognised. Switching off to Amy's babbling about the Irishman's wife, his mind was scheming. He had been instructed by his father Dougie that he would be accompanying him to the Hawk Wind club to make an apology to the dancer and Eamon O'Donally. Tommy had been read the riot act, with the last warning from his father, that Dougie would wipe the floor with him if he did not make good of the situation. Tommy realised that he had to go along with it because his dad would not think twice about reclaiming Tommy's pride and joy, the yellow Lotus, and the apartment that Tommy's mum Denise had been sweet-talked into buying him for his approaching twenty-first birthday. Tommy now had the freedom to come and go as he pleased from his pad, not that his parents' palatial home with its panoramic views of Montgo Mountain and the Mediterranean Sea was anything to be sneezed at. However, the price to pay for living in the luxurious mansion was that his father was there. Tommy's mum was a pushover – Dougie Dugan wasn't.

"I must use the ladies' room. It's the pressure of the baby!" Amy pecked his cheek as she scurried off. While Tommy waited for her to return, he observed Eamon and Marcia gazing into each other's eyes. He intended to drop Amy off and then pay a quick visit to his other girlfriend, Paula. Then he'd planned to meet with his pal Ritchie to discuss what he had in mind to bring the big Irishman to his knees. He smiled smugly to himself, glancing at the Irishman's back. *The Irish has-been has an Achilles' heel,* he mused, watching the couple holding hands.

He scowled, mumbling under his breath, "You are going to seriously regret messing with me, Irish tinker!"

He thought to himself, *Once O'Donally's old lady has dropped the kid and is back at work, I will make an appointment with her to see what she predicts about my future business.* Tommy's mum had recommended that Amy should book an appointment with Marcia. He had heard his mother and her mates rattling on about the tarot reader's accuracy. *There is more than one way to skin a cat,* he thought, knowing what measures he needed to take to seek his revenge on Eamon O'Donally.

18

Later that night, while Eamon was in his at home in his office making business phone calls, Marcia had changed into a long, sleeveless Anita Dongre emerald-green, classic Fayre pattern dress with slits up the side. She sat outside on the terrace in the pleasant breeze, which brought respite from the humid night. Earlier, in the restaurant, she had felt twinges, but she'd not let on to Eamon. She gazed at the star-spangled sky and turned to view the bay in the distance. She had consulted her astrological charts that afternoon. The tide was high and the moon, which had moved into the sign of Aries, was full. The planets were in the right alignment for the influence that Marcia felt would be required to enable her daughters to stand strong in the world that they would be born into. Marcia mused that the planet Mars was placed in the sign of Scorpio, and Venus was conjunct with the sun. She sighed contentedly, raising her arms to the heavens. "Please, dear spirit world, bring my daughters safely into this life tonight!" She spoke to the unseen forces that had guided her over the years. She felt a change in the atmosphere, a sudden chill caused her to shudder, the fronds of the palms that surrounded the grounds danced in unison, and the dog sat up, pricking his ears when the gusts picked up. Marcia smiled at the dog. "There will be two more children for you to protect shortly, Roman!" The dog lay back down, resting his head on his forelegs, alert, scanning the area.

Eamon stood for a few minutes by the terrace doors, taking in the spectacle of Marcia with her arms elevated towards the sky. She appeared to be speaking to the stars. The Belgian shepherd's reaction intrigued him. Marcia, barefoot, wearing the flowing green dress, evoked a childhood memory of one of his granny's tales, which had scared him and his brother Patrick. The Irish folktale told of the King of Munster, who was lured by an unearthly woman whose name was Alice Kyteler. She was a healer who had been condemned as a witch. The tale had been imprinted upon Eamon's mind as a young, impressionable boy. He had been ever fearful of any female who was involved in sorcery. He smiled wistfully, gazing at the vision of the mystical woman who had captured his heart. Marcia and the dog turned to look at him as he slid the door open.

"Look at the beautiful moon," Marcia said, returning to look at the sky.

He came up behind her, embracing her, his hands on either side of her stomach, gently caressing, taking in the bouquet of Turkish rose and oriental vanilla. "Ye need to come in now," he breathed, hands roaming. His resting penis began searching. She relaxed into him. Eamon knew that he couldn't win, however, he could compromise. "I don't want ye to put in any effort!" he turned her to face him. Her belly was preventing his erection from attaining its goal.

He led her by the hand to the bedroom, the full moon illuminating the room as he untied the shoulder straps of the dress. It slipped to the floor. "Stay there!" he said, gazing into her eyes. With her nakedness silhouetted in the moonlight, he began to undress. Eamon laid her on her side on the bed.

"I cannot excite ye with foreplay!" He slowly eased his hardness into her from behind. The jigsaw complete, with measured movements, he filled her. Bearing into him, Marcia tightened her pelvic muscles, clamping, passion taking over. Moments later, they released together. "Lay quietly!" He kissed the nape of her neck, her rapid heartbeat thumping against his hand on her chest.

After her heartbeat had returned to normal, Eamon turned her to face him. Studying her, he said, "I could have hurt ye! I could not allow us to linger on too long for fear of raising yer blood pressure. Marcia, I meet ye halfway, so that we can continue to enjoy our love making. However, ye must understand that at this crucial stage, it is essential l that I can stay in control!" He shook his head. "Furthermore, ye must understand that when ye hold me prisoner inside of yer, I cannot come back from it!" He chastised, smiling warmly.

Her fingertips played across his mouth, she smiled without replying.

Eamon lay awake, while Marcia slept. He observed the rise and fall of her quiet breathing, which could be heard even though there was a thunderstorm raging. He had not mentioned that he had seen her earlier, arms raised to the heavens. He had taken note that Marcia had packed the maternity bag in readiness.

Three hours later, Eamon heard Marcia's groan. Her head was pressed into the pillow, hands gripping the sheets, perspiration forming on her brow. Eamon jumped out of bed to phone the clinic. Doctor Saggio assured him that they would send an ambulance. Eamon insisted that he would drive her there. Although panicked, he helped her to dress. The doctor informed him that the contractions were not yet frequent so there was no need to rush.

He wrapped Marcia's coat around her shoulders, protecting her from the torrential rain, and assisting her to the car. Although speeding, he was mindful of the potentially dangerous conditions on the wet hill roads.

Twelve minutes later, Eamon was relieved to see the medical team on standby at the doors of the clinic ready with a wheelchair.

Eamon paced the waiting room floor, angry at himself for succumbing to their earlier passion. Marcia had to undergo a blood transfusion due to haemorrhaging. He had signed the medical form so that the surgical team could perform an emergency caesarean section. He checked his watch for the umpteenth time when the operating theatre doors suddenly opened. Doctor Saggio smiled. "Your wife and daughters are fine. However, as is normal procedure with premature babies, we have placed them in incubators to aid with their respiration. If you don't mind waiting for 15 minutes, then I will send a nurse to take you in to see your wife."

The doctor said, "Mr O'Donally, I simultaneously conducted the other procedure as well, to prevent any further pregnancies."

Eamon nodded. He was thankful that Marcia had come through the crisis. Accepting the news that they couldn't have any more children was difficult, but he was eternally grateful for the four children they had together.

Eamon donned a white gown and mask and followed the nurse into the room. Marcia held her hand out as he approached. Drawing up a chair next to the bed, he took her hand in his. "We won't be able to have any more children!" she whispered.

He reached forward, kissing her. "We have been blessed with two boys and two girls!"

"Eamon, I have not seen the babies yet. They were rushed to the incubators. Please go to them!"

He nodded. The nurse directed him along the corridor. Through the glass windows, he could see the machines that were aiding his babies to breathe. He had asked their weight and was told that at two and a half kilos each, there was no worry about their survival. He stood in awe at their beauty. They both had a mass of copper-red hair, cupid bow lips, tiny noses, and an English rose complexion. He felt his heart soar, as the two pairs of dark eyes watched him. An isolated tear trickled down his cheek and he let it flow. Eamon had experienced joy at the birth of his two sons, however, he was not prepared for the overload of emotions at the picture before him.

Marcia was being moved to a private suite. Eamon took her hands in his, kissing her fingers. He could not have loved her any more than he did at that moment. "Ye have given me two beautiful copper-headed baby girls!" he smiled.

"Copper-red hair!" Marcia exclaimed, beaming.

"I know that ye have red hair, however, ye have it coloured!" he smiled. "The wee girls have the same copper-red-hair as my granny from County Kerry, who moved to Dublin to be nearer to us and fill me and my brother Patrick with her frightening fables!" he laughed.

"The wee girls' also have an intense look, which reminded me of her fierceness. They appear to hold no fear. It is uncanny!"

"Please, Eamon, I would like to see them, to hold them!" she implored.

"The doctor requires ye to rest for 24 hours. The babies will be brought to ye later. I will check on them before I return home." Eamon did not mention that he had purchased her a gift, one that he had discovered she had been looking at on her laptop. She had put the item in the shopping cart cart, although the transaction was not complete. Eamon's accountant had wrangled the 34,000 euro cost of the gift.

19

That evening, after he had spoken to Marcia, he headed to the club. Eamon's men wanted to go to Irish Michael's bar after the Hawk Wind club closed to wet the babies' heads. When he had run it by Marcia, she had insisted that he go and spend some time relaxing with his men.

He took it easy on the number of celebratory drinks. Although he was enjoying the banter at Michael's bar with Dan, Billy, and Thomas, three drinks was his limit. He returned home just before five am. The motion detector lights illuminated the car as he drove through the villa gates. He could see a glimmer of light from Aye's bedroom lamp. The tiny Thai woman who was a nanny to the children was a treasured part of their family. Eamon showed his appreciation by transferring money to Aye's bank account to aid her family in the north of Thailand. He knew that she was excited that Marcia and the babies would be home in a couple of days.

The dog lay alongside the garden chair. Eamon locked his hands behind his head, stretching his legs out. He pondered names for his daughters. Marcia had asked him to give them Irish names, like their brothers. He favoured Aisling and Aine, although he did not know if he was tempting fate, as the latter was the name of a fabled folklore siren that his granny had warned him of when he was a boy. He smiled wryly, he sensed that his granny's genes had been passed down to the girls. *Heaven help us if the pair will be as formidable as she was.* Eamon looked up at the star-lit sky.

Marcia had explained the planetary cycles to him. He thought about the past seven years in which he had gained Marcia and four children, and wealth beyond his wildest dreams, and yet he knew that he could not take it all for granted. His situation was constantly on a knife edge, and he could at any moment have his happiness wiped out. He decided that he would pay a visit to see Father Sebastian, the Catholic priest. Although he had not attended mass since Niall and Quinn were baptised, Eamon sensed that his last financial donation to the church would make up for his nonattendance. Eamon felt the need to atone for his sins. He silently prayed that there would be no more obstacles in his path that would prevent him from breaking his vow to leave the life of crime behind him. He knew that God would not justify murder to protect his family or any of the other violent methods that he had used in the past.

Three days later, Marcia was home with the babies. Her previous healthy eating and fitness regime had paid dividends. *She is absolutely glowing,* Eamon mused as she emerged from the nursery after breast feeding the babies. He took her by the hand and led her out to the garden. The buzzer at the front gates resounded from the lounge. He turned back to answer it.

Marcia smiled when Eamon came towards her with the gift-wrapped package. He placed it before her on the table.

She began to open it. Upon seeing the address of the sender, she glanced at him, continuing to unwrap the box. Marcia gasped. Jumping up, she threw her arms around his neck kissing him. "Eamon, how did you know that it was the one that I wanted? This is such an extravagance!"

"Finish opening it!" he directed, smiling back at her. He had found the Hermes Birkin bag from Madison Avenue Couture in the web-browsing history on Marcia's computer just before she had had the babies.

"Ye deserve it. It is my gift to ye for the joy that ye have given me!" She put the bag back in the box, turning to face him. Eamon sat down, pulling her gently onto his lap. Her arms encircled his neck – he cupped her rear. "I want ye to adhere to the doctors' orders and don't do anything strenuous. No swimming until ye heal!"

She sighed. Her eyes sparkled. "There may be no sex for me for a while! However, I can pleasure you!" she trailed her fingers along his jawline, moving to his mouth. "There will be no exertion!" she coaxed. They kissed deeply, her full breasts pressing against him, inviting.

He playfully slapped her rear. "My little temptress, without a doubt ye are alluring. Nevertheless, ye are to rest. Once ye are given the okay, I can promise ye that I will give ye what ye want. We will both wait. Please don't tink to put any strategic plans in place in the bedroom tonight!" he warned, laughing, checking his watch.

"I have a meeting wit Greg to sort out a couple of tings at the Hawk Wind." Eamon had agreed with him that hen parties would be allowed at the club due to the numerous enquiries.

. . . .

Marcia waited on the top step to greet Suzette as she drove in through the villa gates. She admired her glamorous friend and took in her signature Guerlain Rouge scent as they air-kissed. Suzette wore a couture designer white box jacket trimmed in black with a knee-length skirt. Her accessories were befitting a Hollywood star, Marcia thought. "You look amazing!" Marcia complimented.

"You, my dear friend, look hot in that sexy flowing number. I love the Asian, seductive look, on you. That man of yours will not be able to keep his hands off you. One would not believe that you have recently given birth!" Suzette slipped her arm through Marcia's. They walked through the lounge, "Speaking of which, where are the girls?"

The women quietly entered the nursery. Both girls were sleeping. Their copper-red hair perfectly framed their fair little faces, and their rose-bud mouths puckered, tummies full, they lay in the cribs contentedly. Suzette gazed adoringly from one to the other. Marcia put her finger to her lips, they left the room.

Marcia took two Voss water bottles out of the fridge and filled their glasses. Suzette took hers and the women went out to the terrace. "They are beautiful Marcia. However, where do they get the red hair and creamy skin colouring from? Certainly not from your dark-complexioned stud?" she laughed.

"Eamon's notoriously scary grandmother. He said that her eyes were emerald-green. We won't see if Aisling and Aine will inherit his grandmother's eye colouring until they are a bit older."

"I love their names! Eamon's choice?" Suzette cocked a brow.

Marcia nodded. "I wanted him to choose Irish names like the boys have."

Suzette nodded. "I will have some free time soon. We can go shopping. Retail therapy will do us both good." She crossed her legs, tapping her red talon-like nails on the garden table "Let us get back to discussing us. I know that you have only just given birth, but," she said, smiling, "one cannot waste time procrastinating. You will need an outside interest. Babies and being on hand for your man's entertainment is all well and good... at times," Suzette added, smiling. "However, one must retain one's independence, Marcia. It is also wise," she grinned "to keep a watchful eye on the prowling she-wolves at the Hawk Wind club. Never leave anything to chance. Our men are powerful – they attract a lot of attention. She put her hand up, palm facing Marcia as she went to speak. "How long are you required to abstain?"

Marcia remained silent.

"Exactly!" Suzette stated. "Weeks!" she added, shaking her immaculately coiffured bob.

"While the cat's away, the mice will play. Remember it, because, my dear friend, there has never been a truer saying. Greg's needs in the bedroom are met by me, although his breathing of late bothers me somewhat. Nonetheless, being the ever-resourceful woman, I do most of the work. On top!" she laughed.

"However, your man's temperament is passionate, unlike Greg's. Eamon will need release. Do not leave it to another woman to allow him to let off steam!" Suzette warned.

She placed her hand on Marcia's arm. "I may have reservations about Eamon, nevertheless, I do not doubt that the man loves you deeply. He flew thousands of kilometres to bring you back to him. However, my dear friend, you must never forget that you are his possession!"

Marcia shook her head. She knew that Suzette dished out her words of wisdom regarding men, however, she did not put into practice what she preached with her own relationships.

"On a brighter note, Marcia, I am going to speak to Lloyd and book you in for the complete works. Hair recoloured, facials etc. A treat on me! I will ring you to sort a time out." She hugged

Marcia. "We women must standby one another!" she blew her a kiss, waving as she drove out of the grounds.

Suzette's words played upon Marcia's mind. She realised that her intention was to pre-warn Marcia of the threat that the dancers at the club presented. They would have no qualms about stepping into her shoes without a second thought about Eamon being married with four children. She resolved to make a stand against the female predators.

20

Six weeks later, Marcia's resolve to lose the unwanted pounds paid dividends. She had regained her pre-pregnancy figure by swimming daily, eating healthily, and following a Hatha yoga regime. She felt great after two visits to Suzette's beauty salon for a facial treatment a body wrap and a hair restyle. Marcia was thrilled with the results.

The orders from London and Milan had arrived. Marcia had also previously signed for two deliveries, one from Bordelle lingerie and another from Carine Gilson couture lingerie – two full-length, silk kimonos in the softest silk, delicate lace, and sheerest chiffon. The expense was for both of their benefits. Their private life was an important part of their marriage.

Marcia knew that there was a problem at the haulage company. Earlier, Eamon had rushed out to meet Billy and Dan with the dog. He'd said that his haulage manager Diego had phoned to inform him that he was having a spot of trouble with one of the HGV drivers. Although Eamon did not tell her, Marcia sensed by the look of urgency on his face that it probably had something to do with a driver being caught smuggling narcotics via one of Eamon's lorries.

Billy and Dan had insisted that Eamon have the night off. They both were going to oversee things at the club. Marcia planned a relaxing evening that night with Eamon to help relieve the stress from earlier in the day. Eamon had been spending more time at the club since the opening night. Working nights and returning home in the early hours was taking its toll on him. Marcia sorely missed their intimacy, although he took her in his arms when he came to bed every night.

That evening Marcia had asked Aye to cook Eamon's favourite Thai dishes. Marcia was happy that Niall and Quinn would be home in a few weeks for half-term. They had not yet seen the babies. Marcia felt unsure as to how Niall would react, although she sensed Quinn would be excited. The girls rapidly gained weight. The breast-fed pair were content and always slept through until the next feed. Eamon took great pleasure in holding, kissing, and talking to them, unlike the way he was with the boys as babies. She knew that he loved all his children, however, Aisling and Aine, as young as they were, had their father wrapped around their podgy little fingers. She smiled to herself and thought, *Eamon is putty in their hands.*

Later that evening, Marcia was swimming when Eamon walked purposely onto the terrace, the dog by his side.

Marcia had already given the girls their last feed before settling them in. The expressed feed was on standby, although they normally slept right through.

Eamon wanted to eat later. She had not questioned him about the trouble at the haulage company, although he appeared perturbed. She did not want anything to mar their evening together. She had dimmed the lights before she entered the walk-in dressing room. He lay propped up on the bed, hands locked behind his head, deep in thought with a towel wrapped around his waist, fresh from his shower.

"Would you like a massage?" Marcia broke his thoughts upon entering the bedroom.

Eamon turned on his side, smiling, observing. Resting his head on his hand. "Dressed like that I don't tink that there would be time!" Marcia untied the full-length silk negligee, letting it slip to the floor, continuing towards the bed. He circled his finger beckoning her to do a turn for him so he could take in the sight of her. "Five minutes tops!" He smiled, releasing the towel.

Marcia straddled him. "I think that perhaps I could help you to relax after all the stress you have had lately." She leaned back on his raised knees, widening her legs to show off the ouvert panties and cup-less matching bra. "Perhaps this position?" she made a quick manoeuvre and turned around, rear facing him. She felt his facial hair, his tongue teasing and teeth nipping between the ouvert silk, while his hands held her fast. Eamon increased the titillation. Marcia groaned with pleasure

"That will do for starters!" He lifted her off, placing her beneath him. As he devoured her nipples she bucked. "Ye are not going to tease me, and allow ye to get away wit it."

She found his penis, rock-hard, straining. She smiled at her capture, while her hand slowly moved along the shaft.

"Ye tink that ye have beat me?" He surrendered while she guided his willing hardness, filling her. Marcia's legs locked around him. He supported himself with his forearms on either side of her head, kissing her, thrusting, and taking them up together with the beginning of the spasm, taking them together. Her fingernails raked his flesh as his mouth fervently sought her breast and milk burst forth. Their hearts were racing together with the climax when a cry came from the monitor. Eamon leaned across to look at the screen. "I will get her!" He withdrew. Wrapping the towel around him, he headed towards the nursery.

Marcia observed the screen. "Are ye wet, or hungry?" Eamon kissed Aisling's mouth, putting her on his shoulder, feeling inside her nappy. He lay the baby on the changing mat, cleaned, and then changed her. He carried her towards the door.

"She requires a top-up!" He put her on Marcia's breast. Greedily, the baby suckled, then sighed and fell asleep on Marcia's breast. Eamon picked up Marcia's phone and took a snapshot, before carrying the sleeping baby back to the nursery.

"Now that we have got the wild passion out of the way…," His hand caressed the silk panties. "Let us enjoy slow love making. Leave the panties on!" he breathed, head between her legs.

They moved in unison with deliberate motion. His fingers trailed her face. "This time ye can have it twice!" he said.

Afterwards, as she lay in his arms, he reached across and picked up her phone. Finding the photo, he had taken earlier. He lay back, holding it before him. "What man could want more!"

"Eamon my legs are open!"

He smiled at her. "My eyes are the only ones that are going to see my wife with my child at her mother's breast!"

Marcia laughed, turning on her side to face him. "The picture of Aisling suckling on my breast, while I am attired in a raunchy, silk, cup-less bra and ouvert panties, with legs open is rather…"

Eamon interjected, sending the picture to his mobile phone. "Beautiful! My child at your breast is the result of our union. As our others were. The picture is priceless!" he replied on a serious note.

21

"I DON'T GIVE TWO FUCKS ABOUT A POX-BALLING LITTLE CUNT THAT'S THREATENED YE!" Eamon spat, towering over the middle-aged driver who had informed him about the muscle-bound young thug that had intimidated the two men, threatening that they would harm their families if they did not go along with their demands. Juan, the HGV driver, hung his head, visibly shaking when Eamon confronted him. Without any hesitation, Juan gave up everything that he knew.

Eamon's loyal manager, Diego, had previously given him the heads up regarding his suspicion that a couple of the drivers were delivering contraband. One of the drivers at the haulage company had overheard the two men talking in the locker room.

The following day, Eamon, Dan, and Billy, with the dog in tow, had lain in wait for the other driver, Jorge, to turn up to begin his shift. The lorry was heading for the Portsmouth docks in the UK. The men waited until the guy opened the cab door. He threw a rucksack into the lorry and went to climb in. Billy grabbed him from behind, commanding the dog to begin his search. The Belgian shepherd barked excitedly at the man's rucksack on the back seat. Billy followed the dog as it investigated every nook and cranny of the lorry. No further contraband had been found. Billy praised the dog for his good work.

While being dragged to the haulage office, the driver protested his innocence.

Eamon opened the rucksack, removing then slamming two one-kilo bags of white powder on the desk. He asked Diego for a penknife. Making a small incision, Eamon tested it and spat out the residue. Wiping his mouth with the back of his hand, Eamon roared, "YE FUCKING TINK THAT YE CAN MESS WIT ME!" Enraged, he glowered into the eyes of the driver. Eamon stepped back. "I want names. And ye better not lie!" he scoffed with an icy detachment.

"There are no names, we, we …" the man stammered, "were having a drink in a bar in Calpe. The big guy must have waited for me to use the men's room. He blocked the doorway when I went to leave!"

Eamon sat on the corner of the desk, arms folded. "Go on!" he commanded.

"He said that he knew where and for whom Juan and I worked and where we lived and that we both had relatives in El Colari. Jorge shifted his weight, glancing towards Dan and Billy who were watching intently. He was built like him!" He pointed at Dan, "Only younger! He looked like a body builder. He said that his boss had our families marked."

"This young thug put the heavy arm on yer then ye get Juan involved?" He raised his voice, "YOUSE PAIR RISK YER FUCKING JOB AND MY COMPANY LICENCE. WHY THE FUCK DID YE NOT COME TO ME!?" Eamon spat, rising to his full height. "How much did he offer to pay ye?" Eamon held Jorge's eyes; the driver lowered his to the floor. "Ye better stop wasting my fucking time because ye are standing on the edge of a very big drop!" Eamon warned. "If I find out ye gave me a load of bollocks that there was no cash incentive, youse both will pay the price!"

Jorge's grasp of English was far greater than Juan's, however, Eamon made sure his warning would be understood by both drivers.

"My wife is about to have a baby. My two-year-old daughter needs me. I could not put my family in danger," Jorge said. "The payment was a thousand euros," he confessed. "Also, I promise that for no amount of money would I take the chance of going to jail!" He straightened up. "Please, understand my problem!" he pleaded.

Eamon sucked air through his teeth. "After youse give me every bit of information about this young prick and the name of the bar that he hangs out at in Calpe."

Jorge told him what he knew. Now armed with the knowledge that the guy had arranged to meet both Juan and Jorge in the bar in Calpe the following week for the next drop-off, Eamon advised them, "Stay away from the bars in Calpe until I have dealt with the matter!"

Studying both men, he exhaled, "I am known to be a compassionate man – at times." Then he said sternly, "However, I am no fucking eejit, so don't ever mistake my kindness for stupidity!" He paused for a few seconds. "Diego informs me that youse two have been loyal to the company, furthermore, yer father's family is known and respected by my manager. Therefore, ye can thank him that I am allowing youse two to keep yer jobs." He paused, glaring at the pair.

"I don't care who ye take wit ye to discover who it is behind this shite," Eamon spat as he threw the two bags of cocaine into the boot of his car. "Hunt them down!" he ordered Dan.

22

Marcia had convinced Eamon that although she loved spending time with the babies, she felt the need to have an outside interest and return to work at the Mystique beauty salon. He had agreed that she could spend one day a week conducting readings and one evening working at the Hawk Wind club.

While waiting in her office at Suzette's salon for her first client Marcia thought about her previous evening with Eamon. Marcia had waited to broach the subject of starting work again after their hours of love making. She had carefully set the scene with low lighting and soft music playing from her playlist – Al Greene, 'Let's Stay Together' and Gladys Knight, 'Best Thing That Ever Happened to Me', also some of Eamon's favourite female soul vocalists. They had both massaged one another before the fervour of their passion took them.

She was brought back to the moment by a loud rap on the door. She sat up straight and said, "Come in." Marcia had been previously informed by Suzette that the client sounded like a young man when he had booked the appointment over the phone. Marcia had instructed Suzette to always take payment in advance before any tarot reading.

A good-looking lad swaggered in. Marcia sensed an air of arrogance as he crossed the room, pulling up a chair. He leaned back in his chair, smile beaming. He had perfect teeth, which she assumed were veneers, blue eyes and fair hair which was combed back. His mode of attire did not speak of the high street but more of couture. She judged him to be in his early twenties. There was something about him that made Marcia feel uncomfortable. His look rested upon her breasts. Marcia did not reflect her annoyance, although she bristled inwardly.

"Have you ever had a tarot reading before?" she asked, her manner business-like. She slid the pack of cards across the desk towards him. "Please shuffle them. When you feel the desire, stop."

He grinned, holding her eyes.

"No, but a couple of people have recommended you. One of my birds is always singing your praises."

Marcia had not previously recognised him, but it suddenly dawned on her that this man was in the restaurant with the young woman who she had previously done a reading for. Marcia smiled briefly. "Please, if there are any queries, do not ask until I have finished," she directed firmly. "You may wish to record the reading in case there is something you might be confused about."

"Don't worry about me, love. I never get confused about anything!" he countered. He shuffled the cards and handed them to Marcia, reclining in a leisurely manner.

Marcia turned the first card over, slowly laying it on the table and pausing. Then she set the next two cards in a line below it. She tapped the first card with her forefinger, without speaking.

He sat bolt upright, giving her his full attention, placing his forearms on the desk. She slowly laid down the next three cards. He observed the tarot cards, brow furrowed in anticipation.

Marcia looked up at him and asked his astrological star sign.

"Gemini," he said, smirking. "I can multitask. My mental and physical abilities are finely honed."

Marcia spoke, "I can see that you are beginning a new venture. The challenge that you are undertaking is fraught with obstacles! The ladder that you aim to climb to reach success has many dangerous obstacles. There is a dark-haired man that will destroy your dreams of triumph!" She ran her middle finger across the card of Le Chariot. "The Grim Reaper faces this card, although they are both water cards, which can be beneficial." She touched the card La Maison Dieu, without glancing in his direction. "This is the Tower next to the Grim Reaper, which I sense will bring about your downfall if you continue on the pathway that you are on."

The 22 major arcana cards were spread out before her. She sat back and said, smiling thinly, "Unless you immediately change direction, the next step that you take will be erroneous." She saw his uncomprehending look. "Your downfall!" she informed him.

He pushed the chair back angrily and said, "What a load of crap!" His neck and face reddened, and his eyes bulged. Marcia pulled away as he leaned into her space. "You have fed me a load of shit! My business is going to be successful." He shouted, "I AM EARNING BIG MONEY! AND YOU SPOUT THAT I AM ON THE WRONG ROAD!" He scoffed, pushing the chair out of the way. As he went to leave, he turned to Marcia and said, "You are a bleeding take-on. It's lucky for you that I paid up front because you would not get a euro from me otherwise!" He glared at Marcia. "I will be the one to have the last laugh!" Sneering, he opened the door, slamming it behind him.

A few minutes later Suzette popped her head around the door, mouth agape, followed by Cindy.

"What was up with him? The prat had a face like a slapped arse?" Cindy declared, hands on hips.

"The young tosser slammed the salon door!"Cindy added.

Suzette slumped into the chair. "Fortunately, the two boys' clients were having facial and body treatments in the treatment rooms, and they did not see anything!" Suzette placed her hand across the desk, touching Marcia's. "Are you alright?"

Marcia, although slightly shaken, exhaled and said giggling, "He did not like his tarot reading!"

"Throwing his toys out of the pram. The kid needs his arse kicked!" Cindy retorted.

Suzette stood up, flustered. "No harm done!"

"Lucky for him it was not me he had a strop with. I would have belted him!" Cindy roared with laughter, her brown eyes flashing.

23

Tommy Dugan was seething on the drive to his mother's villa in Javea. He had lost face by being accompanied by his father to Eamon O'Donally's adult club and having to apologise to the Irishman and the dancer. Furthermore, the big Irishman had accepted Tommy's apology and offered his hand, which Tommy reluctantly shook. The money that Tommy's mother Denise had invested in his business was now lost, due to the Irishman's men and their detection dog finding his goods. He had coerced his mum into putting up the money on the pretext that his new venture was in Bitcoin. She had been disappointed when Tommy explained that the market had bottomed out. His mother, Denise, had no idea that some of her inheritance from her dad's estate went towards purchasing a job lot of narcotics. Tommy had made enquiries and found out that his cocaine had been confiscated and the Irishman's drivers were under O'Donally's protection.

To top it off, the Irishman's wife had told him the biggest load of crap. He was determined to make sure they paid for his trouble. However, he sighed with relief as he approached his parents' gates drive and noticed his father's car was absent.

Crocodile tears streamed down Tommy's face, and he wiped them away. He sat on a stool near the central island in his mum's large kitchen. "Mum, she is a liar. The woman on reception took my two hundred euros before I went to see the fake tarot card reader." He sniffed twice for effect. "I haven't any good luck, mum!" he lamented, "All I ever wanted was for you to be proud of me."

His mother hurried to his side; her ample bosom crushed against him. She patted his back, kissing the top of his head. "Tommy, you listen to your old mum, I have plenty more where that came from. There is also all the jewellery that gramps willed to me, which was grandma's."

"I can't take any more from you, mum," his doe eyes blinked.

Denise melted. "You are going to be successful, like dad." She added, "How much do you need to start a new business?" Before he answered, she smiled and said, tickling under his chin. "Do you want me to ask your dad to give you a few introductions in the property business? Dad knows everyone in the game."

Tommy paled, shaking his head. "I want to make it on my own, mum." He paused, placing his hand on her arm. "I want to surprise him!" Denise grinned in agreement.

24

Suzette and Greg were overseeing the Hawk Wind club, while Eamon took Marcia out to a restaurant. She and Greg would have the next night off and Marcia was to begin work there. Eamon insisted that she could only be at the adult club when he was present. The previous weeks had been manic with bookings for hen and stag parties, not to mention the paid-up yearly memberships.

The staff, for the most part, had become like family members. It was just the two top dancers who constantly bitched about each other, vying for the highest tips.

Suzette opened the dancers' dressing room door, momentarily stopping in her tracks at the scene of Sunni the Somalian riding a stool as if it were a racehorse, with her long legs crouched in jockey position and large, firm rear rising and falling. She was taunting Jenny as she sat in front of the mirror adjusting her makeup, glaring at her adversary. "This is how I would ride our boss, Eamon O'Donally. Then he would only want me!" Sunni announced.

"What in bloody hell!" Suzette said, marching across the floor. Jenny sprang up, making a lunge for Sunni. Suzette pushed herself between them. "This is not a damn playground!" She stared at each hissing she-cat. "Leave now if you don't want to work!" She waited.

Jenny stepped back. Sunni nodded, mouthing, "Sorry" to Suzette.

"What's the matter?" Greg leaned back in the office chair when Suzette burst in. "Lock the door!"

She relayed the scene in the dressing room. Greg smiled, "Come and sit with me." Suzette moved around to his side of the desk, sitting on his lap. His hands encircled her rear.

"If that had been you that Sunni was making sexual references to, she would have lost her job."

Greg cocked an eyebrow. "I don't have the pulling power of my Irish business partner, therefore, my sweet, you have no worries. Furthermore, these women are not attractive to me. Only you!"

Suzette put her arms around his neck and kissed him. Minutes later with Suzette astride him, her panties on the floor and dress raised above her buttocks, they reached their peak. Carried away in her oblivion, Suzette increased her pace. Greg held her to him, stoically grimacing with the sharp pains in his chest.

25

Eamon waited for Dan to arrive at his villa. He had received his call, informing him that he had what he had been waiting for.

Upon Dan's arrival, the two men sat behind the locked office door. Dan faced him across the desk. "The two new security men, Scott Lord and Benny Harris, who I took on from Jimmy Grant, joined us in the hunt in the bars in Calpe. Scott got talking to a barman, giving the lad's description. Fifty euros jolted his memory!" Dan grinned. "The previous night, two young guys were in there, asking if any of the locals worked at the Irishman's haulage company. One of them pestered the boss's niece who was working behind the bar. She declines his invitation to go out, however, to keep him sweet, she accepts his business card. The girl gave it to her uncle. Scott said that the description fit the dark-haired lad who was bragging to anyone who listened that he was the other young guy's minder." Dan produced the card, passing it to Eamon "You are never going to believe it, but Dougie Dugan's lad Tommy is behind the narcotics. Tommy's 'goffer' who he sent out to put the heavy arm on your drivers is some numbskull by the name of Alfie Bond. Apparently, he classes himself as another Rambo – his hero!"

Eamon shook his head, fingers stroking his goatee. He was fuming. "Fucking little toe rags!" he grumbled. "I am going to need to get my head around how we deal with them."

Dan sat back in his chair. "Dougie Dougan was understanding over the turnout with his boy and the dancer at the club, however, intimidation and narcotic smuggling in your lorries are another ball game!"

Eamon nodded. "Leave it wit me. I will tink on it. Then I will ring ye."

Eamon sat in his office contemplating his next move. Tommy Dugan had become a thorn in his side. Eamon realised that the only way to remove the thorn was to rip it from its roots. He picked up his phone.

. . . .

Dan had tried to talk him out of going alone into the lion's den. Nonetheless, Eamon insisted that he would confront Dougie Dugan on his turf. Dan offered a compromise, informing his boss that he and Billy would be nearby on standby.

Eamon pressed the intercom on the outside pillar of the magnificent villa. There was no answer, but the ornate gates opened. He admired the backdrop of Montgo Mountain; the panoramic vista across Javea to the marina was stunning. Eamon had the greatest respect for the man. Dougie and his brother Roy had become successful in the property business many years ago.

Dougie Dugan's over two-metre frame stood on the top step of the villa's entrance. Although his demeanour did not appear menacing, Eamon was under no illusion as to the power that the elder man wielded.

Eamon alighted from the Maserati. The two men held eye contact. Dougie smiled thinly, stepping aside as Eamon entered. Dougie led Eamon across the open-plan lounge to his office. Unlocking the door, he bade him enter. Eamon took the proffered chair opposite the mahogany, Victorian desk.

Dougie leaned back into the office chair, locking his hands behind his head. "We seem to be crossing paths a lot these days. However," a brief flicker of humour played on the corners of his mouth, "tell me if I am wrong, but you don't drive all the way from Altea Hills to Javea just for a little tête-á-tête?" He smiled, but his eyes remained cold. He cocked his head. "Why is it that I smell trouble?"

Eamon placed his forearms on the chair. "Dougie, I have come to yer home to discuss a problem that I have encountered with a couple of drivers at my haulage business. It involves yer son and another lad."

Dougie slowly nodded, pursing his lips.

"I notice that you are not mob-handed, which I appreciate, because, whatever the trouble, Eamon, I am sure that you and I can sort it!"

Eamon nodded. "We are both fathers, although mine are youngsters. Nevertheless, I don't doubt that I will face a few problems wit them in the future!" He shifted in his seat. "Yer boy and his mate have been intimidating a couple of my drivers. The pal of yer lad waylaid a driver in a bar in Calpe, threatening their families, telling them that their homes would be destroyed if they did not carry narcotics on their lorry run to the UK docks. The two drivers are decent family men, one wit a baby on the way!" Eamon added.

Dougie sat up, rigid as a stone statue. He stared right through Eamon and exhaled. "Eamon, I don't disbelieve a word that you have told me." He scoffed, "My brother Roy was in a bar last night having a beer. He bumps into an old mate who whispers in my kid brother's ear that Tommy and Alfie Bond have been trying to intimidate a couple of the local trawler men.

Sounds like your problem. Fucking cocaine!" he spat. Appearing to talk to himself, he muttered, "Where the fuck would the lazy prick get money for narcotics?" He gave a half laugh, shaking his head. "Of course, his mother!" he answered his own question. "Firstly, I want to apologise, Eamon. However…," he leaned forward on the desk and said earnestly, "I am asking you to leave it in my hands. I promise you that'll be the end of it!" Dougie grinned malevolently. "I have the perfect plan to hit the fucking spoiled brat who's still tied to his mother's apron strings where it will hurt him the most!"

Eamon nodded. "I am satisfied with whatever way that ye want to deal wit this, Dougie. I have the packages in the boot of my car."

"Please!" Dougie splayed his arms. "Let me have them!"

On the drive home, Eamon phoned Dan, informing him that the problem was sorted. Five minutes into the drive his mobile rang. He recognised the number of his boys' school. Eamon put the call on loudspeaker. A flustered school principal informed him that Niall had once more been involved in a tussle that he had instigated. Niall had bitten another pupil's ear, and the school would not tolerate such ungentlemanly behaviour.

"The boy's half-term is in a few days. I will speak to my son when he is home," Eamon said, sharply. The principal replied haughtily, "I seem to recollect, Mr O'Donally, that you and I have had this conversation regarding Niall's somewhat disruptive behaviour on more than one occasion."

He did not take well to the principal's pompous tone, but he held back his angry retort.

"I don't make idle threats. If I state that I will deal wit my son, believe me…" He paused for a second before continuing, "Ye do well to listen!"

Eamon clicked the call off. "Fucking prick!" he said aloud. "What the hell is wrong with Niall?" he pondered, not for the first time.

His thoughts turned to Joyce Grant, who was returning to Spain for a holiday. Her exit after Jimmy's demise seven years ago to New York to live with her daughter was a bonus to Eamon's previous stroke of good fortune. Joyce had wanted out of anything that would connect her to her past with Jimmy Grant and she had sold Eamon the haulage company for a 'song'. He held a special place in his heart for the woman who he had known for many years. Although he had not kept in touch, Marcia and Joyce spoke on the phone about once a month.

26

Marcia had not mentioned the young male client who had been abusive to Eamon. She knew that he would put a stop to her working if he knew. She put the incident aside and thought about Niall and Quinn's home coming. Lloyd and Keiron had asked her if her boys could be page boys at their upcoming wedding. Marcia thought with trepidation about how she would broach the subject with Eamon. She sensed that Eamon would not object, however, it was the fact that the boys would be required to wear kilts, matching the wedding couple's attire. Furthermore, the tartan was Scottish, not Irish. Eamon was proud of his heritage. Lloyd's family on his mother's side was from the Isle of Skye.

Marcia could not help but smile to herself remembering the scene the previous day at the Mystique beauty salon, after her last tarot reading of the day. Kieron was restyling Marcia's hair, and Lloyd was relaying their wedding plans to his client who was firing questions about the forthcoming celebration. "We are wearing Scottish kilts, with no underwear as tradition dictates." The client giggled, "Apart from the pageboys!" The woman teased him about the venue and the view that the women would have from below the outdoor elevated platform where the couple was taking their vows. He lifted his apron that protected his clothing from the hair colouring that he was administering. "The female contingent would do better to pray for a windy day," he grinned, tongue in cheek, "because the majority will be in for a treat."

Marcia's thoughts turned to Suzette and the tarot reading that she requested regarding her concern about Greg's health. Marcia had reluctantly agreed, however, when she had laid down the first three tarot cards, she had sensed that Greg's health was going to become problematic soon. She had given Suzette the warning, although she had tried not to alarm her too much. However, she pressed it upon her to book a health check for Greg sooner rather than later.

Suzette promised to coax him to see a doctor, although she wasn't convinced that he would listen. He had told Suzette before that she worried too much and that he was only suffering from heart burn. Suzette and Greg were taking a two-day break. She said that they had booked into a hotel in Marbella. She would ensure that Greg rested.

Marcia silently despaired for Greg's longevity if he did not heed the warnings.

Marcia stacked the dishwasher after dinner. Aye had cooked some of Eamon's favourite Thai dishes, including salads and spicy fish. The smoothies were more to Marcia's taste than Eamon's, although they had persuaded him of late to indulge. Eamon had been out for most of the day. He had told her that it was on business. Marcia never questioned him, although it had fleetingly crossed her mind at times that Eamon could have a secret life, as some of the men in their circle did. She had conducted enough tarot readings for concerned women wanting to know if their husband or partner was being unfaithful. Marcia had to use her eloquence with words to avoid becoming involved in the fallout from an irate client's partner. Marcia put the thought to the back of her mind. She had previously faced that difficulty with Suzette's previous marriage to Max Greenaway when Marcia had to try to keep the balance between the pair. Both Marcia's and Suzette's lives had been in jeopardy because Max had wanted revenge for their duplicity. It was a situation that she hoped she would not encounter again in the future.

Marcia had given the girls their last feed. Aisling had stopped crying for feeds at night. They both slept soundly all night. Marcia showered and changed into the black Tribal maxi flared skirt and a halter-neck top from the Indian designer Rina Dhaka, one of the designers that she favoured. Marcia loved the femininity of the style. Although they were dining at home, she wore the emerald and diamond stud earrings that complimented the outfit. She did not wear any shoes out of respect for Aye's Thai custom of not wearing shoes in the house. However, at times, when Eamon forgot, Aye would chastise him, whereby he obediently removed his shoes.

She wrapped a cashmere shawl around her shoulders and went towards the terrace doors. The dog followed. She slipped her shoes back on, stepping into the biting, early evening wind. The low-level, stratus clouds gathering in the distance threatened rain. She moved towards the pool, small ripples played across her long skirt, which whipping it around her legs. She sent her nightly prayer out to the Universe to ask the spirit world to watch over her children. Roman, who was laid by her feet sat up, ears alert. Dog and mistress turned around when Eamon stepped out onto the terrace, wine glass in hand. She thought that he appeared weary. He came towards her, his free arm encircling her waist, pulling her into him, nuzzling her neck. "Ye look inviting!" He took in the essence of Turkish rose and saffron. He knocked back half the wine and wiped his mouth before he kissed her.

"Ye must be looking at that Karma Sutra book for yer inspiration." He nibbled her earlobe, cupping one cheek of her rear, pressing into her.

"Would you like me to massage you?" She smiled. "Or are you too eager?" Her hand moved to caress his desire, feeling it pressing for release. Marcia held his look. His zip slid down with ease. She slipped her hand inside and softly stroked.

"Ye do not leave me much choice!" he breathed, into her neck. His shaft free, her hand expertly teased.

"I'll check on the babies and quickly shower. Then I am all yers. We can eat later. Leave this on!" he said, running his hand down her back.

"I have been honing the skills I learned from my book," she said, smiling.

Eamon winked. Finishing his wine, he took her by the hand.

"Eamon, please remove your shoes!" she reminded him. He shook his head, adhering to her wishes.

"I thought that you wished me to keep it on!" Marcia breathed as Eamon came up behind her and slowly removed her halter top, letting it fall beneath her breasts. He cupped them, nipping the base of her neck.

"I want to undress ye!" He ruffled the long skirt up above her waist. "Mm, no underwear," he said slyly as he pressed his hardened shaft between her legs.

She leaned into him, fingernails tenderly playing down his face.

He planted kisses along the nape of her neck, his fingers stimulating her nipples. Turning her to face him, his mouth engulfed each bud one at a time.

"Allow me to show you a position that will please you," she said in a hushed tone.

146

Eamon carried her to the bed. She raised her leg. He cupped her buttocks, shifting his position so Marcia could wrap her other leg around him. She held his neck fast between her ankles and Eamon carried on with measured movements deep inside of her, until they both united with moans of pleasure.

27

Cindy phoned Marcia to inform her that Joyce Grant had arrived in Spain. She was staying with Cindy and Dan for the duration of her stay as she would be attending Lloyd and Kieron's wedding. Cindy asked Marcia if she would be able to fit Joyce in for a tarot reading. Although Marcia agreed, she felt a sense of unexplained trepidation. "Joyce has a few concerns that perhaps you could throw some light upon."

"Of course!" Marcia replied, somewhat disturbed at the reference to Joyce's concerns. Marcia had given Joyce her last tarot reading seven years ago, prior to Jimmy going missing. Marcia thought back to that time when Joyce had told Marcia that her husband Jimmy Grant had not returned home and hadn't heard from him. Marcia predicted that Jimmy would not return and that Joyce would go to live in the USA. Marcia had heard via Cindy that Joyce loved their beautiful home in the USA, which her son-in-law Matt had purchased. It was a luxurious property in the New York suburb of Great Neck Plaza. Joyce loved sharing the home with her daughter, Sara, and her beloved granddaughter, Jessica.

Cindy had relayed that Matt and his business partner had expanded their restaurant business and now owned two restaurants. Nevertheless, Marcia could not shake off an ominous feeling – a heaviness in her solar plexus, as she had way back when she had 'sensed' that Jimmy Grant was dead. Although his body was never discovered, the Spanish police closed the file.

Marcia walked down the steps to the driveway as Cindy's car pulled up. Joyce alighted, exclaiming, "My goodness, you look amazing!" Putting her bag on her shoulder, she hurried towards Marcia, hugging her. "I don't need to ask if Eamon and your four children are making you happy. Your radiance speaks for itself!" Joyce put her arm around Marcia's shoulder. "You look beautiful in that nipped-in waist, flowing peacock-coloured dress. The Asian influence adds a touch of the exotic, enhancing the mystical look! That suits you so well, my dear friend," she complemented. They waited for Cindy.

Marcia had assisted Aye in preparing a salad for the women's lunch while the babies napped. "Suzette will be joining us a bit later. Would you like to go out to the terrace? Although the midday heat is stifling today, we will be shaded by the canopy!"

Cindy broke in, "Joyce is desperate for you to have a look at her tarot reading!"

"If that is alright with you, Marcia?" Joyce interceded. "Seven years ago, you predicted the demise of Jimmy and my life in America!" she added.

"I will fetch my cards. Take your seats. I will speak to Aye to tell her that if the girls wake up, I won't be too long."

A pregnant silence hung in the air as Marcia turned over the first tarot card from the pack that Joyce had previously shuffled. Their eyes were fixed on each card as Marcia laid them out. Marcia purposely withheld the first bit of information that she sensed would have an impact on Joyce. "Perhaps you would like to ask specific questions?" Marcia did not want to alarm Joyce. She was playing for time.

"Cindy leaned over the layout, finger hovering over the first card. "You never allow anyone to speak during a reading!" She probed, sitting back in her chair. "What is wrong?"

"This is different as you both are my friends!" Marcia smiled, sensing that Cindy felt her apprehension. She eased her way out of Cindy's prying.

Joyce placed her hand on Cindy's arm, placating her and preventing Cindy from pressing any further. "That is fine, Marcia. There are certain situations to do with my son-in-law that are bothering me. Don't get me wrong, I am not being ungrateful to Matt, who with his business partner has expanded their restaurant business. I live in a fabulous home that he purchased in a suburb of New York City. It is one of the best places to live. Furthermore, the private school that my granddaughter attends is highly rated. I enjoy the lifestyle and living with my daughter. Nevertheless, I have had a nagging feeling that Matt has a secret life – another woman or family tucked away. Marcia, I am an expert in recognising the tell-tale signs. I lived with the biggest player – Jimmy!" Joyce smiled wistfully. "Marcia, all that I am asking you is to give me peace of mind." She paused for a couple of seconds. "I do not want my Sara to experience what I went through with her father – his cell phone," she laughed softly at the use of the American terminology. "Sara said to me that he never takes his mobile phone out of his pocket. He is up to something Marcia. Money appears to be no object. He is very generous to Sara. However, she is on her own with her daughter a great deal. There are signs that he is being devious!"

Marcia quietly inhaled as she scanned the cards. "He is not being unfaithful to your daughter, Joyce."

Joyce placed her forearms on the table. "What is he up to then if there is no other woman?" She waited with bated breath for Marcia's answer.

"Matt does conduct various other types of business." Marcia hoped that her cagey answer would satisfy Joyce.

"Such as?" Cindy demanded.

Marcia looked from one to the other. "Joyce, what I am about to reveal to you, I must ask you to try to handle the situation calmly without informing Sara!"

"Marcia, I am her mum. I can deal with anything as long as my girl and granddaughter don't get hurt!"

Marcia looked down at the 22 major arcana cards. "Matt is involved in dealing narcotics. It is a major thing. Planes and shipment by boats are involved."

Joyce visibly paled.

Cindy roared. "What does that tosser think he is doing? He has his wife and child to think about." she took Joyce's arm.

"Drugs!" Joyce said, voice barely audible. She smiled wanly. "I could have dealt with Matt if it had been another woman." Joyce added, "I could have warned him off!" She shook her head. "However, for you to 'see' planes and shipments, then…" She faltered, exhaling. "I promise you, Marcia, that I won't tell her."

Aye came out of the nursery, struggling to carry both chubby girls. The tarot reading forgotten for the moment, Joyce and Cindy headed towards the babies with open arms.

The girls' eyes flashed, and they yelled as they were taken from Aye. "The pair of you have your father's fiery temper!" Cindy laughed, carrying Aisling to the sofa. "You are built like your dad too; you weigh a tonne!" she spoke to the baby.

Joyce soothed Aine with light strokes across her damp curls. "You are both beautiful," she cooed. "Their hair colouring is like burnt copper and look at those long black lashes!" She kissed the baby's forehead. Aine's eyes watched her every movement. "You two are going to grow into stunning sirens that will lure the men onto the rocks! Formidable girls with a formidable father. I pity their future beaus!" Joyce's words brought a hint of a smile to the corner of the child's lips. She appeared to be taking the compliments on board. Aisling stared quietly.

Marcia showed Joyce photographs of Niall and Quinn. "My God! They are strikingly handsome. The image of Eamon," Joyce exclaimed.

"Eamon is collecting them from school tomorrow. I am looking forward to seeing them. I miss them so much," Marcia added, wistfully.

"I could not imagine how you feel with them being away at boarding school. Nevertheless, we both know the kind of world that you and I have lived in out here. Jimmy and Eamon's past was dicey, to say the least!" Joyce said. "My late husband no longer has to fear the Law tapping him on the shoulder, but sadly, Eamon must still be paying the price for his past endeavours with Jimmy."

Marcia nodded. Aye came into the lounge, taking both girls to feed them.

Marcia laid the garden table while the women sat talking. She heard the buzzer from the front gates and rushed in the press the button to open them. "That will be Suzette!" Marcia said, excitedly.

Two vehicles came in through the gates, Suzette's car and an Interflora van. The bouquet of 30 red roses was passed to her. "From Lover Boy?" Suzette asked, cocking an eyebrow. Marcia smiled, ignoring her touch of sarcasm.

"How are you darling?" Suzette hugged Joyce.

"You are even more glamourous than ever," Joyce gushed. "The three of you are so slim, unlike me. Since I have been living in America the lure of doughnuts has meant I have put on a few kilos."

"Marcia has just received red roses from her lover! She's just putting them in water. She won't be long!" Suzette said, sitting down next to Joyce.

"We have so much to catch up on, Suzette, although Cindy keeps me updated on what you two successful ladies are up to." She took Suzette's hand. "I am happy for all three of you." The women sat talking. "Cindy's man is a hunk and also a gentleman," Joyce said.

"I would not say that Dan is a gentleman at all times, especially when we are behind closed doors!" Cindy said, grinning.

"What about your relationship Suzette? How are things with Greg?" Joyce queried.

"We have just been to a lovely hotel in Marbella for a two-day break. My man adores me, as I do him. Greg is the love of my life, Joyce. As you know, Max was cut from the same cloth as Jimmy. It was in their genes!"

Joyce nodded in agreement.

Marcia topped up the wine glasses.

"You are still being sent roses even after seven years of marriage?!" Joyce smiled warmly at Marcia.

"Eamon is not a man who expresses his feelings easily, however, his romantic gestures are wonderful," Marcia said, beaming.

"Roses!" Cindy intercepted, smiling. "For the number of children Marcia has given him, she should receive the crown jewels, not flowers!" Cindy teased.

"I must concede that her man spoils her. As she deserves to be!" Suzette added. "Furthermore, I must admit that the fabulous Hermes Birkin bag that he had sent from America after Marcia gave birth to the twins is something that I covet," she said, grinning.

Joyce and Marcia left the other two women, who were discussing work. They sat at the far end of the large garden table.

Joyce spoke, "You must not concern yourself with my problems, Marcia. I will protect my girl and granddaughter." She smiled wanly. "You used to say to us, 'forewarned is forearmed'. I will watch points with Matt."

Marcia exhaled without replying.

"I have heard great things about Eamon's and Greg's adult club. How are you coping with him working in such an environment?" Joyce asked.

"I would be lying if I said it hadn't crossed my mind that Eamon is surrounded by young, beautiful, near-naked women. And it has made me feel... uncomfortable!" Marcia adjusted her dress when she crossed her legs. "When I was heavily pregnant with the twins and I couldn't do some things that I could previously, I felt inadequate. Although, Eamon was always attentive." She smiled. "He appears to like me pregnant, but one can never be sure."

"Marcia, I have lived in your world with a notorious philanderer, who flaunted his predilection for women, married and single, young and old," Joyce spoke without malice. "I suffered the humiliation until his death. Jimmy had no morals. Eamon has! Eamon needed help to become legal when he began to rise after Jimmy's demise. I previously discovered that Jimmy had betrayed him with Eamon's Eve." Joyce did not go into details. "Therefore, when I came to a position whereby I could help Eamon, I sold him Jimmy's haulage company at a price that would have seen Jimmy turn in his grave." She laughed, continuing, "It was my way of compensating Eamon for his loyalty to Jimmy that hadn't been rewarded. This world..." she splayed her arms, "is full of secrets. The men keep a tight-knit circle, as I imagine you have come to understand. Nonetheless, women talk among themselves about their woes with their partners and their friends' relationships, but Eamon has never been mentioned in our girl talks." She sat back, observing Marcia. "When you first came to Spain with Suzette, I sensed that Jimmy's eye was trained on you."

Marcia blushed, "Joyce!"

Joyce placed her hand on Marcia's arm to prevent her from speaking. "After Eve's death, I noticed the change in Eamon. He quickly went from being heartbroken to seeming detached regarding the situation. My feminine intuition informed me that somehow Eamon had discovered her and Jimmy's betrayal. He was free to look elsewhere. I spotted his interest in you," she laughed. "I took note that it was reciprocated."

Marcia smiled, remembering when she first laid eyes on Eamon.

"Eamon was besotted with you, even though I sensed that he was trying to fight his feelings. It's understandable after the woman he had been married to had betrayed him. However, Jimmy picked up on Eamon's attraction to you, and sent him to Miami so that his path to you was clear." Joyce looked to the sky. "God had other plans in mind. The rest is history. Marcia, you and your children have given Eamon what he was always searching for. Over the years, I knew that Eamon cared for his younger brother and his family's welfare. Eamon is a protector. Although he must pay the price for his past deeds with Jimmy by constantly looking over his shoulder, so don't judge him because he has sent your sons out of harm's way. Bear with it!" She advised. "The man loves you."

28

The following afternoon, Eamon and Thomas Harper-Watts, whose wife Isabella was due to have a baby shortly, were returning from collecting the boys from the boarding school. Eamon had phoned Marcia to say that they were 19 kilometres away. He had stopped in Benissa as the boys needed the toilet, and he was taking them to have a drink and snack.

Marcia sat in the nursery with the baby girls. She felt overwhelmed with the excitement of seeing the boys soon and introducing them to the twins. Marcia kissed Aine after her feed. She put a new dress on her, placing the contented child in the cot. Aisling smiled as her mother reached for her. Aisling's mouth sought the bud. "Your brothers will be here shortly!" she spoke to the suckling child, who observed with both chubby hands fixed on the breast. Marcia planted a soft kiss on her head. "You also have another big brother who is not here," she confided, wistfully. "He would love you all!"

When Aisling had finished feeding, Marcia wiped the residue from the baby's chin and changed her. Putting her in the same frilly cotton dress as her sister.

The Belgian shepherd's ears pricked up. He got up from where he had been lying in the shade beside Marcia's chair at the garden table where she sat relaxing and padded across the terrace. The dog had heard the car before Marcia had and headed to the front of the villa. Marcia followed.

The 7-seater BMW that Eamon had purchased for his family pulled in. Marcia wore a flowing, lilac skirt and matching top embroidered with scattered Wisteria. Her skirt whipped in the wind as she hurried towards them, putting her arms out towards the boys. Crouched before them, she smothered their faces with kisses, unaware that Niall tried to turn his face away. Eamon missed nothing. "Mummy you look like a princess!" Quinn, beaming, returned her embrace.

"I am terribly excited to see our baby sisters. I have been saving my allowance to purchase them a gift," Quinn added, eagerly taking Marcia's hand.

She ran her free hand across Niall's hair, smiling. "We have missed you both so much!" She walked ahead of Eamon. Niall's face was turned towards the ground, while his brother skipped happily alongside Marcia.

Eamon had a plan in mind for his eldest son. One in which he silently hoped would work.

Dom and Maureen would be arriving in a couple of days. They were booked into a 5-star hotel in Calpe that overlooked the Mediterranean Sea. Dom had refused Eamon's offer to stay at the villa, insisting that he did not wish to impose upon Eamon's large family.

Billy also had company at his house. Jane's niece, Kalita, was also visiting for Lloyd and Kieron's upcoming wedding. Eamon had received two packages the previous day, however, he was waiting for the right time to reveal them. But first, he wanted to try to resolve the niggling problem with his son.

"Go up and changed," he directed the boys. "When youse are ready, come to the lounge!" Eamon smiled at Marcia and said, "Come and welcome me!"

She crossed the lounge, falling into his open arms. He cupped her backside and kissed her. "Once the boys have met the babies, I must attend to some business. Niall will accompany me, while Quinn stays at home wit ye!"

Marcia beamed. "Niall will like that. I will join Quinn in the pool."

Eamon held Marcia at arm's length. "Tonight, I would like ye to wear this!" He ran his hands up her back, nuzzling her neck. Quinn skipped down the stairs, and Niall trailed behind. "I will get the girls," he said, discreetly patting her bum.

Aisling opened her eyes at the sound of his voice. Aine wriggled in slumber. Eamon kissed her cheek, "Come to papa, ye little porker!" He scooped Aine up with his free hand. She smiled sleepily, snuggling into his neck. Kissing their damp curls, he carried the twins into the lounge.

Quinn squealed with delight, rushing towards them. "Papa, they are so pretty!" He took both of their free hands cooing at them. Niall stood statue-like, his dark eyes reflecting his disdain.

"May I hold one?" Quinn asked, kissing each girl's hand.

"Both of ye sit back on the settee because they are heavy and will wriggle."

Eamon passed Aisling to Marcia. The baby happily went into Quinn's outstretched arms, her mouth clamping his nose. Giggling, he gently moved her head.

Aine squealed, gripping her father's shirt when he tried to place her in Niall's arms. She clung limpet-like to him, and tears flowed.

"She does not like me!" Niall said, scowling at Eamon.

"Don't worry, she will get used to ye, Niall," Eamon explained.

Niall did not respond. He stared at the child whose arms were around his father's neck, while Eamon soothed her. "In a moment I must attend to my business." He spoke to Niall, "I would like ye to join me. Quinn can stay wit Mummy and swim in the pool."

Niall nodded.

"May we take the babies into the pool, Mummy?" Quinn asked.

Marcia smiled. "I will ask Aye to take them onto the terrace where they can watch you swim. You can entertain them."

Quinn beamed. "I will go change into my swimming trunks."

Niall sat in the passenger seat of his father's Maserati. "I would like ye to see how my businesses are run, Niall, because when ye are grown ye and yer brother will take over from me!" Eamon sensed a change come over his son. He was showing some interest, scanning the yard as they parked near the lorry bay.

Diego stood up, smiling when Eamon opened the office door. He held his hand out to Niall. "It is a pleasure to meet you," the elderly Spanish manager said, taking the small boy's outstretched hand.

"Encantado de conocerte," Niall replied.

Diego's smile spread from ear to ear. "May I show your son around?"

Eamon nodded.

Eamon stroked his goatee beard, watching from the office window at Niall pointing at lorries as he spoke to Diego. Eamon observed his boy's latent authority, which was yet to bloom. He could see some of his personality traits in his son. Niall's stoicism Eamon could relate to, but his inherent jealousy of his sibling, he could not. The attitude Niall had towards his brother was unlike Eamon's towards his sibling Patrick. However, he was determined to forge a bond between his sons. Furthermore, he felt a disquiet beneath Niall's composure. He would try to unearth his son's problem.

Eamon stood back, holding the club's door open to allow Niall to walk ahead of him. "Are you the proprietor?" Niall asked as he stopped to glance at the stage of the Hawk Wind club.

"I am in a partnership," Eamon said as he raised his hand in greeting to Dan and Billy who were changing barrels and stock checking behind the bar.

"What are the poles for?" Niall queried.

"They are dance poles!" Eamon did not elaborate. He touched Niall's shoulder, guiding him towards the men behind the bar.

"Hi, boss!" Billy smiled. "Would you like me to show your son around?"

Niall interjected brusquely, "My father will show me. Thank you!"

Billy nodded, catching Eamon's eye, who nodded in return.

Eamon led Niall into the office and opened the safe to show him where the books were kept, explaining how the clients paid a yearly subscription.

Niall appeared to take it on board. They moved across the floor of the club. He told Niall about the two bars and the staff that worked there. Niall took in the dressing tables, with makeup strewn atop them. He walked towards the mirrors. "Why are there so many stools?" Do people work in here?"

Eamon sat him on a stool. "The dancers prepare for work in here."

Niall looked around, then faced him. "Papa, are you a criminal?"

Momentarily shocked, Eamon composed himself. "Why would ye ask that, Niall?" He spoke softly, not wanting the boy to clam up.

"There is a boy at the school who tried to intimidate me and others. It did not work, although others were afraid."

Eamon's mind raced. He crouched down to Niall's eye level so as not to intimidate the boy. "Ye are a good boy to tell me, Niall. I am proud that ye stood up to the bullies…" He paused for a few seconds. "Did anyone hurt yer brother?"

Niall's eyes questioned his father's. "Boswell hurt Quinn. When I was told by another boy. I went to find him, then I struck Boswell. He then left Quinn alone. He said that his father told him that our father was nothing but an Irish criminal! I told him that our father was powerful and if he tried to hurt Quinn again that you would kill his father!"

Eamon froze but carried on listening to what Niall had to say.

"My friend Jones reported the situation to his father, who threatened the principal with legal action against the school. For extortion!"

"Extortion?!" Eamon controlled the inner rage at the revelation.

"Boswell demanded our allowance. He had his gang backing him." Niall met his father's eyes. "They assumed that I would be intimidated, like the others!"

Eamon reeled. He could not believe that he had sent his small boys to a top private school to be protected only to become threatened. Eamon ruffled his son's hair, smiling, and helped him from the stool. "Let us return home son. Ye will have time to swim."

Niall smiled. "Boswell informed us that his father is wealthy, and he owns many properties in England and Spain. Are you wealthy, Papa?"

Eamon clipped his seatbelt in after checking Niall's.

"I am wealthy in the fact that I have two handsome sons and two beautiful baby girls. Your mother and I have a wealth of happiness."

Niall smiled.

"Go and change into your swimming trunks," Eamon said. As Niall went into the villa, Eamon walked towards the pool where Quinn was jumping into his mother's arms from the edge. Marcia fell back with the impact, laughing. "Quinn, I would like to speak with ye!" Eamon said.

Marcia looked up, concerned. Eamon smiled at them. "Ye can rejoin Mummy in a minute." He kept his tone light, picking up a towelling robe for Quinn as he made his way to the steps. He winked reassuringly and Marcia's concerned look dissipated.

Quinn stood as Eamon shut the office door. "Did yer sisters watch ye swim?" Eamon asked, sitting Quinn on the chair and crouching before him.

Quinn smiled and said, "Papa, they grew excited when I called to them and I jumped into the water!"

"How do you like yer school? Is everything grand wit ye?" He asked tentatively, observing Quinn's reaction. Quinn cast his eyes down, and Eamon lightly cupped his chin. "Dadda is not angry, Quinn. I want ye to tell me if ye have been upset at all by anyone at school."

Quinn's dark brown eyes met his father's. "Niall stopped Boswell from trying to take my allowance. I would not give it to him. I was saving it for a gift for my baby sisters. Boswell pulled my hair and shouted at me!" Tears formed in Quinn's eyes, and he sniffed. "One of the boys reported it to Niall…" He hesitated. "Niall hit him and bit his ear!" Quinn's eyes darted away. Eamon contained his rage. "Papa is going to make some changes regard-

162

ing yer school. Perhaps we can find somewhere nearer to home," he said, smiling.

Quinn jumped from the chair, hugging him. "Papa, I miss you and Mummy. I would be happy to see the babies every day." A huge smile quickly replaced his tears.

Eamon rose to his full height. "I will let Mummy know a bit later. I can promise ye and Niall that youse won't be staying away anymore!" He checked his watch. "Ye go back to the pool for a while." Eamon exhaled, watching the small boy cheerily move towards the terrace. He locked the office door.

Thomas Harper-Watts answered the call. Eamon recounted the conversation that he had with his sons. "I am withdrawing my boys from that school and that fucking principal is going to pay for his underhandedness. The cunt knew all about the boys being threatened by another kid. I will require yer father's assistance again. I will get Billy to delve into this Boswell's whereabouts. And I want to find out if Lord Arthur's 'friend', Chief Inspector Ross Lowe, has any dirt on him!"

"My father is always on hand to assist. I will telephone him." Thomas reassured. "I will question my sons to see if there have been any problems."

Eamon placed a call to Billy. "I will get on to it boss. This guy will have a paper trail, and my pal is an expert at IT paper chases!" he laughed.

Eamon took another sim card from his safe and placed the call to Big Dave Broadbent, who answered after two rings. "I require ye services. I want every bit of information on Doctor Alberto Sanchez. He is a school principal!" Eamon gave him the address of the boarding school.

Dave replied, "No problem, I will get back to you ASAP!"

Later that evening, Eamon checked in on the children. He joined Marcia on the terrace, drink in hand. He took a large mouthful of the sauvignon blanc, enjoying the crisp, dry notes of the refreshing wine.

"You appear to have needed that," Marcia said, before pausing for a couple of seconds. "Is there anything wrong, Eamon?"

"It has been a long day!" He sat at the table, taking her hand, stretching his long legs out, and sitting her on his lap. Her arms encircled his neck. He took another swig of wine, putting the glass on the table. "I have three gifts for ye!"

Three?!" she said, smiling.

"One is news." He pushed her long skirt up to her thigh, cupping her bare buttocks. He smiled. "I took note of the book that ye keep reading or studying." His fingers explored.

"It is extremely informative in the ways of pleasure," she countered. "Have you ever read The Karma Sutra?"

Eamon gave a soft laugh. "In parts. More so the pictures," he said, smiling.

"Do ye want the news before ye practise on me?" he grinned.

She gasped when his forefinger entered, taking hold of his face, her tongue searching.

He broke away, holding her face on either side. "The boys will be sent to a local school so that our children will grow up together!"

Marcia threw her arms around him.

"Do ye tink that ye can leave that dress on while ye perform some of the moves in that book?"

"Eamon, I am so happy! Have you told them?"

He nodded.

"I tink that ye should have one of yer other gifts. Ye can earn the other." He lifted her off his lap. "I will get it!"

He returned with a small box, standing before her while she opened it. "Cartier!" she exclaimed. The box held a white-gold, diamond-encrusted love bracelet. He had had it inscribed. 'I will always love you. Eamon.'

She gasped. "Eamon, the love bracelet is stunning! The words are beautiful."

Eamon smiled, helping her put it on her wrist.

"When I made the purchase, I was informed that the small screws on the bracelet have significance. They hold the love interest tightly together." He took her by the hand, leading her to the bedroom.

She watched him as he stripped off his shirt and trousers and stepped out of his underpants. She still admired his powerful physique. Nothing much had changed since the first time she had seen him naked, except his once jet-black hair was now streaked with silver. He entered the shower. A few minutes later, under the streaming water jets, he turned when the door slid open and Marcia entered. He noticed she had not removed her jewellery.

"I thought that perhaps we could celebrate the anniversary of our first union as we did seven years ago," Marcia purred.

Eamon pulled her to him as his penis stood to attention. "Do ye want an all-nighter just like we did back then?" He leaned her up against the steamy wall. She opened her legs and wrapped one of them around to accommodate him as he entered her. "Ye have given me four babies since then! Also, many years of pleasure, my little mystic!" he breathed, softly biting the nape of her neck. He carried her through to the bed, still inside, kissing, holding her firmly.

He straddled her on the bed and held her arms above her head. "That night was when you introduced me to multiple orgasms."

He stimulated her nipples, circling his tongue around each one. "Ye taught me what true love meant!" he confessed. Moving slowly, he planted soft kisses down her body. Reaching her mound, he parted her legs, tongue teasing. She bucked beneath him, fingers clutching the pillow.

She raised her legs and rested her ankles on either side of his neck. She guided him into her. Eamon ran his hands down her thighs, relishing each motion. She raised her buttocks and groaned with pleasure. "Oh, Eamon," she whispered, digging her fingernails into his arms.

He watched her reaching her peak, pumping with gentle deliberation. He smiled as she was overcome by the powerful climax. Removing her legs from his shoulders, without withdrawing, he lay on top of her. "Ye have taught me many tings!" he told her, locking his legs around hers. He kissed her, feeling both their hearts pounding.

Afterwards, Eamon rose from the bed to check the children's monitors – they were all fast asleep. He wrapped a towel around his waist and made his way to his office. He could no longer walk around the house naked, in case Aye or the boys came out of their rooms.

"This is also for our anniversary!" he said when he returned to their bed.

She looked at him, then back to the diamond and emerald bracelet. She held her left hand up. "It matches!" she ran her fingertip along his mouth. "Eamon, it is beautiful!"

"Ye have had a great deal of Irish in ye over the years!" he said, laughing. "Hence the emeralds!"

29

Tommy Dugan was angered by his mother's phone call, however, she was his financial backer, and he could not ignore the call. "For fuck's sake, Paula, can you get a move on?" He tried to get back to the moment.

"Relax, Tommy." Paula's fingers caressed Tommy's scrotum.

He pushed her head back, then holding either side of her face, he shuddered. "There you go. Buy the baby something!" He threw two hundred euros on the bed. Paula got up from her knees. Adjusting his fly, he pecked her on the cheek. "It's my old mum. She wants to see me!"

Paula had not told Tommy that she has spoken to his mum about the baby that she was having. Paula's mother, Shirley, was best mates with Denise Dugan. Shirley had invited Paula over when she knew that Tommy's mother would be visiting. She knew that Denise was all about family and thought she would appreciate knowing that Paula was pregnant with Tommy's baby.

On finding out, Denise had told Paula, "Tommy will have to sort it out with the pair of you. After all, both you and his fiancée are having my boy's babies."

Dougie Dugan was furious when his wife told him that Tommy had got two women pregnant. Denise wanted them to have a father-and-son talk. Dougie scoffed at the thought. He couldn't wait to get away to the hotel in Barbados, where he and his other woman, Julie, spent ten days together every year.

Tommy knocked on his father's office door. He was hoping that he was in a good mood, as he needed to ask for a rise in his allowance. Dougie was in the dark that Denise paid for Tommy's household bills.

"Come In!" Tommy popped his head round the door, smiling. Dougie scowled. Tommy tried to make light of the heavy mood that he sensed his father was in. "How's you and Roy's business going?" He sat opposite his father's desk. Dougie viewed him with distaste. Tommy shifted in his chair, trying to ignore the steely look in his father's eyes.

Dougie exhaled. "What have you been up to?" He continued "You don't need to answer that, because from what I hear, you have been very busy!"

Tommy was unsure as to where the conversation was heading. He said, "This and that, Dad. Trying to make contacts. Networking is the way to go."

Dougie elevated his brow. "Networking!" Dougie repeated, then said in a low and menacing tone, "I am going to do the talking and I don't want you to utter a word. Do you understand?"

Tommy nodded.

"There are certain issues that I need to clear up. To be honest," he smirked, "I don't know where to start." He locked his hands behind his head, glaring at Tommy. Dougie shook his head. "I think that I should get the most important issue out of the way, then I can deal with the others."

Tommy squirmed in his seat when Dougie leaned forward on the desk.

"Let me begin with your two young ladies…" he smirked when Tommy's face paled, "that you have got in the family way!"

Tommy shrank into the chair. He went to speak. Dougie put his hand up. "Fucking rest it!" he ordered.

Tommy clammed shut.

"The way I am seeing it, you need to explain the situation to your fiancée, Amy… or perhaps she slipped your mind. Although, it will save you a journey when they both have their babies on the same day at the same hospital. YOU USELESS CUNT!"

"But Dad!"

"QUIT WHILE YOU ARE ON TOP!" Dougie roared. Then lowering his tone, he said, "We are not even halfway done." He relaxed into his chair. "This next issue is the one that concerns me most because it involves my associates – decent people who are trying to earn a living for their families. I have heard it from the horse's mouth that the poor excuse of a Rambo wannabe, Alfie Bond, whose IQ is lower than a skunk's, has been spreading his stink, threatening honest men to smuggle YOUR FUCKING NARCOTICS!"

Tommy moved his head back when his father lunged at him, grabbing his shirt and shoving him. Dougie smirked, opening the desk drawer and smacking each parcel down on top.

Tommy glanced at his goods.

"You make me sick to my stomach. However," he tapped the cocaine, "you are going to accompany me and your uncle Roy when we make the final delivery. Unlike the destination that you originally had in mind, this time the Mediterranean will be the recipient!"

Dougie sat back down, projecting icy rage. "You and your mate should thank your lucky stars that the sea was not your early grave. Anybody else would have been beaten and topped. Nevertheless, Eamon O'Donally is old school. The man has respect. I had to apologise to him once more due to you infringing on his haulage business." Glowering, Dougie continued, "The man had the decency to confront me on his own, with no backup. He is swallowing it due to our association. That's what mates are for. Unlike you and your scummy ponces! The narcotics will be dispersed in the sea tomorrow at 8 pm. Ensure that you are here!" He grinned. "Furthermore, seeing that you are not mature enough to know the difference between respect and disrespect, you will return the car and apartment keys to me. The summer house is your new abode, and you can use the old Clio in the garage that was your granddad's."

Jaw dropping, Tommy stood up.

"FUCKING SIT DOWN!" Dougie growled, "DO NOT UTTER ONE WORD UNTIL I SAY SO!"

Tommy slid the keys towards him.

"NOW GET THE HELL OUT OF MY SIGHT!" Dougie shouted.

....

"THAT CUNT IS GOING TO PAY!" Eamon spat. Big Dave Broadbent had come back within 48 hours with the information regarding Doctor Alberto Sanchez, the school principal. Eamon stopped pacing his office floor. He sat back down at his desk, exhaling. His voice calm, cold with threat, he muttered under his breath, "That pox-balling, pretentious prick is going to be knocked off his perch. Let's see how he handles the impact from ground level when I stomp on the bastard for allowing my sons to suffer!"

Eamon drummed his fingers on the desk, sucking air through his teeth as he listened to Dave on the other end of the phone. Dave informed him that the boys' school had previously paid an out-of-court financial settlement to one of the other parents whose son was being continually threatened by a pupil by the name of Boswell.

"That cunt swept that under the fucking carpet. I will lay money on it that the kid's father 'bunged' a hefty wedge to keep the school sweet! How much do I owe ye, Dave?" Eamon arranged to meet up with him the following day.

Running his fingers through his hair, Eamon sat back in the office chair. His phone rang, and Thomas's number flashed up on the screen.

"I have spoken to my sons. Mathew confided that he had also been threatened. Atticus informed me that although Boswell and his associates had tried it with him, he had warned them off. My father is going to withdraw his financial funding for my sons' school fees and advised me to look elsewhere."

"I fucking knew it! We must deal wit this, Thomas."

Thomas replied, "My father has received a great deal of information on the boy's father. Adrian Boswell is of interest to the Law and taxman in the UK.

"Go on!" Eamon sat up.

"I have his address."

Eamon picked up a pen and note pad, scribbling the information down. "Thank yer father for me!" He would give Thomas a bonus for his father's help, as Lord Arthur would not accept any remuneration. He phoned Dan to tell him that he needed him and Billy to come to his home ASAP. Eamon thought about what to tell Marcia. She was thrilled that the boys were changing schools to be nearer their home. Niall and Quinn both appeared happy with the situation that they no longer were separated from their family. He had noticed a slight change in Niall since he had involved him with his business. Nevertheless, the boy did not acknowledge the twins as Quinn did.

Quinn was so like his mother. He had her gentle manner and warmth. Quinn was tactile, as was Marcia. On the other hand, Niall was an enigmatic child, like Eamon had been. He had an inherent powerful presence, which Eamon recognised.

He mused about his daughters. At three months of age, they were both showing traits of their strong will. Although, he thought that Aisling had the edge over her sister. He smiled to himself as he remembered his feisty copper-haired granny, with her emerald-green eyes flashing as she relayed the stories of sirens to him and Patrick as young lads, putting the fear of Christ into them both. His daughters had inherited her genes through his DNA.

Marcia was his siren. She had lured him with her quiet, mystical air. He wondered at times how he could have ever survived without her. He was not foolish to think that he ruled his domain. Behind closed doors his woman wrapped her tendrils around him, imprisoning him. She reigned supreme. Eamon realised that Marcia would be devastated if she discovered that he had sent the boys away to a school where they had been threatened. He would get on the case and make enquiries right away about the boys attending a local school. He would ensure that only he or Marcia would drop them off and pick them up from the school unless he gave his permission otherwise.

30

Dan and Billy sat opposite Eamon's desk, listening to his instructions. Billy handed Adrian Boswell's paper trail to Eamon. He studied it. "This tosser, for whatever reason, appears to feel the need to take an interest in me and spout rubbish to his kid, whereby the kid shouts the odds at my boys about me being 'an Irish criminal', while the kid is trying out his old man's games of extortion."

"I think that the father needs to be taught a lesson." Billy replied, "One that he will never forget!"

Dan nodded in agreement.

"My thoughts entirely!" Eamon replied, resting his forearms on the desk. "There is also the matter of the school principal, who knew about this racket with Boswell's boy. I have a big surprise in store for him too. Furthermore, Thomas's father, Lord Arthur, is not very happy about his adored grandsons being threatened by the Boswell kid. He has plenty of legal sway. However," he grinned malevolently, "I will handle the principal once the Christmas period is over. Nevertheless, this prick, Boswell, will be paid a visit. He lives in L'Ampola, over 300 kilometres from here. So we'll need to rise early if we are to catch the worm. From what I am told, Boswell has made a name for himself in the London area. He then went on his toes to Spain when the UK taxman started chasing him for some unpaid dues from his property business, which he had attained using heavy arm tactics. The Law also became interested in his extortion racket and money laundering. Apparently, the man is up to his old tricks out here in Spain too. He owns an estate agent. As yet, I don't know where exactly, however, if ye get on it, Billy, I should imagine that it's near where he lives. But I will leave that in yer hands!"

"No sweat, boss!" Billy replied. "It won't be hard to find. Perhaps it would be wise to use Thomas as a potential buyer!" He grinned. "Thomas's upper-crust voice would draw the bastard out with his feigned interest in purchasing an expensive property. For cash!"

Eamon and Dan exchanged looks, smiling. "Grand idea. Do ye tink that ye can get on it ASAP? I want to leave in the morning. Thomas will do his part once you get the details. It should be straightforward tomorrow, but ye never know!" Eamon sat back. "Youse two have been working flat out, what wit the club being so popular. Also keeping a lookout at the haulage company. Now I spring this on youse. It goes without saying that I appreciate yer loyalty. There is a nice bonus coming for all three of youse." He smiled at Dan and Billy. "Lord Arthur will not accept any payment, therefore, Thomas can reap the reward." Eamon stood and rose to his full height. "That's it, boys!" The men took their leave.

Going out the door, Billy turned to Eamon and said, "Hopefully it won't take me long. I will ring you, boss." Eamon gave a sharp nod.

. . . .

"Nice whistle, boss," Billy remarked when Eamon strolled towards the club doors that night. Eamon nodded in acknowl-

174

edgement of the compliment on his suit. Earlier, Billy had phoned him with Boswell's estate agency's details, which he had passed to Thomas. Thomas then called them after scanning the properties for sale on Boswell's website. Insisting on speaking to the owner of the company, Thomas said that he would only commit to a cash transaction on the luxury property that he was interested in. One point two million euros clinched it.

"The club is heaving tonight!" Dan said, opening the door for Eamon. "There is a large group of men inside, celebrating a stag party. A couple of them look as if they are fuelled by something other than alcohol. Thomas is inside with some of the security guys who are keeping an eye on them because they are a rowdy bunch." He smiled. "The women are also out in full force, boss."

Eamon entered the club, catching Greg's eye. He was speaking to Suzette at the cocktail bar, which was five deep with men and women. He had to hand it to Suzette, he thought, as he scanned the bar. He was impressed with the amount of male attention that Lloyd and Kieron were getting. The pair put on a good show for the customers. Both men and women found them entertaining. He admitted to himself that even he thought their banter was amusing. Suzette had employed them. Her business acumen was spot on. They were an asset to the club, he concluded.

Eamon passed a group of women as he made his way to the club office. "Excuse me, ladies," he said as he moved sideways to squeeze through the throng. He felt his arm being tugged. He turned.

"Hello, handsome!" an attractive brunette said as she moved in front of him, cleavage on display, her blue eyes holding his. Running her eyes over him, she cocked her head.

"He is married, Alison!" a voice called from the group. "Wedding band!" She held her left hand up, waggling her fourth finger. The women laughed when she shrugged.

"I don't mind, with this one," she called over her shoulder.

Eamon politely slipped away, smiling and nodding to the crowd. "Have a grand evening, ladies."

The woman swooned. "The hunk is Irish!" She feigned fainting, to the roaring laughter of her friends. "Can't I persuade you?" she called after him.

Eamon cocked an eyebrow, continuing towards the office.

Greg entered a few minutes after Eamon. "You are very popular with the females. I saw that woman accost you," he said, grinning. "Suzette is not amused with the attention that I get, but you certainly get the lion's share!" he laughed, pulling up a chair. "Does it bother Marcia?"

Eamon pursed his lips. "To be honest, I can't be sure. However, I tink that Marcia realises that she has my full attention!" He shook his head and smiled. "Although, if the shoe was on the other foot, and Marcia had the men coming on to her, then that would be a different story!" Both men laughed. "On a more serious note, Greg. How is yer construction business going?"

"I've been working flat out. I have work contracts to deal with. I have recently taken on a big contract for a villa renovation job in Urb Urlisa for an American guy. However, I have a reliable manager, a Spanish fella, married with kids. Speaks and writes fluent English, which, out here in my business is an asset." He unbuttoned his suit jacket, rubbing his hand over the left side of his chest.

Eamon thought about what Marcia had told him about her concern about Greg's health.

"Problem?" Eamon asked.

Greg laughed. "Don't you start. I have it in the ear from Suzette. Like I tell her, it is nothing but heartburn!" he said, smiling.

Eamon slowly nodded.

"To be honest, Greg, this burning the candle at both ends was grand when we were younger! Perhaps ye should have a health check. My wife previously insisted that I have one. Doctor Saggio is yer man!"

Greg did not answer.

Eamon took on board his disinterest and changed the subject. "I will soon be in a position to sort ye out wit my half share that I owe ye for the club, Greg!"

Greg put his hand up, leaning forward.

"Eamon there is no rush. This place is a goldmine. We run a tight ship here. Everything is legit. On paper, you are my legal partner. Your name and mine are on the deeds. Leave the money side of it for another 12 months. You are not going anywhere, are you?" he laughed.

"It's all about trust, mate!" He stood up to leave.

Eamon thanked him. A couple of minutes later, there was a tap on the door. "Come in!" He sat back in his office chair; a hint of a smile played on the corner of his mouth. "How can I be of assistance?"

The woman who earlier had badgered him smiled, closing the door. He judged her to be in her late thirties. He proffered a chair, all the while she did not flinch under his glare.

"Please do not think that I am being presumptuous, but I wanted to ask you if there are any management vacancies in your club?" she asked.

Eamon tugged at his goatee beard. "I have men to step in when required. The dancers are employed by my wife and my business partner's fiancée. If I heard correctly, your name is Alison, isn't it?"

"You remembered?" She smiled at Eamon, but he did not return it. "Perhaps, you have some other opening for me?" She cocked her head, the pink tip of her tongue resting on her veneered teeth. Her black dress rode up her thigh, revealing a tattoo.

"I assume that ye are not enquiring about working as a dancer because there is an age limit."

She bristled at the slight.

"However, if there is nothing else, I am afraid I cannot help ye." Eamon locked the door after she stormed out. He shook his head. A series of text messages pinged in on his phone one after the other. Moving back behind the desk, he picked up the phone and opened the first attachment. It was from Marcia. Scrolling through each one, he studied her various positions and poses. He smiled, unbuttoning his suit jacket. She stood against the wall in the bedroom, legs parted, wearing a white lace cup-less bra and matching ouvert panties. 'I thought that white would be more suitable…!' The message read. He smiled. The colours of the lace underwear varied from black to red, along with the different views and positions – rear view, legs apart, reclined on their king-size bed. He zoomed in to look closer, adjusting himself.

He replied, 'I won't be late, and the white is appropriate, for starters,' inserting three emoji love hearts.

His two-way radio crackled, distracting him from his thoughts of his wife. He heard Dan's voice, "Trouble, boss!"

Eamon was surprised to see that the trouble was not with the rowdy group of stags, but over at the cocktail bar. Dan and Thomas were among the fray, trying to break up two men, one was dressed in a red suit, the other, in a citrus green and floral shirt. Women were jeering, egging them on. Another male's fist struck Thomas on the side of the temple. Eamon's large hand, grabbed the assailant by the throat, lifting him inches off the ground. The man screamed out when a kick to the crotch knocked him to the floor. The security guards jumped in in a flash and frog-marched the perpetrators to the exit. Eamon followed. The two males who had previously been fighting, put their arms around one another's shoulders and hobbled away. Billy shook his head and said, "That guy who took a kick to the balls will be sore for a while!"

Eamon added, "With the impact of that powerful kick to his bollocks, I would tink that he would be banjaxed for life!"

"Jane would not be a happy bunny if that had been my 'tackle' that had taken that strike!" Billy laughed. "However, it appears that the male couples seem to be far more protective over their partners than we are with our women!" Eamon cocked an eyebrow. Both men smiled, knowing that there was no truth in the comparison.

Dan and Eamon came back inside the club. They walked to the far end of the bar where the stag party was in full swing. "Do you want a night cap, boss?" Dan asked.

Eamon shook his head. "I can't have any drink tonight. I require a clear head for the early rise and journey in the morning. I need to ensure that poxy 'gombeen' gets the message."

Dan raised his hand in Jane's direction to order half a lager. She was working behind the bar, standing in for Cindy, who was taking some time off due to Joyce Grant's visit.

Eamon glanced at the stage and caught Jenny's eye. She smiled, while upside down on the pole, legs horizontal, her full breasts and G-string between firm buttocks, tantalising. The men around the stage roared, whistled, and clapped. He gave a sharp nod. She winked.

Dan perched on a stool at the bar, taking a swig. "Some of the women do not make any bones about who they covet!" Dan smiled. "Although, she certainly has some form!" Dan eyed up Jenny's toned body. "Give me my trustworthy woman any day!" Dan finished his drink.

"My thoughts exactly!" Eamon replied.

Eamon observed Benny Harris and Scott Lord standing near the far wall on the other side of the stage. The pair were reliable security guards, both single good-looking men. However, he had taken note that of late they seemed to have taken more than a fleeting interest in two of the dancers. His thoughts turned to Marcia who had previously stated that she had seen Benny's eyes linger on the Irish dancer Martha, and Sandy was Scott Lord's interest. She had predicted to him that there would be serious relationships shortly between the two couples. He smiled to himself. From what he was seeing, he tended to agree with her.

31

As Eamon came in the front door of the villa, the dog greeted him, tail wagging. A shaft of light came from the bedroom door. Easing it open, he saw Marcia perched up on the king-size bed. She wore a white satin negligee and white lace underwear. A little copper head clung to her breast, chubby hand clasping either side as she suckled.

"Aine," Marcia mouthed.

Eamon undressed, holding up five fingers, and walked to the shower.

Marcia had returned the baby to her cot by the time Eamon had finished showering. He lay stretched out on the bed, towel wrapped around his waist, hands locked behind his head.

Marcia's white satin negligee, embroidered with translucent blue and green dragonflies, floated behind her as she crossed the large room

Eamon smiled. Marcia released the towel from around his waist and straddled him. She leaned forward, nipples brushing his. Eamon reached for her, feeling satin on flesh, caressing her body as they kissed.

"You look tired. Let me soothe you." Marcia said as she ran her fingers through his hair, down to his shoulders.

"I am all yers!" Eamon sighed, relaxing back on the pillows. Marcia removed her negligee, and sat back astride him, buttocks facing him, her tongue and mouth encasing his hardening shaft, teasing, pleasuring. He sighed and she took him deeper. A few minutes later, Marcia gasped as she felt his tongue between her legs.

"Don't move!" he whispered, as he flipped her over, widening the opening of her ouvert panties with his fingers. He felt her tighten as he slowly entered, filling her.

With her head thrown back, she gripped and released the coverlet with each measured action. His hands clamped on either side of her buttocks as he gently but firmly triggered their climax, taking them both over the edge in a frenzied passion.

....

5 am the following morning, Eamon opened the back door to the black Audi A7 that he had instructed Billy to purchase from Joey B. Once it had served its purpose that day, the motor would be scrapped.

Billy was at the wheel and rubbed his hands together when the chill of the damp pre-dawn air filled the car. Thomas was in the passenger seat. The men knew that they could draw attention to any suspecting Guardia Civil, however, they all carried on them their required documentation, along with details of the properties for sale that Thomas had printed off.

Billy followed the signs for the AP-Valencia in the direction of Calle de la Ampola, where Adrian Boswell's villa was situated. Thomas had scoped out the place on Google Earth. He turned to speak to Eamon in the back seat. "The residence is surrounded by high walls. The only exit is through large, metal gates. I had a bird's eye view of the cars that are parked inside the grounds – a Mini Countryman and a silver Aston Martin.

The Aston is a powerful car, however, the rough terrain and country lanes nearby, which would be used by farming vehicles will prevent Boswell from putting his foot down until he exits to drive to his estate agency office in the town centre." Eamon nodded. Thomas continued. "The area is pretty much secluded, from what I could see it looked like an ideal hideaway. The man appears to value his privacy," he said, smirking. "The seven-bedroom property has the obligatory swimming pool at the rear, pool house and mountainous backdrop. My intuition tells me that Boswell will arrive for our appointment on time. I used the alias, Archibald Hendry," Thomas added, "who happens to be an associate of my father's, who Boswell assumes is going to conduct the cash transaction for the six-bedroom property in Tortosa. The polite assistant got back to me and reassured me that my request to pay upfront in cash would be met. I was told that the owner of the establishment, Mr Adrian Boswell, reiterated that he will personally show me around the property and that there is also another similar villa on his books."

Billy, instructed by Thomas, took exit 336 for E-901/A-3 towards Madrid. Billy and Thomas chatted among themselves throughout the long journey, reminiscing about some of the good times that they had spent together in Libya and Afghanistan. They had both experienced life-threatening situations and there was an unmistakable bond and camaraderie between the former major, who was born with a silver spoon in his mouth, and the former sergeant in the Special Forces. It reminded Eamon of his relationship with his own brother, Patrick, with their shared experiences growing up.

Eamon mulled over the situation at hand. He had a deep-rooted, intense dislike of bullies. Both he, and later down the line, his brother had experienced physical abuse and intimidation at the hands of their drunken father. They both lived in constant fear as children, hearing the front door bang shut at night, then the unintelligible roaring and furniture crashing. Eamon would quickly move from his bedroom to hide in the outhouse, terrified in the darkness, praying that the monster would not wrench open the door. No one was able to save him. His mother stood by, helpless. The thoughts fuelled his anger. He was not going to stand by and allow his sons to be assaulted and threatened. He intended to teach Adrian Boswell that encouraging his boy to use extortion was a big mistake where Eamon's sons were concerned.

Eamon was brought back to the moment. "At the round-about take the third exit onto CV-31 towards the CV-365 and Godella." Thomas directed. "We are nearly there, boss!"

Eamon checked his watch. It had taken them less than four hours. Billy had put his foot down when he could. He had told Marcia that he had business to attend to. As per usual, she did not question him. Marcia had fallen asleep in his arms in the early hours, however, he had not slept, the adrenalin pumping at the thought of what he was going to inflict upon Adrian Boswell.

They parked out of view to the right-hand side of Boswell's property. It was surrounded by barren land, with farming buildings scattered around. However, the road was shaded by trees and shrubs. Thomas had joined Eamon in the back of the car because the passenger side of the Audi would later get damaged.

"Perfect." Billy indicated their vantage point. "If luck is on our side, I will let him get ahead of us, then hit the dirt to the right. The bushes will cover us. Then I'll meet him – head on!" He grinned. "I would advise wearing seatbelts. It could get a bit bumpy as this terrain looks rough."

"Here we go!" Billy switched the ignition on, the purr of the engine barely audible. The men prepared themselves. "He appears preoccupied." Billy nodded towards Adrian Boswell, who drove slowly through the gates, arms flapping, head shaking. "Looks as if he is having a 'ruck' with someone over the phone. Great, could not wish for a far more advantageous situation."

The Aston Martin turned into the lane. Billy declared, "Hold tight, this is going to knock the guts out of us and the motor!" Billy expertly manoeuvred through the dips and troughs, shaking his passengers' bones. Nevertheless, the car withstood the battering. He drove through a clearing at the end of the lane, facing Boswell's oncoming car.

"He is still at it!" Billy stated when the car came into view. "I would lay money on it that is Boswell's bit on the side he is arguing with for so long. He is taking his time. He is trying to wriggle out of something!" Billy laughed. "Let's see if we can make his day even worse!"

Billy put his foot down and the powerful Audi sped towards the oblivious driver. The impact to the passenger side of both vehicles shunted the Aston Martin. Thomas leapt out, opening the shocked Boswell's door. He grabbed his phone and stamped on it, simultaneously dragging the portly man from the car. Billy joined in to help.

Struggling, Boswell cried out when the two men fought through the bushes and found a small clearing. Billy's foot was on his chest. Terrified, Boswell's bulging eyes scanned the three men. "I have money! Take my wallet!" He tried to get to his inside jacket pocket. Eamon brought his foot back. Boswell screamed when the powerful kick knocked his hand away and Thomas put his foot on it. "Please, I can get you cash – plenty!" he pleaded.

"Listen to me!" Eamon growled, glowering at his victim. "Ye give me a pain in my bollocks." He stood before him. "Money? Ye pox-balling cunt! Do ye tink that we look like we would get out of our beds way before dawn to drive for three hours for a few quid? This early morn visit is to teach ye a lesson!"

Eamon's malevolent grin triggered Boswell's begging. "Whatever you are upset about, we are grown men, we can settle it!" he implored.

Eamon crouched down, his face inches from Boswell's. "Men?!" Eamon scoffed. "This lesson that ye are going to have drummed into ye is about kids – boys. My fucking sons, and his!" Eamon hissed, pointing at Thomas, without taking his eyes from Boswell.

"B...boys? he stammered. "I don't understand!" Boswell's eyes darted from one man to the other, bewildered.

"Let me enlighten yer," Eamon continued in an artic tone. "Ye seem to know me, or so yer kid informed my boys. Allow me to introduce myself. The Irish criminal, Eamon O'Donally," He paused. Boswell's face fell, paling, registering who he was dealing with. "Ye can teach yer brat to be like ye, however, ye scummy cunt, unlike ye, I have never stooped so low as to use extortion, as ye and yer toe rag boy put into practice."

Boswell was shocked into silence. Eamon grasped his shirt front; buttons flew open revealing a fleshy paunch. "Ye need to sort yerself out yer slob, in more ways than one!" he sneered. "I want to know how much ye settled out of court with the principal, Dr Alberto Sanchez."

"Five years' loss of the pupils' school fees," he said, quietly, eyes downcast. Eamon forced his head up.

"Hmm," Eamon smiled thinly. "Ye part wit the money to cover the loss of the school's fees, the principal sweeps yer kid's extortion racket under the table!" Eamon slowly nodded. Billy and Thomas stood on either side of him.

"Please let me compensate you," Boswell pleaded with earnest. "I give my word that your sons will not be approached

186

by my boy ever again. Boys can get out of hand. However, I will chastise him," he said, his eyes beseeching, beads of perspiration forming on his temples.

"Yer fucking words!" Eamon scoffed, "Do ye honestly tink that the word of a pox-ridden jackeen such as yerself is worth anything but 'jack shite'? I am going to ensure that ye teach yer kid to not threaten and hurt other youngsters. Extortion may be yer game, however, I promise ye that ye would not like the game that I play!" In a split-second reaction, Eamon gripped Boswell's flabby jowls. Eamon's head went back, and at lightning speed his forehead struck its target, smashing into Boswell's nose. Boswell yowled as blood poured from his nose. Thomas's boot struck Boswell's ribcage and Billy drop-kicked his chest.

Eamon stood over him. "If ye don't want any further lessons on how to teach yer kid manners, then ye would do well to remember that there will be more of this treatment!"

With blood and tears smeared with dirt streaking his face, Boswell tried to raise his hand but slumped back down onto the ground.

32

Later that night, Eamon and Marcia were dining in Eamon's restaurant. He nodded to the maître d', who poured the cabernet sauvignon. Relaxing back into the chair, Eamon took a mouthful, swilling the notes of plum, blackberry, and pepper over his palette. He observed Marcia with interest as he placed the glass on the table.

Earlier, when he had returned from dealing with Adrian Boswell, the boys were at Jane's having horse riding lessons. Marcia had taken the girls to visit Isabella, Thomas's wife, who had recently given birth to a baby girl. A thrilled Thomas, who had wanted a daughter, had named her Raine. He had received a phone call from Dan informing him to recheck the wine in the cellar at the club as he could not make it tally up with the stock check.

Although Eamon had had no sleep the previous night, he wanted to spend some time with Marcia away from the domestic environment. "Ye are looking very sexy," he smiled at her. "The red dress..." he paused for a few seconds, "is very provocative." He glanced at her matching nail colour. Her eyes followed.

"What gives wit ye!" He took a small sip, and his eyes smiled. He continued, "Ye have not worn a scarlet-red dress wit matching nail colour in all the years that we have been together!"

"I want to feel sexy when I am out with you. At home, Eamon, I am a mother."

He pursed his lips, slowly nodding.

"Don't you like it?" she asked.

"To be sure, ye look classy, hot, and sexy. Although, somewhat promiscuous!" he added, smiling.

"Promiscuous!" she repeated, laughing. He knocked back the wine as the waiter hovered. Marcos the maître d' refilled Eamon's glass and topped up Marcia's water.

Eamon cut his steak. "Ye wear a scarlet-red dress like a second skin, stilettos, red talons, adorned wit emeralds and diamonds. If I had met ye out, there would be no doubt in my mind that ye were a wanton woman!" He smiled, eating a forkful of the steak.

Feigning shock, Marcia laughed. "Eamon, that is worse than saying that I look promiscuous!"

He pointed with his fork, "Eat! Please don't act the innocent, my little mystic. Ye are hot between the sheets!"

He laughed when Marcia blushed. "Yer coy act does not fool me." He cut another slice of meat. "Not when ye can plea-sure me wit such ease."

Marcia held his eyes as she began eating her salad.

"Eamon, I have purchased a short, red dress to wear in the bedroom for you!"

"How short?" He continued eating.

"A pleasurable length. I have also purchased you another gift!"

"Intriguing!" He winked. "Nevertheless, allow me to change the subject because I am feeling hot under the collar! I have been making enquiries regarding a new school for the boys. The one that has shown the best prospects has sent me an email. I have made an appointment for us to view it and run through the prospectus with the headmaster the day after the Christmas holiday. The boys will be driven and collected by either one of us unless I give my permission for anyone else to pick them up!"

"Have there been any problems with Niall and Quinn at the boarding school?" Marcia queried.

Eamon shook his head, continuing to chew. He put down his fork, taking a sip of wine. "The boys are grand. However, ye know that the reason I sent the boys to that school was to protect them!" He smiled, reaching for her hand. "I want my family to be safe. The children will grow up together. No more separation! Finish yer meal. I am eager to view this short dress and the gift!" He winked.

Later that night, Marcia was getting Aine and Aisling settled, who were both cutting their teeth. She had told him that she would change into the dress once they had been fed.

Eamon lay on the bed, the sheet covering the bottom half of his naked torso, mulling over the information that Dave Broadbent had gleaned about Alberto Sanchez the boarding school principal. Eamon had discovered that the pompous head of his boys' school had a secret life and family. His mistress and 12-year-old son, Miguel Sanchez de Leon, were secreted away in a three-bedroom property in San Sebastian, in one of the more upmarket neighbourhoods near the beach, port and town. The principal also had a wife and two grown-up daughters living 50 kilometres in the opposite direction to his undisclosed other family.

The arrogant prick is going to pay! Eamon silently vowed. He smiled when Marcia came out of the walk-in wardrobe, "Yer description of short is not really accurate, rather, more tantalising, bordering on obscene, although not offensive to the eye." He grinned, turning on his side to observe her. "Yer ouvert panties are in line wit the hemline; the neckline plunges to yer naval." He twirled his finger, and Marcia did a turn, 360 degrees. The back reveals yer flesh to the top of yer thighs. If ye wore that type of dress out, it would see ye being taken up against the wall in some alleyway!"

She bent over him for effect, taking a small parcel from the dressing table and passing it to him. Unwrapping it, he jangled the handcuffs, holding up a tube of lube and smiling at the condoms. "These are for some serious enjoyment!" Eamon said as he threw back the sheet. He made a lunge for her, and she stepped back, laughing.

"I have never experienced sex up against a wall in an alleyway!" she said, standing back and bending to touch the tip of the stilettos.

Eamon leapt from the bed, grabbing her waist with one arm and lifting her. "I am not going to take ye up against the wall tonight – some other time! Tonight, my little mystic, I am going to teach ye a lesson about flaunting yer wares!" he teased. He removed her shoes, laid her face down on the bed, and hand-cuffed her wrists to the bedposts. He straddled her, kissing and slowly massaging, starting on her neck and working his way down her back. Marcia groaned, arching into his erection, which slid between her legs. He prepared himself, laying across her, taking his weight with his forearms. Upon entry, Marcia yanked at her bonds. "Relax!" he sighed, moving slowly.

Marcia's fingers gripped and released the pillow as Eamon took control. In a barely audible voice, she called his name with each stroke that took her to the summit.

"Stay wit me," he whispered, nibbling her earlobe. "The next one will be deep, and I will join in with ye!" Clamping her between his thighs, he gently kissed her face, which was wracked with ecstasy as they came in unison.

33

Eamon had not been pleased when he found out what his sons would be wearing to Lloyd and Kieron's wedding. Their page boy outfits were Scottish Black Watch kilts and white frilled shirts, to match Lloyd's and Kieron's.

"My sons are half Irish, not Scots!" he had railed when Marcia broached the subject. However, Eamon had eventually given in to her coaxing.

Suzette had helped Lloyd and Kieron to plan the wedding. She had paid for the venue and catering as a wedding present. Marcia, Jane, and Cindy had clubbed together to cover the cost of their honeymoon. Greg and Eamon closed the club for a night, at their expense. Six pole dancers were the lads' brides-maids. Eamon had booked a villa in Monte Pego for two nights, 8 kilometres from Pego, where the ceremony was being held. The 12-minute drive would give Marcia time to feed the girls. Cots were supplied at the villa for the babies, and the boys would sleep in an adjoining room. Aye's room was on the far side of the villa.

One of Suzette's clients was a seamstress who had made Aisling and Aine's dresses and floppy hats for the occasion. Aye dressed them while Marcia changed.

Eamon walked to the 7-seater BMW with Niall and Quinn. Settling the boys in the back, he had to admit that his sons looked striking in their Scottish kilts.

"Mummy and the babies look pretty!" Quinn exclaimed as they approached. Eamon held Marcia's eyes, smiling, giving a nod of appreciation. He took Aisling from her arms and Aye joined the boys in the back of the car. Aine smiled at the boys. Quinn tickled her under the chin, and she chuckled. Niall looked straight ahead without acknowledging the twins at all. Eamon opened the passenger door for Marcia. She bent forward so as not to crush the emerald-green, wide-brim hat she wore.

"Nice touch wit ye and the girls!" He winked. Marcia smiled without replying. She had emerald-green, frilled dresses and cream floppy hats specially designed for the girls. Their copper-red curls peeked out from beneath the hats. Marcia's soft cream, classic fitted dress matched her stilettos. The emerald and diamond studs completed the outfit.

"You look pretty, Mummy!" Quinn repeated.

"Khun du hix!" Aye interjected, speaking to the boys.

"Kop-Khun," Quinn replied, bowing his head, palms together. The small boy thanked her for the compliment that they looked handsome. She smiled, giving a pleased nod. Aye placed her hand on Niall's shoulder, tapping affectionately. He smiled thinly, then continued to look straight ahead.

The magnificent 18th-century farmhouse was stunning. The grounds were spread out, with a backdrop of the mountain. A languid breeze rustled through the rows of trees. Eamon sat next to Marcia, with a baby asleep on each one of his shoulders. Suzette and Greg crossed the lawns, heading towards where the O'Donallys sat.

"It looks as if the couple has invited many of their flamboyant friends. Their suits have more colours than a peacock!

And the dancers from the club are barely recognisable in their pink bridesmaids' dresses!" Greg laughed. "I have booked into a villa just up the road from here. Suzette and I are going to make the most of our time off."

"Ye should take some time out, Greg. I keep having to remind ye about burning the candle at both ends!"

Greg shrugged the comment off. "I plan to take Suzette away shortly. However, today I plan to let my hair down and tonight my lovely woman and I will dance the night away!"

A few moments later, Marcia leaned in towards Eamon and whispered, "When we were speaking to Greg just now, I had a sense of foreboding, a warning shadowed in darkness."

Eamon watched as Greg and Suzette walked towards their seats. He exhaled. "I know that ye have these feelings at times. However, I have known Greg for many years and the man will tread his own pathway. Ye tell me that ye can't change yer destiny. How do ye tink that a man like Greg could be persuaded to see a doctor against his will?"

Aisling opened her eyes and began sucking her father's earlobe. He smiled. "I keep on top of my health because I want to enjoy my time wit my wife and family. Unlike me, Greg does not have a mystic for a wife... or four babies."

Suzette and Greg hit the dance floor. Tune after tune, they boogied the evening away. Marcia observed Suzette leading him by the hand to a row of seats. Face ashen, left hand holding his chest, Greg slumped on a chair. Suzette waved to Marcia. She was going to ring a taxi to return to the rented villa. Eamon offered to drive them, but Suzette declined his offer, telling them that they would have an early night.

Marcia watched Greg and Suzette get into the taxi. Darkness filled her mind and she was overcome with a feeling of sorrow, sensing that Greg would not be with them for much longer. She thought, *Suzette will be devastated if she loses him.*

34

A week after the wedding, Marcia had fed the girls and was in the bedroom completing her yoga routine, holding the position of the headstand. Eamon walked naked from the shower, drying his hair.

"That position could get ye into trouble!" Eamon said as Marcia opened her legs wider, smiling up at him as he stood before her. He trailed his fingers along the inside of her thigh and held her gaze, exploring between her legs "Ye have not got the control to let me finish," he grinned, "I could slip into ye."

He knelt behind her, supporting her. He slid the straps of her top down, removing the top, then her brief panties. Marcia's mobile rang, they ignored it, but it persisted.

Eamon slapped her rear, playfully. "Ye had better answer that. We can resume later!"

Marcia saw that it was Suzette calling. She tried to make sense of her words; she was incoherent due to her sobbing. "Please stay calm, Suzette. I cannot understand what you are saying!" Marcia slumped on the bed. Eamon began dressing. "Give me the name of the hospital!" Marcia said urgently, opening the bedside drawer to grab a pen and notebook so that she could scribble the address down.

"What's the matter?" Eamon queried, zipping up his fly and reaching for the shirt. Marcia hurried to the walk-in wardrobe to find something to throw on. "Greg has had a stroke and is in ICU battling for his life. I must go to her Eamon; she won't be able to cope!"

"Get dressed and I will speak to Aye about looking after the girls. They have recently been fed, so that will give ye a bit of time to spend with Suzette. Get on the phone to Jane as soon as ye are ready. Ask her to help wit the boys!" Eamon directed.

On entering the hospital room, Marcia stopped in her tracks. Her hand flew to her mouth. She stared at Greg in the bed. Suzette's face was awash with tears. Black mascara ran down her face in rivulets. She was holding his hand, pleading for him not to leave her.

Marcia inhaled and braced herself. Suddenly, Suzette stood up and threw herself into Marcia's arms. "Marcia please help him. I cannot live without him!" she implored. "Greg would not listen to me when I told him about your health warning," she babbled. "This is not the end, Marcia. Please!" Her eyes beseeched, begging Marcia to tell her that Greg would overcome the crisis.

Marcia and Eamon looked on at the burly man who lay motionless, his pallor grey. His face was drawn down on one side from the stroke. Marcia did not reply. Suzette resumed her position by the side of the bed, taking Greg's hand in hers.

Two hours later, after Marcia had tried to no avail to get Suzette to have a break and get something to eat, she promised Suzette that she would rally everyone round to ensure that the beauty salon ran efficiently. Her words fell on deaf ears. Suzette was lying across Greg's arm, speaking words of encouragement. Marcia and Eamon quietly left the room.

Marcia and Eamon were both deep in their private thoughts and did not speak until the car left the carpark.

"Eamon, I will speak to Lloyd, who will take over the running of the salon, and now that Joyce has returned to America, Cindy can be relied upon to work on the reception. I will be able to take the girls with me when I help."

Eamon shook his head. "Marcia, I am trying to get my head around how suddenly our lives can change. Greg is one of life's 'true grit.' The man is one of the best!" Eamon said with deep sadness. "Greg is no age!" he spoke more to himself.

Marcia placed a hand on his arm, but she did not reply. She understood loss from an early age having lost both of her parents when she was a teenager, and Andrew, her first husband, who had died young. She sent a silent prayer out to Suzette for strength to help her overcome what Marcia sensed was inevitable. Suzette had lived with Greg for seven years. Marcia felt that her friend's destiny was about to change.

Eamon drove to Jane's to collect Niall and Quinn who had been having riding lessons and helping to muck out the stables with her and Billy.

"How is Greg?" Billy asked, ordering the barking dogs back to the veranda when Eamon got out of the car. Eamon shook his head as they walked together to the back of the villa. "It doesn't look none too good for him. To be honest Billy, I'm gutted. Nevertheless, he is in good hands. Let's pray that he pulls through to the other side!"

"The man is a diamond!" Billy expressed, smiling warmly.

"Impressed!" Eamon pursed his lips, nodding in approval at the new block of stables and kennels that Billy built.

"Jane was my 'lackey' and tea lady," he teased.

Quinn and Niall, with pitch forks in hand, were in separate stables.

"I tink that I have got it all wrong, Jane. My boys seem to love the hard work by the smiles on their faces."

"The boys know that after they ride the horses they must be fed and watered, and the stables kept clean. The horses know and trust them. Quinn waved; Niall continued to lift hay with the fork.

"Do you want a cup of coffee while you wait for them to finish?" Jane asked, "or something stronger – wine or a cold beer?"

"A cold beer would be grand! Thank ye, Jane," Eamon replied.

The two men took a seat at the long, wooden garden table. "We are on hand to help in any way we can, boss. Jane enjoys having the boys over, as do I. We should have had kids of our own!" he spoke with an element of wistfulness. Then he smiled and said, "It's selfishness on my part. I wanted Jane all to myself." He shook his head. "Fucked up childhood and all that."

Eamon gave an understanding nod.

"You made up for us not having kids, boss," Billy said, grinning. "With your four beautiful kids and plenty of hassle to come from them in the future!"

Jane returned with two beers on a tray and two bottles of water. She took the water to Niall and Quinn. "Gives you food for thought, this sudden turnout with Greg!" Billy said, taking a swig of his beer, as did Eamon.

Eamon's mobile phone rang. He nodded solemnly after answering Marcia's call. He stood up and called to the boys to prepare to leave.

Billy stood up and asked, "Greg?"

Eamon nodded. "He's gone!" Both men remained silent.

Billy and Jane waved goodbye to them as Eamon drove out through the gates.

Eamon could see that Marcia had been crying when he and the boys arrived back home. "Go and shower!" He patted the boys' shoulders.

"May we swim afterwards, Papa?" Quinn asked.

"To be sure," Eamon smiled warmly at the boys. "Youse both have worked hard at Jane's!" He checked the time. "Ye can have an hour, then it's time to eat!"

Quinn skipped towards the doors waving gaily to his mother. She blew them a kiss. He stopped in the doorway and asked, "Papa, before we go to bed tonight, may we play with our new game console that Maureen purchased for us?"

Despite the way he was feeling after hearing the news of Greg's passing, Eamon smiled, nodding. Quinn clapped his hands. His face lit up and he glanced at his brother. Niall returned a thin smile, following him.

Eamon walked towards where Marcia was sitting at the garden table. She rose as he approached, unable to stem the flow of tears. Eamon embraced her, stroking her hair. His silent empathy comforted her. "Eamon, Suzette is broken. There is no consoling her. She is alone at her villa!"

He raised her head, wiping her tears with his fingertips. "Ring her and tell her that once ye have seen to the girls ye will fetch her. She can stay wit us until she feels stronger."

"Thank you!" Marcia kissed him and went inside to call Suzette.

Eamon phoned Dan, who said that Billy had informed him about Greg's death. Dan insisted that he, Billy, and Thomas would take over the running of the required extra security that night. There were two stag parties booked in at the Hawk Wind club that evening. Dan said that Cindy and Jane were standing in for Suzette. Cindy had also organised the running of the Mystique beauty salon. Lloyd and Kieron were eager to help.

Eamon stretched his long legs out at the garden table. He poured himself a glass of wine, swallowing a mouthful, feeling the effect of the sauvignon blanc relaxing his troubled mind. He smiled wistfully at his sons who were happily leaping onto the pool inflatables. He had been to the nursery to cuddle his beautiful daughters before they went to sleep for the night.

Marcia then left for Suzette's to help her pack. He raised his glass to the heavens, silently sending his prayers to his longtime pal, Greg. His thoughts returned to his family. He took a small sip, smiling as Quinn waved at him. *Marcia had known all along,* he mused. It wasn't that he had not believed her concern regarding Greg's health. He had not wanted to believe that the man who had helped him on his way to becoming financially legal, without any remuneration from Eamon was ill. Greg had financed and made Eamon his legal partner in the Hawk Wind club. He realised that Suzette had no knowledge that he owed Greg for his 50 per cent share. Nevertheless, once things were dealt with, he would repay his debt to her. He had had his differences in the past with Suzette, however, he felt that by helping her it was the least that he could do for the man who had been like a brother to him.

He felt eternally grateful for his good fortune, as he observed his two sons play and swim happily. His copper-headed baby girls were sleeping soundly in their cots and then of course there was Marcia who completed the picture. Eamon knocked back the wine. He could not envisage his life without them. Topping the glass up, he thought back to the life that he had previously led – hungry for money, ambitious for status and the luxurious lifestyle that importing narcotics with Jimmy Grant had given him. *Others' misery!* he silently, remorsefully concluded. For all of Eamon's efforts to turn his life around and shun the criminal world that he had previously lived in before meeting Marcia, he realised that he would never have God's forgiveness because he would go to any lengths to ensure that nothing came between him and his family – murder included.

35

The boys were happy with the new school that Eamon and Marcia had agreed upon. However, Eamon and Thomas were going to visit Dr Alberto Sanchez. Eamon had called the school to speak to the principal, but his secretary had answered. Giving his name, he demanded an appointment the following day. Testily, she rebuked him. "Listen to what I am telling ye!" he directed. "Inform the principal that if he does not return my call within half an hour, he will wish that he had!" he said, cutting off the call before she could respond.

Within five minutes, Eamon's phone rang. The haughty principal spoke, "I understand from your son's masters that Niall and Quinn have not returned to the school after half-term."

Eamon broke in, "If ye want to keep yer position at yer school, ye had better ensure that ye are in yer office for our appointment around 3 pm today."

There was a momentary silence from the principal, who then reluctantly agreed.

Eamon stormed into the secretary's office with Thomas Harper-Watts in tow. He needed no introduction. She put her head down as he went to the principal's office. He did not knock. Upon entry, the principal rose from behind his desk. His forced smile and proffered hand towards two chairs were ignored by Eamon. He leaned across the desk, getting right into the man's face.

The principal recoiled from the icy glare. Eamon listed the issues and the compensation that both men demanded for the bullying and extortion that their boys had endured at the hands of the Boswell boy. He informed him that he knew about the money that Adrian Boswell had paid so that the principal would let his son's misdemeanours go unpunished. The principal paled when Eamon revealed that he knew about his secret life, naming his mistress and his son, and giving the details of the property and area where they were secreted.

When Thomas stepped forward to say that his father, Lord Arthur, who paid his grandson's tuition, was informed of the bullying and would stop payment, Doctor Sanchez sank into his chair. Eamon and Thomas both demanded a full refund for the four boys' previous years' tuition fees. The head of the school promptly confirmed that there would be no problem with reimbursement.

36

Suzette kept a low profile when Eamon was at home throughout the weeks of her stay, although he went out of his way to
include her in his family's life. She had appeared as a shadow of
her former self after Greg's death. Eamon took control of Greg's
construction company for Suzette. Running through the contracts with the manager. Eamon was satisfied that the Spaniard
was an honest guy. There was not much that the manager did
not know about the building business and legalities.

The funeral was over and the reading of Greg's will final-
ised. Greg had left Suzette all his possessions, money, and businesses. Eamon attended the reading at Suzette's solicitor's office.
Greg had stipulated that upon his death, Eamon's financial slate
was to be wiped clean. Nonetheless, Eamon had insisted on re-
paying the money that he owed for his share of the Hawk Wind.
However, Suzette refused. She wanted to abide by Greg's last wishes.

Suzette felt ready to return home. She insisted that she
was feeling stronger and wanted to get her life back on track. She
thanked Eamon and Marcia for letting her stay, asking Marcia if
she would visit her the following day.

Marcia drove through the gates of the gorgeous villa that
Greg had built for Suzette. The three-storey property boasted

breath-taking views of Altea Bay and the cities of Altea and Albir, like Marcia and Eamon's home.

Suzette appeared to be back to her old self – confident and business-like, dressed in the latest in-vogue Italian designer couture. To the outside world, she projected bravado, which Marcia knew was only a mask. She portrayed herself as a warrior. She knew that to succeed in the world that they lived in, pain needed to be hidden.

Suzette kissed Marcia on both cheeks. "You look beautiful, Marcia. The Asian couture suits your shapely, feminine figure. The leaf green complements your emeralds," she said, smiling. "Take a seat on the terrace and I will get some wine, and Voss water for you." Upon her return, Marcia sat down, while Suzette stood near the large garden table. "Marcia, I owe you and Eamon an apology."

Marcia frowned.

Suzette sipped the wine, then continued, "I have berated your husband for being controlling with you. And many a time I implored you to leave him, telling you the man was not good enough for you. However, I have seen first-hand that Eamon is a loving husband and doting father. My time living under your roof has been an eye-opener. To have the privilege of being a part of your family has made me realise what I have missed out on by not having children." She spoke wistfully, "Greg always spoke highly of Eamon," her tone was filled with sadness. "I did not ask you here only to apologise," she smiled warmly, taking a seat opposite Marcia. "I have been to visit my lawyer, who informed me that once the inheritance taxes are paid from Greg's estate, and his two children have had their share…" she paused for a couple of seconds, "I will be worth somewhere in the region of seven million – pounds not euros!" She grinned.

Marcia's jaw dropped. "Wow!"

Suzette held her hand up to stop Marcia from speaking. "That is not what I dragged you here for. I have had the legal paperwork drawn up for the transfer of Greg's partnership in the club, which he willed to me. Once the Spanish legalities are dealt with, which should take no longer than a few months – six at the most and the gift tax is paid, the Hawk Wind club and Greg's entitled yearly profits will be yours, Marcia!"

Mouth agape, Marcia tried to take in what Suzette was saying. "MINE?!" she exclaimed.

Suzette clasped Marcia's hands in hers. "I am gifting you my share of the club. You will be your husband's business partner. However, there is one stipulation. Your husband cannot buy you out. One must not forget that Eamon O'Donally is a master of his ship. However, this vessel is now half yours. If you wish to sell your share in the business after five years, then that will be fine."

Marcia shook her head. "Suzette, I cannot accept such a gift!"

Suzette interjected. "Too late, your name is on the deeds. It only requires your signature, and once I receive the call, you and I will go to Calpe to visit my solicitor to complete the transfer." Suzette raised her wine glass, clinking Marcia's water glass. "We are now at the top of that ladder that we started to climb nearly eight years ago."

"I am eternally grateful, Suzette." They laughed, hugging one another.

Marcia decided that she would wait until later that evening, when they were alone, to tell Eamon the news. Greg's death appeared to have had a profound effect on Eamon. His mood was often pensive, his lovemaking solicitous and tender. Marcia sensed that it had made Eamon aware of his mortality. She was unsure how he would respond to the news that she would be his business partner. Upon her return, she saw his

Maserati parked in the drive. The dog wagged his tail in greeting when she got out of her car; sentry-like he walked protectively beside her. Eamon sat under the awning on the terrace, both girls on his shoulders, one contentedly sucking an earlobe, the other baby girl snuggled into the nape of his neck. He smiled, she raised her sunglasses, positioning them on her head. She leaned forward, kissing him. The girls were sleepy; their eyelids flickered, however, the pair clung on to their father. Marcia was having second thoughts about leaving the news until later. "I am going to feed and change them," she said, taking them in her arms.

Eamon was on the phone when she stepped back out through the terrace doors. She could hear him giving orders to Dan at the Hawk Wind club. Sitting down opposite, she waited for Eamon to finish the call.

"How is Suzette coping?" Eamon asked with genuine concern.

"Suzette has returned to her beauty salon. She is keeping herself busy. She informed me that she has been read the contents of Greg's will, although it will take a few months to be settled." She braced herself. Tentatively broaching the subject. "Suzette has given me her share of the club, which Greg willed to her along with his construction business and financial assets!" She waited.

Eamon shifted his position, eyebrow cocked. "Run that by me again? Did ye say that ye have been given Greg's half of the partnership?" His dark eyes searched hers.

Marcia nodded. "Including the yearly 50 per cent profit." She faltered, "If you do not wish for me to accept the offer, I…"

Eamon jumped in, "I am grand wit that!" He smiled happily, it seemed to Marcia, for the first time since the death of his partner and friend. "To have my wife as a partner, and a rich one at that! The club is a goldmine! Come 'ere till I tell ye!" He held his arms out.

She put her arms around his neck. "That is what I would call recompense for Suzette's past injustice to ye."

Marcia did not reply. There was no point.

"Ye can take me out to the restaurant before I go to work, now that ye are minted!" he laughed.

"You will need to pay me first!" she giggled.

"The only payment ye will be having tonight is in kind!"

"I will take you up on your offer!" she grinned.

"Welcome to the real world of pressure, now that ye are a business owner."

"My business as an adviser is legal," she feigned indignation. "I realise that I will need to cut back on bookings at the Mystique beauty salon, Eamon."

The fact that ye class pre-warning of criminal activity as 'legal," he smiled, "is debatable! The law courts may not see it as ye do if ye were up before a prosecutor on a charge of preventing the course of justice!" Eamon smiled, allowing it to sink in. "There is no 'grey area', my little mystic."

Her eyes questioned. He elevated his brow. "Tink on it!" Eamon playfully tapped her rear. "I realise that ye love ye work, however, ye should cut back. The Hawk Wind club and our family, including myself, will take up all yer time." He hugged her, cupping her chin. "It has been a while since ye performed the head stand in the bedroom, and ye were showing me yer control before we were interrupted last time!" He grinned. "Perhaps my tongue might be too much for ye?" His fingers explored circling beneath the layers of her skirt. She threw her head back, enjoying the pleasure. "Ye are wet!" he breathed. Eamon's tongue and mouth moved slowly from her throat to her breasts. "Tonight, ye will be a pushover!" He held her at arm's length, smiling. He glanced at his watch. "After I pick the boys up from school, I have business to attend to. Tonight, we can eat out. I will take over at the club at about 11 pm, and won't be home until 2 am." He smiled and said, "However, if ye will be too tired…"

She interjected. "I won't be!"

"That's grand." He brushed her mouth with his fingertips, lifting her off his lap.

"I will swim before the boys return," Marcia said. "Niall and Quinn take over the pool entertaining Aisling and Aine with jumping onto the inflatables and practising diving!"

Eamon nodded. "Don't cool off too much!" He smiled, winking as he left for the school run and Marcia went inside to change.

Marcia completed the last lap of her daily routine. She knew that Eamon wanted another dog. He had spoken to Jane who had a Belgian shepherd that she had trained in detection. Roman was now approaching eight years old, and the faithful dog had visibly aged, with his grey muzzle. Nevertheless, he remained as alert as when he had first arrived to live with them. She had to agree that having another dog like Roman would bring her reassurance in knowing that the children were safe.

37

Tommy Dugan was consumed by thoughts of how to take his revenge on Eamon O'Donally. The humiliation was crippling his ego. He was back living in his parents' summer house at the bottom of their garden. His prized possession, his car, a yellow Lotus, had been confiscated by his father. Tommy had no other means of transport other than the old car that his grandfather used to drive. Tommy's father and uncle Roy had thrown the bags of cocaine that Tommy had invested in into the sea, however, unbeknownst to them, Tommy's mother had unwittingly given him the money that financed the drug purchase. To top it all off, Tommy's two pregnant girlfriends were on his back, vying for his attention. Tommy realised that he would need to tread carefully where his father Dougie was concerned. His dad was spouting off about principles and loyalty, drumming it into his ear that he was a man of morals. *My old man has me fucked from every angle since I was grassed up by that fucking Irish tinker! he fumed to himself.*

Dougie had given Tommy a last warning to get a proper job and steer clear of drugs. Tommy realised that his dad had eyes and ears everywhere. He rolled a joint, putting his feet up on the coffee table, leaning into the soft leather sofa that his mum, Denise, had given him. Tommy laughed out loud as he toked on the Afghan Black spliff. He was determined to come up with a plan to outwit his father. Then, he would topple the Irishman. The solitude of the summer house and knowing that his father was still abroad on business for another week filled Tommy with a sense of bravado. His father's absence had enabled Tommy to work on his mother. Tommy's crocodile tears and reassurance that he was going to make his mum and dad proud of him worked. Denise had given him a further 250,000 thousand euros, which was all that was left of her father's inheritance.

Denise, never one to keep things to herself once revealed to Tommy that his father Dougie had, over two decades ago, given her jewellery that was worth a small fortune – large diamond rings and a tiara, pearl necklaces and ruby earrings from a heist back in the day. Denise said that she was keeping them for a rainy day. Tommy's father's preaching and righteous moral code that he rammed down his throat irked Tommy. His train of thought was interrupted by the ping of a text message. He lazily reached for his mobile phone, fingers scrabbling. The message was from his mate, Richie Bryant, who was on holiday in the Bahamas with his girlfriend, Sienna. The two-week break had been paid for by Ritchie's mum and nan for his 21st birthday. He opened the message. Picture after picture came pinging through of the couple at the luxurious hotel. 'I am bringing you the best present. See you tomorrow.' Three smiley-face emojis followed the message. "I expect the silly bastard is bringing me a stick of rock!" Tommy said aloud, dropping the phone on the table without replying. Although he had to admit that he had missed his old school pal Ritchie since he became involved with his bird, Sienna, he was not under the thumb, and Ritchie was of the same mind set as Tommy – ambitious.

....

Ritchie Bryant and his girlfriend, Sienna, were at Alicante airport waiting for their flight to London Gatwick where they would get a connecting flight to El Salvador International. Sienna had wanted to use the toilet. Richie was excited about the trip of a lifetime. He sat on the row of seats nearby, waiting when he spotted Mr Dougie Dugan. He knew that his mate Tommy's dad was going abroad on business. Although his father was always friendly to Ritchie when he visited the Dugans' villa, Ritchie was aware of Dougie and Roy Dugan's fierce reputation. Ritchie's father, Bob, informed him that he held the two men in high esteem. Ritchie had sympathised with Tommy's predicament, however, he had agreed with Tommy that upon his return from the Bahamas, they would begin their plan of action.

A shapely, attractive blonde Marilyn Monroe look-alike who was coming out of the toilet caught his eye. Ritchie judged her to be in her forties. Glancing around, she smiled, making a beeline towards a smiling Dougie Dugan. Ritchie acted quickly, snapping away while the couple kissed each other. Dugan's hand fondled her rear as she put her arm around his waist and they strolled towards duty-free. *Caught on camera!* He smirked to himself. He turned in his seat, unobserved. He zoomed in when Dougie put his arm around her shoulder and pecked her cheek, smiling into the blonde's eyes. Ritchie was elated. However, he decided to wait until the end of the holiday to give his pal Tommy the ace card.

Ritchie and Sienna sat at the back of the departure lounge as the first and business-class passengers joined the short queue. Dougie Dugan and the blonde stood side by side, holding hands. Sienna looked in her compact mirror and reapplied her lipstick. Mobile on silent, Richie snapped a few more incriminating pictures. Ritchie had prayed throughout the flight that Tommy's dad was not staying at the same hotel as him. His prayer was answered hours later when the plane landed and Ritchie, at a distance, walked behind the couple through the airport doors. The man with the placard with Mr Dugan's name on it directed them to a white limousine that had the hotel's name on the side. Ritchie sighed smugly after he had taken two more photos.

. . . .

Despite himself and the situation that he was in, Tommy returned the smile from the suntanned Ritchie when he knocked on the door of the summer house. "You're a cunt if you have brought me a stick of fucking rock!" Tommy said, laid out on the sofa, stoned. Ritchie opened the windows to let some air into the dope-fumed room. Ritchie indulged in cocaine, however, he did not partake in smoking 'weed' because if his father detected the strong stench of dope on him, he would stop his allowance. Ritchie kept a change of clothes in the boot of his car whenever he visited Tommy. Ritchie's mum did his washing for him. Like Tommy's mum, she spoiled him.

Ritchie grinned, getting the pictures up on his phone, and passing the mobile to Tommy. "A stick of rock will give you cavities!" he smirked. "Get your teeth into this little lot!" he laughed "This is your fucking ticket to freedom!"

Tommy shook his head, taking the phone. He glanced at the screen, then sat bolt upright. Scrolling through the pictures, he jumped up. "The old cunt has a bit on the fucking side!" he spat. "There he was preaching to me about having two women!" Tommy sneered. "Once I inform my dear old mum and show her the pictures, she will throw the old bastard out!" Pressing the phone into Ritchie's hand, he said, "Send them to me!"

"Calm down, Tommy!" Ritchie stated while carrying out the transfer of evidence.

"Take a seat mate," Tommy said, as Ritchie sat on a hard chair. Tommy slumped back down on the sofa, eyes bulging with anger.

"Revenge is best served cold!" Ritchie advised, grinning. "This was the reason that I did not send the photos earlier, knowing how you would react. As you know, I have more control than you. Do not let your temper get in the way. Forget what your old man is up to with this bird. Use this!" he tapped his temple with his forefinger. "Speak to your dad, let him know that you understand. He is a man. One of us! However, get it across that in exchange for your silence, you want your car and apartment returned." He splayed his hands. "Voilà!" he laughed.

"You are a fucking genius, Ritchie. I owe you, mate," Tommy beamed.

Two days later, 24 hours after Dougie returned from his trip, his wife Denise asked him if he would go down to the summer house to speak with Tommy. "Your son wants a father and son talk," she said.

Dougie held back his retort. He marched down through the garden and opened the summer house door. Clouds of hashish smoke filled the room. Dougie was steaming, throwing open the window. "You are a fucking lazy shit, fit for fuck all!" He turned on his son, eyes glaring. Tommy put the partially smoked spliff in the ashtray. Dougie snatched it, throwing it out of the window.

Tommy snapped. "HOW WAS YOUR FUCKING BAHAMAS HOLIDAY WITH YOUR WHORE!" he shouted.

Dougie lunged, grabbing Tommy by the throat, lifting him and then shoving him back down. "You are extremely fortunate to continue to breathe, you cretin!" he growled.

Tommy realised that he had the upper hand with his dad this time. He got the pictures up, holding the mobile in front of him. Dougie glanced fleetingly at the first picture of him and Julie.

Tommy was shaking but continued, "You have betrayed my mum with that tart!"

Dougie stepped forward. "GET THE FUCK UP THERE AND TELL HER THEN!" He pointed towards the villa. "THE LIKES OF YOU, OR ANYONE WHO THINKS THAT THEY CAN HAVE ONE OVER ON ME IS A CUNT!" Dougie railed, spittle forming at the sides of his mouth. "One more thing…!" Dougie warned ominously. "Don't ever let me hear you call my woman a tart again. She is a decent woman who I hold in high esteem!" He grinned malevolently.

Tommy had heard enough. "I want my car and my apartment returned."

Dougie slowly nodded.

"You are fucking welcome to them. Furthermore, do not think that I am going to finance your women and your kids." Removing the keys from his keyring, he threw them on the coffee table, and then stormed out.

38

Marcia enjoyed her new position as her husband's business partner in the Hawk Wind club. The dancers knew that she occasionally continued to work at the Mystique giving tarot card and astrology readings. She had become fond of the girls, and although they pressed her at times for advice regarding their personal lives, Marcia was reluctant to become involved.

Nevertheless, it did not prevent them from demanding her attention.

On occasion, Eamon's past feelings of jealousy would come out again, like when he overheard a customer remark on Marcia's sexy rear, stating that she looked like the actress Sharon Stone.

Eamon once saw a young guy waylay her while she was on her way to the dancers' dressing room. He had asked Marcia for a date. She laughed it off, telling him she was old enough to be his mother. Eamon did not take it lightly, however. He asked Marcia to come into his office. "These men have the drink in them, Marcia!" He moved to the other side of the desk. "Ye dress too sexy. Ye attract attention!" he declared.

Marcia smiled, moving around the desk and standing before him. "Eamon, I do not wear revealing clothes in public," she countered. "Only when I am with you in the privacy of our bedroom."

He remained silent, lounging in the office chair, his dark eyes holding hers. Marcia knew that he had no argument. Raising the black knee-length dress to her hips, stepping out of black lacy panties, and kicking off her stilettos, she straddled him. Releasing his fly, she held the tip of his flaccid penis between her thighs, reviving it. She quelled his misgivings and put her arms around his neck, tongue searching his. Eamon caressed her rear, cupping each cheek, aiding her rise and fall. Eamon unzipped the back of her dress, removing her bra as their passion began to heighten. He held his fingertips to her lips, suppressing her cries of pleasure when they reached the summit. Moments later, a sharp rap on the office door brought them back to the moment. Marcia hurriedly dressed. Eamon zipped up her dress, handing the panties to her. She gave him a small wave, walking to the door.

The following day, Eamon returned to the villa after collecting Niall and Quinn from school. Quinn, excited about the trip to Maureen and Dom's in Marbella did most of the talking on the way home. Although Niall was non-verbal, Eamon knew that both boys cared for the couple who treated them as their own family.

A short while later, Marcia came in from shopping with Suzette. They had been to the children's boutiques to purchase new outfits for the boys, and Eamon helped her carry the bags in from the boot of her car.

The boys were upstairs changing from their school uniforms into swimwear. Aye was feeding Aisling and Aine in the open-plan kitchen. The twins were approaching ten months old and were beginning to walk. They were both eating three meals a day and did not appear to refuse anything that was put before

218

them, however, Marcia still breastfed them every evening before they went down for the night.

Eamon's phone rang; he walked to his office to take the call. Marcia went to see the girls then she was going to sit and watch the boys while they swam and played in the pool before their evening meal.

"Hi Al," Eamon said cheerily to Alphonso Gabrette.

"Long time no see," the old Italian replied. "How are ya doing lad, and ya four babies? Unless there are any more that you have added to your brood since the last time we spoke?" he chuckled.

Eamon relaxed into the office chair, feet up on the desktop "We are all grand. We stopped after the twins due to a health risk wit Marcia if she was to have any further pregnancies."

"It is ya wife that I am ringing ya about!" Alphonso's timbre became serious.

"Marcia?" Eamon asked, feeling somewhat concerned by the old boy's change of tone.

"There have been ripples across the pond…" He paused. "Instigated by Jimmy Grant's widow who informed her daughter that her husband was dealing in narcotics."

Eamon took his feet from the desk, sitting upright. "What has my wife got to do wit it, Al?"

"Word has it that ya wife informed her!" He continued, "Jimmy Grant's son-in-law Matt was involved with Franco Gennaro junior. The man went 'stool pigeon', however, the lot of them are locked up. Young Gennaro and his men are in a different prison from Matt. The Law is taking no chances with them because of the high risk of someone aiding them to break out. The Law could not infiltrate their circle, until this breakthrough. Therefore, Gennaro's lot are in USP Florence ADMAX, the federal supermax for tight control. However, Matt, being the stool pigeon, is in New York's main jail on the 413-acre Rikers Island in the East River between Queens and the Bronx. As ya can imagine, Frank Gennaro senior, in Manhattan, is pissed off with him, and your wife, who he thinks revealed it!"

Eamon, shocked, stood up trying to make sense of what he was hearing. "Grant's wife had her fortune told by your wife. She blurts out the revelation to Grant's widow, who then informs her gal when Matt begins to get a bit slappy with his wife. Mother steps in to protect her daughter. Then Matt's wife slams him with a visit from the Law, whereby he is arrested. To make it simple, son, Matt's wife informs on him. In return, he informs on Franco junior. Nevertheless, your wife was at the root of it! Gennaro senior is not a happy bunny. From what I hear, he is curious to know how a woman who is thousands of kilometres away could have such inside information. The thing is, lad, Franco Gennaro senior is like an octopus, with long tentacles that can reach far and wide!"

Eamon was rendered speechless.

"It is a warning for ya. If Gennaro's boy is found guilty, he will be seeing his days out in Sing Sing. Importing narcotics on the scale that he has carries a hefty prison sentence." He exhaled. "Therefore, the 'stool pigeon' needs to be silenced!" Alphonso added, "I will make a few discreet enquires. Furthermore, if there is any way that I can help ya, ya can rely on me!"

"Whatever the cost, Al!" Eamon stated, then thanked him. Slumping into the office chair, feeling momentarily numb by the turn of events, Eamon began going over the scenario in his mind. *Marcia must have given Joyce Grant a 'reading' when she last came to Spain.* He concluded, shaking his head at Marcia's stupidity. He realised that he could not confront her until they were alone in Marbella. He would not ruin the holiday, nonetheless, he had to get to the bottom of it.

Marcia had been perplexed by Eamon's change of mood. He appeared distant whenever she spoke to him throughout the nearly six-hour journey to Marbella. Eamon drove the 7-seater BMW in stern silence, with Marcia, Aye, and the twins in the car. Billy and Jane travelled in Billy's Land Rover Discovery; Niall and Quinn had wanted to go in the car with them. The boys were going to stay, along with Jane and Billy, at Dom and Maureen's villa in Marbella, a few kilometres from the villa in Benahavis where Eamon and Marcia would be staying. Although Eamon would have preferred to have the boys stay with them, he felt that he could not begrudge Dom and Maureen, who doted on the boys, the joy of having the children stay with them.

Marcia was struggling to cope with Eamon's reflective mood. His lack of conversation and stilted replies were dampening her enthusiasm and she was beginning to worry about the family's two-day break.

On arrival at their villa, Marcia had fed and settled the girls in their cots. Aye had sung them a Thai lullaby. Aisling and Aine were soothed by her sweet voice, just as the boys had when they were babies. Marcia showered and changed into a turquoise-blue, thin-strap linen dress. She came out onto the terrace. Eamon was lounging at the table, long legs stretched out, wine-filled glass in hand. He took a gulp, watching her. Her back towards him, she gazed out at the beautiful scenery. Eamon had introduced her to Benahavís, the mountainous village on the southern face of the La Serrania de Rhonda mountain range when they had first met. The stunning tranquil scenery filled her with nostalgia. It was there where he had proposed to her. The diamond and emerald engagement and wedding rings were from the area. Those were treasured moments.

She inhaled, trying to make sense of the change in him that she noticed after he had taken a private phone call in his office. Before that, his mood was light. She sensed that the call had something to do with his mood. Marcia knew that there was no point in questioning him.

"Marcia!" He broke her musing. She suddenly felt emotional, turning to face him. He crooked a finger, beckoning her. She hesitated. "I want to speak to ye!"

Her eyes searched his, as she was uncertain of what Eamon was going to say. She walked towards the table and sat opposite him without speaking.

"Marcia, did ye give Joyce Grant a tarot reading when she last visited Spain?"

Marcia tried to read the motive underlying the question.

"Joyce asked me. I could not refuse her. She has been a good friend. To both of us!" she added.

He slowly nodded. "Ye gave her information about her son-in-law, Matt," he said.

Marcia flushed as 'the penny' dropped and she realised where the conversation was going.

Eamon put his hand up when she tried to continue. "Ye have put us all in a dangerous position through yer dabbling!" he accused. "Franco Gennaro senior's name may not be familiar to ye, however, the man is head of one of New York's most powerful families. Because of ye, his son and men are looking to end their days behind bars. Joyce Grant's son-in-law will eventually be freed and given a new identity once the prosecutor has had his day in court."

Marcia was dumbfounded. "Eamon!" she exclaimed.

"Let me finish!" he continued. "Alphonso called me to say that ye gave Joyce information about her son-in-law's involvement in narcotics, which had a domino effect when Joyce told her daughter after Matt became heavy-handed with her. Sara then informed the police." Eamon paused for a few seconds. "Need I go on?" He sank the rest of the wine, pouring another.

Panic rising in her voice, Marcia tried to explain in her defence, "Eamon, Joyce wanted confirmation that her daughter was not being emotionally betrayed. How could I refuse to tell her? She said that it would go no further!" Marcia threw in.

Eamon shook his head, brow elevated. He stroked his goatee beard, exhaling. "Marcia," he spoke wearily, "Joyce informed her daughter after a heated situation between Matt and Sara got out of hand. Joyce gave her the ammunition that ye supplied!" Momentarily silent, Eamon took another swig. "Irrespective if Matt was having an affair or involved with narcotics, how in hell could you imagine that a mother who was armed wit that kind of information would be able to withhold it from her daughter?" Eyebrow cocked, he waited for her answer. None came.

Tears forming in her eyes, Marcia stood up, moving to Eamon's side of the table. She stood before him. "Eamon, I did not intend to cause problems for Joyce and her family. She was distraught to think that Sara was married to a philanderer like her father was."

"Now this issue has landed on my doorstep. Ye are an intelligent woman, Marcia. Ye have dealt wit the likes of Jimmy Grant and Max Greenaway in the past by withholding information, and now you have done the opposite!"

"Eamon," Marcia spoke softly, reaching out, and touching his arm, "I am sorry." He nodded slowly, placing his hand on hers. "If this situation can be dealt wit, ye will owe me!" A hint of a smile played on the corners of his mouth. He pulled her onto his lap. "Let us put this behind us this weekend. There are four children and our friends who are all looking forward to this break." He lifted her in his arms. "I want us to relax and enjoy ourselves."

Eamon walked naked towards the floor-to-ceiling doors, sliding them open. A faint breeze filtered through the room. Marcia lay on her side, admiring Eamon's taught rear and powerful thighs. As he turned to face her, her eyes alighted on his resting penis. They both smiled at each other.

"Would you like me to perform the yoga headstand?" Marcia asked.

Eamon's penis answered. Sliding naked from the bed, she sat crossed legged on the floor, hands resting on her knees, her breathing controlled. Marcia slowly rolled back, taking her weight on her shoulders, arms straight, supporting her torso as she lifted and opened her legs. Eamon knelt before her, holding her thighs. His warm breath and tongue teased between her legs. She held the position, cries of pleasure escaping. He manoeuvred himself and entered her. She gasped upon entry, tightening her inner muscles as his shaft began to fill her.

"I won't go too deep!" he breathed, observing his motion. Her body, controlled, held him as he continued pumping and took her with him to the climax.

39

Eamon parked next to Billy's black Discovery at Puerto Deportivo de Luio en Marbella marina. The area was busy even though it was only just after 10 am. He passed the twins to Marcia and Aye. Both girls wriggled to get down. They had got to the stage where they wanted to walk.

"Bejesus, youse two are porkers!" Eamon kissed each girl. Marcia adjusted their sunhats. Marcia and Aye walked behind him towards the others who were climbing onto Dom's boat. Jane and Maureen took the twins onboard. The baby girls put their arms out to Quinn when he playfully nuzzled under their chins. Niall ignored them.

The children were all safely buckled into lifejackets, and Dom was at the helm, with Eamon and Billy on either side of him on the bridge. Dom expertly steered the cruiser away from its mooring. The south-westerly wind brought warm air from the tropics and the sun's rays were glistening on the aqua-blue Mediterranean waters.

"We will only go a few kilometres out. Drop anchor, have a spot of lunch," Dom said, turning towards Eamon. "Maureen has been up for hours preparing Irish recipes. She's prepared your favourite Guinness beef pie and home-baked soda bread.

Maureen filled Billy to the brim last night." He chuckled. "She said that he needed some meat on his bones. Poor bleeder ate dish after dish." Billy and Eamon laughed.

"I am seriously thinking about selling my golf club – too much commitment. I decided that I want to retire and let my hair down!" he grinned, rubbing his partly bald pate. "I am going to get myself an apartment. A bit out of the way," he winked, "for some entertaining, away from prying eyes. Nevertheless, there is a fella who rang me. He appears to be interested in the club. I thought that maybe he could join us for a meal." He nodded his head. "Kill two birds with one stone!"

"No problem, Dom," Eamon responded.

A short while later, Dom steered the cruiser towards the coastline of Puente Romano Beach Resort in Marbella and dropped anchor. Eamon turned to observe his family. The bridge gave an unobstructed view. He was only half listening to Dom talking to Billy regarding his sexual needs. Eamon had heard it all before about Dom's extra marital flings. Maureen and Aye were sitting cradling the twins. The sound of an Irish lullaby caught on the wind. His daughters' eyelids drooped. He smiled. He cast a look at the boys, who were playing with their video games. He mused that Niall seemed to be more settled in the new school. He hoped that it would continue. Marcia and Jane emerged from the cabins below deck. They had their swimsuits on. He watched the pair jump from the side of the boat into the sea. They appeared deep in conversation as they swam. To the women's left, a synchronised pod of dolphins began to move nearer. Marcia and Jane quickly headed back to the boat, relieved to get out of the water.

Marcia had gone back below deck to change. Eamon knocked on the cabin door. Marcia, wrapped in a towel, opened it and stepped back to let him in. "I don't like ye swimming in

226

these waters." He sat on the bed. "Ye and Jane appeared to be deep in conversation while youse were swimming."

She knew that it was a question, not just an observation.

She let the towel drop and began to dress. Eamon took her hand. She moved in closer. "Maureen is concerned that Dom is being unfaithful. She asked me for a tarot reading. I explained that my tarot cards are at home."

He nodded, pulling her to him, fingers caressing her breasts. He playfully patted her rear and rose to his full height. "I tink that there has been enough revelation recently!"

Marcia did not reply.

"If anyone has suspicions regarding their private affairs…" he paused, "let skeletons remain in cupboards. I have enough problems to deal wit!" he warned, through the hint of a smile.

Later that evening, back at the holiday villa, the energetic toddlers slept soundly after being tired out from playing in the pool with Marcia. Eamon instructed Aye to ring them immediately if the babies awoke and couldn't settle. He drove on the A7 expressway the short distance to San Pedro, a broad stretch of coastal lowland surrounded by a semi-circle of rugged hills on the east side of the Sierra Blanca of Marbella. The area held poignant memories for Eamon and Marcia.

The car moved through the gates of Dom's stunning five-bedroom villa. Dom came out to greet the couple. "Your boys are in bed. Maureen and the others are having a drink in the lounge." They followed him through to the sumptuous open-plan lounge and kitchen area. The others, sitting on overstuffed chairs, waved. Eamon and Marcia smiled and ascended the stairs.

Quinn looked up from his video game when Eamon and Marcia entered the bedroom. Beaming, he sat up, spreading his arms open. Marcia embraced him. "Mummy you look pretty," Quinn said, smiling. "Papa, do you want to get into Mummy's knickers?" he continued unabashed. "My friend Dwight at school overheard his mother on the telephone speaking. She said that she thought you were rough, Papa, although she would not mind you getting into her knickers!" He looked innocently from one shocked parent to the other.

Eamon did not respond. Marcia tousled Quinn's hair and said, "There are some things that should not be said," she said patiently, and smiling kindly. "Let us forget what your friend overheard, darling." She kissed him.

"I beat Billy and Niall in a race in the pool earlier," Quinn said cheerily. "Then Niall raced Billy, beating him also."

Eamon smiled. "Not too long!" he indicated the video game.

Niall looked up, placing the consul to one side. Marcia hugged and kissed him. No response came. She sat beside him. "Maureen is spoiling you both. Quinn said that you beat Billy in a pool race!" she said, smiling. Niall nodded without looking up.

"Another half an hour wit the game!" Eamon directed. Niall nodded again.

As they left the room, Marcia raised her eyebrow at Eamon, who smiled. "I object to being referred to as a bit of rough by my sons' friend's mother," he teased, guiding her towards the stairs.

Marcia could see that Maureen was well on her way to being inebriated. Her tight-fitting, red dress revealed too much cleavage and did not sit well with her rotund figure, even though she had recently lost 26 kilos. The large glass in her hand was nearly empty. "Let's put some music on. There is plenty of food!" she called over her shoulder, teetering on high heels. She stumbled, righting herself. Dom shook his head. Indicating for the men to join him at the bar. Music from the Beach Boys filled the room. Maureen joined the women, squealing in delight when Jane revealed that Billy had proposed earlier.

"Marcia, I need your guidance!" Maureen spoke conspiratorially, due more to her being tipsy. The men were out of earshot. "While Dom was in the bath earlier, I looked at his mobile phone messages. He thinks that I am not savvy with technology, however," she grinned, "I am clued up where my Dom is concerned. His memory is not what it was. Therefore, I punched in 1234 and bingo! Unlocked!" Her smug smile showed red lipstick on her teeth. "A text message I read confirmed that he is meeting a woman named Eliza on Monday. The sly old bleeder. Up to his old tricks. Carry on!" she continued. "When he sells the golf club and I get my 50 per cent share, I am going to have the works done – breasts and face lifted! Furthermore, I will look for a new bloke. Not an oldie like him. Nonetheless," she placed her hand on Marcia's arm, "I must know what he is up to!" She added, "You need to help me, Marcia."

Jane threw Marcia a look of caution.

Marcia inhaled before she spoke. She was adamant that she was not going to be drawn in. "Maureen, please don't ask me to interfere." She continued, "I am sure that you are wise enough to come out on top of any situation. You have been married to Dom for a lifetime!"

Maureen waggled her head, patting Marcia's arm. "You are right!"

Marcia inhaled, relieved. She steered the subject to Jane and Billy's forthcoming wedding. "Have you thought of a venue for your wedding, Jane?"

Jane shook her head. "I am still reeling from Billy's proposal. I assumed that because he has been free for most of his life, he would not be the type to commit. I know that we have been together for a long time, but…"

Marcia intervened, "Jane, Billy was a wanderer. He loves you. Anyone can see that!"

"Don't count on it, Jane!" Maureen slurred. She had topped up her glass with neat vodka. Marcia took the glass from her hand before she knocked it back. Tears rolled down her cheeks. "I am sorry, Jane. Billy is a decent fella, like Eamon," she threw in. The two women took Maureen outside to get some air.

Eamon was deep in thought about Alphonso Gabrette. He knew that he had to help him in preventing Joyce Grant's son-in-law from getting up on the witness stand, and time was of the essence. Eamon was brought back to the moment when Dom tapped his arm. "This bloke that is interested in buying my golf club comes from Dublin. I have asked him to join us at the restaurant to-morrow night. You might know him. Old pals like," he grinned.

Eamon looked up, interested. "Who is he?" he asked.

Dom shook his head. "Brendan, or something like that." He shook his head. "My old swede is not what it used to be!" He tapped his temple. "Cormac Brendan! No, bloody hell, it's Brennan, not Brendan," Dom chuckled.

Eamon paled.

"Do you know that name? I don't want no time waster. No tyre kicker." Dom said.

Eamon did not respond immediately. "I knew him from way back."

"From what I was told. His young wife fucked off with a much younger stallion. The man wants a new start!"

Eamon remained silent.

"Well, you are a good judge. When we meet up tomorrow, you can give me the nod if you think that he is a time waster."

Eamon sank the glass of wine. Billy caught his eye. Eamon nodded when Billy took his glass for a refill. "Let me go and have a word with my old woman!" Dom said.

"Blast from the past?" Billy remarked, handing him the wine.

Eamon nodded. "The guy was a prick. I had a run-in wit him years back in Dublin. We were only youngsters. However, do leopards change their spots? I don't tink so," he said, answering his own question. Billy nodded in agreement.

They had not stayed late at Dom's after he had put Maureen to bed. Eamon was not looking forward to seeing Cormac Brennan the next day. Nevertheless, he would tolerate him for an hour or so while Dom dealt with him. It still rankled with him, although Eamon had previously given Cormac Brennan a beating on two occasions.

The mention of his name brought back the anger that he had felt way back then when Brennan had tried to poach Eamon's girlfriend Jodi at the time. Although he only saw her on occasion, when it suited him and she had been available, they were both up for it – in any darkened alleyway. Jodi Bryant had informed him once after they had finished their business that Cormac Brennan had asked her out. Eamon had recently been set free from the juvenile correction centre. All he wanted was to relieve his sexual frustration. Then Brennan started sniffing around his girl. He sneered, thinking about how he had waited for Brennan. He had discovered that Cormac Brennan's route was to pass St Laurence O'Toole's school that was nearby to his road. He smirked, remembering as if it was yesterday, the shocked look on Cormac's face when Eamon stepped out of the shadows. The first blow to his jaw saw Brennan scream out. Eamon did not hear. Blinded by rage, he beat him into submission. Another time, Eamon had thrashed him again, throwing Brennan into the River Poddle in Dublin. Eamon put Brennan on the back burner, punching in Dan's number.

"How's tings. Any problems?"

"I sense a potential problem. There was a bit of hassle with Dougie Dugan's lad Tommy and his mate. He was back at the club trying it on with a new dancer that Cindy called in from Marcia's list, to replace one of the girls that called in sick. Young Dugan got 'chopsy' with Scott Lord. However, the new pole dancer appeared to be able to hold her own. She gave him the brush-off outside the club when he followed her to her car. Nevertheless, it did not stop him from doing the usual. Shouting the odds that he had your name on his list."

Eamon sucked air through his teeth. "I allowed him back into the club after the last episodes. I don't want to fall out with his father Dougie. But the little prick is beginning to give me a pain in my bollocks!" Eamon added that Dan should ring him if he was needed.

"Is there anything wrong?" Marcia asked, coming out onto the terrace after changing into a flowing, cream silk negligee, embroidered with butterflies.

He sat at the garden table, gazing up at the star-spangled sky. He turned his head. "I am grand. Come 'ere till I tell ye!" Smiling warmly, he held an arm out, stretching his legs out for her to sit on his lap.

Marcia put her arms around his neck.

"Ye obviously know that Billy and Jane are to be married?"

She nodded.

"I offered our villa as the venue. Billy is keen. We will provide the catering. The man is due a bonus," he added.

Marcia kissed him. "How could I not love a man like you?"

He smiled thinly, brow raised, running his hands over the contours of her body. "I have a few bad traits," he countered.

"I would not be without you for the world, Eamon. You have provided us with a wonderful life. It is I who has caused you problems."

He put his fingers to her lips, quietening her. "I have faith that it will be sorted." Eamon returned her kiss, untying the negligee. "My little mystic temptress, who uses silk as a weapon," he breathed, kissing her throat. He adjusted his position, allowing her fingers to free his bulge. His shaft thickened with each stroke, easing into her, while he unbuttoned his shirt. "I want to enjoy ye in bed,"

Her pace quickened, her hardened nipples against his chest, knowing that his words were lost to their passion. Tongue seeking tongue, hands clamped on her bare buttocks, he surrendered to her.

40

Marcia had finished her early morning swim. Eamon and Aye came through the doors onto the terrace, each with a twin in their arms. They were dressed in pink swimsuits that covered their arms and legs, with matching caps to protect their fair skin against the sun's rays. Eamon adjusted their armbands and stood them on the edge of the pool. Both girls wriggled when Eamon entered the water, eager to join him. Marcia and Aye stood by as he coaxed them to jump into his awaiting arms. Eamon swam on his back with Aisling and then Aine sat on his broad chest. Their podgy little fingers held onto his neck. Marcia thought once more about how Eamon interacted with the girls. She observed how he rubbed his facial hair under their chins, kissing and hugging them. She did not doubt Eamon's love for his two sons, however, he was not tactile with them like he was with his two copper-red-headed daughters. They had him tied up in knots. A pout or tear would see the pair having their way, she mused, wondering how he would cope with the headstrong twins as young girls. Aisling sucked his earlobe and Aine snuggled into his chest when he walked up the steps with them in his arms, both ready for their nap.

That evening, when Marcia was getting ready to go out to dinner, he wolf-whistled his approval. Dressed in the midi, black,

Balmain dress that fit like a second skin, she turned, showing the racer back, full-length zip. "For easy access!" she smiled, moving into his arms.

He cupped her bottom. "Ye have no underwear on!" he chastised, playfully. "Leave the dress on tonight, in bed!"

Checking his watch, he exclaimed, "We are running late! The restaurant in San Pedro was booked for 7 pm." Eamon did not want his two boys out too late.

The restaurant was busy, the maître d' showed them to the gallery where Dom, Maureen, and the boys were already seated. Eamon smiled at Niall and Quinn. Both boys were dressed in navy trousers and sky-blue shirts. They stood when Eamon approached – he tousled their hair. Marcia leaned across to kiss them.

Eamon caught Cormac Brennan's eye ogling his wife's rear. He bristled, past anger resurfacing. He nodded to Billy, who didn't appear to be happy in Brennan's company. "Sit here lad!" Dom pulled out the chair next to him. Brennan sat on Dom's other side. So as not to lose face, he took the seat, giving a sharp nod briefly in Cormac Brennan's direction.

A waiter gave them all their menus and Niall spoke to him in Spanish, Quinn followed.

"It is grand to see that ye have such handsome sons. Clever wit it. A lovely wife. They are a credit to ye. How has life been treating ye Eamon?" Cormac spoke as if they were old associates. Eamon studied him, his warning shot bounced off Cormac, who continued to smile.

"Grand!" he replied shortly, quietly inhaling.

Cormac turned his attention to Jane. "Dom informed me earlier that ye train detection dogs. I should imagine that would be no mean feat. However, a dog like that could be something that would be of interest to me. I live alone," he said, grinning. "One never knows if there are intruders around!"

Jane turned her head to face him. Unsmiling, she responded, "You must be vetted before adopting one of my dogs. Have you ever owned one?" she asked flatly.

He shook his head. "I have had neither pets nor any children, sadly!"

"I didn't think you were an animal person," she shot from the hip. "Therefore, I decline your interest in one of my dogs."

Billy smirked. Cormac remained unruffled. Giving a sharp nod towards her in response. Eamon caught Billy's eye. His inconspicuous nod did not go unnoticed.

Food orders were placed and Eamon listened more than joining the conversation when Dom continued to speak to Cormac about the golf club.

Eamon forced his steak down, his appetite diminished due to Cormac's presence.

"I hear that ye have twin girls?" Cormac said to Marcia, who smiled weakly, nodding.

"The babies have beautiful copper-red hair!" Quinn chipped in. "They are pretty!" he added.

"Red-headed girls!" he aimed once more at Marcia. "Yer sons are their father's image. Where does the copper-red hair come from? Ah, I seem to remember being told about yer feisty flame-haired granny that terrorised folks wit her tales, Eamon!"

Eamon fumed.

Cormac, unfazed, continued. "Those were the days. How is yer younger brother?" He paused. "His name escapes me. Good looking lad, married young to the girl who pestered him if my memory serves me well!" Cormac did not wait for a reply. There was none. Eamon glared.

"We were kids, young pups back then. Tings change!" Cormac said with a fleeting glance in Eamon's direction.

Eamon's ire was building. He saw his opportunity to leave when Quinn yawned after finishing his meal. "Boys, it's way past yer bedtime." He rose, moving towards his sons.

Billy was driving them all to Maureen's while Dom stayed behind with Cormac Brennan. Eamon curtly nodded in his direction, guiding Marcia down the stairs from the galley towards the exit.

Marcia left him to his thoughts on the short drive back to the villa, sensing Eamon's anger that was directed at Cormac Brennan.

He stood on the terrace, glass of wine in his hand, staring straight ahead. A gentle breeze rustled the trees. Marcia came up behind him, arms encircling his waist. "Please do not let him ruin our weekend. It was obvious to me that you do not like him. Whatever your reason."

Eamon nodded. "The prick has not learned his lesson!" He appeared to be speaking more to himself. Eamon sipped the wine, turning to face her. "If Dom decides to sell his golfing club to the man, that is his business. Brennan will do well if he stays on the Costa Del Sol, out of my way!" he declared, knocking back the wine and placing the empty glass on the balustrade.

"Would you like to have your way with me?" Marcia offered, playfully, kissing his mouth softly.

He smiled.

"I can supply restraints!" she coaxed. "You could take me up against the wall. The choice is yours."

He laughed. "Yer horny dress warrants the wall now, however, the cuffs will go on later!" Scooping her into his arms, he carried her to the bedroom. He stripped before unzipping the back of her dress. He lifted her, Marcia's legs around his waist, moving towards the back wall. She knew that his passion was partially due to his suppressed hostility. Although he thrust hard, his pumping did not hurt her. He took her twice, then he joined her in orgasm.

She slumped onto his shoulder, and he placed her on the bed. "Satisfied?" He lay beside her.

"I like being fucked on occasion," she said coyly.

Eamon smiled. "Don't get too accustomed to having me take ye up against the wall. I am no longer a young buck!" He grinned.

"I wanted to experience it. It is very…"

He clamped her mouth with his, straddling her. "I am a man who enjoys our lovemaking. A man who savours. My rampant days are over!"

Her fingers caressed his flaccid member. Eamon relaxing, Marcia slowly continued, her mouth aiding, tongue pleasuring until he involuntary shuddered.

He pulled her on top of him, studying her. "Ye are something else!"

41

Cormac Brennan seethed. The smile he projected gave nothing away. He clicked his fingers to a hovering waiter, ordering Dom a double cognac.

"My old woman is not going to be happy if I come home seven sheets to the wind, Cormac," Dom said, nodding to the waiter as he took the golden liquor. "Mind you, she had a few under her belt last night."

Cormac interjected, "You were saying that you first met Eamon O'Donally through a contact?" He smiled at the inebriated Dom.

"Jimmy Grant, vile piece of shit. Mr Big down at Costa Blanca. Well, was!"

"Ye say was! Go on Dom!"

"Jimmy Grant came here to look at a boat that I had for sale. Eamon was with him, being his right-hand man." Dom took a swig. "I invited the pair back to my place. My Maureen took to the Irishman, who wasn't married to the sort that he has now, but some blonde bimbo. However, it became commonknowledge that Jimmy Grant was knocking her off, and everybody else's woman too, for that matter. Sorry, Cormac, you have been having your fair share too, what with losing your woman to a younger bloke!" Dom apologised.

Cormac shook his head in dismissal, projecting a fake smile.

Dom continued, "Jimmy and Eamon's wife both end up dead. They deserved it if you asked me!" Dom took another sip. "The lad ended up having the last laugh. Eamon owns a big haulage company and an adult club. His business partner died recently, and he took it over with his wife." He grinned. "Could you imagine seeing all that young bare flesh nightly? Lucky bastard!"

Cormac nodded.

"Anyhow, the first time that I met Marcia, not long after him being widowed, Eamon gets engaged to her. Spent a fortune on the ring. At it like rabbits on the top deck of my boat. Maureen heard them at it. Mind you, could you blame him?" Dom chuckled. "He soon knocks her up with the boys, then down the line, she gives him the red-headed babies." Dom pursed his lips. "Different class of woman, she is. Straight gal," adding, "not like the other one."

Dom slurped another mouthful. "Predicts the future. Women are into all that mystical stuff" He waggled his head. "Mind you, Marcia, from what I hear, is the business. Brains and a looker. I wouldn't mind a bit of that myself!" Dom guffawed.

I certainly would not mind a piece of her, Cormac thought, *the ultimate payback to O'Donally for beating on me.* Seeing Eamon after all those years inflamed a simmering hatred. Cormac had received a broken jaw from O'Donally. However, that was when they were young men. Cormac was fit. Taking care of himself had paid off. He was a man of influence. Having powerful Arab backers and London contacts would enable him to have his retribution. The arrogant confident swagger that

Eamon O'Donally retained, and his underlying threatening manner no longer intimidated him, he thought. His musing turned to O'Donally's wife. He would make plans to ingratiate himself into O'Donally's circle. He felt horny visualising fucking his wife, O'Donally bound, forced to watch the anal act.

He put his arm around Dom. "Let us get down to business. We can shake on it!" he said, grinning, "If you are satisfied with my offer Dom?"

Cormac smiled caustically, pleased with the deal and the information that he had gleaned from Dominic O'Reilly, he shut the taxi door, paying Dom's fare. The driver knew the address. Dom was a regular.

Cormac placed a call to London. The recipient answered although it was nearly midnight. Shane Reid, Cormac's business partner was a night owl, what with the time differences of the various countries the narcotics and gun-running pair's lucrative company dealt with. It warranted their success, and it was a small price to pay. "Shane, I need a man!" he said.

"He won't come cheap!" Shane replied.

"I won't quibble!" Cormac ended the call, knowing that it would not be too long before his plan would be activated.

42

Tommy was getting hot under the collar, even though his car and apartment had been returned to him. His thoughts were occupied with the pole dancer, Gemma, from the Hawk Wind club. He had waylaid her once again and she finally succumbed, and gave him her phone number, instructing him to text and not ring her as she was studying. He looked at the blank screen once more. No reply to his text. He had sent numerous, all remained unopened. He took himself to hand, visualising her near-naked form. A few minutes later, he involuntarily shuddered. His two pregnant girlfriends had become tedious. He wanted Gemma, no matter the cost. He jumped up to grab his phone when the ping of a text came through, fist-pumping the air when he read that she had agreed to meet him.

He phoned his mother. "My car needs work on the engine." He left it in the air, waiting for his mother's expected reply, "Don't worry Tommy, Mum will pay for it!"

"Are you sure, Mum, because you are so good to me?" After her assurance, he fist-pumped the air for the second time. He would buy a new suit and shoes and book a high-class restaurant to take Gemma to. His old mum was a good sort, he concluded, getting up Ritchie's number to tell him that he owed him 50 euros. It was a bet that the pair had made when Ritchie declared that he was punching above his weight.

....

Angel, stage name Gemma, was thrilled to be asked back to the Hawk Wind adult club. She was going to be in permanent employment, which would aid her in financing her university studies herself. Although her father was generous to her and her mum and provided their lovely villa, cars, and lifestyle, she wanted to start paying her way. She had gone to a good school and done well. At her dad's insistence, Angel had attended karate lessons from a young age and was now a brown belt. She could take care of herself in any situation. She was determined that her father would not discover the type of work that she did. He would be horrified. He was proud of her achievement in passing each level of the exams that would lead her to become a veterinarian. Her mother was in on the secret, although none too happy, in case Angel's father found out. Angel was strong-willed, like her dad. She had known about the situation with her parents from a young age, accepting that her dad loved her, although there were times when he was absent. She smiled to herself as she sent the reply to Tommy's text, one of many that had been unopened. She was making him wait. Now that she felt the time was right, Angel agreed to go out for a meal with him and test the water. She thought that he was cute, but his 'cock of the walk' attitude irked her. He needed to be taught a lesson, she concluded.

Angel was going to park her car a kilometre from her home, a short distance from Moraira. Tommy had asked her to meet him halfway as he was coming from Javea. She'd texted him and said that if he could not drive the 23-minute route, then he should forget it. He did not argue. Tommy said that they could have a drink afterwards at his apartment that he owned near the beach. She sensed that he was bragging about the property. Angel was not going to put herself in a compromising position by being alone with him.

She smiled to herself on seeing Tommy's yellow Lotus parked in the shade under a row of trees. She parked her black, soft-top Audi, which her father had recently bought for her 21st birthday. She also knew that she was going to have the keys to her own apartment soon; her mum had coaxed Angel's dad into letting her have her freedom.

She had to admit, apart from his arrogant attitude, Tommy, with his fair hair and blue/grey eyes, not unlike her father's, was quite good looking, although not overly tall.

Tommy leapt from his car, beaming, white teeth flashing her a smile, eyes appreciating as he watched her body sashay towards him. The classic, short, black dress revealed too much thigh, although the neckline was modest. Angel wore no makeup; she did not need it. Her dark hair, sweeping black eyelashes and height came from her dad's side. She had her mother to thank for her curvaceous figure.

Tommy flashed the Jaeger-LeCoultre watch that his mum had loaned him from his father's collection. He had cajoled her into letting him wear it for a fabricated job interview. He had to return it before morning so his father wouldn't notice it missing from the safe.

"Your watch is stunning," she said, getting into the Lotus and straightening her dress as it rose when the seat belt clipped in. "My dad has one similar." She placed her small Gucci shoulder bag on the car floor by her high heels. Tommy was not listening. His thoughts were on to devouring, and not the meal that awaited.

"You look ravishing, Gemma!" Tommy said.

"Ravishing!" she repeated, eyebrow cocked, smiling.

"Stunning!" he corrected, smiling as he fired up the Lotus.

He asked her about her studies. He showed an interest and complimented her on her looks and intelligence. It did not wash with her. Her father had raised her to be confident. Her mother taught her to value herself. Angel had an abundance of both. She placed her hand across the top of the wine glass when he tried to refill it. Two was enough. "I have an exam in the morning!"

Tommy nodded.

Angel checked the time after finishing her dessert.

"Bed calls! I cannot disturb my parents. My father is strict, although adorable."

"Disturb your parents? At this time of night?" He held his wrist out to show that it was 10 pm.

"They won't be sleeping," she laughed softly. "They adore one another. They seem to think that I can't hear them. A new bed is needed!" She stood up. "I won't be long. I am going to the ladies' room."

Tommy adjusted himself for the third time that evening, observing the curves of her buttocks. He felt as if he was busting out of his trousers. He wanted her. That night.

His hand gripped the gear stick, blood pumping, erection straining. His peripheral vision took in her thighs, hemline inches away from what he knew he had to have. Under the shadow of the trees, on the quiet road where only the odd light from a villa shone through, he stopped the car behind hers, showing his compliance. He turned in the seat to face her. She released the seat belt.

"Do I get a goodnight kiss? I will sleep better," he smiled.

She hesitated, smiling. He leaned across inches from her face. Just a light one – her lips brushed his. Testosterone took over and Tommy forced his tongue into her mouth. His hands grappled and fingers fumbled to reach between her legs. She tried to free herself, biting his face. His fingers stabbed inside her panties. She ripped at his hair, but he felt nothing. When she twisted his scrotum, he cried out.

"MY DAD, DOUGIE DUGAN, WILL KILL YOU WHEN I TELL HIM!" she shouted.

Tommy recoiled, eyes blazing. "GET THE FUCK OUT OF MY CAR!" he growled.

Angel bolted towards her car and locked it.

Creeping into the lounge, carrying her shoes in her hands, she shuffled across the marble tiles. She could see the glimmer of light under the door of her father's den. Suddenly the door opened, and her mother had two empty wine glasses in her hand. Her mum's scream brought Angel's dad running.

One heel broken in the tussle, dress torn, hair askew, face tear stained, Angel looked terrified. Dougie rushed to her side, cradling her to his chest. "Who the fuck is the slimy cunt that did this to you?" He demanded coldly, looking from Angel back to Julie.

Angel sobbed, "His name is Tommy. He drives a yellow Lotus…"

Dougie roared, "HE HAS FUCKING DONE HIMSELF THIS TIME! See to her, Julie. I'll be back within the hour. It won't take me long to sort it!" Dougie stated, quickly putting a shirt and shoes on, and snatching up his car keys.

His car headed towards Javea's coastline apartments.

Tommy put his hands to his face after he opened the door to his rage-filled father. "I didn't know that she was your bastard kid!" he cried out when the foot lifted him inches from the floor. He scrambled to get away. Dougie yanked him by his shirt front.

"I'll do fucking time for you if you come within a mile of my baby girl. Don't utter one word. I promise that you will regret it, you fucking low life. Stick to your two pregnant women." He kicked Tommy in the rear.

43

"The dress speaks of promises to come!" Eamon said, smiling when Marcia came outside onto the terrace where he was waiting to drive her to the club for work. His car was being serviced and Marcia was leaving the club earlier than Eamon. Billy would drop him back.

"Too sexy!" he stated.

She laughed. "Eamon, it is an olive green, slightly above-the-knee dress, with a normal slashed neckline."

"That fits like a second skin. Yer mound protrudes!" he continued to smile. "I find it alluring. However, we are entering a testosterone-fuelled building, where rutting males are stimulated by dancers!" She moved into his arms. "Can ye feel the effect that ye have on me?"

Her hand slid down, slowly caressing his erection. "Would you like me to change my dress? Afterwards?" Her fingertips continued teasing.

Checking the time, he kissed her. "Come to the club office when it's quiet."

Marcia went back into the villa to change.

He shook his head when she emerged in a black dress.

"The change of colour makes the same statement!" he smiled, taking her arm and guiding her to the front door. The dog lay on the tiles outside the kitchen area waiting for Aye to throw him some titbits while she was cooking.

The club was heaving with young revellers out on a stag party. Eamon and Marcia parted company once inside. Marcia headed towards the women's changing room. Although it had taken a while, Jenny and Sally, who had been off hand with her at first, called out from the other side of the room. The two Irish sisters raised their hands and said in unison, "Good evening, Mrs O!" Sunni sauntered naked towards her. Marcia smiled at them all.

"When can I book a reading? I am desperate for a new man," Sunni asked her, not for the first time.

The women laughed. Sunni had had more men than most of them. "Sunni, my life is busy, I have four children to see to!" Marcia brushed her off. She was concerned about the problems her readings had caused previously. Eamon had not mentioned it again, however, she knew that until the coast was clear, she would have to be careful.

Sunni pouted. "I will dry up!" she said to her audience. More laughter. "We don't all have your luck to have a handsome, loyal stud!"

"Are there any problems… apart from Sunni's needs?" Marcia smiled when they shook their heads, laughing.

Marcia sat on the stool at the end of the bar, waiting for Cindy to finish serving a customer. The new barmaid, Anne, was kept busy helping Cindy get through the demand for top-ups.

"May I join you?" Marcia turned her head, she smiled at the handsome fair-haired man who she judged to be in his mid to late 40s. He pulled up a seat. His knee touched hers.

Marcia adjusted her position. "I work here! Also, I am married."

He didn't respond. He held her eyes, making her feel uneasy. "A classy woman like you, working in a place where so many men would find you tempting!"

Marcia flushed. "My husband owns the club!"

He nodded his head, smiling. Marcia sensed Eamon's presence before she spotted him making his way from the cocktail bar, towards her. She stood up. "Please excuse me!"

Eamon stopped halfway, glaring at the man. The man quickly made his exit. Marcia followed Eamon to the office. He locked the door. Walking behind the desk, he sat down. Leaning back, he studied her. "From where I was standing, it looked as if ye were enjoying that prick's attention!" he accused flatly.

She came to his side of the desk. "I told him that I was married!"

"Only seven words. I don't tink so!" he threw back.

"I said that you were the owner of the club."

He slowly nodded. "It did not seem to deter him. Until ye see me coming towards ye!"

"There are no problems on the floor." She slowly raised her dress, removing her panties. Eamon watched her. Marcia unzipped his fly, releasing him. He remained still as Marcia straddled him and kicked her heels off. She held his face, fingers playing across his mouth. "I waxed earlier," she said.

His penis responded to her teasing. He picked her up, laying her across the desk on her back, gently pulling her in closer towards him. Kneeling before her, he parted her legs. Marcia bucked under his warm breath and tongue, crying out. He hushed her, stifling her moans of pleasure with his fingertips when he entered her. Supporting her back, he held her to him.

She bit his neck as a deep orgasm took them over the edge.

He helped her up from the desk, smiling. Marcia's mobile rang from inside her bag on the chair. He passed it to her. She jumped up when Aye told her that Aisling would not settle. She had more teeth coming through and although Jane was staying with Aye to help with the children, Aisling, more so than Aine, would only find comfort from Marcia's breast at times such as this.

"Put these on!" Eamon picked up her panties. She went to put them in her bag.

He held her arm. "Wear them. It could be cold out there!" he jested, kissing her. "Ring me, once she has gone back to sleep!" Marcia dashed out the door, refusing Eamon's offer of having Billy escort her home.

44

"Keep back. Don't let her see you until she has passed the bend!" Tommy directed, rubbing his hands with excitement with Ritchie at the wheel of Tommy's Lotus. The pair had been to an Indian restaurant. Tommy had wanted to drown his sorrows after his discovery that his dad Dougie had fathered the girl that he had taken out on a date, as well as the humiliation of Dougie Dugan defending her. Tommy had received two blows from his dad. It was something that Tommy could not swallow, although he was wise enough to realise that he could not take revenge on his dad. However, this was a golden opportunity that he was not going to miss. Ritchie did not drink and had his drug habit under control. Tommy, however, had snorted cocaine and drunk vodka on the rocks.

Tommy had spotted the Irishman's wife driving away from the Hawk Wind club. The Lotus hung back. "That flashy fucking Irishman O'Donally is going to rue the day that he caused me so much grief with my old man." He pointed to the windscreen towards Marcia's car. "Her up ahead in her Mercedes soft-top, she robbed me of 200 euros for a tarot reading that was a load of bollocks!" Tommy Dugan sneered. "She is heading to Altea Hills. I am going to get my money's worth. Let's see how her old man wants her after I have finished with her!" He patted Ritchie's leg, smiling. "You can have your turn too since Sienna chucked you out for having that love bite on your neck from that tasty sort that you had the other night. She won't be putting out to you until she has calmed down. Beggars can't be choosers!" Both laughed.

The balmy night sky was full of stars. The waxing moon threw shadows as Marcia drove along, with the hilltops in the distance. She had the top down on the Mercedes. She hummed along to Enya's 'The Memory of Trees' on the car's sound system. The road was quiet, with only the odd passing car. Normally, the drive took her 18–20 minutes. Marcia realised that there was no need to panic. Even though Jane had no children of her own, like Aye, she was naturally maternal and sensible. Although the twins were both teething, Marcia felt that it was more the case that Aisling was beginning to project her strong will. Marcia passed the signs for Club de Golf, just after turning left onto Calle Noray and turning slightly right onto Calle Principal de la Serra, she was in Altea Hills. She briefly thought of Eamon, knowing that she had reassured him earlier that there was no need for jealousy.

She panicked when a car suddenly came up alongside her and swerved. She tried to keep control of the Mercedes, but the other car sideswiped her, causing the Mercedes to skid off the road into the undergrowth. She sat stunned for a moment. When she saw Tommy approaching, she tried to put the roof up but there wasn't enough time. She tried to lock the doors, but the grinning Tommy Dugan lunged at her, gripping her dress by the shoulder strap. His free hand pulled the door open. She tried to bite his hand. Another hand gripped her hair, dragging her kicking and screaming out of the car. Tommy clamped his sweaty hand over her mouth. The pair then dragged her away into the undergrowth.

"Pin her arms, Ritchie, kneel on them!" Marcia twisted and bucked. Her dress rose to the top of her panties. Tommy sat on her thighs, restraining her, unzipping his fly. "You are going to have it both ways. You have a firm butt for an old bird!" He smiled caustically. His fingers pushed between her legs.

Marcia was wild with fear, her struggling in vain.

"She's been got at already!" Tommy grinned. "Your old man had you at work?" He rubbed his fingers together.

"For fuck's sake, Tommy!" Ritchie stated, "Get a move on, mate. I am straining here!"

Tommy released his hold, crouching, pulling his trousers down. "She is going to get it rough like I bet her old man gives it to her."

In an amazing show of strength, Marcia's knee struck his testicles Tommy yelled, holding his crotch. Momentarily stunned, Ritchie loosened his grip on Marcia's wrists and Marcia managed to wriggle free. Jumping up, she lashed out. The side of her foot caught Ritchie's chest. The force of the blow sent him staggering backwards, landing him in the dirt.

She ran barefoot, heart racing. She jumped in the car and fired up the engine, pressing the button to raise the roof. Her car bumper scraped against the yellow Lotus as she sped off. She continually looked in the rear-view mirror, her blood pulsating in her ears. She jumped out of the car and punched in the code to open the villa gates.

She sat at the steering wheel, shaking, tears running in rivulets down her face. Even though the nightmare situation had been averted, the adrenaline continued to pump through her.

Minutes later, her car door opened. Jane stood in shock at the sight of her. The dog nuzzled Marcia's leg.

In between sobs, Marcia told Jane what had happened, begging her not to phone Eamon. Jane helped her out of the car.

She said that she had managed to get Aisling off to sleep. Aye had retired to her room.

Jane helped Marcia out of the ripped dress and left her alone so that she could have a shower. Jane told her that she was going to phone Billy, brooking no argument.

Thirty-five minutes after receiving the news of Marcia's attack, Eamon quietly opened the bedroom door. He appeared calm on the surface, but his cold rage was hidden. He vowed that no stone would be left unturned in finding his wife's assailants. He would ensure that they were exterminated. The room was dark except for the small bedside lamp. Marcia lay on her front, face hidden in the pillow. He moved across the room. She did not look up when he sat beside her.

He lifted her tear-stained face towards him and cradled her against his chest. No words were spoken. Jane had filled him in with the details. She had shown him the torn and mud-stained dress. She told Eamon that Marcia had given her the names of the men and that they had been driving a yellow Lotus. She had even had the presence of mind to partially remember the car registration as she sped away. Eamon had taken note of the yellow paint on Marcia's Mercedes driver's side bumper, which was now dented.

He gave Billy the directive to send Scott Lord to his villa. This was something that he would not leave until the morning. He lay alongside her in the bed, waiting until she fell asleep. Upon his insistence, Marcia took two sleeping tablets and soon drifted off, her nightmare forgotten. Easing from the bed, he left the room.

A short while later, Dan and Scott Lord advised Eamon that they would bring Jackie Cooper in to help track down the conspicuous car. Benny Harris had vouched for the club's new security recruit, Jackie Cooper, having previously given Dan the run down on the man's military history. Dan, under Eamon's instruction to employ another security guard had taken the man on. Jackie had arrived on the Costa Blanca with his wife a few weeks earlier. The two men had met in a bar and had got talking, realising that they both had a military history. Benny later introduced Jackie to Dan. Jackie immediately gelled with the ex-paratroopers. It was a given that he would join Eamon's security team.

Before the dawn began to filter through across Altea Bay, Jackie smiled triumphantly at Scott Lord and Dan. He had typed in 'yellow Lotus' on social media. Facebook revealed numerous photos of Tommy Dugan leaning against the car and sitting behind the wheel. He scoured his friends list. Bingo. Ritchie Bryant. There was nothing private about Tommy Dugan. His family and friends gave the men everything that they required. Jackie Cooper downloaded Google Chrome. Dan and Scott sat on the corners of the Hawk Wind office desk while Jackie got up Google Earth. Armed with the address, he zoomed in, tapping the screen and grinning at the image of the yellow Lotus parked in front of the property. The three men high-fived. Jackie took a picture on his phone of the building. "They are at home!" Jackie said, proudly sitting back in his chair.

Dan directed, "We will wait until the cunts surface!"

Jackie wiped the computer's history, shutting down the computer. Dan phoned Billy. Billy would see to it that the hard drive was destroyed. Replacing a computer was easy.

At 10 pm Scott Lord and Jackie Cooper pulled up outside Tommy Dugan's beachfront apartment in Javea. Jackie had not let his eye stray from Google Earth all day. The yellow Lotus had remained parked outside of the building.

At 10:23 pm, two young lads came from the apartment block, both laughing. Jackie recognised Tommy Dugan from his photo on Facebook. His pal Ritchie Bryant was with him. Ritchie got in the driver's seat.

"They look smart!" Jackie grinned.

Scott switched on the engine. "Let's see what the pricks are up to tonight!" He let the car idle while he waited for them to pull out. The car turned right onto Avenida del Mediterraneo, cruising along at a steady speed. The two men knew that the Lotus could outrun them, however, it appeared that the lads were in no hurry to get to their destination. Scott stayed behind leaving two cars between him and the Lotus. They tailed the yellow Lotus for 13 kilometres. Scott continued until the car drove into Denia town, parking next to a white Clio. Two young girls got out of the Clio and spoke briefly to Tommy and Ritchie before returning to their car and following the Lotus.

At 2:43 am Scott nudged Jackie. They had been waiting further along the road from a small villa in Denia, where the two young couples had previously entered.

Tommy punched Ritchie playfully in the arm, smiling, making gestures with his crotch as they left the villa. Both lads put their arms around one another, stumbling and then supporting each other. Ritchie fired up the Lotus. Scott remained at a distance.

An hour later, the quiet waters of the bay received two cocaine-overdosed lads, who had been sitting on the deserted beach near the Cabo San Antonio Natural Reserve snorting cocaine. Scott and Jackie had crept up, unseen. The 50,000-volt Taser held to the pair's testes had helped persuade Tommy and Ritchie to continue with the narcotic. Within 36 hours of their attack, Marcia's assailants had become shark bait.

Two weeks after Tommy Dugan and Ritchie Bryant had been reported missing, Thomas Harper-Watts translated the Spanish newspaper report for Eamon and Dan. "The bodies of two young men were caught in trawler nets by two fishing boats. The only way that they were identified was by dentistry. Crustaceans had eaten his eyes and ears. No fingers or toes remained!" The post-mortem would come later, nevertheless, there was much speculation that drugs were involved in their demise. A plastic bag filled with white powder was concealed in an inner pocket of the leather jacket worn by one of the men, which tests later confirmed to be cocaine. Drug dealers?" Dan thanked Thomas, who returned to the club floor.

Dan said to Eamon, "Word has it that Dougie Dugan has split from his wife, however, young Tommy has left behind his legacy, with two of his kids on the way. Both of his pregnant women are now in residence at Dougie's villa. Roy Dugan's wife who is a client of Cindy's at the Mystique beauty salon informed her that her brother-in-law Dougie had had enough and moved 20 kilometres away. Apparently, he is living with his lover and their daughter. Although the gossiper told Cindy that this was confidential!" Dan smiled and Eamon gave a sharp nod.

"I want ye to give Scott and Jackie a bonus," Eamon said, opening the safe and removing some money. He divided it into three piles, sliding one toward Dan. "Take two well-earned days off with Cindy. I have already seen to Billy's. I am impressed with Jackie Cooper. Make him permanent staff."

45

Marcia sat on the terrace on the yoga mat in the lotus position after completing her yoga routine, her breathing and mind controlled. It had been two weeks since her assault. Her resolve was strong in not allowing the attack to affect her.

When she had first come to Spain, she endured a similar situation at the hands of her landlord's son Mario. She had put it behind her, as she would this. Marcia realised that Eamon would not have let the situation go. She allowed her thoughts to return to Tommy, who had once been a client, albeit an unsatisfied one. The clarity of Marcia's dire warning to him remained fresh in her mind. Marcia had had a haunting dream on a couple of occasions of Tommy's drug-crazed eyes leering at her. Her screams awoke Eamon, who had cradled her in his arms until she fell back to sleep.

Marcia went indoors to change into a bikini, feeling the need to swim. Aisling and Aine were asleep, the boys were staying at Jane and Billy's villa overnight as they were having horse riding lessons in the morning, and Eamon was at the club.

The cool early evening breeze and the chill of the water enveloped her. She swam beneath the surface from one end to the other. In the past, she did not like to swim underwater, however, since the night of the assault upon her body by Tommy Dugan, she had felt it helped to cleanse every trace of the violation to her body.

Eamon, with the dog at his heels, slowed his pace when he came round the corner of the villa, observing Marcia's form immersed below the surface of the water. He nodded to himself, going inside the villa to check on his daughters.

He came back out, glass and wine bottle in hand. Stretching his legs, he filled the glass. Marcia stopped at the end of the pool, smiling. He winked, holding her dark eyes that matched his. The black bikini top floated to the surface, and panties followed.

He sipped the sauvignon blanc, savouring the bouquet. "Do ye tink that it is wise to taunt me?" he jested. "Come 'ere till I tell ye!" he directed, taking another mouthful. "'Tis for ye benefit!" he coaxed.

She climbed out of the pool, wrapping the dressing gown around her naked form. She smiled, walking towards him. They had made love from the second night after her attack. It had been Marcia that had instigated their love making. Eamon had tried to refrain, thinking that she might not be ready, however, she was determined that nothing would come between them. She untied the belt of her gown. He nodded his approval, running his eyes down her body.

She straddled him and put her arms around his neck. He put his glass on the table, cupping her rear. "Would ye like to hear the news first, or open the gift that I have for ye?"

She held his face in her hands, breasts pressing against his chest. She kissed him and began to unbutton his shirt. "Is the news good?" Marcia asked, running her hand down his chest, fingertips fluttering over his nipples.

"Mm," he drew her closer, nuzzling her neck. Her body moved against his erection.

"The problem across the pond has been dealt wit!" he breathed.

She sat up, eyes questioning.

"We no longer have to worry about any repercussions from your revelation to Joyce Grant about her son-in-law." He smiled back at her.

She widened her legs as his fingers explored. Her tongue found his. He patted her rear. "Let us continue in private. Yer gift can wait. This can't!"

Marcia threw her head back, groaning with pleasure as he placed her on the bed and began stimulating her with the tip of his shaft. She bucked and he moved inside her, filling, then moving slowly, smiling at her first orgasm. Clamping her thighs with his, he continued. "This one is about us!" he rasped as they peaked together, their heartbeats racing.

He lay on top of her, arms on either side of her face, taking his weight. "Have I earned my gift?" Her eyes sparkled.

"I have arranged a two-day break in Lake Como, Italy, just the two of us. I am told the scenery is beautiful."

She ran her fingertips across his top lip. "Eamon," she paused, eyes searching his, "I love you so much."

He kissed her fingers. "Once Billy and Jane's wedding and honeymoon are out of the way, Jane will be able to help Aye wit the children. Dan, Billy, and Cindy will step up wit the running of the businesses." Rolling off her, he pulled her to his chest.

Although it had remained unspoken, Marcia knew that Eamon had dealt with the two thugs who had attacked her, and he had closed the door on the incident. Nonetheless, she was aware of her husband's temperament. Eamon did not forgive or forget anyone who trespassed against him or his family. The Grim Reaper from the tarot deck came to Marcia's mind.

46

Shopping for clothes was not one of Jane's favourite pastimes. Suzette, Jane, Cindy, and Marcia were taking her to look for a wedding dress and a suitable wardrobe for their honeymoon. Jane had suggested they go to Dubai for their honeymoon, however, Billy stated that he would take her anywhere but. The Persian Gulf held no interest for him, as he had travelled there many times in the past when he was in the military. Instead, they settled on Sorrento in southern Italy.

Suzette's wedding gift to Jane was a make-over. Lloyd would restyle her long, blonde hair. Keiron would apply his cosmetic artistry including eyelash tinting, eyebrow shaping and a deep facial, which Jane had agreed to.

The three glamourous women coaxed Jane into numerous boutiques, although she eagerly purchased the sensual lingerie, as did Marcia. She finally found the dress for her special day. Suzette insisted upon paying for the dress, along with two linen above-the-knee skirt suits, and accessories. Jane gasped when the assistant told Suzette the amount. Suzette brushed it off. Cindy encouraged Jane to try on a pantsuit. The women were all wowed when she paraded it for them. Cindy brooked no argument when she paid the bill. Jane profusely thanked them all.

Laden with purchases, the women drove to the marina. The restaurant's maître d' welcomed them, showing them to a table. They quickly placed their orders, as Suzette had only a short time before she had to return to work. Suzette looked wistfully at the three women. "I envy you all." She took the Voss mineral water from the waiter. "I know that Greg has been gone just a short while, however," she sipped from the glass, "I want a man's arms to hold and support me. I may have financial independence, however, it is not what I long for!"

The three women listened without replying. "I know that I won't be very popular with the men in our circle who knew Greg." She glanced at Marcia, Eamon having been Greg's friend and business partner. "Nevertheless!" she smiled, "my grieving is over. I am on the hunt for a new love!" No one responded. They ate their salads in silence.

Cindy left with Suzette to go back to the beauty salon. Jane smiled and said, "I don't blame Suzette, although she is right that the men will judge her." She ordered two organic filtered coffees. Marcia nodded. She knew that Eamon did not have a high opinion of Suzette, even though she had gifted her 50 per cent share of the Hawk Wind club to Marcia to make amends for her past wrongdoing. However, it had not changed Eamon's mind about her.

"I cannot thank you and Eamon enough, Marcia, for offering your villa as the venue for our special day. It will be my dream come true. I can't even imagine the expense…"

Marcia placed her hand on Jane's arm, interrupting. "You and Billy are like family. My children adore you both. How could I work if you did not help as you often do? Aye could not cope without you. Eamon and I are showing you both our appreciation. Suzette has not been as lucky as we have with our relationships. Cindy and Dan also have something special. I hope that Suzette finds what she is looking for…" she inhaled, "if she does not rush into the arms of the first man that takes her interest. Suzette will be fine. In six months, Suzette will be settled!" Marcia predicted.

She heard a familiar loud belly chuckle and turned in the direction it was coming from. She saw Joey B, the car dealer who was a dear friend to Eamon walking through the door. Marcia paled when she saw who came in behind him.

Joey B spotted her. Waving, he made his way to their table with Cormac Brennan in tow. Marcia stiffened. Upon seeing the Irishman, Jane turned back towards Marcia. Both women gave each other a knowing look.

"Ladies!" Joey B exclaimed, beaming.

"May we join ye?" Cormac did not wait for a reply, pulling up a chair next to Marcia. Joey B sat next to Jane. "How is Eamon?" Cormac twisted in his seat, his knee brushing Marcia's.

"He is fine!" she replied quietly, moving her knee away.

Joey B smiled. "You know Eamon?" he asked Cormac.

"We have a past connection. We came from the same area in Dublin." Cormac smiled at Marcia. "I had the pleasure of meeting these two lovely ladies in Marbella when I was about to purchase my golf club. And now we meet again as I am about to purchase a new car from Joey B, who, I might add, has a reputation for honesty that reached my ears all the way down the coast!"

The car dealer shook his head, smiling. "You boys like the top-of-the-range motors, Eamon is no exception!" he grinned at Marcia. "Eamon purchased Marcia's Mercedes from me too."

"Have you been busy, girls?" Joey looked at both women. "Out shopping, just like my wife and daughter?" he asked, grinning.

Cormac clicked his fingers at Marcos so he could order some wine.

"We were just leaving!" Jane said to Joey, ignoring Cormac Brennan.

"Please, I insist that you stay and have a glass of pinot noir. The smoothness remains on one's palette," Cormac invited.

Jane glared at him.

"Thank you, however, Marcia and I rarely drink alcohol during the day." She threw Cormac a challenging look. "I am running late, and I have animals to see to," she said firmly.

"Before you go, girls, I have been meaning to phone Eamon to invite you all to my Sophia's wedding in four weeks," Joey B said.

"Thank you, Joey, I will tell Eamon," Marcia replied, stepping out of reach of Cormac Brennan. She did not want him to touch her. Jane raised her hand to the waiter for the bill.

Cormac took the bill from the waiter. Jane's look of disdain was wasted. Cormac leaned towards Marcia. "Hopefully, we will meet again soon," Cormac added.

Marcia smiled thinly.

Joey B turned to Cormac when the women left. "Small world, Cormac!" he said, cutting a slice of steak and forking two chips. "Seeing as you are an old pal of Eamon's, why don't you come to my daughter's wedding reception too? You and Eamon can catch up, go over old ground!" He crammed the food into his mouth, putting his hand up while he continued to chew. "Bring a partner," he said, through a mouthful of food, "If you have one?"

Cormac willingly accepted the invitation. Not believing his good fortune at being able to infiltrate Eamon O'Donally's circle with such ease.

Wiping his mouth and hands, Joey B took his mobile phone from his pocket. "Excuse me for a minute. I am going to ring Eamon in case his wife forgets. My Mel will have a go at me if I don't get confirmation from him. We are both very fond of the lad."

After the call, Joey B put his phone away. "My wife will be pleased that Eamon has accepted!" Joey B patted his paunch. Cormac smiled smugly.

"Getting back to business, now that you have had a test drive in the Mercedes cabriolet convertible, my man can deliver it to you tomorrow and drive your Audi back to my showroom – if that is convenient?" Joey B said.

"That is grand!" Cormac raised his glass. "Let us drink to many more years of knowing that you will be the man who will supply my vehicles! Trusted men are hard to come by!" They clinked glasses.

47

Marcia had not spoken as they walked to their cars. As she opened her car door, Jane said, "Don't let him spoil the lovely time that we had today, Marcia."

Marcia shook her head. "Why did he feel the need to come here, Jane? I know that Joey B is the main car dealer here, however, Cormac Brennan lives in Marbella. I sense that he is up to something!" She said heavily.

Jane nodded. "Billy does not like him, and Eamon did not hide his dislike of Cormac Brennan when we were in Marbella. It would be foolish of him to come here." Jane checked her watch. "The animals need feeding!" Both women hugged.

Eamon was curious about who Joey B was with at the restaurant. He had said that they had had lunch with Marcia and her friend.

"Papa!" Quinn called out for Eamon to watch him dive off the side of the pool. Niall followed, swimming further underwater than his brother. Both boys surfaced.

"Grand, boys!" Eamon congratulated them both. Roman's ears pricked up. Rising, the dog padded towards the side of the villa. Eamon knew that the dog must have heard Marcia's car. Marcia, laden with shopping bags came round the corner. Eamon rose to help her, without taking his eyes from the two boys.

Quinn waved to her. Marcia blew them a kiss. Niall looked briefly, then took off to the end of the pool. She kissed Eamon. "I will take these inside, then join you."

Marcia returned to the terrace, smiling at the boys as they raced one another. She took a seat opposite Eamon. He did not mention the phone call from Joey B. "Did ye eat out? Aye has prepared a meal." He caught the flush on Marcia's face. He was intrigued. He waited.

"We went to the restaurant at the marina. Suzette and Cindy only had an hour to spare. Jane and I remained." She paused. "Joey B came into the restaurant with..." The flush spread as she continued, "Cormac Brennan." Marcia halted, seeing Eamon's face pale.

His dark eyes hardened. "What the fuck is that prick doing here?" He growled at her.

She remained silent. Pushing his chair back he turned on his heels, towards the terrace doors. Marcia sighed.

Eamon phoned Thomas Harper-Watts. He asked him if they could meet at the Hawk Wind club. Privacy would be required for what Eamon needed to say to him.

Thomas opened the office door; the club's silence permeated the building. It would be a few hours before opening the doors to the public. Eamon returned Thomas's smile despite the anger that he was feeling. He proffered a chair. Resting his forearms on the desk he said, "I require some information. Yer father is the man who has the contacts. I need to find out if this fella Brennan is up to anyting!"

"My father is always willing to help," Thomas said, smiling. "Give me his Christian name and any details that you may have. My father will contact the Chief Inspector once I have spoken to him. He finds it all rather exciting!" He smiled.

Eamon gave Thomas Cormac Brennan's name, description and approximate age, and area where he was from in Dublin, as well as the name and address of the golf club that Cormac Brennan had purchased in Marbella from Dominic O'Reilly. He had little to go on. Eamon reclined back into the office chair after Thomas had left to make the call to his father. He sensed that Cormac Brennan was up to something, nevertheless, he could not put his finger on exactly what. Joey B had a reputation as an honest car dealer, but the Costa Blanca was 583 kilometres away, a five-and-a-half-hour journey from the Costa Del Sol, which Eamon knew had its own reputable car dealerships.

There was no reason that Brennan should step on his turf, he concluded. The man obviously had not learned his past lesson from the beating that Eamon had given him years ago. Eamon was grateful to Thomas. He and his father, Lord Arthur Harper-Watts, were good men to be acquainted with. Eamon would reward them, although the jovial man had tried to dissuade him in the past regarding payment.

Billy had told Eamon that Thomas was having marital problems. He said that Thomas's beautiful, Chilean wife wanted another child, even though the youngest one was still only a few months old. He told Billy that he could not do enough to please her. Eamon had seen the attention that Thomas got from the women. His upper-crust voice and looks like Oliver Reed charmed the ladies. He drew them like bees to a honeypot. Although Billy said that Thomas was not a player, he didn't think it would be long before he began to look elsewhere. It was not the case that Billy was a gossip. He was usually tight-lipped, as most of the men were, however, on occasion he would keep Eamon up to speed regarding his men's personal lives to ensure Eamon's ship sailed smoothly in calm waters.

Eamon exhaled as he thought about how he had reacted to Marcia earlier, by storming out of the villa without saying a word. He felt a pang of guilt. It was not her fault. The fault lay with him and the grievance that he had against Brennan. She had been through so much, stoical throughout. He was determined to make it up to her. He phoned a hotel to make a reservation and booked some flights. After Dan and Cindy returned from their two-day break, he would get away with Marcia. Then he got on the phone with Jane, who asked him to visit.

Although Eamon was used to his Belgian shepherd, Roman was showing signs of ageing. His back legs were getting stiff. Eamon had spoken to Jane about introducing another dog, without upsetting Roman. Her dogs barked when he got out of his car in her grounds. After a sharp command from her, the five dogs returned to the veranda.

Jane confirmed that she would step into help with the children while he took Marcia away for a couple of days. Then she turned the subject to the dog. The Belgian shepherd that she felt would be suitable for his family was called Caesar, who was 18 months old and fully trained in detection work. She reassured Eamon that the young dog would not cause any problem with Eamon's old dog. She advised that he wait until they returned from their break to introduce him.

Eamon returned to the villa to the happy scene of his family all playing in the pool. The girls wore Inflatable armbands, their copper-red curls peeking out from beneath pink floppy hats. Their chubby, flailing arms smacked the water. Quinn and Marcia surrounded them. Niall was throwing the weighted water toy, diving to retrieve it.

Eamon entered the villa without being spotted. Minutes later, after changing into his swimming trunks, he strolled towards the pool.

"Papa!" Quinn called, setting off a chain reaction. Both girls held their arms up, squealing with delight when Eamon came down the pool steps. He smiled at Marcia, taking both babies in his arms. Aisling held his face, giggling as did Aine. He rained kisses under their chins, tickling them with his facial hair. Tinkling laughter rang out when he jumped up and down in the water. A short while later, a hovering Aye took both girls' hands, leading them from the pool. Eamon watched them toddle along-side her. Aye was speaking to them in Thai. Both girls smiled, eagerly entering the villa to get changed and eat. Eamon turned back down the steps. "Niall, Quinn! I will give ye 10 euros for every race that ye beat me in!"

Marcia retreated, leaving her husband with the boys. She sat at the table on the terrace, observing. She smiled at Niall's beaming face. Each boy won a race. She knew that Eamon was a powerful swimmer and that he had allowed both sons to win. All three dove under the water at the last challenge. Eamon surfaced just ahead of them. "I owe ye 100 euros each. Race ye back. Double or quits!" Eamon climbed out of the pool. "Come to my office before bed and I will pay my debt," he told the boys. The beaming boys picked up their towelling robes before going inside to change. They both returned Marcia's wave before disappearing through the villa doors.

Marcia ran her eyes down Eamon's torso as he dried himself.

He elevated his brow. "Ye appear hungry? Would ye like me to feed ye before we go to work?" he teased. "It will be a busy night. Two stag parties... no time for an interlude in the office!"

Eamon gently pulled her up from the chair sliding the straps down on her racer back swimsuit, revealing her breasts. He held her to his chest, feeling her nipples and his erection both pressing. "Ye wore a swimsuit like this when I first saw you swimming in Jimmy Grant's pool eight years ago. I wanted ye then as much as I desire ye now!" He pressed harder against her pubic bone.

Marcia ran her fingertips along his jawline. "Eight years ago, I was naive, sexually inexperienced."

He kissed her. "You were a very quick learner because if my memory serves me right, it did not take long before yer beautiful mouth was pleasuring me!"

Marcia blushed at the memory.

"Bear in mind that was our first time together!" he laughed.

"That was the first time I had done that sort of thing for a man," she confessed.

"Wow!" He feigned shock, laughing "Ye were a born natural. To have taken me deep wit such ease!"

She blushed again. Eamon scooped her up in his arms. "I am going to see the children and pay my debt to the boys. Once ye have topped up the girls before they sleep. Then I will quench yer hunger pains!" He winked placing her on the chair.

She watched his retreating back. Not much about him had changed since the first time that she had seen him, apart from his once coal-black goatee beard being now mostly sil-ver-grey, and his once trim waistline being slightly thicker. He still held that same fascination for her. Her desire for him had not waned over time.

His touch continued to ignite the flame as it had the first time that he had kissed her on the dancefloor in the marquee at the wedding of Jimmy Grant's daughter. Eamon had given her a life of happiness with four beautiful children, wealth beyond her dreams and a passionate love that she reciprocated – and yet her soul ached.

Marcia looked out across the bay at the distant bluffs of the mountain range. Her thoughts travelled beyond. She hoped that her firstborn son, Reuben, would hear her prayer for his safety.

Marcia stepped into the bedroom from the walk-in-wardrobe. Eamon was propped up on the bed with a towel wrapped around his waist. He turned to face her. "Red silk!" he said, smiling. He ran his eyes over the cup-less bra, travelling down to the scanty underwear. He smiled at the stilettos. "This getup tells me that ye want hot sex!"

"I thought that we could have an enactment of the first time that you and I made love. However, you may find that I have improved upon my technique!" Marcia said as she sauntered to the bed.

"Our first night was lustful and passionate. We made love… twice," he added, releasing the towel. Marcia smiled at his erection, straddling him, fondling the girth, feeling his shaft thickening.

He removed her shoes. "I would like to make one request," she breathed, her tongue teasing across the tip of his hardness. "The second time, I would like you to take me from behind!"

Eamon smiled at her, relaxing onto the pillow, watching her mouth and tongue move down to his scrotum. She knelt before him, taking him deeper. He caressed her hair, involuntary shuddering.

A while later, Marcia asked him to record a video – he obliged. Afterwards, she lay in his arms, both watching the footage. "I did not realise that I was so noisy!" Marcia giggled.

Eamon glanced back at the screen at Marcia on all fours, with her head thrown back, moaning as he pleasured her. Cries for him to continue filled the room when they reached the plateau. He clicked it off and rose from the bed to lock the evidence of their love making in his safe.

48

It had only taken just over 48 hours for Thomas Harper-Watts to phone Eamon with news on Brennan. They arranged to meet up at the Hawk Wind club so Thomas could fill Eamon in.

A smug smile played at the edge of Thomas's mouth when he sat opposite his boss. "Cormac Brennan's life makes for interesting reading," he said, smiling. "One would find it difficult to know where to start. Each chapter is as intriguing as the next. My father made enquires with his influential associate the Chief Inspector, on the pretext of his son's financial business investment with Cormac Brennan."

Eamon leaned forward, interested.

"Drugs and arms trafficking, also involvement in human trafficking – Arabs, with a fellow in London who is his business partner, also a Dubliner!"

Eamon pursed his lips, giving two sharp nods.

Thomas continued. Shane Shepherd was the main man, and then Brennan came on board. The two have been under investigation for over two years."

Both men grinned.

"My father informed me that Chief Inspector Ross Lowe has a personal vendetta against Shane Shepherd, who has eluded his attempts to bring him to justice. However, London HQ, he said, will now up their surveillance – on both men. They are aware that Cormac Brennan has purchased a golf club in Marbella, with laundered money. Furthermore, your friend Dominic O'Reilly who sold it to him is in the clear. The man pays his taxes!"

Eamon rose, walking to his safe. "Tank yer father for me, Thomas!"

Thomas hesitated at the five wads of 1,000 euros.

"Ye deserve it!" Eamon pressed home.

Eamon sucked air through his teeth, contemplating the human trafficking that Brennan was involved in. He had no qualms about destroying Brennan if he continued to step on his turf unless the Law got to him first. Either way, he was on to a loser, he concluded, locking the Hawk Wind doors after he had set the alarms.

....

Marcia relented and agreed to give Suzette a tarot reading. She was apprehensive, due to the problems that she had caused with her revelation to Joyce Grant. Both women sat in Suzette's lounge. Suzette expectantly waited after handing Marcia the shuffled pack. The air of suspense filled the expansive room. Marcia laid out three cards. She looked at her friend. "Suzette, love will smile at you in the not-too-distant future. A man who has dark skin," She tapped the picture of the Le Chariot. Marcia smiled at Suzette who was staring at the tarot cards. This relationship will be successful, as the man is with business. Suzette inched forward, smiling. "However," Marcia's inflection altered, "there is a warning! Before this new love comes into your destiny, you need to be wary of a traitor, a man who will bestow favours. He will be a Judas, a deceiver," Marcia emphasised, placing her forefinger on the Le Pope card. "Keep your emotions in check with any form of business proposition with this man. Do not be taken in by him." She added, "He is a striking figure. Tall, dark, and handsome. Nonetheless, his charms hide a devil within."

Suzette nodded, forearms on the table. With her hands palm to palm, she clapped her fingers gleefully, beaming. "I cannot thank you enough, Marcia. To hear you tell me that I will not end up on my own is gratifying."

Marcia smiled warmly and explained, "Please do not rush into anything. The man is waiting in the wings of your destiny. He is only a few months away."

"Fabulous!" Suzette exclaimed. "Where would I be without you, my powerful friend!" She reached for Marcia's hand.

"Suzette, I understand that you feel lonely without Greg." Marcia had been through situations with her in the past, such as with Suzette's first husband, Max Greenaway, and then the affair that she had been embroiled with Gary, who worked for Max. Then Greg came on the scene, a chapter that lasted over eight years. Suzette could not be without a relationship. Marcia empathised, as she could not envisage herself being with any man other than Eamon. She felt that what they had together was irreplaceable.

Suzette stated that she required a new wardrobe. "To impress my new man!" Suzette laughed. Marcia shook her head smiling. Although Marcia had a large walk-in-wardrobe with designer dresses, shoes and accessories, Suzette's was on an even grander scale. "I have received an invitation to Joey B and Mel's daughter Sophia's wedding. The women are both clients at my beauty salon. Also, Jane and Billy are getting married. Two big social gatherings!" she laughed, dark brown eyes twinkling. "Hopefully, my new man will be in attendance!"

Marcia was thrilled to see her friend smile easily, after losing the love of her life, Greg. His sudden demise had shaken them all to the core. However, Marcia knew Suzette. It would not take her long to set her sight on a new beau.

. . . .

Eamon sat in his office, resting his elbows on the desk, forefingers pressing either side of his temple, trying to relieve a forming headache. He had received news about his son Niall's disruptive behaviour at school again. He inhaled. He thought that his boy's recent good conduct had been a turning point, however, he realised that it had been only a lull from the battle that Eamon had thought he was winning. Eamon was at a loss as to what method to use with Niall. The school head had informed Eamon that Niall had given Atticus Harper-Watts, Thomas's son, a black eye after a tussle over a young girl. Eamon was gobsmacked, although the two boys were strong willed, they had grown up together and had a strong friendship. The head informed Eamon that the school would not tolerate such behaviour. He exhaled, shaking his head in disbelief that two seven-year-olds would vie for a young girl's attention. Eamon had agreed to come to the school to discuss the matter.

Eamon took the proffered chair, trying to remain cool at the head teacher's overbearing manner. He held the man's eyes, with a steely glare. The head teacher coughed nervously behind his closed fist and spoke more to the room than to Eamon. "The crux of the issue between Atticus and Niall is a fellow pupil, a girl whom, Atticus informed me upon being questioned, Niall had pressed his attention upon. Niall has not defended himself. In fact, your son did not respond to the charges. Eamon smiled caustically. "Are ye trying to tell me that the boys, who I would like to inform ye are friends, are fighting over a girl? Boys will argue!" Eamon stated. Eamon put his hand up, interjecting when the head went to speak. "My son and Atticus have had their disagreements, but our families have a strong connection."

"That may be the case in the world that Niall lives in, however, when at school, physical violence is not accepted."

Eamon's neck reddened. He stood to his full height. The pompous head teacher moved back a step from behind the desk.

Eamon jangled his keys. "I will discipline my son," he said, sneering, "when I see fit!" He paused. "I do hope that we understand one another!" The head teacher remained silent. Eamon turned on his heels, slamming the office door.

Eamon fumed as he strode to his car, clicking the key fob. Upon firing up the engine, he glanced at the school building. He sensed that the head teacher looked down on him and Niall. *The pretentious prick had better be living a clean life, because if he so much as hands Niall a detention, he had better think again,* he thought to himself. He drove with speed out of the school gates. There had been no mention of Atticus being punished for the part that he had played, not that Eamon would have wanted it. However, Thomas Harper-Watts was from the English upper-class. Eamon was not.

He decided that he would not mention it to Marcia until he had had a word with Niall. "How the fuck do you chastise a young lad over a harmless dispute over a girl?" he said aloud. "Seven-year-olds!" He blasted the horn at the driver in front of him on the AP-7 to get out of his way. It was not the incident with Atticus that disturbed Eamon. Niall had given Atticus a black eye. Eamon knew that Atticus could hold his own and that Niall would not have walked away from a blow without fierce retaliation. But the head teacher had not mentioned to Eamon that Niall had been injured in any way.

He placed a call, giving the name of the school and the name of the head teacher.

Later that day, Marcia said that she would collect the boys from school, but Eamon insisted that he would do it. He wanted to speak to Niall without her knowing. Quinn and Niall came through the school doors, their heavy satchels swinging from their shoulders. Quinn was speaking to a boy, the boy laughed, and Quinn waved to him as they parted company. Sullen-faced, Niall walked towards his father's Maserati. Quinn skipped gaily alongside.

Eamon threw Niall a heavy look. "I will speak to ye in yer room when we get home."

Niall nodded, looking at the ground as he opened the back door and got into the car. Making sure the boys were strapped in, Eamon looked at Quinn in the rear-view mirror. "How was yer day?" he asked them both. Niall did not answer.

Quinn beamed. "Papa, I had a great day, although I did struggle somewhat with Latin. My friend Frederick assisted me. The master allowed him," he added. Eamon smiled. He felt there was no point in asking Niall. His son would give him answers behind closed doors.

"I am eager to see Aisling and Aine," Quinn chirped. "May we swim later, Papa?"

"That's grand!" Eamon nodded. "The girls love the water as much as youse boys do!" The sneaky look of disdain that Niall shot Quinn did not go unnoticed. Eamon failed to comprehend Niall's lack of brotherly love for Quinn. He had always had a fondness for his own brother Patrick in Northern Ireland. The distance between them did not prevent them from speaking on the phone regularly. Their bond was strong. Unbreakable. He had hoped that Niall, being the eldest, would have looked out for his brother. Up until now, Niall's jealousy had got in the way.

Marcia came down the villa steps as Eamon arrived with the two boys. The dog padded towards the car. "Mummy your dress is pretty!" Quinn exclaimed, pointing at the leaf-green skirt embroidered with yellow, pink, and purple flowers that swished around her ankles. The bracelets along her forearm tinkled with her quick movement as she embraced both boys. Quinn hugged her with his free arm. She took his satchel. Unresponsive, Niall continued to walk towards the villa.

Both boys ascended the stairs. Aye came out from the kitchen, calling out to them, "Tam gup kaow, gin kaow."

Quinn turned, smiling, holding his hands palm to palm in front of his chest, head bowed. "Kap khun krap," he thanked her for cooking the food.

Aye nodded in response, "Mai pen rai," no problem, she smiled happily returning to the cooking. Marcia went to the nursery while Eamon followed the boys up the stairs.

Niall hung his jacket up and turned to face Eamon. Eamon moved to the bed, sitting down and facing his son. "Niall, I had a phone call from your head teacher today." He chewed the corner of his lip. When Niall hung his head, his heart melted. "Niall, I know that ye and Atticus for the most part are friends. We fall out at times. However, some things will not be tolerated at school. Tell me, son, what brought this on where youse two ended up fighting?"

Niall shifted his position. "Jemima Barclay-Smith is my friend," he said in a near whisper.

Eamon sighed, getting the picture. "The young girl is your girlfriend? Atticus wanted her for his girlfriend too?" Eamon could not believe that he was having this type of conversation with his seven-year-old son.

Niall shook his head. "Jemima said that Atticus's grandfather is a Lord. She wanted Atticus to be her friend!"

Eamon shook his head in disbelief. "Come 'ere son!" Eamon beckoned. Slowly the small boy moved to stand in front of his father. "When ye grow up and meet girls, some want nice, expensive things, however, there are girls that will want ye for who ye are.

"Mummy wears rings and bracelets!" Niall said.

Eamon scratched his goatee. "To be sure!" he tried not to smile as he explained, "Mummy and I are married. Her jewels are gifts from me!" *She certainly did not want me for any titles* he wanted to say. Eamon did not know if Niall understood. Nevertheless, Niall nodded, almost smiling.

"Ye have plenty of time in the future to find a nice girlfriend." He rose from sitting on the edge of the bed, tousling Niall's hair. "Change into yer swimwear and join yer brother and sisters."

Marcia was in the pool with the children when Niall walked down the pool steps. Eamon smiled back at her as she twirled Aisling and Aine in the rubber rings that supported them. He stretched his long legs out, observing. He had met women in his time who had wanted the high life. Eve, his previous wife was no exception. Marcia was different. Although she wore designer dresses now, it had been different in the beginning. She had not wanted to step into his world, his life of crime. He gave it up for her. At the time, the money made from shipments of narcotics had afforded him a certain lifestyle, allowing him to dine at the best restaurants without a thought as to the cost. A twist of fate had boosted his financial situation further, meaning he could purchase his wife anything that she desired. However, he knew his wife. Marcia wanted him and the children rather than diamonds and designer clothing. He classed himself as an extremely fortunate man.

Marcia aided both girls to walk up the steps to a waiting Aye. "Gin khao," Aisling raised her arms to Aye who replied in Thai. Both girls, without a second look, toddled away.

Marcia came up alongside him. Discreetly, he caressed her bottom, keeping one eye on the boys in the pool. "Get our suitcases out. In two days ye and I are going to Lake Como. I have asked Jane to help Aye with the children." Marcia threw her arms around him.

49

Hours before their departure to Italy, Marcia and Eamon were trying to pacify the girls. Both were teething, but Aisling began to vomit. Eamon called Doctor Sanchez, who rushed to the villa. He had checked the girls over. Aisling's previous high temperature began to drop after Marcia had administered some medication. Although Marcia, for the main part, used homeopathic treatment for herself, she went along with the medical advice for her children. After reassuring them that the girls would be fine, the doctor took his leave. The baby girls just wanted to be cuddled. Marcia and Eamon ended up postponing their two-day break for a few weeks. For both, their children came first with them both.

....

The temperature was mild with a balmy, pleasant breeze for Billy and Jane's wedding reception in Eamon and Marcia's villa grounds, which looked spectacular. Eamon had pulled out the stops for his loyal employee, who he classed as a friend, along with Dan. Both men were Eamon's right-hand men. Dan and Eamon were Billy's best men. Eamon had closed the adult club for the night. Marcia wore a Katherine Elizabeth wide-brimmed black hat with two large peacock feathers, the emerald-green, classic capped sleeve dress was coordinated with the colour of the accessories.

Niall and Quinn stood on either side of their father. Eamon's tailor had made the boys' black suits in the same style as Eamon's. Both girls, in Eamon's arms, wore boater hats with an emerald-green ribbon around the crown, and frilly, cream taffeta dresses. Aisling sucked her father's earlobe and Aine snuggled into his neck, eyes drooping. Eamon kissed them both as Aye and Marcia took the girls inside the villa for a nap. Thomas Harper-Watts's sons Atticus and Mathew waved to Niall and Quinn. Eamon smiled at Thomas, as the four boys moved across the grounds together. Eamon noticed Atticus put his arm around Niall's shoulder, their previous tussle forgotten. Quinn and Mathew had their heads together, talking. Eamon took note that Isabella, Thomas's wife, was not with them, although she had been invited. The grounds were packed with friends of Jane and associates of Billy and Eamon. The entire staff of the Hawk Wind were in attendance.

Marcia made a beeline for the bride. "Jane, you look fabulous in your wedding dress!" Jane's newly styled, bobbed hair, just above the shoulders, looked chic. Lloyd and Kieron had transformed her look. Her violet-blue eyes, framed by tinted dark eyelashes, sparkled with happiness. Although Marcia had previously seen the fitted, off-the-shoulder, pearl embossed wedding dress when Jane had tried it on in the shop, it was not until Jane walked towards a smiling Billy at the ceremony, that Marcia noticed her stunning figure. No one was used to seeing Jane in anything other than horse riding attire. The sight of her walking down the aisle brought gasps and smiles from all the women. Billy was also transformed in a black, three-piece suit, handmade shoes, and a black silk tie against a white shirt.

"Billy and I cannot thank you enough, Marcia. When I think back to my previous wedding," Jane laughed. "To marry such a wonderful man and have a wedding like this. I…"

Marcia placed her hand on Jane's arm, interjecting, "Jane, in our circle, we pay it forward!"

Jane, understanding the philosophy, nodded. Marcia watched her walk towards her guests. She waved at Jane's niece Kalita who had arrived for the wedding from England on her own. She was staying to help her look after her aunt's animals while the pair honeymooned in Sorrento, Italy.

Later that evening, the tempo changed. Maureen and Dom arrived late. They had missed the ceremony earlier, due to their daughter returning to America. The children had been put to bed. Quinn and Niall were leaving the next day to stay with Dom and Maureen for a couple of days.

Marcia was taken aback by the transformation in Maureen's appearance. She told her that she had undergone plastic surgery, and nothing, she said, had been omitted. "You look 15 years younger!" Marcia exclaimed to a beaming Maureen. "I am playing Dom at his own game!" she replied. "I went clubbing with my friend Joanie. We both met two fellas. Tell you about it later!" She took her leave. Marcia smiled. Maureen teetered on her too-high heels across the turf towards Jane and Kalita.

Suzette came towards Marcia. Her royal blue, fitted dress, was obviously haute couture. Her scarlet lipstick matched her nail colour. Suzette oozed elegance, no matter the occasion. Both women complimented one another. Suzette scanned the crowd. "I see that Lloyd and Keiron's handsome new friend Lorenzo is here. It is such a shame that women hold no interest for him!" Suzette remarked playfully.

Marcia shook her head at her friend. The young lad was many years younger than Suzette and had recently lost his male partner. His death, Lloyd had told them, had left him bereft. The two hairdressers had met him at a club. Lloyd had taken him under his wing and Lorenzo was working at the reception at the Mystique beauty salon. Marcia thought that Lloyd had other intentions that were other than altruistic. She knew that a handsome man would turn Lloyd's head. On a previous occasion, when Marcia had given him a tarot reading, Lloyd had confessed his digression. She had kept her thoughts to herself about Lorenzo. "Let us join them?" Suzette took Marcia's arm, guiding her towards the group of men.

When Marcia and Suzette entered the marquee, the adults were in full swing. Lloyd was up on the stage with a microphone doing his bit as emcee. The Hawk Wind dancers, wearing low tops and short hemlines were gyrating on the dancefloor. The exception was Sandy, and Martha, who were both dressed in classic dresses. Marcia observed Scott and Benny Harris; both men were focused on the two women. Marcia predicted that it would not be too long before Scott made his move on Sandy.

Marcia was fond of Sandy. She often confided in Marcia and told her that she was not interested in a relationship. Her son's welfare was her priority. *If Scott has patience with her...,* Marcia mused, sensing that they would become a couple. She was a bit uncertain regarding Martha. She had a keen interest in Benny, and although he seemed to reciprocate, Marcia felt that Benny seemed hesitant.

"Penny for them!" Eamon said, circling his arm around his wife's waist. "Silently match making?" He smiled, glancing at the two men standing with their glasses in their hands, watching the women.

"How well you know me!" Marcia said, turning towards him, smiling. He cupped her chin, brushing her mouth with his. Eamon was not normally openly affectionate in company, however, the milling crowd was otherwise occupied, busy talking and drinking.

"It is looking like yer prediction about my men will come to fruition shortly!"

Marcia nodded her head. "Benny will drag his heels with Martha." She paused. "They will eventually become a couple. Both men will have a family with their intended!"

Eamon cocked an eyebrow. "My little mystic has done enough predicting!" he teased. "I tink that I underestimate ye. I tend to forget that ye do not require those cards!"

Marcia slipped her arms around his waist. Although his waistline had expanded since he had put on weight, Marcia was not in the least perturbed. It was his well-being that was at the forefront of her mind. However, Eamon's suits had gone up a size. He had four new ones made, one for the wedding and three for their upcoming two-day vacation in Italy.

"Ye look stunning. I see what you've done matching the emerald-green ribbons on the girls' hats with your dress. Nice touch. A nod to me?"

"Of course!" she replied. "Although I am going to change my dress later."

He pulled her into him. "Leave it on! I like to see that I have put my stamp on ye!"

"You impressed your mark upon me from the moment you first kissed me," she countered.

Eamon nodded, smiling. The music changed to salsa. Cindy's raucous laughter rang out. Keiron had her in his arms, both gyrating, body to body, swaying, bumping, and grinding. Sunni, the black pole dancer wore a dove-grey dress that fit like a second skin and left nothing to the imagination. She hooked her powerful thigh around Lorenzo when he dipped her backwards.

"I have my man for the night!" she called out to the other dancers, who laughed.

Eamon smiled at the antics, although he caught sight of Dan observing Cindy from the side-lines – he wasn't smiling. Lloyd sashayed over, placing his hand on Marcia's arm, and looking at Eamon for approval. Eamon gave a sharp nod. He kept his eye on the man in the jacket embroidered with birds of paradise, whose hands cupped Marcia's rear, his groin meeting hers. Eamon stiffened, changing stance. He had to remind himself that his wife's dancing partner favoured males. The dancers from the Hawk Wind club surrounded them. Marcia's gay laughter could be heard when Lloyd momentarily held her in his arms inches from the floor. Her dress rose too high up her thigh for Eamon's liking – he sucked air between his teeth.

Eamon joined the grouped men near the door. "She would give a man a good night locked in those thighs!" Billy nudged Benny Harris in the direction of Sunni. "Look at those limbs! It would take you a week to prise yourself from her grip once she had you in a headlock!" he laughed. "Why don't you try your luck, mate?"

Benny shook his head, brow raised. "Not for me, Billy. My preference is for a woman to act like a lady in public!" he threw in, smiling.

"What about you?" Billy turned to Scott. "Fancy trying your luck?"

"Leave me out of that one!" he laughed, scouring the crowd. He spotted the dancer who he had been watching earlier talking to Thomas Harper-Watts. "Excuse me, boys!" Scott pushed his way to the other side of the marquee.

Thomas smiled and nodded when Scott approached, taking his leave of Sandy. Scott stood in front of her. "May I get you a drink, and we can get some fresh air?" He asked her, grinning. She studied him for a moment, then agreed.

Scott Lord was surprised at how readily Sandy had agreed to have a drink with him. He took two glasses from a waiter's tray, guiding her to the far end of the terrace to a wooden bench beneath the palm trees. She took the proffered glass, sipped the champagne and pulled a face. "I am not used to drinking!"

Scott took a large mouthful. He felt nervous for the first time in his adult life. He had a lot riding on the conversation that he was about to have with her. "May I take you out to dinner sometime?"

Sandy put her drink aside. "I don't socialise. I have a son to care for."

Scott held her doe-like eyes. Behind them he sensed fear.

He nodded. "Dutiful mothers can have the occasional evening off," he pressed. "I promise that I will bring you home at a reasonable hour!"

She smiled back at him. "I am not one of these women men think will sleep with them after one date," she shot straight from the hip.

"What about after the second date?"

Sandy laughed.

"I like you, Sandy. You caught my eye a good while back, however, you appeared unapproachable. Until I thought that I would make my move when I saw you speaking to that handsome bugger, Thomas."

Sandy blushed when Scott placed his hand on her bare arm. "Give me a chance, Sandy?"

She stood, inches from his face. "Let us dance!" she said, handing him the glass.

Scott beamed.

Lloyd called Billy and Jane to the dance floor for their wedding dance. "This rendition of Etta James's 'At Last' is for two very special people, Jane and Billy!"

Billy led his wife by the hand to the middle of the marquee. Piano accompaniment played through the speakers and Lloyd's beautiful voice filled the marquee. The couple danced, and Lloyd raised his hand inviting the bystanders to join them. Marcia enticed Eamon to dance with her, tapping his shoulder. Watching Billy and Jane embracing, and Scott talking to Sandy, Marcia smiled at Eamon. "Are you cross with me?" she asked.

"Are ye referring to making a spectacle of yerself wit the fella with parrots on his jacket?" Eamon smiled, but Marcia knew that he was not joking.

Eamon went outside to speak with Thomas and Jackie Cooper. Marcia stopped near the entrance of the marquee to speak to the two Irish sisters, Martha and Bridie.

"I love ye dress, the colour suits ye!" Martha said.

Marcia thanked her. The natural redhead was friendly, unlike her sister, Bridie, whose eyes, Marcia noted, projected a hardened element to her personality. She returned the compliment about their dresses to them both. Most of the dancers often confided in Marcia about their personal lives. Marcia gave them advice, up to a point, without becoming overly involved.

Martha had told Marcia about her and her younger sister's life before they ran away from their home in Dublin in the middle of the night. Their drunken, physically abusive father was the reason.

Benny Harris came through the entrance near where the three women were talking. He stopped. "Good evening, ladies!" He looked directly at Martha. "Why are you not on the dance floor, enjoying yourselves?"

Bridie scowled. Martha beaming, took his arm. "I will if you join me," she said.

Benny shook his head. "I put away my dancing shoes years ago."

Marcia stood back, watching Martha coaxing Benny to the dance floor, who did not appear to put up too much resistance. Marcia smiled to herself, watching Martha's arms go round Benny's neck. She excused herself to Bridie.

The two dancers Sandy and Martha, both had previous difficult lives, which had brought them to Spain. The two men Scott and Benny were both wanderers, hardened men who had fought in war-torn countries and faced personal battles. Benny had lost a wife and young daughter to another man while he was away fighting. Scott had been a stuntman, a martial art expert and an Arabian horse trainer for a wealthy guy in the Middle East. *Two young women catch their eye. Their fighting days are over.* Marcia thought, smiling to herself. She walked across the grounds to check on the children. She stepped onto the terrace and saw Eamon standing with a group of men at the far end. As if sensing her, Eamon turned, smiling and winking.

Eamon was listening to Thomas Harper-Watts. Atticus had confessed to his father that the scuffle over the girl had been his fault. Eamon waved the situation away. Nonetheless, he did not forget that it was his son, not Thomas's, who had been hauled across the coals by the head teacher. It was clear that due to Atticus's grandfather being the peer Lord Arthur Harper-Watts, who financed his grandson's education, the incident had been brushed to one side. Eamon had been informed about the head teacher's private life, which made for interesting reading. Eamon was keeping the information on the back burner until required.

50

Eamon spent 35,317 euros for the two-day break to Italy, which was a no-brainer, and he did not break a sweat. Having a private charter jet meant he could be back in Spain within a couple of hours if needed, and he could just write it off as a business expense.

Fortune had shined on Eamon over the years and money was no object. The haulage company and the Hawk Wind club were both successful businesses. The restaurant was also turning a profit. He had various offshore accounts on the Caribbean island of Nevis, Switzerland, and Gibraltar. He also invested in gold bullion and art. There was also the 150 million that he had 'inherited' from overseeing Jimmy Grant's narcotic deal eight years ago.

The King Air 350 jet taxied on the runway after the two-and-a-half-hour flight from Alicante airport, having landed at Milan Malpensa Airport. MXP airport was further away than another airport to their destination, however, the thirty-four-mile journey warranted spectacular scenery and he wanted Marcia to enjoy every moment of the two days that he had arranged for them both in Lake Como.

The chauffer driven black Mercedes moved with expertise through the narrow streets. Torno was 28.1 kilometres further than Bellagio where Eamon had at first wanted to go, however, he had ended up booking the penthouse suite at the Hotel II Sereno Lago di Como for its outstanding views and reviews and Michelin-starred restaurant.

When they arrived, Marcia began unpacking. She had brought two large cases as she wanted to purchase clothing for the children from the numerous shops on the other side of the lake. Eamon had read aloud from the list of the various types of massage available at the hotel. Marcia had come prepared. She was not going to allow anyone to massage her husband, other than herself.

Eamon lay naked on the large bed, relaxed. Marcia thought that, of late, he looked tired. She wore a black, short silk wrap-around as she approached the bed with two small bottles of Contour body treatment oil and Tonic body oil to help drain the lymphatic system. Both were recommended by Lloyd who used them on his clients at Suzette's beauty salon.

Marcia glanced at his resting penis, which would normally be showing interest in such a situation. "Turn over onto your back," she said softly. He complied. Marcia's fingers worked the taut axillary muscle in his neck. Marcia knew that Eamon lived under a lot of stress. Her hands slowly worked along either side of his spine loosening the whole area up.

Eamon closed his eyes. Marcia continued for nearly an hour. He had not responded when her fingers massaged his inner thigh. She realised that Eamon was exhausted and had fallen asleep. Slipping quietly from the bed, she went to the wardrobe to get a robe to cover him while he slept. She changed into a long, cream silk robe and pulled the white muslin curtains across the floor-to-ceiling windows, leaving them ajar.

She stepped onto the balcony. The scene that spread out before her, took her breath away. Eamon had pulled out all the stops for the two days that they would spend away. Eamon had also booked a day trip for them for the following day. The hotel manager had recommended a train journey up to Brunate towards Switzerland to the west. He had told them that the views were magnificent. She picked up the information leaflet on the coffee table next to a large garden chair that would seat two people. The opulence of the hotel and the stunning view of the mountains surrounding the lake seemed surreal to her. Her mind drifted to her life before Eamon. Her son Reuben's face appeared in her mind. The years had passed yet he had not been in contact. Mother and son were in different countries. Just over 3,000 kilometres separated them. She raised her head gazing at the mountain top opposite, sending her silent prayer to him.

The warm, lazy breeze instilled in her a sense of inner peace. A feeling of contentment overcame her. Marcia hoped that she was receiving energy from her son after her prayer for him. She heard an approaching helicopter holding wooden structures in a cradle held fast by chains. Over the next two hours, five trips had been made to the left side of the mountain where large villas were scattered. The last load swung precariously on the chains. Marcia glanced at the boats below. One slip from its anchor and all below would be obliterated. Marcia sat back and thought of how Eamon carried a heavy burden. She knew that his life was precarious due to his past as Jimmy Grant's right-hand man. The Law, at any given moment, could wipe him out, taking her and their children with him.

Marcia left him to rest until the sun began to disappear behind the mountains. Shadows began to fall across the quiet waters. The door slowly opened, and Eamon stood smiling with the towelling robe around his waist.

"Ye should have woken me," he stifled a yawn placing his hand over his mouth. He said, "Marcia, I planned…"

His mobile phone rang from inside the room, and he hurried towards the persistent ringing. Eamon had kept his phone on in case there was a call about the children. He looked perplexed as he stepped back onto the balcony. "Patrick!" he said in surprise. A moment later his demeanour changed. "My condolences to ye. How are ye coping?" Eamon remained silent, phone to his ear. He leaned against the surrounding metal railings. She is free from pain. Life will go on, Patrick!" He stood up, turning to face Marcia. "Do not apologise. I am yer brother!" Eamon looked up to the sky, "I don't hold it against ye, Patrick."

Marcia saw Eamon run his fingers through his hair.

"Ye are not on yer own. I will always help ye," he stated. Eamon clicked the call off, placing the phone on the table. "Patrick's wife has passed away. As ye know, she had breast cancer, and he had been nursing her for over 18 months."

Marcia held her hand out to him. "Patrick has Anna to help him. I know that she has her hands full with her small son." Eamon jumped in. "Patrick has told me that he had lied about the parentage of Anna's two-year-old son. There was no father to Anna's boy living in the nearby village. Young Eamon is his son. I should not have sent her to County Armagh," Eamon chastised himself. "Patrick and Anna will be married, after a reasonable time. He told me that they are deeply in love."

Marcia knew how much Eamon loved and cared for his younger brother. He had given him the deeds to the small holding in County Armagh. He regularly sent funds to aid Patrick and his family. Eamon looked hurt by his brother's confession.

Marcia went to the mini bar, removing the sauvignon blanc that had been chilling in there for over two hours. She knew that Eamon needed it. He took the wine glass without saying any more about his brother's deception. He smiled thinly after taking a gulp and placing the glass on the table.

"Eamon, you told me that Patrick was never in love with Rosie. Yet he did the honourable thing when he made her pregnant. I know that he said that Anna named her baby after you because you helped her and her young daughter by sending them to Northern Ireland to help Patrick and Rosie out."

Eamon elevated his brow, picking up the glass and sipping the wine. "I never intended for them to sleep together though," he countered. "The wee boy is my nephew, my namesake. Rosie must have known, especially if the small boy looks like Patrick, as Conner does. There would be no denying it!" he added.

Marcia rose and switched the Jacuzzi on, returning to take his hand. Knocking back the rest of the wine, he required no persuasion. Arms resting on either side on the edge of the tub, he smiled when she let the negligee slip to the floor. Her nakedness against the backdrop of the dusky mountains as she climbed in was a sight to behold. "People cannot deny when they love each other, as we know."

Her breasts pressed into his chest. She held her arms around his neck.

"I do not deny him. Patrick deserves to be loved!" The heat filled his groin. "Ye win!" He smiled, his tongue searching her mouth. The bubbles stopped and Eamon carried her out of the tub across the balcony towards the bed. Darkness fell, a wind blew up out of nowhere, a flash of lightning lit up the room and thunder clapped on the other side of the mountain. The heat of their passion reflected the brewing storm. Marcia's cries flew on the wind each time that he took her to the peak, eventually crashing together into the oblivion of bliss.

Eamon slept until nearly 8 am the following morning. Marcia had never known Eamon to sleep so late. He was normally an early riser.

After breakfast, they purchased tickets for the top deck of the car ferry. The sun's rays after the previous night's storm played across the lake. A few small boats had broken free from their moorings. Marcia had insisted that they cancel the railway ride to Switzerland. She wanted Eamon to rest, they could return another time she had told him.

Marcia and Eamon got off the ferry at Tremezzo and took a tour of the magnificent architecture of the Villa Carlotta. After two hours of walking, admiring 70,000 square metres of botanical gardens and the museum, Marcia could see that Eamon had had enough, even though he did not complain. She noticed that his breathing had become laboured. Alarmed, they returned to the car ferry to go back to Como. She had wanted to go shopping, but she didn't want to drag Eamon along if he was tired, so she asked him to wait at the restaurant by the edge of the lake. He needed no persuading. Marcia headed off alone to the children's boutiques to buy them presents.

When she returned, she found Eamon preoccupied, gazing across the large expanse of water. The short sleeve white muslin shirt that Marcia had recently purchased for him now strained against his paunch. There was perspiration on his brow, and he looked hot. Marcia was now concerned about his health. She realised that she would have a fight on her hands trying to get him to have a full health check. She sat opposite him, parcels and bags full of the latest children's fashions at her feet. He smiled.

"The girls will be pleased," Eamon said, glancing at the pink shopping bags. The boys are not interested in clothes, but the baby girls do love their dresses. They must get that from their mother!"

Marcia packed while Eamon had fallen asleep for an hour. She was determined to get him to comply with her wishes that he have a health check. They had four hours before the car came to collect them to take them to the airport. She tried not to think of the drive with so many hairpin bends. Eamon stirred, joining her on the balcony.

"I have loved it here with you, Eamon!" Marcia said. He stood behind her, his arms encircling her waist. She turned to face him. "Eamon I am concerned about your health!"

He shook his head. "Marcia, it is stress. I have caught up wit the lack of sleep since we have been here."

"Eamon, Greg passed quickly. He too waved Suzette's fears away. I do not want to have to face my life without you – the children with no father. The boys need your guidance!" she pleaded.

He nodded, exhaling, "Okay!"

She threw her arms around his neck and kissed him.

. . . .

Marcia had taken on Bonita, the sister of Suzette's cleaning lady. Aye, although friendly to the woman, made it clear that it was she who made the household rules. Marcia had left her to it. Eamon's appointment with Dr Saggio was at 2 pm. Marcia wanted to go with him.

Eamon did a urine sample and had blood tests, which Marcia insisted on. The tests covered most things: diabetes, as Eamon had a sweet tooth, blood pressure, pulse rate, height, and weight. Eamon went on the surgery treadmill to have his heart rate measured. His full report was ready the following day.

Marcia sat next to Eamon in the doctor's surgery the next day. Dr Saggio smiled. "You are a very healthy man. Everything has come back fine. Although your BMI is higher than it should be."

Eamon frowned.

"Body Mass Index," the doctor explained. "If you cut down on your intake of calories, do more exercise and drink more water, then I can foresee a long and healthy life ahead of you."

Marcia beamed, thanking the doctor. Eamon gave a sharp nod.

Sitting in his Maserati in the surgery car park, Marcia hugged him. "I am so happy, Eamon. Aye and I will help you to change your diet. I will order more Voss mineral water."

Eamon held up his hand and protested, "If ye women tink that I am going to eat the rabbit food that ye appear to relish, you've got another ting coming!"

Eamon drank the fresh fruit and spinach smoothie. He ate the natural yoghurt with nuts and fresh figs at breakfast. He began swimming in the early mornings, and he was often seen with a bottle of Voss mineral water in his hand. By the time Joey B's daughter Sophia was to be married, Eamon had shed 10 kilos. The new suits that he previously had made were put to one side as they now hung on him. His wardrobe housed his shirts and suits from before his weight gain. He had been measured by his tailor Eugene for a new wardrobe, altering a suit that he required for the upcoming wedding reception.

"You look 10 years younger!" Marcia exclaimed, standing behind him as he dressed, adjusting his tie in the mirror, and smiling at his reflection. "I will have many rivals. The women at the club will be drooling, more than ever!"

He straightened his tie, turning to face her. Placing his hands on her hips, gently pulling her to him.

"My little mystic, don't ye tink that I have enough to contend wit, let alone fighting off females that would offer any man their wares. Ye and the children are my life. I have it all!" He kissed her and added, "Ye get plenty of attention, from men of all ages. Ye are hot!" He pressed into her groin. She reciprocated. "Ye reinvent yerself all the time. One day it's sexy, flowing Asian-style dresses, then red-hot, low-cut mini dresses behind closed doors or seductive, second-skin couture. Classy, yes, nevertheless, ye look horny!" He laughed. "And that cup-less, crotch-less lingerie that ye treat me to when you practise those Karma Sutra positions. Not to mention the handcuffs. Ye are a man's dream!"

She threw her arms around him.

"Ye will need to help me out before we go to work!" Deft fingers released his fly, caressing his swollen shaft. He undressed, slipping the shoulder straps from her black dress and letting it fall. He picked her up, fingers exploring as he laid her on the bed, his body covering hers. "This is a matter of urgency!" he said, smiling.

She gasped upon his entry, taking his measured movements. Passion took over and she bit into his neck, nails raking his back. Joining one another they released in unison.

Still inside her, gradually shrinking, he looked at her and said, "I give ye enough pleasure that ye bite into me, tear my back to pieces and cry out my name as I am taking ye to the edge, and ye worry about my stamina?" he questioned, smiling, cocking an eyebrow.

51

Gun shots rang out along the street from the Hawk Wind club. The club had only opened just over an hour ago. Dan and some of the men stood in the club doorway to see what the noise was. Some African Caribbean young men had been kicked out of the club for causing a disturbance. Billy had heard one of them say that the lads were from rival gangs. Dan and a couple of the security men had stepped in between the two main troublemakers before it got out of hand. However, verbal abuse from both sides continued outside. One guy threw a punch and mayhem ensued. Girls were screaming as a lad slumped to the ground. Dan and Thomas watched as an older style, black Mercedes drove past, with a young lad leaning out of the window, shouting the odds, gun in hand.

"Fucking hell, it looks as if that kid is dead!" A girl was leaning over the lad screaming murder. Both groups of men ran off.

"Ring for an ambulance!" Dan ordered Thomas, who spoke fluent Spanish. Dan knew that the Guardia would not be long in coming. He was also concerned about the club's licence. He did not bother ringing Eamon who would be coming in later. He would deal with it. He informed each security man to deny that they had seen the shooter because it had happened so fast.

Thomas went to try to calm the young girl who was now kneeling on the ground over the body.

Sirens wailed, screeching to a halt when the ambulance and police arrived within minutes of one another.

Dan and Thomas Harper-Watts walked with the police officer into the club office. The officer wanted a statement. Inside, the crisis had gone unnoticed. Pole dancers carried on performing, and men carried on drinking, leering at the women.

Dan closed the door. Thomas quickly gave the officer the run down in Spanish. The officer took notes, however, he told him that the gangs were known to them. The lad that had been killed was the younger brother of the guy that ran the narcotics gang. Both groups were from Javea. No blame was put on the adult club. The officer explained that it was the norm for the two rivals to disrupt any venue that they frequented. Dan gave the officer two complimentary yearly memberships to the adult club, which were gladly received.

Dan, relieved, high-fived Thomas and Billy. The three men went to the bar and ordered three half-pints of lager from Cindy, who was in the dark about the shooting.

An hour later, Eamon, followed by Marcia, entered the club. Dan caught his eye and Eamon nodded, heading towards the office. Dan moved across the floor, smiling as he passed Marcia who was making her way to the dressing room.

Dan went into detail about the night's events. Eamon, sitting in the office chair slapped his hand on his thigh in disbelief. "What would I do witout youse men? If it is not the punters wit the drink in them, and fuck knows what else they throw down their throats, now we end up wit the bastards having a shoot-out."

Showing his agitation, Eamon said, "Let's get the night over and hope that we have heard the last of it!"

Eamon stood at the bar, observing Lloyd and Keiron entertaining the men and women as they juggled cocktails. Lloyd was singing and exaggeratedly sashaying for effect. The women laughed, and the men looked longingly at his rear in the tight cherry-red trousers that left nothing to the imagination.

Eamon had to hand it to the pair. They were a draw. People flocked from the surrounding areas to see them.

Marcia had just gone to the ladies' room when Cindy saw Eamon and called him over, mouthing, "Trouble!" indicating the dressing room. Martha stood by the door as he entered. She hurriedly left to go on stage. Eamon ordered Sunni to leave and went to help Sally up off the floor.

Marcia came out of the ladies' room, crossing to where Cindy was washing glasses. "Eamon is in the dressing room. Cat-fight!" Cindy said.

Marcia marched to the dressing room to see what was happening. She opened the door and, without hesitation, grabbed Sally's arm, which was resting on Eamon's shoulder. He was astride a chair talking to her. The topless girl's face dropped as Marcia spun her round, her face furious. "How dare you disrespect me!" she shouted.

Eamon put his hands up, leaving. Marcia turned on her. "That is my husband. I am the mother of his four children. Don't you or any of the others forget it. Get your things. You are sacked!" Marcia shook with rage.

"Please!" Sally begged, "I have my young daughter to keep back home. My mum can't afford to feed and clothe her."

Marcia poked her. "You must think that I am blind and do not see you eyeing up my husband. You would not care for anyone, only yourself!" Marcia spat.

Tears ran down Sally's face, streaking her mascara. Marcia exhaled, staring at her. "My girl's father left us here in Spain. I had to send her back to England. However, I support her with what I earn here. She only has me to financially depend on!"

Marcia remained momentarily quiet. "This is the only warning that you will receive from me!" Marcia glared at Sally. "Get back to your job!" Marcia stormed out, ignoring Sally's thanks of gratitude.

Eamon was reclining in his office chair when Marcia entered and locked the office door behind her. He raised an eyebrow, tilting his head to one side. "Come 'ere," he smiled, opening his arms. Slowly, she went to him. "I will not be insulted!" He sat her on his lap.

"Did ye give Sally her marching orders?" he asked with a hint of a smile playing at the corners of his mouth.

"At first... then I relented. Due to the fact that she has a child to support. This is her final warning though!"

They were interrupted by a knock on the door. Marcia slid off his lap, straightening her dress. "That will be Scott," Eamon said, patting her rear playfully.

Eamon had spoken to Billy earlier to ask if there were any problems. Billy was concerned about Scott, who looked dejected of late. Eamon knew that Scott and Sandy were an item ever since the pair got together at Billy and Jane's wedding. He asked Billy to tell Scott that he wanted to have a word with him. Eamon sat upright when Scott came in, nodding to Marcia on her way out.

Eamon thought Scott looked as if he had the wind taken out of his sails. "Take a seat, Scott," Eamon rested his forearms on the desk. Although he did not like to interfere in people's private affairs, he asked him how things were going in general. Scott scratched the back of his neck, waggling his head, exhaling.

Eamon continued "You and Sandy, okay?" Billy had remarked that the usual carefree man had become tetchy over the past week. Scott hesitated for a minute. "It does my head in to see Sandy being leered at practically naked, dancing around the poles. To top it off," he looked sheepish, "every time I try to get close to her, she backs away."

Eamon nodded, understanding his plight.

"Do ye want a bit of sound advice?"

Scott smiled, nodding.

"Have ye taken her boy out? Marcia said that he is a big lad who Sandy has looked after on her own. Get to know the boy. Once ye become closer, ye will find that Sandy will also!" Eamon smiled. "Take one step at a time. I will speak to Marcia. If Sandy agrees, maybe Sandy could work behind the bar."

Scott beamed. "I will keep you in the loop, boss!" Scott thanked him. Eamon realised that it was sexual frustration that was behind Scott's mood. Eamon understood how he felt, he would not be able to tolerate seeing his woman tantalising other men by dancing topless for them.

At closing time, Scott approached Eamon at the bar. "Sandy has accepted Marcia's offer of bar work. I am taking her lad out tomorrow, get him into self-defence, horse riding. Sandy seemed happy that I asked!"

Eamon nodded, smiling. He went to walk away, but Scott stopped him. "Sandy asked me to stay over. She is cooking me breakfast in the morning!" Scott grinned.

Eamon pursed his lips, giving a sharp nod of acknowledgement.

52

"My gal is in the family way, my Mel tells me!" Joey B chuckled to Eamon, "I cannot wait to have grandchildren. Did not expect one this soon, nonetheless, me and Mel are thrilled."

Eamon and Joey B stood in the cool late afternoon air; a lazy breeze brought Joey some relief. Joey's luxurious home was located on the other side of the Altea Hills to Eamon. Joey B's reputation went before him; his was a name that people knew and trusted. His successful car business had attracted customers from the surrounding areas to purchase top-of-the-range vehicles. Joey B smiled, turning towards his wife, Mel, who was with a group of women, Marcia among then. "I remember when that gal of yours, Marcia, first came to Spain with her mate, Suzette. Greg Davidson bought a car for each of them, however, your gal was having none of it. She insisted on paying for her car!"

Eamon nodded.

"Decent gal. Good catch!" Joey threw in.

Eamon smiled to himself. He observed Marcia. Suzette appeared to be holding court with the women and laughter could be heard. Running his eyes over Marcia's rear, he smiled to himself. Earlier when they dressed for the reception, Marcia had shown him a preview of her in the

Alessandra Rich, long-sleeved, pink, light-reflecting midi dress, minus her panties. She looked amazing, stunning, however, the figure-hugging dress showed off her curvy rear a bit too much.

The vision rose before him of Marcia with only an hour to spare before they were due to leave, the dress raised to her waist as she mounted him. They had come together. Eamon was brought back to the moment when Joey said, "Sophia's fella Emmanuel appears to have it up top!" He tapped his temple. "University degree of some sort to do with business." He waggled his head. "A bit down the line, if the lad is kosher, I will step back and let the kids help to run the show, while me and Mel enjoy the grandchild. Mind you, I need to lose weight, although Mel calls me her cuddles!" he chuckled. "Nevertheless, I won't be able to run around with my grandchild if I don't get rid of some of this!" Joey patted his paunch, smiling.

Joey B spread his arms wide. "This little lot cost me an arm and a leg." The two marquees filled the grounds. Rock music from a band that Joey had paid to play at the reception blared out. Young people milled around the grounds. "This din will stop later," he shouted when the band increased its tempo. "My Mel saw your twins out shopping with Marcia and that little Thai woman who lives with you. A pair of carrot-tops with green eyes, my Mel informs me. Real beauties!" He mopped his brow for the third time. "Wait until those baby gals of yours are grown. They will give you the runaround." He mopped once more. "Let's hope that they don't get married at the same time, being twins and all!" he chortled. "Here come your pals. I will see you a bit later!" Joey B, a jacket thrown over one shoulder, headed towards a group of people that had just arrived.

Eamon nodded to Jackie Cooper who had just come in. Scott Lord, with Sandy on his arm, came towards them. She broke away, moving towards the group of women and the raucous laughter.

Suzette scanned the crowd. "Suzette is on the hunt!" Cindy teased her. Suzette laughed. "Greg would not have wanted me to live on my own!" Suzette feigned indignation and flicked her thick, dark bob. "There are many good-looking men here. I am going to the other marquee where it is quieter." She waved to the others, determined to look for a new partner, heading in the direction of some older men who were filing into the marquee.

Marcia smiled at Sandy as the rest of the women, dispersed. "Marcia, you look stunning, so chic! I love your hair swept back. The red and auburn glints in your hair are lovely. You never cease to amaze me with how you always look so elegant. You have four children and work at the Hawk Wind club!" Sandy complimented.

Marcia smiled, shaking her head. "I have a lot of help with my children and the running of our household. I don't do it all alone"

"I cannot thank you enough for your help, Marcia!"

"Sandy, you did it yourself. The choice was yours. It was apparent that you wanted Scott as much as he wanted you." Marcia was happy for her. Sandy looked radiant. Her dark brown eyes sparkled. She placed a hand on Sandy's arm. Sandy, blushed. "Have you told him yet?" Marcia did not come right out and say that she thought that Sandy was pregnant.

A dark shadow moved across Sandy's eyes. "I am two weeks late!" she chewed the corner of her lip. "I am always regular," she fleetingly glanced across to where Scott was talking to Eamon and the men. Marcia put a hand on her shoulder. "Sandy, Scott will be thrilled. Tell him tonight. Do not leave it. You will both be happy. I feel that Scott is in for the long haul," Marcia reassured.

Sandy beamed, hugging Marcia.

Suzette took her time in perusing each eligible man. Wedding bands were dismissed, however, she was pleased that so many who she assumed were single were also pleasing to the eye. She had purchased the deep-red, one-sleeve fitted dress, dismissing the hefty price tag. On her, she knew that it looked stunning. Suzette stood near the back; her vantage point gave her a clear view.

"Would ye do me the honour of accepting to have a drink wit me?"

Suzette turned upon hearing the Dublin brogue. Her smile lit up, as did her eyes, as he held her look. Suzette eagerly took the proffered champagne flute. He was over two metres tall, handsome with dark hair peppered with silver streaks, which she thought added to his sophistication. Suzette judged him to be in his fifties. His broad chest and trim waist indicated that he took care of himself. All in one swoop, her eyes missed nothing – the cut of his suit, the insignia on his cufflinks. Glancing at his handmade shoes, her smile increased.

"May I introduce myself?" He did not wait. "Cormac Brennan." He looked briefly over the heads of the crowd. "I do not know anyone, apart from Joey B, who invited me after I purchased a car from him. I could have used another dealership in Marbella where I live, nevertheless, I would prefer to spend my money with a reputable man such as Joey B. Not that I am a man who is a penny pincher!" He laughed. "My golfing club is being upgraded. The millions do not concern me. Underhandedness does, however!"

Suzette swooned. She glanced at his fingers – bare of rings. "I am Suzette," She held her free left hand out, ensuring that he noticed that it was free of rings. "I own the Mystique beauty salon, which I opened when I first came to the Costa

310

Blanca. It has been extremely successful over the years, to the point that I am seriously thinking about purchasing a property in Puerto Banus. Marbella is part of my future business vision."

"Destiny appears to have put us together!" Cormac Brennan flashed his perfect, white porcelain veneers that had cost him a thousand pounds per tooth. "I hope that ye do not tink that I am jumping the gun." He flashed his smile. Suzette shook her head and he continued, "I have contacts in real estate in Marbella if ye need assistance?"

Suzette profusely thanked him. "I cannot believe that a beautiful woman such as yerself has not captured a man's heart!" He indicated her wedding ring finger. "My wife left me for a younger model. She wanted someone closer to her age." He confessed, "It can get lonely at times, even though my life is busy with business." He placed his hand on her bare arm. "Please do not allow me to burden you with woeful stories about my wife leaving me!"

"I was in a relationship for many years with a wonderful man. Sadly, he passed away." Suzette stopped at that; she did not want to ruin anything with this new encounter. She had no intention of letting him slip from her grasp.

Cormac Brennan had previously been keeping a low profile. He had seen Eamon O'Donally on the other side of the grounds, speaking to two men who he recognised as the Brinkman brothers, who owned a night club in Benidorm. Cormac had been introduced to the pair by his business partner Shane Davis when Cormac and Shane had visited a club that they also owned in the West End of London. The brothers, Shane had informed him, were renowned for their extreme violence if anyone stepped on their toes.

Cormac had seen O'Donally's wife. He had taken his time admiring her. Sexy and classy. He had rubber-stamped her.

He would enjoy fucking her. His plan was underway. Cormac had spotted the attractive woman in the red, one-sleeve dress with black-bobbed-hair and curves in all the right places.

He smiled into Suzette's dark brown eyes. Her black false eye lashes fluttered. Assured of no obstacles with Suzette, Cormac laid down the next step of his plan. "Would you like to go out for some air?" he asked, fanning himself. Suzette allowed him to guide her towards the entrance. Cormac was aware that Eamon O'Donally would see him. Unperturbed, he crossed his line of vision, making a beeline to the perimeter of the grounds where there was seating.

Cormac stood before Suzette, back turned to the eyes that he sensed were on him. Suzette crossed her shapely legs. He admired her. She certainly was attractive. His experienced eye ran over her attire. At a guess, the dress was from one of the big fashion houses. He could see the fire behind her dark eyes, which excited him. He smiled. "I would like you to see my latest venture when you visit Marbella. Not for one moment would I tink that ye would be interested in golf though!" He gave a soft laugh, continuing, "I decided to change direction when I was introduced to Dominic O'Reilly's associate, who informed me that the golf club was on the market!"

Suzette raised a quizzical eyebrow. "Dom and Maureen O'Reilly? Do you know them?"

Cormac smiled. "Yes, and Eamon and Marcia O'Donally. Eamon is from the same district as I am in Dublin. However, our paths separated. I met up wit him and his family when Dominic invited me to a gathering at a restaurant prior to purchasing the golf club."

"That is wonderful that you and Eamon have a connection," Suzette enthused. "Marcia O'Donally is my dearest friend. We have a history!" Suzette beamed.

Cormac nodded, smiling, his mind churning. A south-westerly gust rustled palm-fronds. "Would you like to dance?" Cormac asked.

Scott Lord had not taken his eyes off the big guy. Something made him suspicious of the guy who he had previously seen ogling Marcia O'Donally, his look lingering on her. Scott thought that he had recognised his face, although for the moment he could not place where he had previously seen him. Scott had watched him follow Suzette into the marquee. A short while later, Scott's attention was trained on the man when he exited the marquee with Suzette. The pair were under his observation as they moved to the perimeter. He turned his attention back to Sandy, however, his mind was checking for the memory of Scott's previous connection with him.

Eamon sucked air through his teeth after catching sight of Cormac Brennan who strolled across the lawn towards the marquee. Stomach churning, he nodded to himself. *Ye tink that ye can push yer luck wit me,* he inwardly fumed. Marcia came into his vision, and he returned her smile as she approached.

Linking her arm through his, she asked, "Is everything alright?" She noticed the icy, dark look in his eyes.

He exhaled, "That prick Cormac Brennan is here!" he nodded towards the marquee. Marcia froze, knowing how intensely Eamon disliked Cormac.

"Eamon, we can make our excuses…"

He interjected, "Fucking make our excuses?!" He shook his head. "He is on my turf. If anyone is to leave, that prick will!"

Marcia remained silent. Scott and Sandy came towards them. Scott pulled his boss to one side while the women talked.

"It's that guy that I spoke to you about earlier, the one who looks a bit suspicious and is eyeing up the women." Scott did not mention that he had seen Cormac ogling Marcia. "I remember where I have seen him before. He had dealings with Mohammad Aaryan in Saudi when I worked as a horse trainer for his Arabian horses." Scott told Eamon how he had ridden past the two men on his way out of the stables. He remembered that Mohammad had stopped and introduced him to Cormac Brennan, who admired the stallion. "I thought that he looked shifty back then. The Arab is into arms dealing. Like attracts like! He would be mixed up with that lot!"

Eamon nodded. "Let us enjoy the evening!" he said, returning to the women and taking Marcia by the arm. Scott grinned.

The 70s and 80s soul music played, and couples slowly danced, bodies entwined, to Barry White's sexy, gravelly tones. Eamon took Marcia's hand. Scott and Sandy followed them to the dance floor. Eamon moved to the left side of Cormac Brennan, who had his arms around Suzette. She was gazing up at him, smitten. Scott Lord and Sandy were to the right of Brennan. Eamon and Scott glared at him. He seemed unperturbed and smiled smugly at them. But there was a flicker of recognition as he met Scott's hazel-green, hardened eyes with flecks of gold. He remembered that Mohammad had referred to this man as Cobra. Mohammad had informed him that the name was well-deserved as the man was as lethal as his namesake.

"Are there not any women to yer liking in Marbella, that ye must travel so far to get yerself one?" Eamon's Arctic glare matched his tone.

Marcia stiffened. Eamon's gentle but firm grip held her fast as they continued to dance. Suzette looked up, smiling. "I would have missed out on this charming lady if I had refused Joey B's invitation!" Cormac threw back, ignoring the slight.

Eamon caught Scott's look of disdain. Cormac dismissed both men, smiling into Suzette's eyes, gradually moving away from them.

Marcia was relieved that Cormac Brennan was leaving, however, she could not believe that Suzette was going with him. *How could Suzette be so foolish?* Marcia wondered. She had advised her to wait before jumping into anything, but her words were wasted. Suzette, as in the past, never heeded her warnings.

Later that night, after returning home, Eamon checked on the children, satisfied that they were sleeping contentedly. He entered the master bedroom where Marcia stood silhouetted next to the floor-to-ceiling window. She wore a short, black silk negligee wrapped loosely over a matching cup-less bra and ouvert panties. She gazed out across the vista, sending her nightly silent prayer to her son Reuben. She turned to him, smiling.

Eamon undressed silently, his eyes locked on her. Marcia sensed that he was perturbed. She could understand why. Greg had been his friend and loyal business partner and Suzette had just gone off with a man who was Eamon's arch-enemy from the past.

She slipped the silk wrap from her shoulders and went towards him. His resting penis stood to attention. He swept her into his arms and lay her across the bed. Her fingertips ran along his jawline, and she stroked his hair as he went down, bucking when his tongue softly flicked her clitoris. She tightened her grip on his head between her legs. Breathlessly, joyously, she began to climax. He took her nipple in his mouth, and she arched when his pulsating member entered her, causing her to climax again and again, deeper with each measured thrust.

They held each other in an embrace, tongue seeking tongue with a soul kiss. He stayed inside her. His hands held either side of her face. "I would haunt ye if ye ever took another man into yer bed after my death!" he said, smiling thinly.

Marcia knew that he meant it. He was referring to Suzette. She did not want to spoil their time together and knew she needed to choose her words carefully. Eamon arched an eyebrow, waiting for a response.

"Eamon, I could never replicate what we have together with anyone else." She brushed his lips with hers. "My love for you runs so deep that I know it will stay with me until the end." She held his eyes, feeling him grow thicker inside of her once again. Marcia sensed that she had appeased him. They made love again, slowly, coming together.

53

Marcia had received a text from Suzette the following day, asking if she could visit her at her villa as she had the morning off work. Marcia guessed that Suzette wanted to tell her about her evening with Cormac.

Eamon had gone to the haulage company with Dan, Billy, and the new detection dog Caesar, who Marcia immediately fell in love with. Eamon had dropped the two boys at school. Aye and Bonita were entertaining the girls. Within the hour, Aisling and Aine would have a nap. Roman, the faithful old Belgian shepherd walked with her to her car. She tickled his ears. Although he was ageing, Marcia felt assured that the canine could still protect them for a long while yet.

Suzette looked somewhat tired but happy, giving it away that she had spent half the night in bed with Cormac Brennan. Marcia sighed inwardly. Suzette slipped her arm through hers. "Come through. We can sit on the terrace. Coffee or Voss?" She picked up a bottle when they passed the open-plan kitchen.

"Coffee, please." Marcia felt that she would need the caffeine to bolster her resolve once Suzette had bombarded her with talk of the new man.

A few minutes later, Suzette came out, cup and saucer in hand and sat opposite Marcia at the large table. "This place no longer feels lonely!" she did a 180-degree twirl with her arms outstretched. My life has changed since yesterday. Furthermore, so has my previous non-existent sex life!"

Marcia shook her head, but Suzette did not notice. She told her that Cormac had stayed until just before dawn. "The man is virile. When he showered after our return from the reception, I was ready for him on the bed. But I was unprepared when he dropped the towel that he had wrapped around his waist. The length! The girth!" She held her hands apart indicating the size. Marcia shifted uncomfortably in her seat. Suzette, oblivious to Marcia's discomfort went into detail about how he had hurt her, but she had found it pleasurable.

"Thank goodness that I had shaved. He said that he favoured no hair."

Marcia coughed, more out of embarrassment. Suzette had always been open and too explicit about her previous sex life with Greg and her lover before him, but it was too much for Marcia this time. "Thankfully, I had some lube in the bedside cabinet left over from Greg. Cormac went on for hours. To please him, we finished off by having anal, but he was gentle." She smiled.

Marcia put her hand up, anger showing. "Please, Suzette, enough! I have known you for a long time. It is not your sexual exploits that are causing me concern. It is the man. Why have you never listened to me? You ask me to give you a tarot reading because you want advice, yet you jump in with the first man who shows you attention. I warned you about him. You did the same when you were with Max. I warned you about Gary, however, you ignored it and he betrayed you, as Cormac Brennan will!"

Suzette looked hurt. Marcia leaned across and patted her arm.

"Marcia, I am lonely on my own. What is the good of having all this wealth that Greg left me if I have no one to share it with? I need to be loved, to feel reassured in a strong man's arms. If this new relationship peters out…" her smile returned, "then there will be another."

Marcia felt that there was no more to say to her friend. "Please take it slowly. I know that you are going to be very happy with another man who is waiting in the wings of your destiny. However, the timing is not right yet, and you will have to wait."

"Allow me to say something, Marcia," Suzette said, taking Marcia's hand in hers. "You have your man, a beautiful family. I have no one. Only you. My dear friend."

Marcia nodded, knowing that she would be there to catch Suzette when she fell, which Marcia sensed would not be too long in coming.

"Cormac has invited me to stay at his home in Marbella. I will ask Lloyd to look after the salon for me while I am there. I can look around for any suitable premises for another beauty salon while I am there."

Marcia knew that Suzette had been thinking about expanding her business for a while. She wanted to advise Suzette not to get involved in a business venture with Cormac Brennan, but knowing that her warnings would fall on deaf ears, she remained silent.

54

In Eamon's office, Billy informed him that Scott said he was thrilled at the thought of becoming a father. He and Sandy were making plans to get married before the baby's arrival. "The man talks of nothing but the changes he is going to make to the villa that he has put a deposit down on in Calpe. Benny Harris introduced him to a guy in the property business. Strings were pulled, and he said that a deal was struck under the table. Scott has taken Sandy's boy under his wing, training the lad at Elliot's gym."

Eamon smiled. "They are welcome to have their reception at my home, as ye and Jane did. I will foot the bill. If that is acceptable to the couple. Speak to him."

Billy left to join the rest of the club's security team.

Eamon sent a text to Marcia who was at home with the children. He had arranged to take Marcia out for a meal midweek. Billy would be standing in at the club, alongside Dan. It was Eamon and Marcia's wedding anniversary. They always kept their birthdays and anniversary private, celebrating quietly together. They had married while Marcia was pregnant with Quinn. He smiled at the memory of Marcia in her wedding dress with a baby bump, breast feeding Niall. He had never seen anything so beautiful. Blood rushed to his groin as the vision came to his mind, and he adjusted himself. He understood how Scott felt about his forthcoming child. He remembered that when Marcia was pregnant with Niall, he had sent her to Thailand until the baby was born, because of the danger of a 'grass' who was pointing the finger at Eamon's associates.

There was a knock on the door. "Come in!" Eamon said.

Scott Lord entered, beaming from ear to ear and taking a seat. "Billy has just told me about your generous offer for our wedding reception at your home!"

Eamon nodded. "I have spoken to Sandy. We are both thrilled."

"That's settled then!" Eamon said. "I will see to the catering. The bill will be covered by me, once ye and Sandy give me figures. I know that ye have a lot on wit yer new home and a baby on the way. Ye can take yer woman away for a few days. I can highly recommend Lake Como in Italy. Marcia and I will return there someday."

"I'm afraid that is out of my financial league at the moment, boss!"

Eamon put his hand up. "The honeymoon comes as a gift from the men. Furthermore," he said, smiling, "once ye return, I am sure that yer services will be required!" Scott shook his head again with a look of amazement at Eamon's generosity. He held his hand out and Eamon shook it.

Locking the door behind Scott, Eamon heard his mobile pinging. Marcia had sent several picture messages. Settling back in the office chair, he perused the first one. The baby suckling at her breast, which was becoming less frequent of late unless the girls were fretful, the leaf-green silk negligee and matching cup-less bra, the baby's hand on the free breast. Eamon zoomed in on his wife's parted legs. The vision of what lay between the opening of her ouvert panties caused a rush of heat to his loins.

He loosened his tie and unbuttoned the top button of his shirt. He could not look any further. He sent a reply. 'Rest before I come home. It is going to be a very long night.' He sent five heart emojis.

His walkie-talkie crackled to life, breaking his thoughts. "Spot of trouble, boss! Footballers!"

Thoughts of Marcia put aside, Eamon sighed, joining the security men, who were trying to calm the group of celebrity footballers, worse for wear for celebrating their victory win at the bar and demanding private strippers.

. . . .

Two days later, Marcia was faced with a dilemma. She had spoken on the phone to Suzette when she had returned from her stay in Marbella with Cormac Brennan. Marcia had hoped that Suzette's enthusiasm for the man would have waned, but Suzette had gushed down the phone about the amazing time that she had spent with him. Marcia was going to go to the salon and have a coffee with her. She realised that she would have to break the news to her about Cormac, as Eamon had threatened to inform Suzette if she didn't.

Suzette looked radiant when Marcia came into the busy salon. Cindy and the two male hairdressers waved in greeting. Lloyd's client was laughing as he continued to gesticulate. Marcia missed the camaraderie and the buzz. There wasn't the same vibe at the Hawk Wind club.

"Come into the staff room," Suzette said. Marcia followed. Suzette busied herself making two coffees. Marcia took a seat. "I have some exciting news. I have put a 250,000-euro deposit on a property in Puerto Banus. It will become my second salon. It has a large one-bedroom apartment above it. It's all thanks to Cormac and his contact in real estate. Cormac took me to see it. You will love it, Marcia. I am so thrilled. I thought that I would name it Voodoo Woman, to keep in theme with this one."

Marcia took the coffee cup, thanking her.

Suzette continued, "Cormac loved the name!"

Marcia shifted in her seat, feeling uncomfortable.

Suzette changed the subject. "Sandy from the Hawk Wind club came in to have her hair restyled. What a transformation for the lovely girl. She told us that she is pregnant and getting married to that handsome security guy, Scott. He looks rather randy – a man with sex appeal." Her eyes sparkled mischievously. "I hope the girl will be able to handle him. Those eyes of his are scary. I love a wedding! She invited me, plus a guest, also all the staff here received invites."

Marcia knew that she had to get it over with. It was better coming from her than Eamon, who would not pull any punches. "Suzette, Eamon has offered our home for their reception. As a wedding gift, he is paying for the catering."

Suzette clapped her hands. "You and I need to go shopping. Perhaps Barcelona, or Rome!" she sipped her coffee.

Marcia braced herself. "Suzette, you cannot bring Cormac Brennan to the villa."

Suzette looked astounded. "Why not!"

Marcia quietly exhaled. "Eamon and Cormac are not friends. There was some form of dispute between them in the past. Eamon is unforgiving."

Suzette shook her head. "You are wrong. Cormac holds no ill feelings for Eamon. He told me that they had fallen out when they were young men. However, he feels that it is water under the bridge." Her eyes searched Marcia's.

Marcia was silent for a few seconds. "My hands are tied, Suzette. Eamon will not tolerate him!"

Suzette stood her ground, dark eyes blazing. "Who the hell does Eamon O'Donally think that he is? This wedding is Sandy's and Scott's, not his. He has always governed your life, Marcia."

Marcia rose, picking up her shoulder bag.

Face aflame, Suzette continued to rail against Eamon.

Marcia slowly turned to leave. "Please do not let this come between us, Suzette."

Suzette sneered, "If he thinks that you and I will fall out and I will be out of your life, he can think again. Thankfully, I had the common sense when I gifted you my 50 per cent share of the club, to put in the stipulation that he can never buy you out!"

Marcia walked out through the salon. There was laughter throughout from the lad's banter. Thankfully no one had heard Suzette and Marcia arguing. Marcia hoped that Suzette would not bring Cormac Brennan to the wedding ceremony. She had done her bit. Marcia wanted to enjoy the rest of the day with the children, then Eamon had booked a table at a restaurant to celebrate their anniversary.

The girls splashed in the pool; the boys had gone to help Jane with the horses. Jane suggested that they stay the night, so Eamon and Marcia could go out. The boys had school the following day, so Marcia had packed their school uniforms and swimsuits. Eamon was going to collect them in the morning and drive them to school. Jane's niece Kalita was staying for a few days. While Jane entertained the boys, Kalita gave Marcia a tarot reading. Marcia had found some of the predictions unsettling, however, she put them to the back of her mind.

Marcia could not resist putting on the black, ruched Mugler dress. It was mini on one side, knee length on the other. The asymmetrical design, although classy, with long sleeves, had a cut-out neckline, which previously Eamon thought was too

sexy to wear in public. However, the passing of time had soft-
ened his outlook.

Eamon turned when Marcia came through the terrace
doors. "Ye seem to need to project ye sexuality!" he stated, the
hint of a smile forming at the corners of his mouth. "I hope that
ye are wearing underwear! Just because it's our special day, don't
tink that ye can use it as an excuse to show so much flesh." He
checked his watch. "Our table is booked for 7 pm." He drew her
to him, nuzzling her neck, hands clasping her rear. Her arms went
around his neck "Ye can leave the dress on when we get back
tonight. I tink the evening calls for handcuffs!" he breathed, softly
nibbling her neck. "There are two sets in the bedside cabinet."

The restaurant was busy for mid-week. The waiter
showed them to their table. The owner of the restaurant in Calpe
came through the kitchen doors as they were seated. His smiling
face welcomed them as they sat down.

"Luigi!" Eamon said, shaking the Italian's hand. Eamon
had known the proprietor for years. Although Eamon made
use of his own eatery, he also ate at other restaurants, including
Luigi's

"You both look as if you are celebrating," Luigi remarked,
looking from one to the other.

Eamon glanced at Marcia and then back to Luigi. "We
are quietly celebrating our wedding anniversary."

Luigi snapped his fingers to one of the staff, mouthing
an order. "Meraviglioso!" he enthused. Minutes later a waiter
brought a bottle of Krug champagne to their table. "Enjoy your
evening!" he bowed, leaving the waiter to pop the cork and pour
the champagne into two crystal flute glasses.

Earlier, Billy had informed Eamon that Jane's niece
Kalita was staying at their home for a few days. Knowing that
she had an interest in the mystical arts, as did Marcia, Eamon

wondered if Kalita had given Marcia a tarot reading. "When ye took the boys to Jane's today, did ye see Jane's niece?"

Marcia blushed, picking up the flute and taking a sip. "Yes. Kalita was not busy; she gave me a tarot reading." She took a bigger sip. Eamon nodded.

"Did she say anything interesting?" He drank, eyes on her.

"She spoke of America for both of us. You will travel there. I will travel later." She omitted the part about a warning of two women connected to Eamon.

"I cannot read the tarot cards for myself. My intuition plays a big part." Marcia added as they placed their orders.

Eamon was curious. He had seen a bank statement of Marcia's. Eleven thousand euros was paid to a jeweller. He always purchased her jewellery, so he was intrigued as to why she felt the need to buy expensive jewellery herself with her own money that she earned from her half share in the club. Furthermore, she had not mentioned it.

They ate their meal. Eamon had a slow-roasted lamb dish with rosemary and oregano. Marcia had fish – bacalao with chickpeas. He asked her if she had spoken to Suzette. He was satisfied that Marcia had said what needed to be said. Nothing more was mentioned on the subject.

Eamon smiled at the small, wrapped box that Marcia took from her bag. He opened it. "They are grand!" he exclaimed, removing one of the Tateossian rare stone cufflinks.

"I thought that the black diamonds complimented the white gold and looked so suave!" Marcia said.

Eamon's smile spread, realising what the mysterious bank account entry was. "I have a gift for ye too." He produced a box, sliding it towards her.

She gasped upon opening it. "Eamon!" she breathed, taking the emerald-encrusted ring from the box. You have given me so much!"

He leaned across, and took it from her, slipping it onto her finger. "The stones are the colour of the baby girls' eyes." He returned her brief kiss.

"Before we go home, can we drive to the top of the hills? The panoramic view is breath taking!"

Eamon nodded. Marcia excused herself to go to the ladies' room.

They sat in Eamon's car under the star-spangled sky at the highest point of the hill. "So much has happened since we first met!" Marcia said. She turned to face him. "I know that there have been times when I have caused you problems. I understand how precarious your life – our lives – are. I will never do anything to hurt you, Eamon!" She reached across to kiss him.

He gently eased her across his lap. "Neither will I hurt ye!" he countered. The zip on her dress slid down easily. He unbuttoned his shirt and opened his fly. He pushed her dress above her waist; his erection found her. Marcia rode him. "Ye lied to me. No panties!" He held her buttocks, meeting her with thrusts.

"They are in my bag," she sighed. She cried out with his last thrusting.

A sharp rap on the car window suddenly brought them back to the moment.

"For fuck's sake, Marcia. It's the Guardia!" Hurriedly, they dressed.

"I am driving!" Marcia mouthed, knowing that Eamon would be over the legal drink-driving limit.

Eamon got out of the car. The young officer pointed his torch, indicating for Marcia to get out of the car too. He shone the flashlight over them, momentarily resting his gaze on their left hands. "Documentos!" he ordered.

Marcia returned to the car to get her residence document and driving licence from her bag. Eamon produced his from his wallet. Shining the torch over the green documents, the officer studied them and nodded.

The officer took out the breathalyser to test them. "Hawk Wind?" He glanced at Eamon's work permit. Eamon nodded. Eamon exhaled in relief as the breathalyser was put away. "Good club," the Guardia said, a hint of a smile playing on the corners of his mouth. Eamon knew that off-duty Guardia frequented the adult club.

"Muchissimas gracias." Eamon thanked him. He knew very little Spanish, only basic words.

"De nada," the officer said, half turning in the direction of Altea Hills below. "Go home now! Illegal!"

Eamon exhaled when the Guardia drove away. Both remained silent until the rear lights of the police car disappeared down the hill. They got in the Maserati and Eamon fired up the engine.

Eamon turned to Marcia. "How humiliating. That young Guardia could only have been in his late twenties!" He drove on. "No more. Ye planned for us to have sex up here. Yer panties were in yer bag!" he accused, momentarily turning to look at her.

Marcia put her hand across her mouth to stifle a giggle.

"Marcia, do ye realise how serious the Law out here is for indecency!" She placed two hands over her mouth as she burst out laughing.

55

Cormac Brennan had kept the staff on when he had purchased the golf club from Dominic O'Reilly, bringing in only a new manager, Jack Reynolds, who came highly recommended by Shane Davis, his business partner in London. Shane had informed him that Jack had managed two pubs in the past for Shane. The man had a reputation for being a ladies' man, however, that went with the territory. The guy had also previously been a male stripper. It was Jack's discretion and ability to teach a lesson to anyone who trod on Shane's toes that interested Cormac.

Shane and Cormac had worked many scams together. He owed his turn of good fortune to Shane, who he had bumped into at a luxury hotel in the rainforest in Bali while on honeymoon with his young wife Angelica. Cormac had been infatuated with the blonde beauty with the perfect body and looks, but she was insatiable. Cormac had to keep her in the style that she demanded. There was also the problem of all the younger studs vying for her attention. She thrived on it. What Angelica lacked in eloquence and intelligent conversation, she made up for with unbounded knowledge of beauty products and the latest designer gear.

They had been leisurely lounging around by the pool, bored, when fate played its hand and Cormac felt a tap on his shoulder. Cormac turned. The man raised his sunglasses. Both men smiled, shaking hands. Shane Davis and Cormac Brennan had a history. Both were brought up in the Ballybrack council estate, located in Dun Laoghaire-Rathdown, Dublin. They reminisced about how they had stolen lead off the church roof and had not confessed their sins to Father O'Boyle or the fact that they had taken themselves to 'hand' as youngsters. They both admitted that the mortal sin that the father preached to the boys had terrified them, albeit, not enough to get them to confess. They rolled back the years with much laughter.

Shane gradually took Cormac into his confidence, speaking to him about potential new business ventures, while their wives went on day trips together. They had been fascinated with the Tirta Wat. The temple, which was 19 kilometres away, drew them daily. Both women wanted to learn about Buddhism, much to the delight of both men. Their absence gave them hours of freedom to talk privately.

Cormac stepped into the world of arms dealing, which took him to Africa, Libya, and the Middle East. It had become his bread and butter. Cormac went from financial strength to strength with his new business partner.

More recently, Cormac had asked Shane for a favour, giving him the name of the man who he detested.

"I can't say that I recall an Eamon O'Donally. That name eludes me," Shane said.

Cormac pressed on. "Do ye remember that pretty girl that I was seeing? Ye used to rib me that I was punching above my weight!"

Shane laughed. "Jodi, big tits, nice arse." The penny dropped. "Ye got to be fucking mental!" he gasped when the memory came flooding back. "Ye are talking about the dark-haired, good-looking fella that was in the correction centre for a time. Upon his release, we lads couldn't get a look in with the girls. He had his pick of the local lasses. That Jodi had the hots for him. I remember the hiding he gave ye for trying to get in on the act. Although it was well known that he only used her. Then there was the second time, as I recall when he gave ye a leathering and threw ye in the river Poddle! Thank fuck that ye could swim!" Shane chuckled at the memory.

Cormac bristled. "We were boys, young bucks then. He wouldn't get away with it today!" Cormac countered.

"Fucking steer clear of him. Eamon O'Donally would come back at yer like an 8-tonne digger on speed!" he warned. "The guy was nearly the death of ye. Don't push yer luck! Leopards don't change their spots. That one had no stop button!" he added.

Cormac dismissed Shane's warning.

"Be it on yer own head!" Shane said, accepting that Cormac would not heed his advice. He would send Jack Reynolds to Marbella to aid Cormac if needed. Cormac was pleased with how the situation was beginning to unfold. He was looking forward to Suzette's visit. She had told him that she had been invited to the wedding of one of Eamon's security guards. When she had asked him if he would like to join her, Cormac readily accepted the invitation. Suzette suited his plan nicely. He enjoyed her in bed, although he had only tested the water with her sexually. She had ticked all the right boxes – good figure, attractive, successful businesswoman. She was the key that would open a gateway for him. He had shown her the building in Puerto Banus town with the one-bedroom apartment above it, which Suzette had eagerly snapped up. His associate Brian Morley had given him the keys so that he could take her there. He grinned to himself.

Jack Reynolds did not disappoint. He was over two metres tall, a good-looking guy, on the wrong side of 40. He had a muscular physique, manicured nails, and a winning smile. Cormac summed him up upon their first meeting. He could see that Jack was a ladies' man who wanted the high life – the typical champagne taste but lemonade money, money that Cormac would provide.

He smiled, shaking Jack's hand. Jack filled him in about his past. He had married young and had three children by the age of 20, living in a council flat in Ilford, Essex. Jack was never at home. Twenty years later, Mandy, his long-suffering wife, at age 36, went to the Caribbean on a three-week cruise, paid for by her sister, and met a new man. She now lives the high life with her Barbadian husband and five-year-old in the Caribbean. Jack tagged her as a whore. Cormac sympathised. Jack went on to name as many women as he could remember that he had slept with from the time he had met Mandy. Cormac congratulated him. Jack did not go into too much detail when he told Cormac that he had helped rid Shane of a couple of guys that had become a nuisance. Satisfied, Cormac made plans for his next step. He needed to rid himself of the need to scratch the itch that had been irritating him ever since Eamon O'Donally had thrashed him, twice.

Jack Reynolds did a double take when the beautiful, young brunette walked into the golf club. Well above average height, with shoulder-length hair, she had a confident air. He noticed her unvarnished, manicured nails, with no rings on her fingers. Jack took an inventory, sizing her up. The girl was classy. Not his normal choice, but he could not look away. Chantelle, the barmaid waved to her.

Approaching the barmaid, he indicated to the brunette. "Who is she?" She smiled warmly towards the subject. "That is Sheila O'Reilly, the previous owner's daughter. She has been staying with her sister in America. Landed herself a rich guy out there. She won't be back here for long!" she predicated. Jack nodded. He loved a challenge. He walked to the other side of the club where Sheila was seated by the floor-to-ceiling windows that gave a view out to the green. He introduced himself. He was hooked. Sheila was not. However, making small talk, she informed Jack that she was eager to see her parents' friend's children. Niall and Quinn O'Donally were arriving the following day to spend the weekend with them. "I owe Eamon O'Donally a debt of gratitude for helping to save my life," she said. Sheila left it hanging in the air. Jack was dumbstruck. He couldn't believe that she had such a close connection to the man who Cormac wanted to obliterate. He decided to wait and see how it panned out with Sheila.

She made a phone call. A short while later, a man, who Jack judged to be in his early 50s, came towards them. Sheila said goodbye and waved to the bar staff, leaving with the man. Perplexed, Jack sought out Chantelle. "Eddy is her driver. Sheila was seriously ill, near death's door at one point, which left her with a problem with her vision and prevents her from driving." Chantelle then added, proudly pumping her fist in the air, "Girl power! Sheila is ballsy. Takes no prisoners!" Chantelle concluded, smiling. Jack wanted to find out more.

56

Marcia felt a lump in her throat. At any moment, Sandy would walk through the doors wearing the Roberto Cavalli wedding dress that Marcia and Cindy, along with Jane, had been given a preview of when it was delivered. Scott had driven Sandy to Madrid especially, so she could try on the dress that he had seen her looking at on the Internet. She had tried to dissuade him, "It was only a fanciful dream," Sandy had told the women. Nevertheless, Scott drove nearly 500 kilometres from Valencia to Madrid. He managed to do the journey in under four hours; one of Scott's previous jobs was as a stunt driver for a film company in California. Scott had waited for Sandy in the car after insisting that he wanted her to have the dress of her dreams, no matter what the price tag. Their marriage was going to be for life, he had told her.

Sandy had informed the manageress when she had tried it on that she was pregnant and was concerned that the dress would not fit come her wedding day. Scott had driven her back to the shop again two weeks later for the waist to be adjusted to accommodate the growing bump.

Marcia had been to the Mystique beauty salon earlier for a facial, eyelash tint, and brow shaping. Lloyd had recommended that she have gold highlights with soft red tones. Her short, thick hair was away from her face, defining her cheek bones. Eamon said that she looked chic. Lloyd had been rehearsing the songs he would sing at the wedding in the salon's staff room. Keiron wiped a tear, touched on hearing the emotion of his husband's beautiful tenor voice.

Sandy had been concerned about having a white wedding dress. She said to the women that she felt like a hypocrite. They allayed her fears. Marcia informed her that she had been pregnant with Quinn and Niall had been at her breast on her and Eamon's wedding day.

Scott Lord turned his head when the wedding march played. He adoringly watched Sandy come towards him. Her son Brady, in a three-piece suit, stood alongside Scott. He was his best man. Benny Harris walked proudly by Sandy's side, her arm resting on his, proudly escorting the stunning bride. There were tears as the beautiful young woman and her handsome man looked lovingly into one another's eyes. A silent hush filled the Oficina de Registro when they both repeated their vows and kissed. Once outside, the pole dancers erupted with applause and congratulations. Confetti fell like snowflakes over the couple. Sandy turned, throwing her bouquet as the girls from the club gathered, vying for the prize. Sunni, the tallest, easily caught it. "I am next!" she called out. "I will be seeing him later!"

The men shook Scott's hand. Marcia was happy for the couple, sensing that Scott would look after Sandy and Brady. Sandy had previously confided in Marcia that she had fled to Spain with her boy to get away from Brady's father who was a drug addict and heavy drinker. He had physically abused her, forcing her to have sex with guys he brought home, to earn money to feed his addiction. Sandy had said that Brady had seen things that no child should see.

Marcia had been on tenterhooks, praying that Suzette would not bring Cormac Brennan with her. She took Eamon's proffered arm as they followed the couple to the reception at Marcia and Eamon's home.

Everything was in place for the wedding. There had been a hiccup, however. Shelby, the sought-after West Indian DJ had his equipment stolen from his van while loading it after playing at a beach venue the night before the wedding. When Benny heard about it, he made a tour of locally known, second-hand music equipment dealers. With the second name on his list, he hit gold. He did not need to make threats. Benny's intimidating demeanour spoke volumes. The man relinquished his stolen goods without a fuss. Shelby returned the good deed by playing at the wedding free of charge.

The weather could not have been better. There was a lazy breeze, bringing relief from the heat. Everyone was happy, the couple was well-liked, and friends brought many gifts that Marcia stored in one of the spare bedrooms for the wedding couple. Cindy had sent a message out that items for their new home would be appreciated. Many had gifted money. Sandy walked towards Marcia who had just settled the twins.

"You look stunning, Sandy!" Marcia complimented her, smiling at the radiant bride.

"I am so happy, Marcia but fat!" She placed her hands on her baby bump. She turned to where Scott was talking to the men. "Scott does not want to stop at this baby. I won't have time to regain my figure," she chuckled. She turned her attention to Marcia. "Your dress is beautiful, classy!" she added. "Red suits you. It complements the highlights in your hair."

Marcia thanked her. She had purchased two red Alexandre Vauthier dresses. The one she originally wanted was a sexy, asymmetrically cut dress that Eamon thought she looked hot in. He informed her that if she wished to purchase the thousands of euros dress, she should only wear it in the bedroom, therefore, she also purchased a more classically cut one for the wedding. Marcia wore the red, classic above-the-knee, slashed neckline dress, adhering to Eamon's suggestion. The sexy asymmetrical one she kept for when they were alone.

Sandy's tone became serious. "May I ask you a personal question?"

Marcia nodded.

"Do you find it difficult with your husband being surrounded by near-naked women when he is at work? He is very handsome. It concerns me with Scott. Not only the dancers but also the women who come into the club."

Marcia smiled, looking across to where Eamon was holding court with the men. His silver-fox hair and goatee gave him a look of maturity, which she knew would be an added attraction. She realised that there were women who would step into her shoes at the first opportunity. "I try to focus on our relationship. I respect Eamon and the way he needs to protect his family. In return, he is a wonderful husband and doting father. Eamon has morals and strong principals, which I adhere to. I hold on to our mutual respect. I do not take him for granted. Marriage requires work; it's a partnership. This all sounds long-winded!" she laughed, "However, the combination of love and knowing your man appears to work. Only think of what you and Scott and your family will have. That is what Scott wants."

Marcia added, "You can dance for him in private!"

Both women laughed. Sandy was suddenly distracted, and Marcia looked to see what had taken her attention. Brady, her son of 15, who could pass for 18, was deep in conversation with Bridie, the younger Irish sister who danced at the club. Sandy voiced her concern. "There is no mistaking his interest!" her declaration was more to herself.

Brady is a big lad, an old soul, far more mature than his years, Marcia concluded with a tad of wistfulness. Sunni came into their vision. Waving to them. There was a strikingly handsome young guy on her arm. His ebony skin was a few shades lighter than Sunni's. There was obvious chemistry between them. Sandy walked towards them, and the other dancers from the club homed in on them. The two Spanish dancers Katia and Alda came round the corner of the terrace, approaching Marcia. Introducing the two young men who were with them. Marcia could see the family likeness.

"Identical twins!" Alda stated. Valentino, then Felix, kissed Marcia on both cheeks. "The boys love the fact that we are dancers at the adult club!" Alda beamed towards their partners.

Marcia smiled. She loved the rhythm and cadence of the girls' Valencian accent, mixed with broken English. She thought it added to the sultry pair's attraction. The two couples went to join the others. Marcia inhaled. It saddened her to think that Suzette had missed the wedding. Suzette, as much as the other women, had been excited about the celebration. She felt bad about telling Suzette that she could not bring Cormac to the wedding. But Marcia was in no doubt that if she hadn't said anything, Eamon would have given her a verbal lashing. Marcia knew that Eamon's previous view of Suzette was one of disdain. And since Greg's death, he now despised her even more for taking a lover – "when the man was barely cold in his grave," Eamon had railed.

Marcia knew that his vitriol was fanned by the fact that Suzette's choice of partner was a man that Eamon hated. Eamon, glass in hand strolled towards her. "Nice turn out for the couple!" He kissed her. "Ye look inviting!" He winked. "A seductress!"

She slipped her arm through his. "Is red yer new colour?" His eyes smiled. "I am looking forward to seeing ye in that raunchy red number tonight!"

Scanning the crowd, he sucked air through his teeth when he saw Sandy's son Brady making his way to the dancefloor with Bridie. "Scott is on it. The lad appears overly interested. I should imagine that the girl does not realise that he is still at school!" Eamon shook his head. "The boy's build belies his age. Scott has been teaching him martial arts and how to ride a horse, but it appears to me that it's the girl who is turning his head! Scott is not amused!"

He turned to face her. "I am pleased to see that yer friend took yer advice!"

Marcia did not reply to his remark regarding Suzette.

"Lloyd will sing soon. Would you like to dance with me?" She drew him closer.

"To be sure, if ye promise to behave?" He grinned, leading her towards the marquee.

Lloyd, Keiron, Lorenzo, and Lorenzo's new partner Paulus, stood to the right-hand side of Shelby, the DJ. Lloyd was wearing a flamboyant tangerine and leaf-green floral shirt with a mustard-coloured wool suit. Olive green suede shoes completed the picture. He called for order, microphone in hand, sashaying across the stage to the turntable. Keiron stepped forward, his voice booming, "Lloyd is going to sing a song for the special couple. Scott, you handsome hunk, please take your beautiful bride to the dancefloor!"

Applause resounded, and the crowd parted to allow Scott and Sandy through. Lloyd nodded to Shelby. The music started and Lloyd sang Roberta Flack's version of 'The First Time I Ever Saw Your Face'.

Scott cupped Sandy's chin, kissing her. Sandy's fellow dancers erupted in applause. Keiron, Lorenzo, and his boyfriend wiped away their tears.

Eamon took Marcia in his arms for the next dance. He raised an eyebrow with a hint of a smile when out of the corner of his eye he saw Sunni's thigh wrapped around her man as they danced. Cindy's raucous laughter rang out. Dan smiled at the woman in his arms. Eamon glanced up to see Martha, the Irish dancer talking to Benny Harris. Both were heading to the exit of the marquee. Brady and Bridie were in a tight clinch, hip to hip, swaying to the music. Eamon pursed his lips. Marcia kissed him.

He smiled. "The temperature is hot in here tonight!" He stepped back. "Marcia!" he breathed. "Not in here. If ye fondle me, it will become embarrassing!" She took her hands from his fly, placing them around his neck. He held her dark eyes with his. "My little mystic who predicted that Benny Harris and Martha would become an item. They have just exited the marquee together!" He grinned back at her.

"There will be another wedding, and babies to follow!" She pressed her pelvic bone into his.

"Stop yer fortune telling!" he whispered playfully. "I will make a prediction for ye. Tonight, my little sorceress, I am going to shackle ye. Torture ye with my tongue. Can ye predict how long ye will last before I have ye calling out for mercy?" Marcia pressed closer, kissing him. "Furthermore, if ye continue to tease me in public, ye will pay in private." He returned her kiss.

Eamon left the marquee. He told Marcia that he was going to check on the baby girls. His attention was drawn to the far side of the grounds where Martha stood, hand placed on Benny Harris's arm. He continued watching. The couple separated. Martha walked towards the terrace doors. Benny took the route to the side of the house. Eamon pursed his lips, nodding. He surmised that they were meeting up somewhere. Eamon knew that Benny was a lot older than the Irish dancer. Billy had previously informed him that the man had lost his wife and five-year-old daughter, wiped from his life when she had left him while Benny was away on a mission.

Momentarily, the memory of when he had discovered that Marcia had left him came back to him, unbeknownst to them both that Marcia was pregnant with the twin girls. He could relate to the mental anguish that Benny must have experienced.

Fortunately for Eamon, he had convinced Marcia to return. *Maybe this will be Benny's second chance for happiness,* Eamon thought to himself. Marcia had predicted that Benny and Martha would become a couple as she had also predicted that Scott Lord and Sandy would marry. He opened the nursery door, stealthily moving towards his two copper-haired cherubs. Mouths puckering, chubby arms spread out. He replaced the light coverlets over their legs. "God bless ye," he whispered to both.

57

Cormac Brennan's mood was light, even though he had just had words with Jack. Jack Reynolds was a good organiser – he appeared to run the business like clockwork. Nevertheless, Cormac had underestimated Jack's lure to women. The man was besotted with Dominic O'Reilly's daughter, Sheila. Chantelle, the barmaid, had informed Cormac when he had paid an unexpected visit to the club, that Jack was on a two-hour break. She told him that Jack spent every free moment with Sheila. "They were loved up!" Chantelle happily stated.

Cormac reminded Jack about Eamon O'Donally and the mission that he wanted Jack to undertake. Cormac wanted photographs of Marcia O'Donally's comings and goings. Jack had tried to back pedal. Explaining that his girlfriend Sheila was closely connected to the O'Donallys. "The situation could become difficult!" he told Cormac.

Sensing that Jack was infatuated with the girl, Cormac stated that he would need to replace him if he was not up to the job. Mind whirling, Jack unenthusiastically nodded his agreement.

Although not overly enthused, Cormac was looking forward to spending time with Suzette. He had the evening all planned out and was not in the least bit concerned that Suzette had informed him that she had decided to decline the invitation to the wedding. Brennan knew the reception was being held in O'Donally's villa grounds. Although he would have liked to get one step closer to his arch-enemy, Cormac realised that he could not push his luck by attending with Suzette.

He had invited Suzette to stay overnight. He knew that she was enraptured with him. The woman struck him as desperate to have a relationship with him. First, he had wanted to test the water. The first night of sex, he had toyed with her. He had seen the pain etched on her profile, fingers tearing at the pillow as she stoically allowed him to take her from behind. Cormac had been purposely gentle with her, due to his size. Plus, at this moment in time, he could not risk losing her. He smirked – the vision of what he had in mind for her filled his loins with heat. Adjusting himself, he thought about how his young ex-wife had betrayed him. It worked every time – he was once more flaccid.

Although Suzette was an older woman, he judged her to be in her mid-forties, she had a good body and was glamorous in an old-school way. Nevertheless, he could not but admire her business acumen and her ambition to spread her wings and become successful in Marbella. He mused about how far he had come. At first, he had rented the secluded, lovely home, although he had led his ex-wife to believe that he owned it. The stunning villa in Marbella East was a mere 5 km from the beach front. He knew that he would later have the option to purchase the house, once he had some clean money. With the help of the Arabs and Cormac's business partner Shane Davis, he became legitimate in the transportation business. The container ships carried the cargo on the South China Seas, although the type of goods being shipped was not what was being declared.

Palms were greased, whereby stevedores at the ports were instructed to load the containers. Cormac's ex-wife had discovered that he had lied to her and did not own the villa at that time. It became known to her when she had wanted to make some structural changes to the property. Cormac waggled his head. *Win some, lose some,* he concluded, thinking as to how that had been the first nail in the coffin of their relationship. Nevertheless, his thoughts returned to Suzette. She certainly had a lot going for her. She was wealthy – she had easily parted with the 250 thousand euros for her new business venture. Cormac smiled smugly to himself. He stood on the terrace admiring the view. He loved the seclusion that the south-facing home gave him. He waved upon seeing her car come through the gates. Cormac had given her the gate pass code, encouraging her to believe that they were becoming closer. He required her trust, which would aid him to gain her confidence.

They enjoyed a candle-lit meal, which his housekeeper had prepared earlier. He poured two glasses of wine, asking her to join him on the white leather four-seater sofa. Suzette spoke of the plans that she had for her new beauty salon. Cormac made all the right noises, smiling in all the right places. He was intrigued as to why she had refused the wedding invitation, knowing how she had previously told him that she and Marcia O'Donally were close friends and had a history. He wanted to delve further.

However, Suzette at first hedged her bets, making excuses. He refilled their glasses, pressing her. She began by telling him how Eamon O'Donally controlled her friend, Marcia, going back to the time the pair had first come to Spain.

Cormac encouraged Suzette to drink up. She revealed that when she had inherited the 50 per cent share of the Hawk Wind club from Greg, she had gifted her share to Marcia, on the understanding that Marcia did not sell her shares to her husband. Suzette said that she had her solicitor draw up the legal paperwork. Suzette declared that she was adamant that Eamon O'Donally would never have full control of the club.

Cormac fought to contain his rising anger, but he retained the smile, which was more of a grimace. "What encouraged ye to give such an ostentatious gift?" he asked coldly.

Hesitating for a few seconds before replying, she said, "Marcia and I have a history."

"Many friends do!" he countered, waiting for her to continue.

"I felt that I owed a debt to Marcia for helping me. She had my back with various problems that I had with my first husband."

Cormac frowned. "Please, enlighten me!" he pressed, topping up their drinks and leaning back into the overfilled cushions on the sofa. He took note that Suzette was becoming uncomfortable. He smiled reassuringly.

"You must understand, Cormac, that my husband at the time controlled my life. He was related to Jimmy Grant. They had dealings with one another."

Interjecting, Cormac placed a hand on her arm, "Can ye get back to how Marcia O'Donally helped ye!"

Suzette took a large mouthful. She went into detail from the beginning to the here-and-now. Suzette omitted the part about the emotional blackmail regarding Marcia's son Reuben but included that she had robbed Max Greenaway of £150,000 after he was arrested and sent to prison.

"Marcia is gifted. I could not have come this far without her advice!"

Cormac smiled thinly. "I understand. Ye both joined forces. Commendable!" He covered his mouth with the rim of the glass. Eyes cold, he nodded.

Suzette relaxed and kicked off her shoes. Cormac put his arm around her shoulder. She looked up adoringly, briefly brushing his lips with hers. "I won't be a moment. I need the bathroom," she said.

He pointed to the left. Wiping his mouth, distaste consuming him. *How the fuck could the stupid bitch give away a small fortune like that?* Eamon O'Donally would not care that his wife became his partner and that she was legally prevented from selling him her shares. The couple were one unit. Furthermore, it would have been fortuitous to him. What Suzette had done was to help make O'Donally legal. Although some of the information that he had on O'Donally could be partly hearsay, Cormac would lay money on it that somewhere down the line from O'Donally's time working as Jimmy Grant's right-hand man, that O'Donally had inherited or financially gained when he had taken over Jimmy Grant's turf.

From the time of Jimmy Grant's demise, Eamon O'Donally was most probably getting his financial act together, gradually washing his illegally gained spoils. Dom had told him that ever since Marcia had come into O'Donally's life and they had a family, he had cleaned up his act. Dom had stated that O'Donally was now on the straight and narrow.

Refilling his glass for the third time, he knocked it back. He smirked. He would repay Suzette tonight for her stupidity.

She waved her panties, dropping them to the floor. She straddled him, arms encircling his neck, her black dress rising. Cormac carried her across the room and with his free hand he opened his office door.

"Ye are going to enjoy this!" In a quick manoeuvre, he laid her face down on the desk, one hand caressing her buttock. Freeing his throbbing erection, he parted her legs. His body weight pinned her down, preventing her from moving. Her screams excited him, driving him on as he thrusted. Her sobbing was heard by no one. "Ye are a stupid whore!" he breathed, pumping.

Slumped across the antique Georgian desk, Suzette realised that she should have listened to Marcia's warning. Cormac shuddered. Standing back, zipping his fly, he walked from the room. "Get the fuck out of my house," he called out over his shoulder.

The over five-hour drive home to Altea Hills from Marbella East had been long and painful for Suzette. Halfway through the return journey, Suzette felt overcome by the humiliation of Cormac Brennan raping her.

Locking and resetting the alarm to her villa, when she arrived in the early hours, Suzette dragged herself into the shower. For more than an hour, she scrubbed her skin to rid herself of the toxicity of Cormac Brennan.

Exhausted, she took 530 milligrams of valerian. The herbal extract had helped her since Greg's passing. Sleep took her. Drifting off, the ping of a text on her mobile on the dressing table was unheard.

58

The DJ, the marquee company and the catering staff had left the grounds, leaving no sign that so many people had gathered to celebrate Scott and Sandy's reception. Eamon had taken the dogs out for a walk. Marcia had thrown a cashmere wrap around her shoulders and stood by the pool gazing out at the vista. This was her favourite time, a time of reflection a few hours before dawn. The light from the waning gibbous moon, on its journey back to the other side, illuminated the boats in the still waters of Altea Bay in the distance.

Marcia sent her prayers of protection out to her eldest son Reuben, then to Niall and Quinn who were staying with Maureen and Dom in Marbella that evening. Her younger boys' privileged life was at variance with her eldest. However, there was nothing that she could do to help him. Many years had gone by without any contact from him. She had no idea if he was dead or alive. She inhaled, putting the heavy thought to the back of her mind. Her thoughts turned to Suzette. She would ring her later. She knew she would have ignored Marcia's warnings, as she had in the past when she had an affair with her ex-husband Max's partner in crime. Suzette had put her trust in Gary, and he betrayed her financially and emotionally. Marcia had given her advice not to put her trust in Mikey, Max's driver, but once more, Marcia's words fell on deaf ears. This was part and parcel of Suzette's nature, jumping into situations where angels feared to tread. Nevertheless, Marcia was concerned that one day Suzette could get hurt. Marcia could not help but like her. She owed her life in Spain to her. Without Suzette, Marcia would not be where she was now.

Marcia's new life at first had been bittersweet when her first born, Reuben had gone into hiding in the UK. She began working at the Mystique conducting tarot readings, and due to Suzette's business acumen, money came pouring in. Also, her social life picked up. The night that Eamon O'Donally danced with her, and they kissed to slow soulful music, her fate was sealed.

She turned smiling when Eamon came across the terrace with the dogs. Her heart skipped a beat. He continued to excite her by his presence, as he had done from their first encounter. "I will join ye. The dogs will be thirsty after their run. Roman appears to be struggling wit his back legs." He ruffled their coats, taking them inside.

Wine glass in hand, Eamon moved in behind her. He took a sip, free hand holding her waist. "Penny for them?" he said, tilting her head up.

She remembered when he had first asked her that same question so long ago. "I like to reminisce at this early morning hour."

"Just reminiscing?" he crooked an eyebrow.

"Partly!" She turned to face him. The silence is beautiful. The calm is like a blanket of contentment across Altea Bay."

"The calm before a storm!" He drank a mouthful.

Marcia ran her fingertips along his jawline. "You should be careful what you say. The wind has ears!"

He knocked back the wine, stretching to put the glass on a chair, taking her in his arms. "Do not tink, my wee philosopher, that I have forgotten my prediction for ye. Late as it is!" He nuzzled the nape of her neck.

"To foretell. Is not a foregone conclusion. As your previous statement was!" She laughed when he picked her up in his arms, took her inside to the bedroom placing her on the bed. "Don't move!" he ordered, smiling. I will lock the place up. Marcia quickly changed into the red, asymmetrical dress. Kneeling on the bed she dangled the handcuffs upon his return.

"Panties?" He undressed, watching her.

"Removed!" she replied. "Would you like to video record us?"

He nodded, taking the proffered mobile phone. Switching to record, he placed it on the cabinet at an angle. "And ye wanted to wear that dress in public? It is obscene. I can see where ye have waxed." He laid her on her back, legs raised to his shoulders, finger teasing. "Ye won't be getting foreplay, as punishment for taunting me tonight!"

Marcia held his head, writhing, bucking, dress above her breasts. His tongue and mouth took her, hastily filling her, covering her with his large frame, locking his powerful thighs around hers, securing the depth of him inside of her. Marcia bit his neck as she came for the second time. Eamon timed it, joining her.

. . . .

The following morning at 6 am, before the household awoke, Marcia had joined Eamon for an early swim. Once submerged, she removed her bikini, the patchy rain sensual on her nakedness. Eamon had purposely swum at a distance. Informing her that he knew the game that she was playing. Refusing to take the risk of being seen making love outside. Aye could pop her head out of the door at any given moment. Marcia had entered the shower.

Eamon wasted no time in joining her. The power jet switched off, he entered her from behind. A hand clamped across her mound, he gently but firmly thrust deep inside, passion overtaking them. She fell back into him as the first spasm took her. "That will teach ye to play games wit me!" he smiled, turning her to face him, and kissing her. "I have a busy agenda today. Dan is joining me at the haulage company. New contracts require checking out after I drop the boys to school. That is without having to pleasure my wife!" He playfully slapped her rear. Although Eamon had a manager and his manager's two sons to run the haulage company, Eamon was not the sort of person to step back. He kept on top of each of his businesses.

Suzette played on Marcia's mind. She felt a sense of guilt that her friend had missed the wedding, knowing that Suzette had been as excited as the other women. Suzette had been generous to Sandy, gifting her the hair and beauty treatments, which would have cost hundreds of euros.

The boys had left for school with Eamon. There was a shower of light rain, however, Marcia had looked at the forecast and sunny weather was predicted after midday. The twin girls were occupied by Aye and Bonita. Marcia and Aye planned to take them out after their afternoon nap.

Marcia heard a text come through on her mobile phone on the table. Picking it up, she smiled. It was Suzette, asking Marcia if she was free to come to her villa. Marcia replied that she would be with her in half an hour.

Marcia punched in the code to open Suzette's gates and drove through. Walking to the side of the villa, a sense of foreboding came over her. She did not know if it was the isolation of the large, detached building. This had been Greg's home. He had his construction company build it for them. Greg's villa was nearer to the Sierra de Bernia range that spread for 11 kilometres perpendicular to the sea. The elevated view took her breath away, making her realise how fortunate she and Suzette were. They had both come a long way since their first encounter.

The terrace doors were open, and the feeling remained. She called out, her voice echoing, breaking the silence. Suzette came down the stairs. Marcia took a step back. She had not ever seen her without makeup before. Gone was the glamourous woman. She was wrapped in a silk dressing gown, her hair unkempt, with a heavy-eyed, sullen look.

Marcia hurried towards her. "I am sorry that I upset…"

Suzette intercepted, smiling wanly, "I am the one who needs to apologise to you." She inhaled. "Let us get some fresh air under the awning. I need the rain to help clear my mind." She walked heavily as if she was burdened, Marcia thought. Her mind was racing to try and work out what could have affected Suzette so much. Marcia sat opposite her at the oversized ornate garden table. Marcia let her talk.

"I was deeply upset about not being able to go to Sandy's wedding. I drove to Marbella East to stay overnight with Cormac at his villa. Cormac did not appear to be overly upset about not going to the wedding. He masked it well – at first!" she added.

Marcia reached out for her friend's hand when she saw tears threatening to fall.

"We were drinking, having a cosy talk, which changed to him prying about our friendship, pressing for our history, Marcia. I explained in detail, leaving out a couple of things." She smiled thinly, looking out into the distance. "He seemed to accept it when I told him that I gifted my half share in the club to you. I went to the bathroom, removed my underwear, and returned to the sofa. He took me to his office!" Tears fell.

Marcia stood up.

"Let me finish, Marcia," Suzette's voice broke. "He held me down on my front across the desk!" Rivulets of tears spilt down her face. Suzette continued, "Pinning me with his body weight, he anally raped me. My screams of excruciating pain ignited him to ram more purposely…"

Marcia leapt up, taking the sobbing Suzette in her arms, smoothing her hair. "Don't say anymore!"

"Why did I not listen to you? Eamon was right about him. He is evil! My dress was stained with blood!"

"You must see the doctor, Suzette. I will take you."

She shook her head. "I feel humiliated. I will survive. As I have in the past. He has 250,000 euros, which I transferred into his bank account for the deposit on what I assumed would be my new beauty salon in Puerto Banus." She scoffed at herself. "How stupid can one be?" She wiped her tears. He has sent a text. When I texted you this morning, I noticed it. Not that I read it."

"Where is your phone?"

"Upstairs, why?" Marcia pursed her lips. I would like to see what he has written.

"The text was sent after I got home," Suzette said, showing her the time on the message as 2.45 am. Suzette opened it, putting her hand over her mouth as she read it. "I am truly sorry, my darling. My passion for you overwhelmed my sensibilities. Tears of sadness overcome me, thinking of what I have lost. Please, my darling, forgive me. Cormac. Xxx."

"Perfect!" Marcia stated. "I want you to keep him on the line until he is ready to be hauled in! Do it, Suzette!"

Marcia went to make them coffee. Upon her return, she pressed Suzette to drink it. She watched Suzette type the reply, forgiving him. "Insert four kisses!" Marcia instructed. Suzette pressed send. "Suzette, I think that he will reply shortly. You must continue with the pretence."

Suzette nodded.

"That despicable man cannot be allowed to get away with what he has done to you. I will broach the subject with Eamon when the time is right. He will be angry that you went with Cormac. He despises the man. There will be a price to pay; however, all will not be lost. Leave it in my hands."

Marcia ran a bath for Suzette and phoned Lloyd to inform him that Suzette was unwell and wouldn't be coming to work. He reassured her that he would take care of things at the salon.

59

Maureen O'Reilly had been keeping their daughter Sheila's secret about her whirlwind romance with Jack Reynolds, the manager of the golf club that Cormac Brennan had purchased from Dom. Dominic had heard all the rumours about the new manager's roving eye, warning Sheila about him if he came on to her. Their baby girl had given up on the guy in America and had returned to Spain. Maureen, behind Dom's back, had been introduced to Sheila's new beau. She had admitted at the time of meeting him that she could not blame Sheila for falling for the handsome smooth-talking Jack. Maureen had secretly admired him, wishing that she was a few years younger. But now that she knew he was a phi-landerer, her opinion of him changed. Maureen now wanted Jack Reynolds's blood. Sheila had been seeing Jack at every opportu-nity, either visiting the golf club or sleeping over at his apartment. Maureen comforted her girl when Sheila told her that her friend Karen had seen Jack with another woman in his car. Suspecting duplicity, Karen followed the car. It stopped near the marina, and she saw the couple kiss. Karen had sent Sheila the mobile phone pictures that she had taken to prove his infidelity.

Maureen had suffered in silence over the years with Dom and his cheating. However, this situation was a different ball game. Her young daughter was heartbroken. Maureen told Sheila to leave it in her old mum's hands. Maureen planned to tell Dom. She could withstand the ear bashing if it got rid of Jack Reynolds.

Dominic O'Reilly was lounging on the double bed when Maureen entered. He threw the magazines he was looking at on the floor. Maureen noticed the pages with topless women, legs akimbo. She smiled wistfully at him, sitting on the bed. "Dom, Sheila is upset!"

Dom sat bolt upright. "What's the matter?" he asked, concerned. This was his precious baby girl that she was talking about. Maureen went into detail. He did what she had expected him to do. Maureen shed crocodile tears. Dom informed her that he was about to make a phone call. Maureen took her leave.

Eamon was on his way home when his mobile rang – it was Dom O'Reilly. "How's retirement suiting ye, Dom? Ye must be knackered from yer journey back home after the wedding."

"Eamon, I need your help. My girl is being used by some cunt of a player that is managing the golf club for Cormac Brennan." Eamon, stunned into silence let Dom continue. "Sheila is broken. You know how close we came to losing her. I help get her back on track, and then this fucking playboy who is old enough to be her father wines and dines my girl, winning her over. Sheila may be naive, but her daddy is not!" he said with a threat of menace.

Eamon gave Dom the other mobile number that he only used for certain occasions such as this. Eamon said to give him an hour as he had to check on the Hawk Wind club.

Dom instructed Eamon to remove Jack Reynolds, no matter the cost, giving him the information about where Jack was residing. He would get a picture of him, even if he had to pay a visit to the golf club and take a discreet one on his mobile and fax it through. Eamon informed Dom that he could class the problem as closed as soon as he received the ID. He would keep him updated.

Two hours later, the fax that he had been waiting for came through. Eamon placed a call to Big Dave Broadbent. "Trouble!" Dave chuckled, knowing that was the only reason that this mobile number was used. Eamon filled him in on the requirements. Faxing the photograph.

. . . .

Aisling sat on Eamon's chest while he lay on the sun lounger. Marcia played with Aine in the pool. The boys were at Jane's for a couple of hours of riding lessons. Also, Billy's tireless energy entertained them. The boys had become interested in basketball and Billy installed a post and net.

Aisling leaned forward and tugged Eamon's goatee, he winced, gently releasing her grip. She puckered her mouth, hugging him, nipping his top lip. "Ye little porker, ye would eat me!" He said, nuzzling under her chin.

"Gin khao!" she stared, demanding.

"Marcia!" Eamon called as Aisling sought his nipple through his unbuttoned shirt. "My wee child is demanding food!" He threw her up in the air, catching her.

"Gin Khao!" she said with more force, chin wobbling. On cue, Aye came through the terrace doors. Aisling wriggled, arms outstretched as she approached. Aye placed the child on her hip and pacified her. Whatever Aye had said in the Thai language, Aisling had nodded twice. Marcia handed Aine to Eamon, he followed Aye inside.

Marcia lay in the shade on the double sun lounger, turning on her side when Eamon strolled back outside towards her. "Why don't you join me? The boys won't be back for quite a while." She patted the rattan.

He pulled a chair up beside her. "Ye can't be trusted!" he grinned. "Would ye like to go out tonight before I begin my shift at the club?"

"Not for too long. I would like to spend some time with you in private before you leave."

Eamon replied, "Someting planned?"

"Hm!" Marcia rose, sitting on his lap.

"Metinks, that my wee mystic is up to something!" he accused teasingly, kissing the tip of her nose.

....

Marcia realised that there would be no right time to bring up Cormac Brennan. She knew the reaction from Eamon would be explosive, no matter how long she left it.

They had returned from the restaurant and Eamon had checked on the children, joining her on the terrace, embracing her from behind. He took in the scent of her perfume, bouquet of vanilla, sandalwood, and saffron. He drew her closer. "Ye appear to have something on yer mind," he breathed. Marcia did not reply. Turning Marcia to face him, he looked askance. Eamon held her at arm's length. She broke from his intense glare. Eamon tilted her head. "What is it?"

Marcia inhaled then blurted out, "It's Suzette!"

He elevated his brow.

Marcia took the bull by the horns. "Suzette was anally raped by Cormac Brennan!"

"Raped?!" he said incredulously.

Marcia placed her hand on his arm. "Eamon, I know that she was pre-warned. However, I can understand her loneliness since Greg's death."

Eamon erupted. "Are ye telling me that the stupid bitch is sleeping wit another man, let alone the likes of Brennan? So soon after Greg's death?" He raised his hands to the sky. "The woman could not have walked in Greg's shoes. The man adored her. She is a whore, a Jezebel!" he spat. "That man left her a financial fortune and she didn't even have the decency to show respect to the man's memory!"

He glared, although Marcia knew that his anger was directed at her friend, and not her. "So don't try to tell me that she did not know what she was getting into. Ye told me that ye previously warned her!"

Marcia remained silent throughout his railing. His temper simmered and she knew that she had to tell him everything. "Eamon, he also swindled her out of a quarter of a million euros, on the pretext of helping her purchase a building to expand the beauty business in Puerto Banus."

Shaking his head, he laughed caustically. "She was scammed by him? The woman who tinks that she knows all there is to know about business? Ye forget, Marcia, that when me and Greg took the club on, she stuck her two penneth in!" he scoffed, walking away. He called out over his shoulder. "How the fuck ye tolerate that woman who ye class as a friend is a mystery to me!" He turned at the terrace doors. "Some fucking friend!"

Minutes later Marcia heard his Maserati start up.

Marcia waited for nearly two hours before she sent Eamon a text. "I will wait up for you," followed by three heart emojis. Marcia lay on the bed; she went back to her book. Twenty minutes later, her mobile pinged. She smiled seeing four hearts. She returned five.

At 3.25 am, the two Belgian shepherds greeted Eamon, wagging their tails, when he opened the front door, shoes in his hands. For the most part, Eamon tried to remember Aye's customary requirements not to wear footwear in the house. He let the two dogs out of the terrace doors and waited there while they urinated. Locking up, he checked the children. Although they were monitored, he was not satisfied unless he saw them. He pushed the master bedroom door ajar. Soft beams of light filtered through. Marcia was on her side, deep in slumber. He smiled softly as he undressed. She had prepared herself for him. She wore a short, mint-green negligee, her freed breasts resting on the pillow. She lay sleeping in the foetal position. He made out the curve of her rear, covered in matching silk ouvert panties. Eamon walked to the en suite.

He had thought long and hard about Suzette. He had no respect for her for being disloyal to Greg. Nevertheless, Cormac Brennan would pay the price for forcing a woman to have anal sex and robbing her of a quarter of a million euros. However, he had decided that it would cost Suzette. He had the two men in mind who would be capable of carrying out the job. Drying himself, he moved quietly across the room. Marcia slept on. He slid in behind her. She stirred; eyelashes flickered. Eamon gently pulled her to him, resting his powerful thigh across her limbs. Marcia sleepily nestled into him.

"It will be settled. No more discussion!" he said, continuing with soft kisses at the back of her neck, slowly travelling downward. In one manoeuvre, she was on her back, her legs opening to accommodate him. She gasped upon his entry. They moved in unison, tongue seeking tongue, triggering the ascent to their passion.

60

Marcia met up with Suzette at the Mystique beauty salon. She had an appointment later with Lloyd. The busy staff waved when she entered. Lloyd, scissors in hand indicated to the staff room. Although she was not surprised that Suzette had returned to work so quickly, Suzette's ability to rise above adversity and resume her glamorous persona to the outside world never ceased to amaze Marcia.

"I have received further texts from him. He assumes that all is forgiven." Suzette said, looking as elegant as Joan Collins.

Marcia sat down. "Eamon is going to sort the problem. You will be required to pay the expenses, however. There will be 100,000 euros returned from the 250,000."

Suzette reached across, taking her hand in hers, smiling. "I cannot thank you enough... and Eamon. I would pay double to have that bastard taught a lesson!" She stood up. "Marcia I will heed your advice in the future. I am going to throw myself back into my business and wait for the timing of the next chapter." Suzette moved round to where Marcia was seated, hugging her. "How have you ever put up with me? I have brought many problems to your door."

Marcia shook her head. "If we hadn't met, Suzette, I would not have Eamon in my life, or my four beautiful children...

or the business partnership in the Hawk Wind club," she threw in, laughing. "I would not want to be without you in my life – a little less drama though, perhaps!"

Suzette offered Marcia some free beauty treatments in return for the help that she had given her, but Marcia refused.

....

Eamon had waited for Scott Lord to return from his honeymoon before asking him and Benny Harris to meet him in his office at the Hawk Wind club. "I am sorry to lay this on ye so soon after yer return, Scott, however," He looked at the men. "There is 50 grand in it for ye both." Eamon had their attention. He went into detail.

"The man needs a taste of his own medicine! I'm in!" Scott said.

"Count me in!" Benny added.

Eamon gave them the address in Marbella East and the time that Cormac Brennan would expect Suzette to visit. Suzette had provided the gate code for Brennan's villa.

Eamon thanked them. He sat there for a while after they had left, contemplating. Marcia had told him that Suzette had arranged to return to Cormac Brennan's home. Eamon went and unlocked the safe, removing the photographs that Big Dave Broadbent had taken from Jack Reynolds's apartment.

The only thing that Big Dave had taken was the photographs of Eamon, his wife, and his family. Eamon looked at his wife getting into her car with Aye and his daughters. He glared at a clear photograph of him with his sons getting into his Maserati. This contract was personal. Cormac Brennan would not come back from it. He would ensure that he would join Jack Reynolds.

Big Dave had waylaid Jack Reynolds after two days of watching his movements. He had tailed his car to Puerto Banus marina. Big Dave admired the view and people watched while he waited. At 9 pm the popular area was crowded. He kept one eye on the restaurant door while he waited for Jack to come out.

At 3.40 am, after hours of biding his time, Big Dave saw Reynolds leave with a blonde on his arm. He tailed the couple to Jack Reynolds's apartment. To his delight, as he sat in the shadows, a taxicab pulled up outside. The blonde came out of the apartment. Big Dave moved swiftly. He pressed the intercom. "Taxi driver!" repeating it until a frustrated Jack let him in.

Dave stuck his foot inside the door before Jack could slam it shut. He saw the photographs on the table and picked them up while he held Jack in a firm grip, arm forced up his back. Jack cried out. Big Dave shoved the quaking man onto the settee and demanded answers.

"Cormac Brennan the new owner of the golfing club had paid me to take the pictures! I had no choice but to show willingness or lose my job as manager. Nevertheless, I drew the line at kidnapping and murder!" Pleading his innocence that he had refused the contract of kidnapping Eamon O'Donally's wife. "Cormac Brennan intended to video the sexual assault that he was going to make on Eamon O'Donally's wife, then force him to watch it. My girlfriend, who I plan to marry, is closely connected to the O'Donally family and it would have made things a bit awkward."

Big Dave nodded, smiling courteously, thanking Reynolds for coming clean. He took 500 euros from his pocket and handed it to Jack to show his appreciation.

Jack eagerly took it, not quite believing the turn of events. The man had let him off the hook. Jack, through his nervousness, went as far as offering Big Dave a drink. Jack's eyes lit up when Big Dave produced the 'white'. Lining up the powder with his bank card, Jack hungrily snorted it. Big Dave pressed him to have another line.

Big Dave took back the 500 euros, taking one last look at the man slumped on the settee, mouth agape, a trickle of blood from both nostrils. Big Dave smiled smugly. "I forgot to mention that it was not cocaine but rather heroin laced with arsenic." But he did not expect a response.

. . . .

"You can sit in the fucking passenger seat on the way back, Scott! I will be at the wheel," Benny said, face pale. "You may have been a skilled stunt driver, but stop driving like a cunt and think of your family!" Benny Harris got out of the car, hand shaking, he lit a cigarette.

"I thought that you were quitting?" Scott teased the visibly shaken man.

"Fuck off!" Benny inhaled, holding the moment to calm his nerves after the drive around the hairpin bends that got them to their destination in nearly half the time.

"You have been tetchy since the night of my reception. I would have thought that the pretty Irish dancer…" Scott left it in the air, palm raised, realising that he had touched a sore spot when Benny spun around, eyes ablaze.

"Drop it!" Benny stamped out the butt, picking it up and returning it to the packet to ensure that no evidence was left behind. "Let us concentrate on the job, mate!" he said, his tone softer. He did not want to fall out with Scott. The pair had a history. He also knew that this would be the last time that he would work on a mission with him. Benny planned to leave Spain. He had felt guilty for sleeping with Martha. She had stayed the night at his place the night of Scott's wedding. They had made love into the early hours. When Martha had left, Benny knew that his conscience would not allow him to take her to his bed anymore. She was too young for him. He had stuck to his guns and did not answer her texts or calls. He avoided her at work, although there had been the odd occasion when he watched her dance, hidden at the back of the club. Martha had not seen him.

Two nights ago, he observed her coming out of the club arm in arm with a young, good-looking, dark-haired fellow. He had thought it would be better for her to find someone her own age. Nevertheless, it had done nothing for the heartache he now felt – the longing for the redhead who had confessed how she had wanted him. She had tried to convince him that age was but a number. He had a young daughter out there somewhere, living with his ex-wife who was close in age to Martha. He realised that he could not handle being so near to Martha. He was going to use the money earned for this mission to finance his future in another country.

Scott slapped his pal on the back, handing him a balaclava. "Like old times," Scott beamed. Benny returned his smile.

Scott checked his watch. Dead on 8 pm, he pressed the six digits on the keypad, which opened the gates to the isolated villa in Marbella East. The two men moved along the drive without being noticed. In the distance, they could see that the terrace doors were ajar. The pair knew that there were no dogs to cause them any problems, however, they had been informed that there were cameras and an alarm. The men would deal with that once they had Cormac Brennan restrained.

Scott nodded. Benny followed his direction as they studied the man reclining on the sofa with his arms behind his head, eyes closed. The sound of Ella Fitzgerald's voice filled the expanse of the room. They donned the balaclavas.

Cormac tried to break free from the hold around his neck, eyes bulging from Scott's powerful grip, and a look of recognition appearing in his eyes. "Ye are O'Donally's men. Ye worked for Mohammad Arran!" he gasped.

Benny leaned into him. "Shut the fuck up, you fucking toe rag!"

Cormac changed tactics. "I am expecting a guest. At any moment. If it is cash you want…"

Benny's fist rocked Cormac's head. "Let me inform you, my friend and I are the only company that you will be seeing tonight," he growled into his face. "Give me the code for the alarm and the cameras." He directed Scott to release him. "Give me all your keys."

Cormac hesitated for a second. Benny yanked him to his feet. Cormac opened his safe. Benny shoved him towards Scott. Both men glanced at one another. Benny threw the three heavy packages on the desk. Each one had a name on it. The wads of thousand-euro notes were removed. Scott opened the desk with a small bunch of keys, placing the pictures of Eamon's family on the top.

"Look upstairs!" Scott directed. Cormac Brennan was wise enough to allow the men to take what they wanted without a fuss.

Benny Harris smiled at Scott. He waggled the sex toy in front of Cormac's face. Both men manhandled the big man. Scott's elbow struck him in the neck, leaving Cormac gasping for air. Benny leapt on his back across the desk. Scott undid his trousers, pulling them down. He was commando – no underwear, making things easier. Scott inserted the eight-inch dildo with force into Brennan's anus. His screams eventually faded, and he slumped over the antique desk.

Benny checked his pulse. "Done!" he said. "Leave him like that! Looks like he died on the job."

"Hand them over!" Benny held his hand out when they approached the car. Scott yielded, slapping the keys into Benny's open palm.

61

"For fuck's sake, Marcia, tell me why ye tink that ye must act like Mother Teresa to these girls. They get themselves in the family way wit my men, then cry on yer shoulder and ye ask me to step in to speak to them! The next ting ye will be wanting to open a crèche to help them out. From what I hear, the younger sister, Bridie, and Sandy's boy are getting it on. She will be the next one on yer list!" He threw in, shaking his head.

"Eamon, Martha has no one to lean on. She has recently reunited with her brother who came to the Hawk Wind club by chance a couple of nights ago. She is thrilled that he is back in her life. Within a few days, Martha had said that he would be sailing around the world once his employer's boat is ready."

Eamon looked surprised. "I thought that the young, dark-haired fella that she had on her arm recently was a punter – not a brother!"

"Eamon, Benny Harris will leave Spain without knowing that Martha is having his child. If you could inform him…" she paused for a few seconds, "the decision to remain or leave will be his." She pleaded Martha's case.

He sucked air through his teeth. "Anybody would tink that I don't have enough problems to concern myself wit!"

Marcia reached for his hand, and he took it, thumb automatically caressing.

"Make this the last time!" he relented.

"I will help you relax this evening once the children are in bed." Marcia kissed the back of his hand from across the garden table where they were waiting for the boys to finish having breakfast before Eamon drove them to school.

A hint of a smile played on the corners of his mouth. "I will be looking forward to it," he said, winking.

"Papa, we are ready!" Quinn came running out the terrace doors.

Marcia stood up, moving towards him. He returned her hug and kisses. Marcia went inside to hug and kiss Niall. She knew that he was not tactile. Both she and Eamon showered their love on all their children, but Niall projected indifference. Nevertheless, she would not give up on him.

Eamon set the Hawk Wind club alarm, locking up. He had just paid Scott and Benny the 50,000-euro fee he had promised them.

Marcia had returned Suzette's 100,000 euros. The three packages that the men had given Eamon contained the pay-outs. He had set aside 5,000 to give Marcia tonight. Dom O'Reilly had previously phoned him, pleased that his problem with his daughter had been put to rest. He had sent her off to stay for a while with her sister in the USA.

Eamon had asked Benny for a word in private. Scott left them to it. Eamon knew that Benny was leaving Spain in a few days to work in the Middle East. Eamon broke the news to Benny that Martha was pregnant and that she had told Marcia that Benny was the father. Eamon and Benny silently acknowledged that they understood one another. Just a sharp nod from each. Eamon sensed that Benny and Martha would sort things out.

In the club car park, as Eamon was about to fire up his car, his mobile phone rang. Alphonso Gabrette's name and number flashed across the screen. The Italian sounded broken. Marcella, his wife of over half a century had passed away. He went on to say that he was devastated. Eamon gave his condolences. "Is there anything that I can do for ye, Al?"

"I need ya to help me with the funeral, lad. My Marcella was as fond of you as I am. If ya could spare a few days to come over to Miami and be a pallbearer? She would have liked to have known that you were there on her last journey," his voice broke.

Eamon replied, "I would be honoured. I will make the arrangements and contact ye!"

....

Eamon walked into the first-class cabin, glancing at the packed numbered seats. He was taken by the beauty of the woman who was seated by the window. She smiled at him with her dark, almond-shaped eyes. Eamon looked away.

"Hi, my name is Josephine." Eamon caught the American accent. She proffered her hand, which bore no rings. He smiled, taking her hand without responding, however, he did notice that she had a Hermes handbag, just like the one that he had purchased for Marcia.

He put his hand luggage in the overhead locker. He recognised the designer's logo on the case next to his. Settling in, he sent a text to Marcia. Reading her reply, he put the phone on flight mode. He observed the woman next to him from the corner of his eye – long legs, firm thighs, tailored skirt inching higher with her every movement. Her stilettos spoke of handmade Italian leather. *This is going to be an interesting flight,* he concluded, half turning to face her. "Eamon," he introduced himself.

"Your Irish accent suits you," she said, turning to face him. Another couple of inches of thigh came into view. Eamon unbuttoned his suit jacket. She projected confidence – a seducer. He put her down to being a woman who was used to the finest. He silently hazarded a guess that if she did not run her own business and that she had a man behind her, even though she wore no rings to indicate that she was married or engaged.

An hour into the flight, after she had drunk two glasses of wine, Josephine disclosed that she was the mistress of a powerful Miami boss, Ricardo Barossa, who she said allowed her the freedom to meet other men. Nonetheless, she said that he had warned her to never shit on her own doorstep. Hence, she had met up with a client in Paris and was returning to Ricardo Barossa the following evening.

Eamon did not reveal too much to the inquisitive woman who probed, remarking about his marital status. He had seen her glance at his wedding band. Josephine had not been put off that he had a wife and four children. Eamon had abstained from drinking alcohol until halfway through the long flight. He decided that the two large bourbons would be his limit. Josephine was on her fourth glass of wine. She reached into her bag, handing him her calling card.

Momentarily hesitating, Eamon took the purple card out of politeness. He would dispose of it later. There was not any other woman who took his interest. Marcia was his for eternity. He slipped the card in his jacket pocket.

"If you ever get lonely on a trip, we could have an enjoyable time," she held his look.

Eamon did not answer. He pursed his lips and cocked an eyebrow, smiling politely.

They passed the time on the long flight chatting amiably, helping to fill the hours. Josephine kept ordering drinks for them both. She seemed quite interested in Eamon's life and hung on every word, pressing for more stories about his life with every glass they knocked back.

On disembarking in Florida, they went their separate ways. Eamon had a niggling thought in the back of his mind. He recognised the name of Josephine's man – Ricardo Barossa. He would mention it to Alphonso.

As Eamon got into a taxi, he had a strange feeling that he was being observed. At the same time, back in Spain, Marcia had a sudden feeling of dread overcome her – the same feeling of warning she felt when she had lost Reuben to the Universe.

Acknowledgements

I feel fortunate to have so many beautiful supportive friends who I want to send my heartfelt thanks to. Each and every one of you have helped me. Love to you all. Also, my wonderful children and beautiful granddaughters, Coa and Maya, and Kerry Boettcher my wonderful editor. I thank you all.

Printed in Great Britain
by Amazon